GASLIGHT

BOOKS BY SARA SHEPARD

PRETTY LITTLE LIARS
Pretty Little Liars
Flawless
Perfect
Unbelievable
Wicked
Killer
Heartless
Wanted
Twisted
Ruthless
Stunning
Burned
Crushed
Deadly
Toxic
Vicious

LYING GAME
The Lying Game
Never Have I Ever
Two Truths and a Lie
Hide and Seek
Cross My Heart, Hope to Die
Seven Minutes in Heaven

PERFECTIONISTS
The Perfectionists
The Good Girls

AMATEURS
The Amateurs
Follow Me
Last Seen

STANDALONE NOVELS
The Visibles
Everything We Ever Wanted
The Heiresses
The Elizas
Reputation
Influence (with Lilia Buckingham)
Safe in My Arms
Wait for Me
Memory Lane (with Ellen Goodlett)
Nowhere like Home

GASLIGHT

MILES JORIS-PEYRAFITTE
AND SARA SHEPARD

BLACKSTONE PUBLISHING

Copyright © 2024 by Fonhaus Media, LLC
Published in 2024 by Blackstone Publishing
Cover artwork and illustrations by Tomer Hanuka
Book design by Larissa Ezell

All rights reserved. This book or any portion
thereof may not be reproduced or used in any manner
whatsoever without the express written permission
of the publisher except for the use of brief quotations
in a book review.

The characters and events in this book are fictitious.
Any similarity to real persons, living or dead, is coincidental
and not intended by the author.

Printed in the United States of America

First edition: 2024
ISBN 979-8-212-18922-4
Fiction / Thrillers / Psychological

Version 1

Blackstone Publishing
31 Mistletoe Rd.
Ashland, OR 97520

www.BlackstonePublishing.com

Pain is never wasted. It can be a portal to the divine.
—Ben Rahm, *The Path to Transcendence*

PROLOGUE

TWO WEEKS BEFORE

Certain it's the last day of his life, Toby Sherman gets his tripod ready. He has written a script, but his fingers shake so badly he doubts he can hold on to the paper. Hopefully, he'll be able to wing it.

He turns on the camera and sits on his bed. Behind him is his channel's normal backdrop: posters of metal bands, gaming paraphernalia, books he was supposed to read in high school but didn't, and ripped-out magazine inserts of hot women in bikinis. It's an idealized teenage boy's bedroom—not that he's been a teenage boy in years. This isn't even his old bedroom—it's just a set, a bunch of stuff he bought on eBay and at garage sales to appeal to his viewers. Toby's real childhood bedroom—or where he spent the majority of his childhood, and the place he cherishes most—is at his grandma's house back in California. Or it was, anyway. He doesn't know if his grandma lives there anymore. He hasn't seen his grandma in a long time. For all he knows, she could be in jail—because of what he said and did.

He checks his reflection in the mirror before turning the camera on with the remote switch. Would Gram even recognize him, if she saw him online? He looks so different with this straw-like bleached hair and thick glasses. The changes are a good disguise. People notice what jumps out and not much else. They see the glasses, the hair, and pay little attention to his face. For quite a few years now, it's worked just fine. He's been able to record. He's been able to hide. Able to live.

But today—well, today, he got the warning, and it's all going down. There's nothing he can do to stop it. No amount of running or hiding—it doesn't matter anymore. They've found him. They're coming. And they're going to get what they want.

Toby was eating breakfast when he heard from his old contact Lucas, who still seems to know everything but is out of the world, just like he is. And whether you're in the world or out of the world, no one has the power to stop things. Lucas was terrified he was going to get in trouble just for sending Toby the warning. But Toby wouldn't rat Lucas out. He's known, ever since he left, what they'd do if they found him. He's broken so many rules. He also knows what they want. He has information they're dying to retrieve.

He thought about running, but where would he go? He barely has time. Besides that, he doesn't have any money. Or family. Or friends, unless you count his channel's followers, which he doesn't.

Then he got angry. He'd been in hiding for years, and for what? Good wasn't going to triumph here. Evil was going to win . . . again.

But then, he had an idea. Revenge. Sacrifice. And maybe they won't see it coming.

He breathes in. Steadies the camera. Presses Record Live. There's a little countdown, and then a message on the screen says his video is being streamed. He waits a moment or two as people start to log on.

"Hey, Game Giants." He smiles into the camera, addressing his fans. "It's me, T Greg. Welcome back to my channel, and thanks for joining me for another video. But today, I'm doing something a little different. I hope you'll stick with me. I'm kinda getting into it with you all. Getting real about who I am as a person. But I gotta warn you, I'm going way off topic."

Normally, his videos are just about gaming. His channel is a portal for people to watch him shoot at the bad guys. Toby has a pretty decent following, enough to even earn him a little cash to supplement the job he has at the Stop 'N' Go in the poor excuse this place calls a downtown. It's a meager living, but at least he's not on the streets, and he gets to talk about something he likes.

Well. Not today he isn't. Nevertheless, he needs to get this out.

"This is a thing I don't bring up—ever," he says. "I mean, do you really care about the guy behind the games? I don't know . . . maybe not. But I hope my story touches somebody. Makes ya think. If you know anybody who could benefit from this . . . please pass this message on. 'Kay?"

He waits a beat, as if this is a two-way conversation. *You can still turn back*, a voice in his head teases. He slaps the impulse away.

"Right," he says, leaning toward the camera. "This is going to sound stupid. Really stupid." He pushes his hair across his forehead. "But for several years, before I started this channel, I was in a cult."

There. He said it. The world hasn't exploded. He checks the number of viewers watching live. Over a thousand. And actually . . . the number is growing.

He laughs self-consciously. "You're probably like, *huh? What's this guy smoking?* But it's true. No one knew it was a cult, obviously. Like, my grandma, who raised me, literally thought I was hanging with wholesome role models. I even told her the leader's story—at least the story he gave me. How he'd pulled himself out of adversity, how he cured himself of dyslexia, which I have, too. How he's brilliant and an Olympian and has helped famous people and businessmen be their best selves or whatever. Gram fell for it as hard as I did. Thought he was a good dad figure for me, kind of. Certainly someone who could *help* me get over my shit. Hell, Gram even wanted to take some classes with the group, not that we could scrounge up the money. It was expensive as hell, those workshops. It boggles my mind, how much I spent."

He takes a breath. Should he stop? Maybe. But no. He has to push on.

"So, what does that actually mean? Was this really a cult, or am I being dramatic? This thing I was involved in—called ISB, which stands for *Infinite Spiritual Being*—ticked all the boxes. There was a manipulative and charismatic leader. There were levels and hierarchies, and you had to lay out a bunch of money right off the bat, and there was a promise you'd earn a lot, too . . . not that many people did. I mean, there was some fucked-up shit happening there. And this dude, the leader? He broke down everyone's ways of thinking. We all lived together in this . . . place . . . and sang songs and performed ceremonies and practically had our own secret language about how the world worked. And there were rules—serious rules. There was, um, sex stuff, too. Forced. Though that's . . . that's hard to think about. Because we all just . . . accepted it. We just stood there . . . until we didn't."

He tries to breathe. He's said a lot. A shitload.

"Like I said, I joined this group in high school. Which sounds—I know. Bad. But like I was saying, my life was shitty. My dad was an addict—I never saw him. My mom was off finding herself in the desert or whatever. It was just me and Gram, and though she loved me, she had her own demons.

"I had no focus. No purpose. School sucked, I didn't know what I wanted out of life, and all I was doing was partying, which created this vicious cycle of falling even farther behind in school and always disappointing people and feeling like shit. Sometimes my thoughts got pretty dark. I even thought about suicide.

"But I found them. And I felt saved. Understood. These people . . . they listened to me. And they scooped me up and took me in." He shuts his eyes, remembering how good that felt. "They find you when you're weak. Though, to be fair, isn't every teenager weak?" He shakes his head. "We were all fucked up. I told all my friends they should join. Every single one. I was so . . . *thrilled*, I wanted to help everyone."

Something flashes out the window. His heart jumps. Are they here already? But a moment later, the window is dark. It's probably just headlights. He needs to calm down.

"Anyway, one day, when I turned eighteen, I joined them at their compound. I left home with no forwarding address. I wasn't allowed to tell Gram where I was going. She probably worried about me. I couldn't even leave a note except to say that I was fine and safe. I was eighteen. There was nothing she could do to get me back if I didn't want to. That's part of their tactic, by the way. They get you when you're a teenager, but they wait until you're of age before dangling the carrot of joining for real. They wait until parents or guardians can't do anything, legally, to help. Then . . . they strike."

There's a huge lump in his throat. It all sucks so bad.

"At first, I thought this group was amazing—even at the compound. But then . . . it's like when you pull back a carpet and find mold underneath. There was a *lot* of mold. I tried to tell some people, and some believed me, but a lot of people didn't. And then I left. I ran, more specifically. Ran for my f-ing life and kept my f-ing mouth shut. It's been a long time since I've been out . . . but I *still* feel afraid. This guy in charge is scary. He knows people in high places. He has many, many ways to hurt you—and what's ironic is that some of those ways are things I supplied. I figured if I kept my head down, he'd leave me alone. But I think that was wrong."

He laughs mirthlessly. "You're probably wondering why I'm telling you all this. Like, *keep your mouth shut if it's so dangerous.* The thing is, I think some people are coming for me. This might be my only chance to say all of this. And I want people to know. I'm willing to make the sacrifice. That place . . . it ruined me, and it's still out there. That guy—the leader—he's still out there. I got out, but I still feel the effects, and I probably will for the rest of my life—and I don't want that to happen to someone else."

Tears fill his eyes. *Crap.* He hadn't expected to cry. There are limits to what he'd do on camera—even on the last day of his life.

"Look, they're going to take this down probably really, really soon," he says quickly. "I can only hope that someone will screen-record this while it's still up and make it go viral. Seriously, the more people who see it, the more people who'll know. I'm depending on you, okay? Again, it's a group called ISB. Please, if you know anyone involved, have a serious conversation with them. It's a dangerous organization. You could save their life."

And then he lurches forward and hits Stop.

He sits for a moment, the tears spilling silently down his cheeks. Just like that, and the video is out there in the world. He looks at the stats. There were thousands of viewers, more than he's ever had in his life. And more are watching now.

He looks out the window again. The street he lives on is as dead as ever. A nothing town, in a nothing state, in a nothing life. But that's the trade-off, he tells himself. It's not like he can go back to anyone he used to know. And so, he's here.

And they're coming. He knows they're coming. And he knows what they're looking for. The address.

He shuts his eyes and waits. They're going to make him pay.

He just hopes it's all worth it.

CHAPTER ONE

CARSON CITY, NEVADA
PRESENT DAY

There's a storm brewing.

Danny Martin watches out the window of the cab as the sky turns a curdled yellow. The wind bends branches sideways. Dust pelts the windshield. It's like the weather is psychic.

The cabdriver, a pudgy man in his late forties, puts on his hazard lights and eyes her with concern. "Bad time to be out, miss. Might even get a tornado."

"Sorry to make you drive in this." She sinks lower in the back seat.

"Won't be much longer," the driver says, observing the map on the GPS device suction-cupped to his windshield. "But still. Better take cover when you get there. Your friend got a basement? You might need it."

"She does," Danny lies. She has no idea if Bex has a basement.

She glances at her phone. Bex's address is highlighted in bold. Danny has the directions spelled out, turn by turn, and she follows along with the driver. She needs to know, herself, just how close they are getting. It's hard letting things evade her control, so she has rules. *Touch the light switch four times, or else something bad will happen. Give him at least five compliments daily, or he'll hate you forever. Leave nothing to chance. Trust no one.*

She looks out the window. This town is cute, if you like quaint, Main Street, live-in-a-bubble sorts of places—it's certainly different from the place *she* has been calling home. There's a kid's consignment store that has a cheerful yellow-and-blue striped awning, a charming little bookstore called Scribbles and Things, and an antique shop with a bronzed Buddha—and is that a spinning wheel?—in the front window display. They pass a playground, a fire station, a pretty stone fountain. The streets are abandoned, both because of the storm and because it's not even 8:00 a.m., and the fountain is overflowing with water—so are the gutters. But if it were sunny and dry, this would probably be a nice spot to spend an afternoon.

A perfect place to have a nice life, probably. A perfect place to disappear.

Her phone buzzes in her hand. She turns it over.

Check in, please.

Danny checks her list of directions. *Two turns down, two to go.*

Abruptly, the taxi comes to a stop. "One-oh-five Hartwood Avenue."

Danny looks up, startled. She missed clocking one of the turns. *Fuck.* She needs to do it right, today of all days. She's almost tempted to ask him to go back and do it again.

She turns to look at where the cabbie is gesturing. Bex's house is painted white and has a small front porch. The yard is a patch of green grass that's getting greener and muddier from the storm. There's an iron fence surrounding the back, maybe for a dog. A tire swing careers from a big oak, the wind forcing it against the trunk every few seconds. The oak's upper branches whip wildly, threatening to claw the house. There are kids' toys strewn around the front porch—a plastic shovel, a tricycle, a soccer ball that's rolling farther into the lawn with every gust. Danny also notices the windsock in the shape of a goldfish spinning wildly from the eaves. Her memory flashes with recognition. Could it be the same one? Bex won something just like this at the county fair when they were sophomores. It used to hang off her parents' front porch, right over the door. Somehow it pushes everything into sharp, nauseating focus. Bex really lives here. She was Danny's oldest, best friend . . . until she wasn't.

"Miss?" The driver glances at her in the rearview again. The windshield wipers swish and groan. "This the right place?"

"Uh . . ." Danny pushes a shaky hand through her hair, suddenly afraid. Bex's windows are dark and the blinds are pulled shut. When she looks up the street, all the other houses look similarly buttoned up. It's so fucking early, that's why. She always forgets people don't keep the same schedule as she does. She's been awake for hours—she's used to waking up before the sun anyway, sometimes even in the middle of the night if that's what is asked of her. *Or something bad will happen.*

She clears her throat. "Um, d'you mind if we drive around a bit? Like, maybe back to the bus station, and then come back again?"

He stares at her. "You serious?"

"Or, um, at least back a few streets. Just to kill time." She tries to sound casual. "I'm a little early. I don't want to wake them up, but this weather . . . I'd rather not hang around outside, either. I'll pay you," she adds, noticing his disgruntled expression. "I have the cash. Double, if you want."

The driver's hand creeps to the gearshift. "Better hope the weather doesn't get worse."

He pulls away from the curb. With this temporary reprieve, Danny feels a weight lifting off her. She shuts her eyes and rhythmically breathes. She is steady. She is in control again. For a few minutes, anyway. And when they come back around in fifteen minutes or so, she'll be ready to reconnect the dots in her life for real.

CHAPTER TWO

In her dream, Rebecca Reyes—now Williams—is blindfolded.

A hand clasps hers, and then someone leads her through an unfamiliar maze of rooms.

"Where are we going?" she wails.

The guide—a woman—giggles ominously. She tugs Rebecca's hand, yanking her up a flight of stairs. Rebecca's bare feet skid across a wooden floor. Now there's a carpet underfoot. Her free hand reaches out and touches the edge of a bumpy stucco wall. She knows this wall. She's scraped it, blindfolded, before.

"Can you please tell me what this is all about?" she pleads, the panic rising.

The woman doesn't answer. Rebecca's heart starts to pound. She doesn't want to be here. She doesn't trust this woman. She doesn't trust *anyone*. Not anymore.

"Take off my blindfold," she demands. "Where are my children? I want to see them. Roscoe? Where is Roscoe?"

"He's not yours." The woman continues to giggle.

"What's so goddamn *funny*?" Rebecca asks. "What are you talking about?"

The giggling grows louder . . . and closer, too. Then she feels something wet on her ear. *Blood?*

She jolts up. She is drenched in sweat and lying in bed. Her son, Roscoe, sits next to her on the mattress. At first, the little boy's expression is jarring. His smile is spiky, mischievous, *knowing*. It's like he's looking straight into her. She half expects him to ask her where the woman was taking her in the dream.

But then she focuses: No. Roscoe's giggles are innocent. He points at Rebecca's nose and laughs again. She touches there, pulls something away. Attached to her finger is a red smiley face sticker.

"Gave you a clown nose!" Roscoe declares, waving a sheet of stickers above his head. "Why'd you have to move, Mommy? I wanted to give you clown cheeks, too."

"Sorry, baby," Rebecca croaks, consciousness slowly seeping back in. *Relief.*

Her husband, Tom, appears in the doorway, carrying their eighteen-month-old, Charlie, on his hip. When he sees Rebecca's stickered face, he grins. "Mommy's gotten a makeover, I see. But you know what happens to little boys who wake Mommy up from her precious sleep?"

"What happens?" Roscoe turns excitedly to his dad. His eyes widen with joyful trepidation.

Tom plops the baby on the bed and lunges for Roscoe. "They get eaten by the tickle monster!"

Tom sweeps Roscoe up by his ankles and holds him upside down. The sticker sheet flies onto the floor. After a beat, Rebecca tips forward and does her part in this game, tickling his belly. It takes a lot of effort for her to be cheerful, though. Her head is still so . . . *cloudy.*

"Make the tickle monster stop, Dad!" Roscoe screams. "Her hands are cold!"

"Okay, okay." Tom turns Roscoe upright and sets him on his feet. Rebecca ruffles his sandy hair, feeling a wave of simple pleasure. It's tinged with dread, though, and irritation. Residue from that awful dream is tarnishing the sweet family moment.

"What do you want for breakfast, bud?" Tom squats to meet Roscoe's eyes.

"Pancakes!" Roscoe bellows, his usual request for a Saturday.

"And what about you, Mrs. Monster?" When Tom turns to her again, his smile falters, and he cocks his head. "Everything okay?" He gestures to her shirt. "You're all wet."

Rebecca flinches in horror. *There is blood*. But then she looks down and sees the wet patches on her shirt. Sweat.

"Oh." She tries to keep her voice light as she pulls her shirt away from her sticky skin. "Mind watching them while I get a quick shower?"

"Yeah. Sure. Take your time."

But Tom doesn't move from his spot. He's still studying her like he doesn't buy that everything's fine. Does she blame him? He knows all her tells. Still, she flashes him a reassuring smile and steps toward Charlie in his arms.

"Sorry. I didn't even say good morning to my peanut."

Her baby smells like powder and the full diaper of a child who slept so heavily for eleven hours straight he didn't even realize he was wet. Rebecca is lucky to have such a good sleeper. Her whole *life* feels lucky. This house. This husband. This family. She knows how different things could be.

Finally, Tom and the baby turn toward the stairs, yelling down to Roscoe, who is already in the kitchen. "Don't touch the stove, buddy! I'll do it!"

"Okay, but hurry up!" Roscoe yells back. "I'm hungry!"

Rebecca sighs and trudges toward the bathroom. She stares at herself in the mirror and rubs her eyes. She looks exhausted. *Harried*. It was just the dream, though. *Only* a dream.

She strips off her sweaty bedclothes and sits on the edge of the tub, massaging her temples, trying to chase the dream away. A gust of air presses against the window. The sky is a bizarre color of pea soup, and the trees bend sideways. The storm looks bad. She can't remember the last time they had terrible weather this time of year. It feels like an omen.

But that's ridiculous. It's just weather.

Through the vents, she hears her husband in the kitchen, talking to the boys. Roscoe, as usual, is full of chatter. ". . . So when he snaps his finger, every single character turns to dust!" he declares, in the middle of a story.

"Snaps his *fingers*," Tom corrects. "Snap one finger, and that means he broke it."

"Yeah, and then he says, *I am . . . I am . . .* Dad, what does *ineditable* mean?"

"Inedible? You mean like you can't eat him? Hope not, buddy. Don't think Iron Man would taste very good. Maybe you mean *invincible*?"

"Yeah, maybe. Hey, Dad?" Roscoe's voice now sounds earnest. "Why does Mommy take such *long* showers?"

There's a pause. A clang. Rebecca stops breathing to hear his answer. "Well, long showers feel good," her husband answers.

"Yeah, but you don't take long showers."

Tom pauses a moment. "True," he finally says. "I guess, for Mom, it's her safe space."

"She feels safe in the *shower*? That's weird."

"Not really. It's small, and it's warm—seems pretty safe and nice to me. Your safe space is in your bed, right? With all the stars on your ceiling, and your nightlight?"

"Those stars are awesome," Roscoe says proudly. Rebecca presses curled fists to her chest—her sweet, sweet child.

"Remember when we put them up?" Tom says. "Anyway, that's how Mom feels in the shower, I bet."

"Oh. Okay." There's a pause, and then: "Dad, where's *your* safe space?"

"Probably sitting on the couch with all of you when we're watching a movie," Tom answers, without a hitch.

He is such a good man, Tom. Steady. Reliable. Dependable. Years ago, when Rebecca came to Carson City—*dropped from the sky*, Tom teased—she wasn't looking for a partner. She was ready to raise Roscoe alone. Anything would be better than where she came from.

Their first meeting was an idle chat at the grocery store about ice cream flavors. Tom made her laugh, something she hadn't done in a long time. When she went home to the little rental apartment that didn't feel like hers, she felt a little lighter. She thought, *People are so nice here. Maybe I* can *do this.*

A few days later, in divine intervention, she ran into Tom *again*—this time, in the parking lot of the hospital. Rebecca's OB, Dr. Salley, was concerned about her pregnancy, so he'd sent her to sonography for a quick scan. The scan was fine, but Rebecca was shaky and traumatized after the appointment. She'd waited on the curb for a cab to take her back to her dingy apartment; the longer it took the cab to arrive, the more she'd questioned if she'd made the right choice. Tom had appeared in front of her, babbling that he did marketing for the hospital and just happened to be in the building for a meeting—he wasn't a stalker, he swore! Did she remember him from the Price Chopper?

And then Rebecca had burst into tears.

Tom wasn't scared of a woman crying, though. And he did what Rebecca always wanted someone to do when she cried—not tell her to stop, not try to solve her problems, but just comfort her by squeezing her hand and quietly letting her get it all out. When she was done, he'd asked if Rebecca wanted to take her mind off things and see a movie with him at the local theater. "I was going anyway," he added. "Though . . . maybe you don't want to see what I have tickets for."

It was one of those of car-racing action movies—that actually, back in the day, Rebecca found entertaining enough. Her knee-jerk reaction was still to say no, but she was so lonely. Her instincts were rusty, but she had this feeling Tom was interested in her—*why*, she had no idea, because she felt she looked like she'd swallowed a beach ball and was probably acting like a feral animal. Also, Tom seemed safe. So, after a lot of waffling, she decided to go with him to the movies.

In the dark theater, Tom was a gentleman. He bought her snacks. They laughed at all the same silly jokes. Their fingers bumped when they both went for popcorn—a food, much like ice cream, Rebecca couldn't get enough of after years of not eating it. The wistful, airy storyline did take her mind off things; it had been ages since she'd seen a movie, *period*.

After, Tom asked her out for another date on the spot, but she told him she wanted to take it slow. In the end, though, Rebecca called him the next day. It didn't take long for her to fall for him, and for Tom to fall for her. Despite everything, she still had the capacity to love someone.

As they grew closer, Tom admitted that he was overcoming substance addiction; it was still sometimes a struggle, with lots of meetings and check-ins. At first, Rebecca figured him relapsing was a foregone conclusion—this all had to be too good to be true. She grew cautious around him, hyperaware when he excused himself for the restroom on their dates, always hunting for signs of irregular behavior. It took her a while to believe that he truly wanted to be clean, but, eventually, it seemed like the path became easier. She wondered if that's why he was drawn to her; maybe he could tell from first glance she was running from something, too. Rebecca wanted to be open with him about her past, but she was still always looking over her shoulder, scared of uttering certain names out loud. She gave Tom just enough of a sketch about her past so that he could fill in the rest of the picture himself. Nothing was a lie, not really. But the stuff she left out—it was for his own good.

Sometimes she thinks about her blurring of the truth, though. Do all husbands and wives keep such big secrets from each other?

She steps into the shower and lets the hot water needle her scalp. The room fills with steam. She hugs her body, running her hands down her shoulders, her arms, and to the back of her legs. Tom is right: this is her safe space, usually the place where she can calm down. But the odd images in that dream pound at her, like waves against an ocean shore, again and again, over and over. That woman dragging her. The feel of that stucco. It was more *real* than it has been for a long, long time. *Why?*

She eyes the body scrubber hanging from a hook. *Yes.* She grabs it and starts to scour her skin. It's hard to tell what hurts more, the scalding water or the scrubber. Skin peels off in flakes, heading for the drain. *Good.* Yes. Scrub it clean. She exfoliates her stomach, her shoulders, her back. When she gets to a spot on her upper thigh, she moves the brush to avoid the area, and a feeling of dread bubbles up. She never touches the old wound. She despises when she gets a glimpse of it. It's hidden in such a place that it's rarely exposed on her body; when Tom asked about it, she glossed over an explanation, saying it had been an accident.

Ten minutes later, she turns off the faucet. Water drips from the tap. Her reflection is blurry in the steamed-up mirror. Sound streams from the vent again—Charlie banging on his highchair tray, Roscoe singing along with the TV, and every once in a while, Tom calling out things like, "Syrup or butter? Milk or orange juice?"

Rebecca reaches for a towel. Her mind feels clearer. Her heart isn't racing anymore. A cloud still hangs over her, and she's still so jumpy, but it's just residue from the dream. It always goes away. At least the dreams aren't as frequent anymore; she used to disappear into the shower constantly before Roscoe was born. But those times—they were so different. How often did Tom hear her weeping under the spray? The walls are thin in this old house. The vents echo. When she'd come downstairs after, no matter how cheerful she'd appear, there were always questions in Tom's eyes. She knew he wanted to ask things, but how much do you owe a person, even someone like Tom? "The past is the past," she'd told him when she could feel his curiosity bubbling over. "I'm going forward, not back."

Something catches her eye out the window.

Rebecca stops drying her calves, straightens, and wipes the steam from the glass. A taxi has pulled up to their curb. *That's odd*. They aren't expecting anyone, and they rarely get random pop-ins.

The back door to the cab opens, and someone steps out. Suddenly parched, Rebecca reaches for a glass tumbler on the counter and takes a sip of cold water. Their unexpected guest has light hair and carries a ratty black backpack. Whoever she is leans over and speaks to the driver, then closes the door gently, as if she worries about breaking it. Then, she peers at Rebecca's house with a serious, determined expression. Finally, the cab pulls away, and the woman takes a few tentative steps up Rebecca's walk.

It's only then that Rebecca realizes who it is.

Danny.

No. Her mind must be playing tricks. With trembling fingers, she grabs her phone and pulls up the app for the video doorbell she insisted

Tom install a month ago because of . . . well, because of some things she doesn't want to think about. The live feed appears on the screen. There's a grainy image of a thin, hunched woman walking slowly toward their front porch. It is undeniably Danny Martin. One of the top two people in the world she *least* wants to see.

She sucks in a gasp. The tumbler slips from her fingers and falls to the floor, shattering into a thousand tiny shards.

CHAPTER THREE

Tom masterfully flips the first pancake. "Boom," he says as the underside starts to sizzle. He's always been the breakfast guy. Guys in college used to ask him if he'd ever been a short-order cook. *Yeah, right*, he'd joke with them. *Like I'd ever be able to get up that early.* Of course, that was before he had kids.

Something crashes upstairs. He looks up, startled. "Rebecca? You okay?"

There's a pause, but then Rebecca shouts, a little shakily, "Yep! Water glass—my hands were wet. No big deal!"

"You need a broom?"

"There's one up here. I've got it!"

He heads back to the kitchen, ruffling Roscoe's messy hair as he passes. The boy has changed out of his pajamas and into his Iron Man costume. It consists of a shiny jumpsuit and a plastic superhero mask, though the mask is already pushed back to the top of his head like a hat. Charlie, the baby, sits next to him in his high chair, sucking greedily on a bottle of milk. According to the dozens of baby books Rebecca bought when she was pregnant with Roscoe, eighteen-month-olds aren't technically supposed to drink out of bottles anymore—something to do with the rubber nipples and the formation of their teeth—but sometimes bottles are the only thing that comforts the kid, so Tom sneaks him one every now and again. It's not like the boy's going to go to kindergarten still using a bottle. It's gonna be fine.

He listens for more noises from upstairs. The broom. Footsteps. Did she break a glass? Out of the corner of his eye, he notices Roscoe watching him. He heard the crash, too. Roscoe can be a sensitive kid. Full of worries. Never misses a trick.

"Mom will be down soon, and then we'll start our amazing Saturday," he assures him. "A little cleaning, maybe a dance party, some Lego . . . and how about a movie on the couch later? Disney? Or maybe your mom and I will watch something romantic once you all are down for bed?" He winks. A simple day, just how he likes it. "But first, my friend, you're gonna eat the most amazing pancakes ever. Do you think I should make Mommy heart-shaped pancakes, or Mickey Mouse?"

"Heart-shaped," Roscoe decides.

"I hear that, man."

The wind kicks up again, pressing against the side of the house. The kitchen lights flicker. Roscoe's nearly translucent eyebrows knit together with a new concern. "This storm is pretty bad. Do you think the power will go out?"

"Maybe, buddy. But it's okay. No big deal." He opens the junk drawer. "We'll look for some candles. You don't happen to know where any are, do you?"

"Dad! I'm not allowed to play with candles!"

"Oh yeah," Tom jokes. "I forgot you're only seven."

He opens another drawer, and another. Things are so jumbled that he can't seem to find a flashlight, either. It agitates him, though he isn't sure why. Maybe it's the expression he saw on Rebecca's face that's dampened his mood. He dreads that look because it takes her so long to come out of the fog. And she never talks about what's on her mind.

"What if this wind blows us into another dimension?" Roscoe asks suddenly.

"Another *dimension*?" Tom chuckles as he switches gears from his flashlight search and pours more batter onto the griddle. "Where'd you hear about dimensions, bud? That's Iron Man kind of stuff."

"I read about them in my fact book at school. Like, in other dimensions, there are people who look just like us—but they *aren't* like us, right?" Roscoe reports. "It's called arrow worlds?"

Tom thinks for a moment. "I think you're talking about parallel worlds. Like side by side." He flips the pancake again—*yes*, another perfect flip—and then holds up his hands parallel to each other to demonstrate. "That's what parallel means. It's this idea that there are other worlds out there, and different versions of us are living lives based on all the other things that could have happened to us. Like, say I actually hit a home run my senior year of high school the day the baseball talent scout was watching. What college would I have gone to instead? Maybe I'd be playing in the big leagues! Maybe there's a version of me out there living that life!"

"Whoa!" Roscoe's eyes are starry. "So I'd have a professional baseball player for a dad?"

Tom gets a pang of wistfulness. *I wish, kid.* "You never know."

What he doesn't say is that there's no version where Tom would have hit a home run that day—he'd been high out of his mind on pills, some weed, probably a few shots of tequila, and who knows what else. Even if he'd played amazingly, even if he'd hit another *hundred* home runs that season, he would have never made the big leagues. His addiction stood in the way.

But it didn't hamper him forever. Because there was another crossroad in his life, and that time, he'd chosen the right path. But what if, when he'd met Rebecca, he'd walked away, went back to his old habits? Tom had still been on unstable ground when they met, only a few months clean. If he hadn't chatted her up at the grocery store, and if he hadn't then approached a crying Rebecca outside of the hospital a few days later, he might not have Roscoe or Charlie today.

Thank God he'd taken the chance. In any other circumstance, he would have probably steered clear of a pregnant single woman, but there had been something different about Rebecca. She'd seemed vulnerable but also tough and self-reliant—and he liked how she was totally game for the car-crash movie he took her to on their first date, even though the movie was horrible. Also, in the middle of her crying episode in the hospital parking lot, he remembered how she'd suddenly pointed at his sneaker. "Your lace is about to be untied," she'd said between sobs. "Wouldn't want to trip." It touched him that she could be concerned about other people in the midst of her fear and pain. He could see she was a good person. He was going to therapy as part of his recovery, and he'd learned that for the past decade, he'd been pushing away everyone who cared about him, thinking he didn't deserve them. He was trying to believe that he was worthy of kindness as much as anyone else.

But, on the flip side, he also felt needed, and that felt good. The responsibility set him straight. Having a ready-made family compelled him to get up and go to work every morning, too—which, at the time, had been a shitty starter job in the hospital's marketing department. Parallel Life Guy? He would've quit that job in a heartbeat. By now, Parallel Life Guy might be in a ditch somewhere, high out of his mind.

Another big gust of wind blows the umbrella on the patio table sideways with a crash.

"Uh-oh," Tom says. The umbrella skitters across the yard and comes to a halt at the block fence that surrounds their property. He darts outside, grabs it before it gets damaged, and turns the crank to close it up. Just as he's about to go back inside, one of the chairs blows all the way to the back of the fence and bangs noisily against the iron gate. Gritting his teeth, Tom runs out to rescue it.

The wind presses against him as strong as a shove. He grabs the chair and muscles it back to the porch but then, in his peripheral vision, twin headlights cut slowly through the fog on an adjacent street. Tom stops to look. The car is really creeping along—sure, there's a storm outside, but there's no cause to drive *that* slow.

The rain drips down his neck and into his shirt, making him shiver. About a month ago, Rebecca suddenly got this notion that someone was lurking around their property. She'd heard rumors about break-ins, she said—she wouldn't let up about it. Tom dropped a bunch of money on one of those expensive video doorbells so they could monitor things. Nothing has come up on the camera's feed, per se, but Tom *has* noticed some suspiciously slow cars on the surrounding streets from time to time. He doesn't want to worry his wife, but last week, there was this sedan parked down the block for half the day, and he was pretty sure someone was inside.

"Dad?"

Roscoe stands at the sliding door, peering out the opening. Tom makes a big show of setting down the chair in its proper place. "Coming in now, buddy. Bet those pancakes are done." He peers over the fence to the side street again. The car, whoever it was, has crept away. Good.

The pancakes are just about perfect. He pulls them off, covers them with a paper towel, and steps toward the stairs for Rebecca. "Babe? Breakfast!"

No answer.

"Honey?"

Still silence.

What's she doing up there? She'd seemed so out of it in bed. He can tell she's had another dream. She's always dazed afterward. Talking to her, trying to suss out what she's feeling . . . it's like feeling around in a dark attic, not knowing what sorts of spiderwebs you might touch.

He knows it has to do with the parts of her past she doesn't talk about. Most dudes wouldn't have been able to handle their wives keeping their past fuzzy, but Tom tried to put that aside. It was obvious, that day he'd come upon her in the hospital parking lot, that Rebecca was doing the pregnancy thing alone—she seemed so shaken, like she had no one else to turn to, and then she just lost it in his arms. Tom, a stranger! But he felt flattered that she chose his shoulder to cry on. *Needed*. It also didn't hurt that Rebecca was gorgeous, funny, and really sweet.

Eventually, Rebecca explained that she'd gotten pregnant by a one-night stand; she barely knew the guy, but she said he was an asshole and definitely wouldn't want a kid. Tom wondered if she still had ties to the dude, even though Rebecca swore up and down that she did not. The more he fell for her, the more he looked past it. Shit happened.

Probably better the douche didn't want to be a dad. Rebecca was all in when it came to becoming a mother, and she wanted to bring Tom along on that journey—if he was game.

And . . . Tom *was* game, much to his surprise. In his partying days, he'd never given any serious thought to parenthood—he could barely take care of himself, let alone a little human. But once he was clear-headed, he remembered how he used to babysit the neighbor kids when he was in junior high. He had so much fun making up obstacle courses for them in the basement and writing out the multiplication tables in shaving cream on the bathroom mirror. (The mom wasn't a huge fan, but it sure helped the kids learn.) He would make a good dad. Maybe a great dad. Didn't hurt that Tom's parents liked Rebecca, too; found her steady and sweet. *They* certainly didn't seem to care that she was expecting and the baby wasn't his. In fact, his mom took him aside and said Rebecca was the best thing that had ever happened to him. And though he'd never tell this to his mom's face, she was *never* wrong.

It's why he . . . well, not *overlooked* things about Rebecca, but he didn't push her to talk about stuff, either. It isn't like there are lots of Greatest Hits from *his* past. But now, eight years later, eight years sober, it nags at Tom sometimes, especially when his wife seems to disappear into herself and won't answer his questions. Was her dream this morning about Baby Daddy? When she'd said he was a dick, did she mean he was annoying . . . or *abusive*? Also, why doesn't Rebecca speak to her parents? ("They weren't the best, and we were never really close," she'd told him—case closed.) What's with the lack of pictures of her life before Carson City? ("I'm not really a picture-taker," was her excuse—but that isn't true, because she takes hundreds of shots of the boys.) And why, when he brought up something innocuous like high school homecoming, for example, did Rebecca grow pale and jittery and change the subject? It took Herculean effort for Tom to find out she was from Davis, California—a town, as far as Tom can tell, that looks perfectly middle-of-the-road. He'd googled it; they had a Walmart but not a Target, a very small community park and a nice-sized library, and nearly no crime.

Only once did Tom really try to broach the subject of how he wished

Rebecca opened up more. It wasn't long after they'd met—Rebecca was about eight months pregnant, really starting to get swollen and uncomfortable. Tom was long past tapered withdrawal; he'd moved on to wading through boring, itchy months where sobriety didn't feel quite like a habit yet but he'd beat himself up if he relapsed. One night, he'd felt particularly unsettled, the itch for just a tiny taste so, so bad. So he decided to rely on Rebecca. He'd already told her the broad strokes of his addiction, but that night he told her the dirty stuff, all that gunk hiding in the corners. Like snorting stuff in the middle school bathroom, and passing out at his cousin's wedding, where he was supposed to be giving a speech, because he'd taken too much. Waking up in the ER and being told he was either going to rehab or jail. All the dumb, desperate, dangerous things he'd done to score drugs and get high, including taking all of his mom's meds after her disc surgery. After he'd told her about literally watching his buddy die from an overdose and not being able to help him because he didn't know CPR and considering, in those dark, regretful days afterward, purposefully overdosing *himself* to ease his pain—well, after all that, he'd felt almost naked.

So he'd asked her, gently, if she had some dark stuff in her past, too.

She'd waited a long time before answering. "My past . . . it's nothing that interesting—certainly nothing like what you went through."

And then, idiot that he was, he'd joked, "So if I google *you*, I won't find any skeletons in your closet?"

Her eyes had flashed—but only for a moment. "I don't even have a Facebook page. Never have." She'd started tapping on her phone—angrily, maybe. "Here. Do you want to check? Don't believe me?"

Tom had been flooded with embarrassment. Now she thought he didn't trust her. Then again, was it so much to ask? Later that same night, he *had* googled her. He hadn't before, but maybe there *was* a dark secret he'd missed.

But . . . there was nothing. Or, rather, too many Rebecca Reyeses matching her age and description to find *his* Rebecca in the haystack.

"Hey, Dad?"

When he turns back, Roscoe is frowning at something at the front door, which he can see from his seat at the kitchen table. "There's some lady on our porch," he says.

"Lady?"

Tom walks into the hall. Sure enough, he can see a wavy figure on the other side of the ground-glass sidelight.

"Let's go see what she needs." He scoops up Charlie from the high chair. Roscoe scrapes his chair back and zips down the hall, too, excited for this new adventure.

Tom's halfway to the door when feet pound down the stairs. Rebecca streaks past him, her wet hair slapping against her back, and practically throws herself against the front door, blocking their view.

"Babe?" Tom asks, stopping in his tracks.

His wife spins around. There's a strange, frenzied look on her face that he's never seen before. "Oh! Hi!" Her gaze darts from Tom to Roscoe to the baby.

"There's somebody on the porch!" Roscoe declares excitedly.

Tom frowns. "One of the neighbors, maybe? Maybe because of the storm."

"Let's look at her through the video doorbell!" Roscoe cries. He loves the video doorbell.

Rebecca glances at the door. Tom gets a weird, crawling feeling. She already *knows* someone is at the door. Tom can tell.

Then the doorbell actually rings. Rebecca jumps.

"Should we . . . get that?" Tom asks, jokingly. Whoever it is can see them through the window. They'll know they're home.

"I'll do it." Rebecca lurches to the door, undoing the two deadbolts she insisted he install. Tom can't see who's on the other side, but he hears a woman's voice.

"Bex?" the stranger murmurs. "Hey. Do you remember . . ."

"Oh my God, Danny?" Rebecca cries in a strange, fake-happy tone.

Tom's heart hammers faster. His mind catches on what she said. Danny. *Danny?* Does that name ring a bell? See, that's the thing: with a wife who tells him nothing, he *knows* nothing. But judging by the terror in Rebecca's eyes, one thing's for damn sure.

Danny? She was *not invited*.

CHAPTER FOUR

Rebecca's gaze is fixed on Danny, who is leaning toward her. And then, to Rebecca's horror, Danny starts to *whisper* ever so softly in her ear.

"Play nice," she says. "I'm just here to talk."

Rebecca can barely breathe. She breaks eye contact and looks past Danny into the front yard. The storm is still whipping, but no cars lurk at the curb. No strangers hunch behind the trees, at least from what she can see.

"I'm alone," Danny adds, as if reading her mind. "It's just you and me. I promise."

This can't be happening, Rebecca thinks. *She needs to leave. Now.*

"Rebecca?" Tom steps forward, places a hand on her shoulder. She jumps at his touch. "Everything okay?"

Rebecca shakily turns to him. "This is, um, Danny." What choice does she have except to introduce her?

"You already said that." Tom's brow is furrowed, and there's an uncomfortable edge to his voice.

"Mind if I get out of this wind?" Danny breaks the silence, motioning behind her at the swirling sky. "I'm afraid I might blow away!"

Tom looks at Rebecca for guidance. Against every fiber of her being, Rebecca moves aside. "Uh . . . yeah, sure. Come on in."

"Whew, thanks!" Danny says brightly, dripping her way into the foyer. "Man! Do you always have weather like this? The cabdriver told me we might get a tornado!"

"It's pretty crazy out there," Tom says. Rebecca can feel his gaze returning to her, but she knows if she looks at him right now, she'll crack. He'll see how afraid she is. She'll give something away about Danny. *And then what will Danny do?*

Instead, she looks her old friend up and down. Danny looks the same in a lot of ways: that wavy, golden-blond hair, lots of freckles, the pointy chin people always said gave her a Reese Witherspoon vibe. But there are differences, too. Danny has always been petite, but now she seems withered and wasted. Her legs in her skinny jeans look emaciated. Her oversized sweater swallows her whole. She's wearing the old costume jewelry ring they bought at Joe's Thrift on Main Street when they were in eleventh grade—could it really be the same one?—except now, instead of wearing it on her pointer finger, her fingers are so whittled down it only fits on her *thumb*.

There's something off about her pallor, too—her skin is almost gray, and her fingernails are blue. *Is she sick?* Rebecca wonders. Or maybe she's just cold. The rain drips off her, forming a puddle on the wood floor.

"Let me grab you a towel," Tom says, darting toward the kitchen. He's back in a flash—there's barely enough time for Rebecca and Danny to exchange a look.

As Danny mops her face, Rebecca says, "Danny, this is my husband, Tom."

"Nice to meet you, Tom," Danny chirps. "Sorry to barge in on you like this."

"No problem at all." Tom looks back and forth between them. "So, sorry—you know each other . . . how?"

"From high school," Danny supplies. "We were close. Went on all kinds of adventures, huh, Bex?"

"Tom doesn't want to hear about *those!*" Rebecca trills, her voice unnaturally high-pitched. Is she smiling? She doesn't feel like smiling, but she hopes she is. She can't control her mouth, or her words, or how quickly she is talking.

Tom frowns. "High school. So you're from . . . Davis, is it?"

"That's right!" Danny dries her hair. "Has Bex mentioned me?"

Rebecca just blinks. Her brain is sludge. She can barely think, she's so shocked. "We don't really rehash old times."

Tom gives her an odd look. Then he turns back to Danny. "Well, one thing Rebecca definitely didn't mention is that we'd be having company this morning. Otherwise I would have made more for breakfast."

"I, um, didn't know we *were* having company," Rebecca musters. "But, um, want some coffee, Danny?"

"Yeah, you look frozen," Tom says.

"Oh, I'm fine," Danny trills. "Again, *so* sorry to be just waltzing in here. I'm happy you were even home!"

"Let me get you some coffee. It's no trouble. You need a warm drink." Tom pivots for the kitchen—overzealously, because his backward step sends him bumping straight into Roscoe. Roscoe yelps, and Tom rears back. "My manners! Danny, this is Roscoe. And this guy"—he hefts the baby in his arms—"is Charlie. He's eighteen months."

"Hey, Charlie," Danny coos, touching his nose. It takes every ounce of control for Rebecca not to slap her hand away. *Do not touch my baby!*

But then it gets worse. Danny leans down and grins at Roscoe. "And hey, Roscoe. You're how old? Eight? Nine?"

"Seven," Roscoe admits, but then looks giddily at Tom. "She says I look *nine*!"

"You're a big boy," Tom praises.

Rebecca's smile is a grimace. *Stop looking at him. Stop smiling at him.* Every muscle in Rebecca's body is clenched. *Play nice. Play nice.*

Somehow, she makes it through the foyer on her own two legs, though it feels like she's swimming through slime and viewing the scene from down a long, dark tunnel. Roscoe skips beside them, obliviously excited by the guest. If only she could hide him away. If only she could hide them *all* away.

Danny seems to marvel at each room they pass—first the living room with its sectional couch and huge TV, then the dining room with its mahogany furniture and set table. "You have matching dishes—in a china cabinet, no less," she observes. "You're officially an adult."

"Oh, we inherited from my parents," Tom volunteers. "This is their house, actually—they moved to a smaller place. It's still crammed with their old things."

"It's a beautiful home. And Carson City is adorable—well, I'm sure it is when it's not the apocalypse outside."

Rebecca nods faintly. "Um, yes. It's a great place to live." *It was, until you showed up.*

They enter the kitchen. Danny looks around and whistles. "Could this place be any cuter? Oh my God, Bex, I love this for you!"

Rebecca tries to see the room from Danny's point of view: the stainless steel appliances, which Tom had installed when he inherited the house. The gleaming white cabinets. The expensive knives in the wooden block. The baby's cheerful blue high chair and Roscoe's plastic place mat with math facts up to twenty. A stack of pancakes and syrup, waiting, next to the stove. Then, she notices how Danny absently taps the light switch several times before actually stepping over the threshold. She clocks Tom seeing it, too.

"What do you do for a living, Tom, if you don't mind me asking?" Danny asks, sweet as pie.

"Uh, I'm in marketing and communications." Tom reaches into the cabinet to grab a mug. "But it's a little dry for so early in the morning."

Danny shrugs as she sits down. "Good communication is important. *Always.*" She looks right at Rebecca again—*pointedly*. "So do you work for a particular company?"

Rebecca wants to kick her. Why is she asking? She can't possibly *care*.

Tom stares between them, an uncomfortable smile on his face. Then he does what he always does in a tense situation: he babbles. "I'm the communications workflow manager for a few medium-sized companies in the area, actually. It started out with the local hospital—my dad knows the head of marketing there—but I've branched out since then. It's sort of a consulting gig, but since I work with a bunch of companies, it works out to a pretty good career."

"Cool." Danny rests her chin on her hands. "Good for you."

Tom shrugs. Rebecca can't imagine what he must be thinking. An emaciated stranger shows up on their doorstep and is now praising him for having a job? It's bizarre. She wishes desperately that Tom would just . . . *vanish* for a little while. Long enough for her to clean up this mess and make Danny go away. Because if there's one person in this world who might change Tom's mind about his wife, it's her old friend Danny.

"Rebecca? You okay?" Tom asks.

She jumps. They're both staring at her. "Um, of course," she says, *playing nice*. "Just thrilled."

CHAPTER FIVE

Domestic bliss. This is what Danny thinks as she takes in the rooms of her old friend's house. The blue-and-white crocheted afghan thrown over the sofa. The framed family photos on the walls, Bex's entire family wearing matching white shirts and blue jeans like they're dolls. It's the sort of vibe Danny's mom always aspired to, actually. Wait, has Bex turned into *Janice*? God, how many professional portraits did her mom force upon their little family of three? *Let's take a photo on the beach! Let's do a photo shoot for the Christmas card!* Maybe *that's* why Dad took off—he couldn't stand another feeble attempt at pretending they were happy. But the closer Danny looks at Bex's family photos, she doesn't see the same fake smiles. She feels a pang of envy. Just like Bex to have it all come easy.

Negativity! Danny winces and pushes the thought away. *No more negative thoughts, or something bad will happen*, she tells herself. She worried that being back in Bex's presence would bring her old baggage to the surface. She needs to focus.

She takes in more evidence of Bex's stunningly ordinary life. Magazines about food and decor in a little rack next to the chair. A smattering of bills on the table near the door. A tan, quilted purse—which must be Rebecca's, though she can't imagine her old friend carrying a *purse*—stuffed to the gills with baby wipes and goldfish crackers and other things she needs to satiate two children on the go. She's dreamed about this moment for a while, and here it is. And yet she's finding it hard to remain in the present.

Tom is still talking about his boring-as-oatmeal job. Then he pivots and starts talking about how his whole family still lives in Carson City—his parents, both sets of grandparents, and twenty-two first cousins.

"My family loves that Rebecca and I live here," Tom says. "It's great for the kids to have the grandparents nearby. They spoil them rotten."

"I'm sure," Danny says. "Lucky, having grandchildren so close." She clears her throat. "I guess you don't see your parents, Bex . . ."

"Rebecca's parents?" Tom glances at Bex. "I mean, we don't . . ."

"Not in a long time," Bex says over him, in a cool, forbidding tone. She won't look at Danny. It gives Danny a guilty pause.

Tom brings over the carafe and pours coffee into a mug he's retrieved for Danny. "Really, I'm fine," Danny says, trying to stop him. But Tom doesn't stop. He pours right to the top. He probably thinks he's being nice, but it's kind of annoying. "Um, I'll pour this back in. I don't need all this."

Tom shrugs. "Just don't drink it. No big deal."

"No, I need to . . ." She's feeling overwhelmed. She taps her finger against the lip of the mug five times. Maybe she'll only have a tiny sip. A tiny sip can't hurt, right?

When she looks up, Tom and Bex are staring at her. She smiles.

"Anyway, thank you so much for letting me interrupt your morning," Danny says. "I know it's early, and I've dropped in on you unannounced . . . You're a huge lifesaver. See, I'm sort of passing through, but I missed my ride, and then I kind of remembered you lived here, Bex. I hadn't seen you in so long, so . . ."

Tom sips his own coffee, glances worriedly at his wife, and then looks back at her with an apologetic smile. "Passing through . . . to where? Like, a job?" He looks Danny's outfit up and down dubiously. Danny knows how shabby she must seem. Where she's from, it's okay to walk around in threadbare clothes—admirable, in fact. But Tom is looking at her with pity, like he thinks she's rolled in off the street.

For a moment, she feels ashamed. *Zap! Negativity.*

"Sort of. I'm doing this outreach thing," Danny answers. "But, I'm such an idiot—I left my wallet, ID, all of that on the bus, and then my ride didn't show up." She rolls her eyes. "I just need a little bit of time to regroup and figure out a few logistics, and I couldn't think in the storm."

"Wait, you rode a *bus* here?" Bex asks. She looks skeptical.

"That's right," Danny answers. She stares at Bex. Bex stares back at her. Danny vows not to break her gaze first.

Tom puts his cup down and laughs uncomfortably. "Hey, man, I don't like buses, either. Terrible way to travel."

"But how did you get this address?" Bex asks next. "Was it Toby?"

"Toby?" Tom looks at Rebecca. "Who's . . . ?"

"Just someone from high school," Bex says.

Tom frowns. "Are you in touch with him?"

"No . . ." Bex swallows. "I just thought, maybe . . ." She looks at Danny, wanting an answer, but there's no way Danny's going to go near *that* question. Perceptive that Bex would guess Toby, though. She isn't wrong. Perhaps Bex saw Toby's video—the one that got him into so much trouble.

She takes the tiniest mouthful of coffee just to be polite and swishes it six times before swallowing. It feels like poison in her veins.

"Anyway, even letting me crash for a little bit would be amazing," she goes on once she's done swishing. She gestures to the window. "I literally saw a tree fall on a car on the ride over. Do you know falling tree branches can kill people, if they're heavy enough?"

"I've heard that, yes." Tom glances at Bex. "But it's up to you, honey—I know you had some things planned for this morning, some outings . . ."

"Uh . . . I don't . . ." Bex starts feverishly buttering a pancake, like she can't handle thinking about it. She pulls her little boy onto her lap and holds him tightly. "You all full, baby? Want anything else to eat?"

The boy looks overjoyed. "Can I have another pancake?"

"Sure."

"How about you, Danny?" Tom asks. He takes a loping step toward the sink, where he has presumably left the batter bowl. "Maybe enough for a few more."

"It's fine," Danny says. Like she'd *ever* eat pancakes.

Tom shoots her a glance. "It's no big deal."

"Really. I'm good." God, Tom is really trying to smooth this over, make things pleasant—in a protective kind of way. He cares about Bex, Danny can tell. This makes her envious, too.

Zap. Negativity!

"Did you know we're living in a parallel world?" Roscoe suddenly pipes up, like someone has dropped a coin into his back and he's sprung to life.

A confused, pained smile blooms on Bex's face. "*What*, honey?"

"A parallel world," Roscoe says proudly. "Dad said that there are other us people that made different choices living in parallel universes that are sort of like ours, but not *totally*. Like, there's another Dad, but it's the Dad who went to a different college because he hit a home run. Which would probably mean he might not have met Mom at Price Chopper, and then me and Mom would be living somewhere else."

Danny stares at the little boy. His bangs are in his eyes. His fingers are smeared with syrup. Actual sugary syrup, addling his brain. She pities the poor thing. This is not how one should raise a child.

"Wow, Roscoe!" Tom says proudly. "Look at you and your big brain!"

Danny can't resist. "Where do you think you'd be living in this other world, buddy?"

"Hmm." Roscoe taps his temple in an overly exaggerated thoughtful gesture that only kids can get away with. "I don't know . . ."

"Parallel worlds aren't real," Bex interrupts—sharply. "There's *nowhere* else you'd be living, Roscoe. This is our reality. Nothing else."

Danny looks over at her, surprised by her sudden passion. But then, considering the subject matter, maybe she shouldn't be. Tom's eyes bulge. Roscoe looks as if he thinks he's done something wrong. But then Tom claps a meaty hand on the little boy's shoulder. "Mom's right, buddy. We're in the right world for sure. Things worked out just like they were supposed to."

Danny swishes and sips, tickled with how precocious Bex's little boy is. And how *perceptive*. Far more than he realizes.

Parallel worlds, indeed.

CHAPTER SIX

DAVIS, CALIFORNIA
NINE YEARS BEFORE

The appointment takes place in a spartan study room in her town's dinky public library. After all the amazing things Danny had heard about Ben, she figured he'd at least have a proper office. One like her old therapist, Dr. Rose, who was on the second floor of a building that also housed a plastic surgeon and an architect. Dr. Rose had an indoor Zen fountain, a lot of spider plants, a soft couch with a lot of throw pillows with dumb, obvious inspirational phrases stitched onto them, things like *You Are Special* and *Mind over Matter*.

Then again, Danny despised that woman. Went only once before realizing it was a heap of bullshit.

This makeshift office, on the other hand, is so tiny that it can barely fit a table, four chairs, and a tripod with a video camera in the corner. A man is already in there when Danny enters, sitting comfortably in one of the chairs, legs stretched out in front of him. It can't possibly be Ben, though. This guy has sandy hair that's thinning at the top. His face is drawn and bony. His eyes are deep-set, which makes him look mournful and pouty. He's wearing a lame collared shirt and L.L.Bean chinos and, oh my God, *Crocs*. He also doesn't straighten when she enters, which she thinks is rude. Instead, he just peers at her directly, unblinking.

"Uh . . ." She glances behind her. This is totally the wrong room.

"Are you Danielle? Danielle Martin?" he asks.

"Yeah . . . ?" Danny mumbles.

He smiles. "I'm Ben. Welcome."

He reaches out his hand. Danny just stares. She doesn't have a ton of experience with adult guys after her dad left. Boys her age, sure—but not *men*. All of her teachers are women. She has no interactions with uncles or neighbors or even friends' parents. She can't think of the last time she was with an older man alone. This Ben guy looks pretty harmless, though—in fact, if he dared to try something with her, Danny's pretty sure she'd be fine with laughing in his face and walking out.

It's a letdown, really. *This* was who lots of kids at school were talking to? *This* was what Danny thought she was missing out on? All she's heard about is how amazing this Ben guy is. How *life-changing*. He's a captivating speaker. Developed some sort of life-coaching system that transforms people. Took some IQ test that deemed he's one of the smartest people in the world. Holds degrees from a bunch of prestigious universities, not that Danny really cares. She'd finally agreed to meet with him, accepting that she needed some direction in her life, some *guidance*, but maybe he's just as bullshit as all the other jokers claiming to help people. What kind of life coach doesn't even have an *office*? Even worse, this first session is more expensive than Dr. Rose, and Danny had to use her own money—her mom's rule is that she'll pay for licensed therapists *only*.

Ben is silent, still watching her. Danny shifts her weight. There's a strange, unpleasant scent—mildewed books, rotting plants, unwashed socks—that makes her want to puke. Everyone knows library study rooms are sex rooms. It's not a bad idea, really—it's private, it's quiet, and no one comes back here. She considers Brian Bishop, her latest crush. Not that she actually has the guts to even speak to him, let alone suggest secret boning in the library study room.

"Why don't you sit?" Ben finally says, pointing to a chair opposite. "No need to be nervous."

She scoffs. "I'm not *nervous*."

"You sure?"

"Yeah." She should definitely go. Or would leaving prove to him he was right—she *is* actually nervous? Which she isn't. Not at all. She's not afraid of this guy.

Begrudgingly, she sits. She doesn't break her gaze from his. "I'm not nervous," she repeats. *Fucker*, she adds, in her head.

"Good." His smile flickers. "So, what have you heard about me?"

Get a load of this narcissistic asshole, Danny thinks. "I don't know, nothing really," she says.

"Not *anything*?"

She shrugs. "I heard you were, like, super smart or something." She rolls her eyes.

"You don't believe that, though."

"I mean, intelligence is sort of subjective. Tests are bullshit."

"I agree with you," Ben says. "Such bullshit. What else did you hear?"

"I don't know." Danny feels annoyed. Are they just going to stroke his ego this whole time? "What did you hear about *me*?"

"I heard you're smart, too."

Danny twists her mouth. "No, you didn't." No one ever called her *smart*.

Ben seems puzzled by this. But before he responds, he points to the video camera she'd noticed when she came in.

"Mind if we record?"

Perv alert! "Uh, I do mind, yes."

"We can try it, at least? And if you don't like it, we can stop. I'll never share the tape. It's just our conversation. Your thoughts." Before she can say yes or no, Ben stands and turns on the camera. "Seriously, if we get rolling and you want it off, that's totally fine. Just say the word."

Danny wants to say the word right now, but something holds her back. Curiosity, maybe. She toys with the idea of saying something super offensive on video. She watches as Ben sits back down. He's shorter than she thought, probably only about Rebecca's height, but he has broad shoulders. His hands are small but strong with blunt, square fingers. Maybe he was a gymnast, or a weightlifter.

"So." He settles back down. "I'll ask you some questions, and we'll go from there. I'm glad you've come, by the way. This is a huge first step."

Does he expect her to say *Me too*? Danny isn't about to lie. Mostly she just feels embarrassed—on his behalf.

"Anyway." Ben points at the camera. "It's October fifth. Can you state your name? I know we just did that, but for the video."

"Oh. Um, Danielle. Danielle Martin. Everyone calls me Danny."

"Do you like that?"

She frowns. "Do I like what?"

"Being called Danny. Instead of Danielle."

The question puzzles her. Her mother has called her Danny ever since she was a baby. Everyone else followed suit. She's never thought of herself as a *Danielle*. She wonders why. It's not bad. Much more grown up.

"You can call me either," she says, shrugging. "I don't care."

"I like Danielle," Ben decides. She's kind of pleased that he made this choice. It's like he's read her mind. "So. How old are you, Danielle?"

"Seventeen." Her gaze flicks to the video lens. She clears her throat. "You sure no one else is gonna see this?"

"Oh God, no. It's just that my technique relies on talk therapy, Danielle. And maybe you already know this, but a lot of people have seen a lot of success with my program. Thousands. I'm based here in Davis—born and bred, just like you—but I speak with people from all over the country."

Danny shrugs. "Okay . . ."

"And sometimes, there are things said in these sessions that hold a key to a door you don't need to open yet. But when you're faced with those doors, later, you can go back and watch what you've said. And maybe all will be revealed. So, in essence, these recordings are for *you*."

Danny makes a face. Dr. Rose never talked about keys and doors. Mostly all they talked about was why Danny acted out and why she had such a bad attitude. She suspected her mother called Dr. Rose ahead of time and set the agenda for the sessions.

"So." Ben folds his hands. "How are you doing?"

". . . You mean in school?"

"Maybe. But mostly, I mean *you*. How are *you* doing?"

Danny shrugs. "Okay."

"Lots of friends? Like . . . who's your *best* friend?"

"My best friend's Bex. Rebecca." She studies Ben's expression. He just nods. She wonders if Rebecca likes *her* nickname, or if it was one of those things she'd stumbled into as well. Then again, Bex never seems to stumble into anything. She always knows what to do and say, what music to listen to and what types of jeans are in style—it just all comes so naturally to her. Bex and her perfect family, big house, perfect life, always reaching the finish line before Danny even starts the race. But she never gloats or makes Danny feel less than. She's always inclusive, so willing to share her wisdom with Danny so that Danny can up her cool quotient. Danny loves Bex for that—but she also hates her, too.

"And what about boys? Are you . . . dating?"

Danny laughs uncomfortably, feeling her nails dig into her thigh. There is no way she's going to talk about *boys* on his camera.

"Okay, okay, never mind," Ben says. "We'll skip that. I'm just trying to get a picture of where you *are* in life. What you're into. If you're mature or not mature."

Mature? Danny bristles. "I might not have a boyfriend, but that's not because I'm not mature. It's more because boys my age are undeveloped dipshits." Well, except for Brian Bishop. Or maybe *especially* Brian Bishop.

"Aha!" Ben cries, letting out a laugh. "Well, you know what they say—girls mature much faster than boys." He looks at her then, making steady eye contact. "You talk to your parents about that kind of stuff? Dipshit boys?"

Danny makes a face. "I mean, my dad isn't around. But my mom—no. No way."

"Sorry about your dad," Ben says. "But your mom—do you feel sad that you can't talk to her about those sorts of things?"

There's something about his tone that strikes a nerve. Is it the word *can't*, not *won't*? It's *her* decision not to talk to her mom. Or is it the word *sad*? God, therapists and their sadness. No, she isn't fucking sad she and her mom don't hang out and girl talk. If anything, she's annoyed—not about the talking part, but more because her mom has blinders on most of the time, and only sees what she wants to see. Sadness? That's for people who can't cope. Danny can't even remember the last time she cried. Sadness is for this emo loser and his creepy video camera. She wants to smash things, ground things under her boots, scream really loud—do strong, empowered things. Not curl up into a ball and be a sad, sad, sad little baby. Fuck this guy. Really, truly, fuck him.

"Danielle?" Ben's voice cuts through her thoughts. "Everything all right? Can you tell me where you went just now?"

She eyes him suspiciously. "Nowhere. I'm fine."

"Look, I had parents who didn't understand me either." He shifts, stares at his lap. His eyes get all soulful. What a fake.

Danny scoffs. "Who said I had parents who don't understand me?"

Ben doesn't answer this, just goes on with his story. "Parents who more or less abandoned me, actually. Dad left. And Mom took up with this . . . real fucker, if you pardon my language. I struggled. *Hard*. The boyfriend beat me. I watched him do it to her, too—within an inch of her life. I have the hospital records—I can show you."

He waits a beat. Is she supposed to say yes, please, *show* me the hospital records, I'd love to see them? Like, that *sucks*, and she's sorry it happened—but no thank you. And stop saying things like *fucker*, she wants to add. You're so far from cool it's ridiculous.

"I was helpless," Ben goes on, his voice cracking. "It was such a terrible time. I got into some real trouble. But finally, when I was at my lowest low, begging for some sort of change . . . something . . . *happened*. I was filled with this . . . *sparkle*. This . . . *clarity*. I knew how I could change. And I saw roads. So many roads. Roads not only for myself . . . but for others, too. It's when I came up with the ISB program."

His eyes are shining. He has this weird smile, too, like he's on drugs or something. Danny almost wants to laugh. Is he actually for real? And does he think she's going to buy into his weird little *religion*?

"I can help," Ben says. "I've helped a lot of people. Just ask them.

And if you don't get help here, where are you going to get it? Who's going to help you?"

Oh, like you're God? she thinks. *Yeah fucking right.*

"You deserve to be happy, Danielle. You really do."

And just like that, her walls go up. *Fuck this guy*, Danny thinks, rising from the chair. *Definitely not for me.*

"I have to go," she mumbles, reaching for her backpack and spinning for the door.

"I'm sorry to hear that," Ben says in a quiet, composed voice. When she peeks back, he hasn't moved from his seat. He doesn't seem annoyed. He doesn't even seem that surprised. Maybe he pegged her for a quitter from the start, though.

Whatever, Danny thinks as she flings open the door to the library study room and emerges into the stacks. She doesn't need enlightenment, anyway. This Ben guy? She so, *so* doesn't get what everyone's talking about. What a waste of a hundred bucks.

CHAPTER SEVEN

CARSON CITY, NEVADA
PRESENT DAY

Rebecca's "friend" takes another tiny sip of coffee and then no one knows what more to say. It is, by far, the strangest breakfast Tom has ever experienced.

A phone rings an unfamiliar ringtone. Startled, Rebecca jumps and bangs her knee on the underside of the table. She laughs awkwardly. "Oops! Sorry."

The ring seems to be coming from inside Danny's sweatshirt. She pulls out a phone from the kangaroo pocket and looks at the screen, but then puts it away.

Rebecca straightens. "You need to get that?"

"Nah," Danny answers breezily. She jumps to her feet, phone in her hand. "Mind if I use the bathroom? I've been holding my bladder all morning."

"S-Sure." Rebecca points down the hall. "Back there. To the left."

Danny nods and heads off. A second later, the bathroom lock clicks. Then Rebecca spins around and looks at Tom. Her mouth is slack.

Tom tousles Roscoe's head. "Go play in the living room, okay, bud? I'll come see what you're up to in a sec."

"Okay," Roscoe says cheerfully, then skips into the living room.

Instantly, Tom turns back to his wife, who has crumpled against the table.

"Hey," he whispers. "What's going on?"

Rebecca lifts her head and looks at him like she hasn't understood what he's said.

"You seem . . . upset," he goes on. "Is she really an old friend? Talk to me. Something's wrong, right? That was super awkward."

Rebecca opens her mouth, then shuts it again. After a moment, she shakes her head. "It's just . . . a surprise. That's all. I can't figure out how she even *got* here."

"She told us. The bus."

"I think she's lying."

Tom raises an eyebrow. "She doesn't travel by bus?"

"I highly doubt it."

Tom thinks about this for a minute. "You think she's scamming us? Leaving the wallet on the bus, missing the ride . . . you think she has financial problems?" Something else occurs to him. "Danny was asking about my job, looking around the place, commenting on our china cabinet . . ."

"I don't think she's here to rob us," Rebecca interrupts, snorting.

There's a rustling sound from the bathroom. Rebecca sits up straighter, her mouth settling into a straight line. She definitely looks freaked. Even more freaked than when she woke up from that dream this morning. They should send Danny away . . . but Tom's also a little curious. Here's a literal *person* from his wife's past, in their powder room, claiming to have been her best friend with knowledge of her high school years, boys she knew, even her *parents*. Tom wishes he could ask Danny actual questions.

It's curious to think of Rebecca having friends; it's a side of her he hasn't seen. She's cagey with new people she meets, like other moms at Roscoe's school. She's friendly, and she volunteers for the school library and other activities, but she never gets close with anyone. He worries she's lonely, too much inside herself. Something must have happened to her, back in the day, that made her lose faith in most people. He's wondered about what it could be. Something with her parents? Or a friend? *Danny*? But Rebecca wouldn't let Danny in if she'd done something truly terrible. At the same time, there's definitely some shit that went down between them that Rebecca doesn't want to get into.

Suddenly, another idea comes to him. *Of course.*

He eyes the powder room door. "We don't have anything in that medicine cabinet? You got rid of those pain pills from the root canal?"

"Wait." Rebecca blinks. "What are you saying?"

"Babe, I know all the signs. She's dangerously thin, dirty, she's acting really sketchy, seeking out friends she hasn't seen in years, mentioning stuff that costs money . . . it's classic. Was this what she was like in high school, too? Is that why you're afraid of her?" He never considered Rebecca being mixed up in that kind of world.

Rebecca shakes her head. "Danny's not on drugs. She never has been."

"You just said you have no idea why she's here," he protests. "And you haven't seen her in years . . ."

She breathes in, but then stares at the place mat. "That's true. But . . . drugs? No. I'm sure of it."

Tom turns over his palms. He's not sure if he believes that.

"And anyway, those pills you mentioned, from the root canal—I threw those out." She gives him a loaded glance. "You told me to get rid of pills we don't need, just in case."

Tom looks away. Yes. He had said that. It's something his sponsor insisted upon: No addict is infallible or invincible. Everyone has the capacity to slip up, especially if the opportunity is there. Best to eliminate the chance for disaster.

"Why'd you lose touch with her, then?" he asks.

She shrugs.

Tom's skin prickles. "Does it have anything to do with that Toby dude?"

She laughs, though the laugh sounds forced. "*No*, God. Danny just . . . left one day."

"Left?" He sits back. "Like ran away?"

"Sort of."

"What's that mean?"

"She went to this . . . place." Rebecca traces a pattern in the table's wood grain. "In the woods of Oregon, with this group of people. It was right after graduation. Her mom filed a police report, but there wasn't much she could do. Danny was over eighteen."

This is the first Tom is hearing of any of this. "Was she kidnapped?"

"No . . . nothing like that. It was her choice."

"But why'd her mom file a police report? Were they like the Mansons? Murderers? Is that why you're scared of her?"

"Tom, no. God. And I'm not scared." She looks at him, her mouth twitching. "I'm *not*. I'm just . . . surprised."

It breaks Tom's heart, a little, because she's lying. But maybe she has a good reason. Danny is still here. Maybe she doesn't want to say something with her so close by.

He crosses his arms. "That must have been really sad for you, having a friend vanish."

She cuts her gaze away. "Yeah."

"You must be glad she's okay after all this time."

Rebecca shrugs. She doesn't seem glad. Tom chews his lip. "Do you think she still lives there? She mentioned some sort of workshop or something? Outreach?"

"If she still lives there, I don't think they're allowed to travel."

"*Allowed to*? So maybe she doesn't live there, then."

"No, I think she *does*," Rebecca says. "I just think she's lying about the outreach stuff and the bus. I think . . . I don't know. I'm not sure what's going on."

"What's going on with *what*?" he demands, laying his hands flat on the table. "What aren't you telling me?"

Rebecca holds his gaze for a moment, then gets up and starts stacking the dishes. "With who she is. Why she's here. She . . . she lives in the woods. Her people are . . . weird."

"But maybe she was kicked out. Maybe she's run away. This is exactly what addicts do, you know," he says. "They burn bridges. They cut themselves off from people they care about. And of course they lie. For money."

Rebecca drops the plates into the sink. "Drugs weren't ever her thing. I swear."

The toilet flushes. Tom thinks he hears Danny saying something in there, but maybe not. Then he hears a rustle. A zipper. The tap turns on. "Maybe we should at least see? I just want to know what questions I can ask, babe. How I can help her, and—"

"I need to handle this myself, Tom," Rebecca interrupts. Her tone is sharp.

Tom sits back, cowed. "Oh. Sure. Fine. Just trying to help."

She lets out a breath and leans against the counter. "I'm sorry, baby. It's just . . . she's an old friend, and I'm rattled is all, by the abruptness of it. It's okay."

The coffeemaker burbles. Outside, the wind swishes and swirls. Tom suddenly feels exhausted, and whatever his wife is hiding isn't helping.

"Why does she call you Bex?" he asks.

Rebecca frowns. "Pardon?"

"Never knew you had that as a nickname."

He isn't sure he likes it. It's childish. It underestimates her. But the way Rebecca's looking at him—like he's missing the point—he doesn't push on. Anyway, everyone used to be a different person in some form or fashion, especially back in high school. For a while, people called him *T*, like saying his full name was too much of a bother. It probably was, since they were all so fucked up all of the time. People change. They outgrow their nicknames. He should drop it.

He glances to the bathroom again. Danny *still* hasn't come out. Should they yell for her? Is that rude? If they open the door, will they find this chick in there rifling through their pill bottles or with a needle in her arm?

"Let me talk to Danny alone," Rebecca says suddenly.

"What?" Tom gives her a strange look. "Why?"

"I'll take her somewhere. Try and figure out what's going on without the distraction of kids and things. Maybe you're right—maybe this *is* drugs. But I wonder if she'd rather talk to me by myself since she doesn't know you."

Tom glances out the window. The wind is still bending the trees sideways. There's a ton of standing water in the road. "This weather is terrible. There's probably flash flooding. I'd rather you not drive."

"It's already clearing up. We'll be fine."

"I won't get in your way if you want to talk to her here. We could just go upstairs and play."

She shakes her head. "When we were friends, we always had deep conversations while driving around. It made us open up. She's obviously here for a reason, but she's dancing around it—maybe she's uncomfortable. It could get her to open up. I could, um, really ask her about where she's been living. What it's all about. That place in the woods, you know."

It feels like his wife is making excuses, but he can't figure out why. "Do you think I'd scare her, being around? I've sponsored people, babe, if that's what this is. I can help. I know what to say."

"Danny's private, like I am. Or that's how I remember her. I think I'll have a better chance of getting answers if we were just . . . alone. She trusts me. She must, otherwise she wouldn't have come, right?"

Tom places his palms on the table. "I really wish we could do this together."

There's a *click*, and they both look up, but the bathroom door still doesn't open.

Rebecca turns off the sink and takes a step toward the bathroom. "I'm going to check on her."

"Who is Toby, Rebecca?" Tom asks again.

Rebecca turns around slowly. Her eyes flash. "No one. Just some kid from high school."

"But how would he know our address? Is he . . ." He swallows hard. There's a question he wants to ask, but he doesn't dare. "Why did you bring up his name?"

"Because . . ." She slaps her sides. "It was just a guess. When I knew Toby, he was, um, kind of a hacker, and he was good at looking stuff up about people. That's why. Now can you stop? *Please?*" There's that twitchy, angry smile again. "Let me just take Danny out. I think she'd be more comfortable if we talked alone. And how about this—I'll say we have plans later. To set a time limit for how long she stays. After three p.m., say, she has to leave."

"But where will she go?" Tom asks. "What if she's telling the truth and has really lost her stuff? We're seriously going to turn her away?"

Rebecca scoffs. "Whose side are you on?"

With that, she marches into the hall. A defensive feeling rises in his chest. Why is she mad at *him*? What did he do? Is it so wrong that he's asking questions? Or maybe she sensed he was about to ask her if this Toby guy is Roscoe's dad. Tom feels guilty for wondering—they'd promised not to go down that pathway to the past. But *she's* the one who said the dude's name. She's also the one who keeps all that stuff in a locked box. Isn't it human nature to wonder?

He stands and wanders into the living room to be with his sons. If she can walk away, then so can he. For the first time in years, he wishes, *really* wishes, he could pop something to take the edge off. He banishes the thought from his mind. *Steady, man. Steady.*

CHAPTER EIGHT

"Danny?" Rebecca calls out in her best sweet voice, knocking on the powder room door. "Want to go for a drive? I can show you the town." She shifts her weight. "And, um, we have plans this afternoon, see, so we can only spend the morning together—I don't like leaving people in the house when we're gone."

She glances back at Tom and gives him an assuring smile. Not that she feels assured whatsoever. But getting Danny out of this house is the best move.

"One sec!" Danny finally calls from the bathroom.

In the living room, she hears Roscoe's soft laughter and the click of Lego bricks. It's all so innocent and sweet. She shakes the tension out of her fingers.

Then she realizes something else. *Insurance.*

"Be right back, Danny!" she calls.

Then, taking the stairs two at a time, she bounds to the second level and skids around the corner to her bedroom closet. It's a mess, a jumble of clothes and blankets and randomly stacked suitcases. Heart pounding, she stands on her tiptoes and reaches for the shoebox on the top shelf. *Extra tampons*, it's labeled—a safeguard so Tom won't look.

When she lifts the lid, she's both relieved and repulsed to see that the items are still there. Relieved because she doesn't know what she'd do if they were gone.

But repulsed, too, because they're all things she doesn't like thinking about.

She sets the box on the floor and stares at the contents inside for a few long, tense beats. It's been so long since she's peered inside.

"Honey?"

Tom's voice sounds from around the corner. Annoyed but also terrified of getting caught, Rebecca drops to her knees and stuffs the lid back onto the shoebox. Tom is already in the room. He stops short when he notices her.

"Look, I'm sorry about—" Tom's gaze drops to what she's holding. Rebecca has pushed the shoebox to the back of the closet and reached for the first thing she could find, an old Nike Pegasus trainer. "What are you doing?" he asks.

She gestures to the shoe in her hands. "Um, finding shoes."

He blinks hard. "I don't think *that* shoe has a match. Didn't Roscoe throw the other one out the window that one time?"

Annoyance wells up. "Why do we still have a shoe if it doesn't have a mate?" She tosses it down hard. *Steady*, she tells herself. *Take a breath*. It's probably fine that she can't grab what she needs from that box. She at least knows it's in there. She prays she hid it back there well enough.

"Oh yeah," she says, calmly now, looking at the shoe on the ground. "Roscoe thought the shoe could fly, right? Because it's called a Pegasus?"

Tom smiles weakly. "He was disappointed when it wasn't actually a winged horse." He blinks at her. "I'm sorry about pushing you. I don't mean to sound suspicious. And I didn't mean to raise my voice or accuse you of anything. I just worry, you know? A stranger in our house . . . I just want to make sure it's cool."

Just then, the bathroom door downstairs squeaks open. *Danny*.

"I love you for that," she says to Tom. "But I'm fine. We're fine. Let me grab her, okay? We'll run to the store while we're out, maybe. You're okay with the kids?"

"Sure . . ." Tom's gaze keeps sneaking to the closet. "If you think you can handle this alone."

"I do."

Tom stands aside so she can step through the door first. Rebecca has no choice but to leave the bedroom—and the box—behind. She pecks him on the cheek, closes the closet door, and heads down the stairs, grateful that Tom is following. She finds Danny in the living room, squatting next to Roscoe and looking at the Lego fire truck box. It upends Rebecca's equilibrium. She wants to wrench Danny away by her hair. *Don't talk to my son.*

"Let's go for a ride," she chirps, inserting herself between them.

Danny looks surprised. "In this weather?"

Rebecca wants to groan. "It's not raining as hard. We'll be okay." She guides Danny to the front door, grabbing the car keys. "Bye, guys," she calls out. "We'll be back soon. We'll pick you up some cookies from the store, 'kay, Roscoe?"

"Really?" Roscoe perks up. "Can you get Oreos?"

"Only if you're good for Daddy. You promise?"

"Promise!"

Rebecca pulls the door shut. Out on the porch, finally alone, she whirls around and faces Danny, all of the pent-up terror and fury rising to the surface.

"Now it's your turn to play nice," she whispers to her old friend, her teeth clenched. "Walk to my car. Smile like it's all fine. And then you're going to tell me the truth about why you're here and how you found me. Because I know everything you've said is a lie."

CHAPTER NINE

DAVIS, CALIFORNIA
PRESENT DAY

At fifty-six, Janice Martin doesn't feel like she has gained much wisdom in the past eight years. When she wakes up, she still feels the same dread. At the same time, she still has the same incongruous, irrationally hopeful thought: *maybe today is the day Danny comes home.* Isn't that a sign of madness: doing the same thing over and over again and expecting different results?

Sighing, she slides her feet into her worn fuzzy slippers. It's Saturday, so she doesn't have to clock in at Dr. Morris's office, where she's worked as a nurse for almost twenty-seven years. She started with the primary care doctor when she was pregnant with Danny, as a matter of fact. Janice usually wishes she could go in on the weekends, too; taking care of patients is a welcome distraction from her thrumming loneliness.

Time to clean Danny's room, she supposes—her usual Saturday chore. But as she opens the door to Danny's old bedroom, she wants to shut it again. Looking inside this space never gets easier. There's the bed Danny bounced on as a little girl. The vanity she sat at to do her makeup.

The bookcase filled with math workbooks Janice bought for Danny to encourage her to study harder—not that Danny did. The same clothes still hang in her daughter's closet. The same shoes are tossed under the bed, the floor carefully Swiffered every week. Danny had been halfway through *Zen and the Art of Motorcycle Maintenance* when she disappeared; the first time she went into Danny's room to see if there were clues to make sense of the irrational choice she'd just made, Janice had found it face down on her bed. She'd thumbed through a few pages. Old-fashioned choice, she'd decided. She'd wondered if that Ben person had made her read it.

That Ben person. Her blood boils, even now.

Janice knows it's not healthy—or rational—to keep Danny's things so preserved and untouched. Her husband, Dave, left her and Danny, too . . . and it's not like Janice keeps memorabilia of *him*. In fact, Janice should move from this apartment—she has the money saved. But this physical space is all she has left of her daughter. And if Danny *does* finally come to her senses and decide to come back . . . well, Janice wants to be in the same place, so Danny can find her. The most ironic thing is that Janice actually knows where Danny is. She even sees her, sometimes, in YouTube videos—with *him*. When she first found out Danny and Ben made videos together—public ones, because that man is always eager for more followers and money and devotion—she wasn't sure if she could bring herself to watch. Curiosity took over pretty fast, though. When she'd seen Danny on the screen, she'd gasped and turned the video off. Her daughter had looked so *thin*. Her skin was a strange grayish color. She was smiling, yes, but there was a wildness to her eyes, a hauntedness.

It was the only proof Janice needed to be sure that whatever was happening at that place wasn't right. Oh sure, Danny talked online about how happy she was, how *this* was her family now—that, especially, felt like a knife to Janice's gut—but the girl had to be brainwashed. And what can Janice do? Scream into the void? Her daughter won't see her. She could bang on the gates of that place—and she has!—but it still doesn't matter. Danny doesn't want to see her. Danny has drawn her boundaries. Or, more likely, Ben has drawn them for her.

After she straightens the already-straight bedspread and wipes some dust from the windowsill, she shuts Danny's door again and sits down at her laptop in the kitchen. Then, she does another thing she always does on Saturday mornings: she clicks on the ISB channel. A new video was uploaded this morning. Clenching her jaw, Janice clicks on it.

The video loads. And there Danny is, thanking Ben for sitting down with her today. Just seeing her makes Janice clutch at her chest. "Hi, baby," she whispers. Tears well in her eyes. Such a silly old woman, she thinks, crying at a dumb video of a now stranger. It will never get easier. Never.

Ben is looking as smarmy and self-righteous as ever. "Welcome, everyone," he's saying in his public-radio tone, like he's always so composed and above emotions. "First off, we all have Danielle to thank for a big social media milestone we hit since our last update." He grins at Danny and then—Janice wants to vomit—touches her hand with his stubby fingers. "We hit one hundred thousand subscribers, so I'm told. Kudos, Danielle."

There's a patronizing undercurrent to his voice that Janice doesn't like. Danny doesn't seem to notice. She vibrates with his praise. The man is going bald. He's completely ordinary-looking. Even before these videos started a few years ago, Janice suspected Danny had a thing for Ben, but she doesn't understand the attraction at all.

"I've said all along that videos are a really powerful tool for spreading your lesson," Danny pipes up on-screen. "Some people aren't as lucky as I am to be in your presence on a regular basis. I get to hear your thoughts and teachings *in person*. I still pinch myself at my good fortune."

"Jesus," Janice mutters, while the on-screen Ben humbly ducks his head and waves her off.

"So I want to continue our talks about the value of the ISM workshop, which we now have as an online class," Danny continues. "I thought about one of my first breakthroughs with you—it was *in* the ISM workshop. That's *Internal Spirit Map*, for those of you who are new to ISB. Anyway, we talked about victimhood. I called myself a victim, remember?"

You are a victim, Janice wants to scream. *It's happening to you right now!*

"Of course I remember." Ben nods.

"And you said there's no such thing as victimhood. It's an illusion to keep women subservient."

Why do I watch this? It's like rubbernecking a car wreck. She can't look away.

"Basically, victimhood is a title put on you as a signifier of your status or worth in the culture," Ben explains. "But you don't have to be the victim. That's your choice. However, the pain you feel from what happened to you in a given incident isn't wasted—when we experience severe pain, mental anguish, even trauma, it can be a portal to the divine. A spiritual journey, if you will. But it takes a lot of practice."

He flashes a smile directly at the camera—directly at *Janice*, it seems. She half expects him to wink. Sighing, she clicks out of the video. Her heart is pounding. As much as she yearns to see her daughter on-screen and takes comfort in the fact that at least she is still alive, it's hard to listen to this. Eight years, no change. Eight years, and Danny is still very much in the thick of this mess.

Frustrated, she clicks to the internet browser to check the private social media group she's set up. There are a few new messages, including a group check-in from other family members who have loved ones on the compound, too.

Anyone have good news? they ask.

Nope, comes a response in the chat. *I wish,* someone else posts. *I've heard nothing, but, Janice, Danny's in a new video.* They all know who Danny is by now since she's so prominent online. *I know,* Janice writes back. *I just watched it.*

The only new posts are memes emphasizing what everyone knows to be going on in Oregon, including an acrostic poem that spells out the word *Gaslight*.

> *G: Gradual distortion of truth*
> *A: Avoiding responsibility and shifting blame*
> *S: Sowing doubt*
> *L: Lying and manipulating the truth*

I: Invalidating how you feel and what you've experienced
G: Getting you to question your logic and thinking
H: Hiding true intentions (and maybe more)
T: Twisting reality to suit the narrative

Isn't that the truth, Janice thinks.

She navigates over to her email, expecting it'll just be filled with junk, but there's an email from George, a farmer who lives near the compound who claims to be in the know about the group and their activities.

Hi Janice, George writes. *Just wanted to let you know that I saw a black sedan leave the compound last night. There was someone in the back who looked like your daughter. I wish I knew more, but no one is telling me too much these days—I think Ben and the others in the group are on to me. Anyway, I hope this helps.*

Janice reads the email over and over until her eyes blur. A woman she met through the Facebook group, Jonette, introduced her to George. Jonette had a son in the organization, but with George's help, apparently, she was able to find out that her son went on long walks in the woods around the compound, and that there was one spot, so far unnoticed, where there was a tear in the barbed-wire fence. Jonette drove up there, snuck in, ambushed him, threw him into the car, and, with the help of a psychologist, talked to him about breaking free from the group. It was one of the few miracle stories, and now lots of people Venmo George for tips about their loved ones, too. Not that Janice had heard a single thing from him about Danny before now. She'd begun to think he was a scammer.

But maybe not. *A black sedan. Someone who looked like your daughter.*

Danny? Could it be? Instinctively, she lifts the curtain, half expecting Danny to be walking up the front path. Only, would that make sense? She was just on YouTube, seeming positive and supportive and as devoted to the group as ever.

What could have happened? Has she finally woken up?

The horror of everything that happened wafts back like it was only yesterday. What did Janice *do*, years ago, to make her daughter leave without saying goodbye? How on earth did Danny see herself as the *victim*? Is it tied to Dave leaving? Janice knows Danny blamed her for that. It was a flaw in *her*, not cowardice in him. Meanwhile, Dave was the one who took off and never looked back. Even when Danny went missing, the guy never resurfaced, never called to say, "My God, Janice, you were on the news! How can I help?" For all Janice knows, the guy dropped dead. Actually, that's the more comforting alternative; the idea of him out there somewhere, ignoring her pain and his daughter's troubles—that's worse.

"You're part of the problem, Mom," Danny had said, the day before she took off. "You're part of my problematic cycle."

"Maybe we can go to therapy together?" Janice begged. "*Real* therapy. And maybe you could explain all of this to me? Help me see?"

"I'm just not empowered when I'm with you," Danny said. "I'm not my best self. Ben says that sometimes we need to shed some skin to be our best versions."

"Are you saying I'm *skin*?" Janice shrieked. "That's all I am to you?" She wanted to shake her daughter's shoulders. "This man," she sputtered. "He's a quack. He's a manipulative fake. He doesn't care about you. He only cares about himself. He's . . ." She took a breath. "He's no better than your father."

Danny's mouth fell open. "Don't bring my father into this."

It was the fatal mistake, Janice knew, to bring Dave into the conversation and demonize him like that. Danny was devastated he left, but at the same time, Janice always sensed Danny didn't blame Dave, either. If she could have taken it back, she would have. She *tried*.

But it was too late. The next day, Danny's things were gone. And then came that message. *Don't worry about me. I'm on a good path. I need to remove myself from the toxicity. I hope you leave me in peace.*

What about her was toxic? All she was trying to do was love. Why would Danny push that away? Why would she think that was a *problem*? If only Janice had a solid piece of evidence of something she'd done really, truly wrong. If only she could *see*.

From her perspective, Janice had tried her best. She thought she gave Danny all she needed. And she *loved* her, deeply, desperately—that was for sure. And, okay, she made mistakes—but every parent does. Janice just wanted Danny to have a better life, and the only way out was a good education. She got on Danny's case about it. And, fine, she got impatient about Danny's listlessness and angst—was that really a crime? She wasn't Danny's best friend, and maybe she didn't empathize as much as she could have, but a mother isn't *supposed* to be her child's best friend. A mother is supposed to provide discipline and structure. A mother is supposed to issue tough love.

If only she had found different words that could have gotten through the walls Danny put up long ago, but it seemed like nothing she said mattered.

She clicks to reply to George's email, thanks him for letting her know about this new development, and adds a little more to his Venmo tip. Maybe she should allow herself to hope that Danny went to someone on the outside. Maybe she found Stella, an ex-member who, so the Facebook group says, is now living a quiet life in Sedona. There's also that boy, Toby, who didn't appear to be there anymore—a neighbor of his is a patient of Dr. Morris's, and he swore to Janice that he saw Toby in the old apartment he shared with his grandma late one night, throwing some things into the trunk of a car and driving off. The neighbor said he was going south instead of north, toward Mexico instead of Oregon, but who knows if that's actually true. For all anyone knows, Toby went straight back to the compound and is still there, as brainwashed as the rest of them.

So maybe not Toby. Someone else, then? Suddenly, Janice has a terrible premonition of where Danny might have gone. There's someone else Danny knows on the outside. Someone who used to mean a lot to her.

Bex.

She rises to her feet. Her skin prickles. Call it mother's intuition, but suddenly she's *sure* it was Danny in that car, and she's sure that's where Danny has gone. To Bex. Her old habit. Her old friend.

But this brings forth no comfort. In fact, Janice's heart starts racing like she's drank a whole pot of espresso. Bex is definitely not the best choice.

Bex is a disaster.

CHAPTER TEN

DAVIS, CALIFORNIA
NINE YEARS BEFORE

Danny can see the surprise on Ben's face as they meet in the same library study room the following week. *Ha*, she thinks. Guy thinks he knows all the answers and has everyone figured out, but it looks like she confounded him.

She shoots him a smirk. "I'm back," she singsongs.

"I was so happy to get your message, Danielle," he says after she's settled down and he's turned on the video camera. "What changed your mind?"

Danny sits back in her chair. "A few people told me to stick it out, and what can I say? I'm highly susceptible to peer pressure." It also helps that Ben offered to give her the next few sessions for free because she seems like "such a good candidate." He told her he didn't do that for everyone, though. She was a special case.

Which, okay, felt kind of good. Maybe it's a line, and Danny doesn't get what the guy sees in her, but it's nice that he sees *something*.

Her gaze darts to the camera. "I was told I'd get used to *that*, too.

The tapes are helpful, apparently? Something about seeing how far I've come?"

"That's true," Ben says. "You'll be amazed how far you come."

Their eyes lock. Ben doesn't look as dorky today, in jeans instead of khakis, a fitted T-shirt instead of a polo. He looks younger, less like a Home Depot employee. And those broad shoulders.

"So," Ben says, lowering his gaze to his notebook. "How can I help you, Danielle?"

Danny opens her mouth, then shuts it again. "Damned if I know."

"You don't know *how* I can help, or if I can help at all?"

"Both? Either?"

"Last time, we were talking a little bit about your communication with your mom. But something upset you, and you left. Do you want to talk about what triggered you?"

Danny shrugs. "I wasn't triggered."

"I watched your tape from our last session. Usually, we watch it together, but I didn't know if you were going to come back. To me, it seems you reacted to the word *sad*. I asked if it made you *sad* that you and your mom can't talk about things."

Danny starts to fidget. "Yeah . . ."

"What about that word gets you so riled up?"

Her shoulders hunch. "I don't feel sad."

"So what *do* you feel?"

Out the window, a librarian pushes a cart past the door. Danny concentrates on the sounds of the squeaking wheels. This is why she hates therapy: coming up with answers on the spot and then having the other person pounce on them like they've found a nugget of gold.

She eyes him carefully. "That stuff you said about your mom . . . and your dad leaving . . . and the hospital . . . and dark places—is that really true?"

"Absolutely," he says. Then he leans back, crossing his hands along his waist. "You think I made it up. To garner sympathy. To make myself seem more legit."

She shrugs. He's not wrong. *Her* dad left. Sure, she didn't get beat up, but it's a pretty close parallel. "Maybe."

He presses his palms together. "I'll never do that, Danielle. I'll never lie to you. I promise. Do you believe me?"

He looks so earnest. Like he might fucking die if she says no. But when she thinks about it . . . maybe she does believe him. He really does look . . . *enlightened*, or whatever.

"Fine," she says. "Whatever. Sure. You won't lie."

"Good. *Good.* So. Back to that feeling. It's something other than *sad*. Can you think of a word for it?"

Danny breathes in and tips her head up to the ceiling. "I don't know. I just feel . . . *different*. From my mom. Maybe from everyone."

An excited, almost dazzled look crosses his features. "Do you often feel different from other people, too? Besides your mom, I mean."

"I guess so."

"In what way?"

"I guess I just feel more . . . aware, I guess."

His eyes light up. "Aware as in you don't get how other people can just . . . bop along without stuff bugging them? Happy? Carefree?"

"Actually, yeah." Danny is surprised he gets it. "That's right."

"Tell me when it started. Tell me what it's like."

Danny stares at the interlocking squares on the linoleum floor. When had she started to feel so different? After Dad left? But no, she was okay for a while after that. She had Bex and Toby and her other friends, and it felt like enough. They'd get together for sleepovers, watch horror movies, prank call people. She'd go to middle school soccer games, she'd ride the roller coaster at their local amusement park, she'd smash in for pictures with her friends and they'd all flash a peace sign or devil horns or stick out their tongues.

Eventually, it all seemed like such bullshit. She wasn't sure when, exactly, but all of a sudden, Danny looked around at the kids at school, amazed that most of them didn't feel it, too. Even Bex, even Toby, even the other kids who were talking to Ben or who recommended she talk to Ben, too—even they seemed so . . . *fine*. It felt like she was the only one on the outside. She wanted to shake them, shouting, *Don't you realize this is all really dumb? Don't you realize we're just biding time until something terrible happens?* She didn't know when, or what the terrible thing would be, but it was coming. It was *life*. And there they'd all be, doing some latest dance craze or jumping off the high-dive or sneaking cigarettes when their parents weren't looking, and they wouldn't know what hit them.

"Yes," Ben says.

Danny looks up. Had she said that out loud?

"Yes," he says again. "And how many days a week do you feel like this?"

This isn't some psych ward assessment, is it? "At least a couple, but it's not that big of a deal . . ." He narrows his eyes as if to say *Tell the truth*. She sighs. "Okay. Pretty much all the time. All the freaking time, and it feels like the bad version of being high. Not that I've ever *been* high, of course."

"I won't judge you if you have. That's not what I'm here for." He props his elbows on the table. "You know, I used to feel that way when my parents dragged me to church. I was about fourteen."

Danny frowns. "I thought your parents split up when you were young."

"Yes. Sorry. My mom and my stepfather." He taps his temple and grins. "Good memory. Anyway, I'd go through the motions, and according to everyone there, I was supposed to get something out of it. But I never did. I just went through the motions. That clarity or joy or fear or whatever the hell people are supposed to feel with religion never showed up for me. But I was still expected to attend every Sunday. Still expected to kneel, then stand, then sing, then pray. It was like I was watching myself in the third person. I was completely disengaged."

"Like you were watching your life in the third person." Danny needs to repeat him to make sure she heard correctly.

Ben looks embarrassed. "I realize that sounds kind of . . . bizarre."

"Actually, it doesn't," Danny says in a small voice. She wants to sound cavalier and casual, but she can't help but add, "It's pretty much how I feel all the time."

"Well, then." He smiles crookedly at her. "It's nice to find someone who feels the same as I do. There's a word for us, you know."

"There is?"

"It's called *autoscopy*. Comes from ancient Greek. *Self-watcher*."

"Ancient Greeks felt like this?"

"Feels good to know that, huh? That there's a word attached? Like you're less . . . alone?"

"Yeah." She *has* felt alone. Really alone.

"What are you thinking now?" Ben asks, after a pause.

"Next time my mom accuses me of being on drugs or not motivated enough, I'll tell her I'm just being *autoscopic*."

"There you go."

Ben writes something in his journal. The camera's power button glows. The lens watches her.

"So have you ever tried to explain this feeling to your mom?" he then asks.

"Kind of. But she doesn't get it."

"She's one of the people bopping through life, huh?"

"She just says I'm not trying hard enough. If I did, then I'd get good grades, and then I'd get some confidence . . . and this would all go away. As if that's going to solve all my problems."

"But it's more complicated."

"I think so. But there's no arguing. She forces me to do these prep classes and extracurriculars, stuff that'll look good on my transcript, but it's the same as you. I'm just going through the motions." She shrugs. "It feels like I'm drowning."

"Drowning. So . . . sinking."

She can feel him watching her, and she dares to look at him, too. To her relief, he isn't staring at her with pity or worry. He's nodding like he totally gets it. A strange little thrill passes through her. An unexpected feeling of . . . *understanding*.

"I feel . . . like sometimes I don't know myself. And it gets overwhelming, like I'm really *not* going to know myself—like I'm not going to even know my name, or where I live, or anything about myself, like my memory is suddenly going to go *poof*." She makes an exploding sound with her lips. "It's never gotten to that point, obviously. But when I start thinking about it, I fear it *could*. Like one day the scales are just going to tip . . . and that will be that."

"What's the worst-case scenario, if that happened?"

Danny frowns. "Um . . . *no memory*? No self?"

"Maybe not having any context of who you are and what you're supposed to do? And you'd be afraid no one would be able to help?"

"Yeah." She slowly nods. "I guess that would be it. But it's dumb, right?"

"It's not dumb. Not dumb at all." Ben sits back. "People like you and me, we feel things deeply. We're more highly evolved. I think it's why I knew we were meant to talk."

The fluorescent light buzzes. Danny is suddenly hyperaware of her breath. He's looking at her like she's not crazy. He's looking at her like he and Danny are the sane ones—the rest of the world has it wrong.

A sharp *beep* punctuates the silence, and she jumps. It's Danny's phone, tucked in the pocket of her backpack. She tries to ignore it, but it beeps again.

"It's okay," Ben says, his gaze on her ringing backpack. "I don't mind if you take that."

"Sorry," Danny unzips the pocket where she has stashed the phone and looks at the screen. Her mom sent a text. *Where are you? Made your favorite for dinner tonight. Check in please! Xo*

"Your whole posture has changed, Danielle."

"It's, um, my mom," she murmurs. "She's so controlling. She also doesn't know I'm here. She's one of those 'I don't believe in life coaching' types."

"You look drained. Moments before, you were so alive."

"Yeah, well." Danny heaves a sigh, suddenly struck with deep, deep sadness. Typical Mom, always thinking she knows anything about what Danny needs. She feels sorry for her.

"Sometimes the ones we love most are toxic to our personal growth," Ben says in a voice so soft Danny almost doesn't hear. "Part of growing up is setting boundaries, sometimes even pushing those people away. It's about finding new people. Finding people who understand you. Who love you differently. Who aren't the villain."

"She never *thinks* she's the villain," Danny says quietly. "She always acts like the victim. Big bad world's out to get her."

Ben scoffs. "There is no such thing as a victim. It's an illusion."

Danny blinks. "What?"

"Your mother is not a victim. *You* are not a victim. People put those titles on others, on themselves—it's a signifier of their status. It's *weak*. Victimhood is something you can choose to be—and you can always choose *not to*."

"Oh," Danny says, rolling the idea around in her mind. "But if that's true, isn't it a cop-out? Doesn't that get truly bad people off the hook? Like people who really *do* hurt others?"

"There are bad people out there, sure. But our pain, our experience—it doesn't have to be traumatic when we look back on it. It's all about how we frame what happens. Instead of letting it define us, *keep us down*, we can overcome our pain and turn it into something transcendent. And in doing so, we can eliminate those negative entities swimming around in our beings."

Danny can't help but scoff. "Yeah, like it's so *easy*."

"It isn't easy. Not at all. It takes practice. A lot of practice. But I can teach you. We have workshops. It's what ISB is all about, actually—reclaiming your life, and then passing that along to others—and getting paid for passing along the wisdom, by the way. It took all of us a lot of hard work to get to where we are; we can't give it away for free."

"You're counseling *me* for free," Danny says in a small voice.

Ben looks amused. "Touché. But that's because I see a lot of potential in you, Danielle. You could be a Seedling."

"I heard something about your weird garden hierarchies," Danny mutters with a twist of a smile. She'd heard rumors already—Ben arranged people in his group into seedlings or bean sprouts or whatever. It all sounds a little woo-woo, but she has to admit a tiny part sort of feels like maybe she's missing out. Or she'd at least like to know what the levels *mean*.

"I know, I know, it's a little corny I guess, but I'm into the plant metaphor," Ben says, shrugging. "We all start as seeds in life. And in ISB, a Seed is the first step toward being a real leader in the group—higher up, you're a Seedling. It's someone who plants the wisdom and lets it grow in others who need it, too. My cofounder, Barb, put together the roles with me. She's amazing, Barb. Been with me forever. Not as my wife, of course—as just a business partner. She's a single mom. *Amazing* at that. Cured herself from cancer, too—*twice*. And just . . . so smart. I bet she'd love to meet you. She's always looking for really dynamic people."

Dynamic? Danny wonders, almost wanting to laugh. *Me?*

"We have so many manuals and workshops," Ben goes on. "Our goal is to teach our ideas to as many people as possible so they can go on and teach to others. It's not just about victimization—we talk about self-healing, breaking free from materialism, and learning how to do hard things. All of these are paths to a better, happier self. Can you imagine if we learned how to be free and happy, what kind of society this would be?" He folds his arms. "Those negative entities aren't a part of your DNA. You can wash them off. And when you've mastered that, those experiences that jolted your system and created those negative entities no longer have an effect on you." He leans forward to look at her closer. "If you decide to live fearlessly, Danielle, your whole life will change for the better. I really wish you'd try it. I think you'd do really well."

Danny's gaze lands on the curve of Ben's lips. It looks like a Cupid's bow. He has long eyelashes, too, and such a warm expression, like he'd never, ever hurt her. She recently heard another rumor that he'd made the Olympic diving team when he was eighteen but had to drop out because of a family obligation. Maybe that was the reason for those strong shoulders.

In her mind's eye, she pictures Ben in a swimsuit executing perfect somersaults in the air. He makes only the tiniest splash as he enters the water. She sees his strong arms stroking the surface, his muscular legs flutter-kicking, his broad shoulders pushing him out of the water.

It makes her feel kind of . . . *squishy*.

"I think, maybe, that sounds kind of cool," she finally answers.

"Good," Ben says, smiling.

She slides her phone back into the pocket without texting her mom back. Her body feels relaxed, almost like she's in a trance. Ben's right. Her mother makes her tense. Sometimes she even starts to go to that strange dark place where she's no longer in her body, where she no longer knows what might happen next.

But maybe there's another way to live. And maybe it's a path through this guy. And maybe everyone encouraging her to join Ben's group has been right all along.

CHAPTER ELEVEN

CARSON CITY, NEVADA
PRESENT DAY

Rebecca holds Danny's forearms tightly, her nails digging into her skin. But then she realizes what she's doing . . . and that she's standing on her front porch where anyone can see. No one is out here in this storm, but they could be looking through the windows. Including her family.

Her fingers release. She takes a breath. Ducking her head, she braves her way through the pelting rain to her car, gesturing for Danny to follow. Rebecca unlocks the car doors and slides into the driver's seat. Danny climbs in next to her. For a moment, they listen to the rain drumming against the windows.

"How did you actually get here?" Rebecca asks. "Start with that."

Danny shakes her head pleadingly. "I took the bus."

Rebecca looks Danny up and down. "But you came from . . . *there*. Oregon."

Danny bites her lip. "I . . ."

"Don't bother lying. I can tell."

"Okay," Danny says haltingly. "I did. But you don't understand—"

"Nope, that's all I need to know." Rebecca thinks of the insurance she should have grabbed from the box. Was it a mistake not to grab it, even if it tipped Tom off? "I'll call the cops, Danny. Tell them you're intruding on my property. How about that?"

Danny's eyes widen. It's a 180 from the bright, chatty woman who swooped into her home a half hour ago, grilling Rebecca's husband, drinking their coffee, playing blocks with her son.

"Don't do that," Danny says in a small voice. "*Please.* I'm still in Oregon, yeah, but I came to see you because . . . It's complicated." She sighs. "He doesn't know. He thinks I'm doing this camping thing at the edge of the property—this sort of solo trip for personal growth. I swear, Bex. But he's going to figure it out soon—it's not like I'm staying long."

He. The man still controlling her. Rebecca shivers just at the idea of him. Then she shakes her head at Danny. "You came seven hours just to talk to me?"

Danny shrugs. "I don't know your phone number." She holds up her cell. "I disabled it, so he can't track me. I'm going to say that I got out of range in the woods, but I might get in trouble anyway. But I really wanted to see you. Haven't you missed me, too?"

Part of Rebecca *has* missed Danny . . . but that time when they were friends was so, so long ago. She flashes back to Danny in high school, before things went off the rails. Hanging out in Rebecca's family's pristinely finished basement, listening to music on their state-of-the-art stereo. Trying on clothes from Rebecca's closet—Rebecca had an amazing collection of clothes, not that her mother ever went on shopping trips with her. Rebecca actually preferred hanging out in Danny's cozy apartment. Danny's mom, Janice, always made cookies for them, and though Danny thought she was obsequious, Rebecca liked that she asked them questions and was interested in their lives. Mrs. Martin kept her booze in a cupboard rather than a locked cabinet, too, so it was easy to sneak. She even preferred the little TV in Danny's room over the giant-screen monstrosity in her home theater, especially when it came to watching scary movies. Danny was so into horror—she used to watch the goriest scenes with reverence.

There was something so *dark* about her, always. Perceptive, maybe—she was an old soul.

But then Rebecca watched Danny slowly slip into melancholy. She tried to talk to Danny about what she was going through, tried to understand the root of Danny's issues. It had to be painful that her dad left when she was so young, and that her mother pushed her so hard to be something she wasn't. But Danny shut her out. She tried to endure the pain herself. But then, one day, she broke wide open, and she finally accepted help.

Rebecca regrets that every day.

Still. They're different people now. Danny is part of a whole past that she wants to forget, a past she can't tell Tom about. She weighs Danny's story, the thing about the solo camping trip, checking in on the app. It *could* be legit. But she doesn't buy that Danny would—or could—break free and get all the way here.

"I'm not really interested in catching up," Rebecca says sharply. "I'm driving you back to the bus station." She turns the ignition and shifts into Reverse. But her fingers are shaking. She almost backs into their mailbox.

Danny notices. "You're really scared of me."

"You're just figuring that out?"

"You think I'm going to, what, blow up your life?"

Rebecca swallows hard. "Well, yeah."

Danny looks down. "I wouldn't. Tom's cute, by the way. Seems like a really good guy."

Rebecca feels a rush of defensiveness. She doesn't like Danny talking about Tom. She hates that she even *knows* Tom.

"Must have been lucky, finding him. I can't imagine you had much when you came here."

Rebecca winces. "It wasn't like that. I'm not with him because I was desperate."

"But he has no idea about . . . ?"

Rebecca gives her a sharp look and then stares straight ahead, navigating the car down the street.

"Does he know *anything*?"

"What do you think?"

Danny raises her hands in surrender. "What did you tell him about me? I'm sure he asked when I was in the bathroom. The poor guy looked really confused."

"I said you disappeared into the woods after high school, that's it. By the way, Tom thinks you're looking for drugs. He thinks that's why you're here and saying you lost all your stuff and need a place to crash. You're acting like an addict."

"Drugs!" Danny's eyes widen. "I guess it seems a little odd, me showing up out of nowhere. But is he really okay that you haven't told him anything about your past? Or . . . let me guess. He's got a messed-up past, too, so he let it go?"

Rebecca presses the brake at the stop sign, feeling her toes curl in her shoes. "That's none of your business."

"So I'm right, then."

Rebecca hates that Danny guessed it so easily. "Tom's had some hardships, yeah. Who hasn't? We're both helping each other build a better life."

Danny pointedly looks out the window. The windshield wipers groan, working hard. Rain puddles on the roads and floods the gutters. Another gust of wind kicks up, sending tree branches scattering all over lawns and roads. Few cars are out on the road right now; Rebecca wonders if it's truly safe to drive. But the bus station isn't far. Only about ten minutes away.

"How did you really know I was here?" she asks Danny, after they go through a stoplight and then another. "*Was* it from Toby?"

"Fine, yeah," Danny blurts, after a beat. "It was."

Rebecca's stomach swoops. She knew it. "Was it around the time he made that video? You found him . . . and then you forced him to tell you where I was?"

Danny looks down, which gives away everything she needs to know. "*I* didn't do anything," she says. "I'm not even supposed to know your address. I snuck into Ben's office and found it."

Rebecca navigates around a huge puddle in the road. "I still don't buy that you're here alone."

"I am."

"You're lying about *something*."

Danny chews her lip. "Fine. I didn't lose my wallet. And I'm not doing outreach, obviously. But I need to talk to you, Bex."

"Well, guess what? I don't want to talk to *you*." She shakes her head. "I know you've come a long way, but you need to go."

Danny looks shattered, like this wasn't in her plan. Then, abruptly, she lets out a whimper and puts her face in her hands. Her shoulders shake. At first, Rebecca feels impatience. But then, as Danny continues to sob, she gets a bolt of concern. This behavior certainly isn't *condoned*, where she comes from.

"Hey." Rebecca reaches over. "What is it? What's the matter?"

Danny shakes off Rebecca's hand. "You don't care. Forget it."

She starts sobbing harder. Something inside Rebecca shifts. She pulls into the first parking lot she sees—it's for a coffee place she and the kids sometimes go to called Maude's. "You have to take a breath. Seriously."

Danny swallows hard. "I-I just wanted to talk to someone who got it. I don't have anyone to talk to about it there. Not in the way I want to. Not with my questions."

"What do you mean? Talk to about *what*?"

Danny breathes in raggedly. "I'm in trouble." Then she starts to babble. "Well. Not in trouble, of course. It's wonderful, really. But I'm scared. *So* scared. I'm . . . I'm going to . . . it's my first."

Then Danny's gaze drops to her belly. Her hands travel there, too, cupping a spot over her belly button. It's the only part of Danny's body that isn't skin and bones, actually. Rebecca gasps. She can't believe she didn't realize it sooner.

"Danny. You're . . . ?" She can't even say the words out loud. "*Whose?*" she whispers. But does she really need to ask? The answer is obvious.

A smile flutters on Danny's lips, then evaporates into a grimace. "I don't know what to do."

CHAPTER TWELVE

After Danny drops the bomb, Bex stares at her, agape. But suddenly, Danny can't be part of this conversation anymore. She'd always intended to tell Bex, of course—it just makes it all so real.

"I have to pee," she blurts, and then points at the brightly lit coffee shop they're parked in front of. The place is empty because of the weather, but the lights are on. "Can we go in there?"

"Sure," Bex says shakily as they climb out of the car. She stares at Danny dazedly. It's clear Bex is still trying to mentally sort this out.

Danny dashes through the rain and into the coffee shop, beelining for the bathroom. Inside, the space is drafty and dark. Soft folk music pipes in through the speakers. Once she pulls the door closed and secures the latch, she leans against the door and shudders. She actually doesn't have to pee that badly. It's just a good excuse to grab a few moments alone and collect herself. In the car . . . that was *intense*. Bex is the first person she's actually told. No one where she's from even knows—she hasn't been allowed to say so.

She rests her elbows on the sink and stares at herself close up in the mirror. Her skin is blotchy. Her eyes look tired. Then she steps back, turns to the side, lifts her sweatshirt. Her clothes hide it, but there's a hint of a belly. She's excited. Kind of. Mostly, she's scared. *Really* scared. How did Bex do this? How does any mother do this? *Be strong*, she tells herself. *You can do hard things.* It's been her mantra since she found out.

Still, it's strange to think that there's been a life growing inside her for several months now. Empowering, too, of course. Same as the empowered way she has faced Bex. She's held her own. She shouldn't feel guilty about manipulating Bex's emotions. Bex manipulated hers, too, once upon a time. How lost she'd felt. How abandoned.

She whisks the thought away quickly. *No negativity.*

Her phone buzzes in her pocket. It had been buzzing silently during that whole conversation in the car, but she didn't feel like she could break their flow and answer it. Anyway, they're supposed to be using the app, not text. She pulls out her phone and finally stares at the messages.

Check in.

Check in.

Check in.

Danny shuts her eyes. She pictures Ben sitting in his little office, his view of the tall Oregon pines out the back window. She can smell the sap in the air, hear the ringing bells. She wants to hold his hand right now. And she wants him to squeeze back to give her courage. In Ben's presence, she doesn't feel she needs to do her rituals. It's only once out of his orbit that she starts to feel so untethered.

You're not doing this right. You're slipping. She taps the light switch the appropriate number of times. If she doesn't, *something bad will happen.* It doesn't make her feel much better, though. It feels like something bad has *already* happened. Things feel out of control. Maybe she isn't strong enough.

Tap, tap, tap. She messes up, has to start all over.

Danny needs to tune into her strength. And so, she closes her eyes. Pictures her blood flowing through her body. The cells in her muscles twitching. And . . . *there.* She feels it. She feels . . . *good.* It astonishes her that she can harness her strength like this; it's one of the ISB principles. Eight years ago, when Ben introduced her to the idea, it seemed laughable. A magic trick. But now, she can easily focus on a single organ at a time and give it the love and strength it deserves. People have healed themselves from major illnesses this way—people Danny *knows*. It's supposed to work for mental stuff, too—the brain healing itself completely without toxins or medication—though that's sometimes trickier. Mental illness, Ben always says, is slippery to treat because it's not actually a condition at all—it's one's mind not being strong enough to overcome your adversity and get out of your own way. Mental illness, Ben says, is a condition of the victim. And no one at ISB is a victim.

Including Danny.

She opens her eyes again and listens to the noisy groan of an espresso machine. But instead of feeling fully cleansed, like she usually does after a strength exercise, she's hit with a wall of sadness. She thinks of Bex in the car, trying to process everything. It makes her feel so shaky and unstable. Being here, not there. Talking to Bex, not Ben.

Keep going, his voice whispers in her mind. *You have to keep going.*

She knows she has to. Otherwise, she might lose everything.

CHAPTER THIRTEEN

Tom checks on the baby in the living room. Charlie is absorbed in a pile of wooden blocks. Good. He paces to the back porch. The storm hasn't knocked over any more furniture, but it's sure creating a river in the backyard, and it shows no sign of letting up.

His phone rings, finally, and he pounces on it.

"Hey, babe," Rebecca's voice is crackly. There's noise in the background.

"Where are you?" he demands.

"Maude's. Danny needed to pee. I'm at the counter, grabbing another coffee." Rebecca pauses a moment. "But . . . I think I've figured out why she's here. I need to take her to see Dr. Salley. Today, if possible."

Tom blinks. It takes him a moment to realize who that is. "Your OB? Why?"

"She's . . . in trouble."

Tom frowns. That young, *skinny* woman, *really*? "She told you she's . . . ?"

"Yeah. And she's scared. She doesn't have anyone else to turn to."

He starts to pace again. "Who's the father?"

Rebecca doesn't answer, but there's weight to her pause. She knows,

Tom suspects. She just doesn't want to tell him. "It's important she sees a doctor," she says instead. "I don't think she's gone to one yet."

"You mean while she's been in the woods? How far in the boonies *is* this place?"

"Dr. Salley's office has Saturday-morning hours. I'm calling the front desk next to see if they can squeeze her in. My hope is that people rescheduled because of the storm. You okay with the boys for a little longer?"

Obviously, the only answer he can give is yes. "So I guess that time limit you set is out the window, then."

"I'll have to see how long the appointment takes and what she needs."

"You sure she's actually pregnant?"

Rebecca scoffs. "I guess we'll find out at Dr. Salley's, won't we?"

And then she hangs up.

Tom stares at the phone before putting it into his pocket. He had so many more questions. But now his wife is gone again.

His head hurts. Something feels so off about all of this. He walks back into the living room, his hands shaking so badly he has to stuff them into his pockets. Charlie is still stacking the blocks. Roscoe is puzzling over a page in the Lego instructions. Tom should see if he needs help, but his brain feels too addled. It's like he's walked into the middle of a mystery movie and no one has told him how it began. Rebecca knows things about Danny. Rebecca, at least this morning, seemed *afraid* of Danny. But now they're just driving off into the sunset, *la la la*, to the OB's office. What the fuck?

He pulls his phone from his pocket and pulls up Google, though when he looks at the search window, he has no idea what to type. What is Danny's last name? Did Rebecca say it? He's pretty sure she didn't.

Into the search engine, he types *Danny*, *female*, and *Davis*—the town where she and Rebecca grew up—and the year Rebecca said they graduated. It's a hodgepodge of results. There is a listing for a Danny Rosen, Certified Nurse Practitioner. There is a story about a woman named Danny Crosby, who won a bodybuilding competition. Is her real name Danielle? And wait, Rebecca said she ran away after graduation. Could that be something?

He types a new search. *Danielle + CA + Oregon + missing* as well as a date eight years before. To his astonishment, something comes up. *Mother's Heartbreak Over Missing Teen.* And a photo of a girl who looks a lot like Danny.

Jackpot.

He clicks on it. It's not an article but a YouTube clip. After an ad about solar paneling, the story appears. On an internal set, a reporter in early 2000s makeup sits with a middle-aged woman. The tone is somber.

"I'm speaking with Mrs. Janice Martin, the mother to Danielle 'Danny' Martin, an eighteen-year-old girl who has suddenly gone missing," the reporter says. (*Martin!* Tom makes a mental note.) "Mrs. Martin is insisting that this isn't a simple case of a young adult leaving the nest. Mrs. Martin? Can you tell us what's going on?"

Janice Martin perks up. "Thank you for having me. Yes, I'm afraid my daughter is involved with a dangerous organization called ISB."

The reporter frowns. "What makes you think this group is dangerous?"

"She started going to this ... life coach, he called himself." The corners of Janice's mouth turn down. "His name is Ben Rahm. I was all for my daughter talking to someone, but I would have rather it was a licensed therapist." She glances at the interviewer for validation. "At least, with a therapist, they go through training. They know how to handle kids, not steer them down the wrong paths. Not, um, take advantage of them." Her voice breaks.

"Of course," the reporter says, full of empathy.

"As it turns out, it was a whole group thing, not just coaching. Danny got involved quickly." Her posture stiffens. "She seemed happy, but when I asked her about what they discussed, she said some outlandish things."

"Such as?"

Janice looks pained. "Like how medication was corporate manipulation. And how she could heal her body with her mind."

A cut to the reporter, crossing her arms.

"And how the world was full of victims, but that was all a construct, too." Janice throws up her hands. "To be honest, I couldn't follow some of the things she was saying. It was nonsense, though. Victims didn't exist? So if my daughter were raped, she'd think—what? She deserved it? The rapist did nothing wrong?"

"That's very concerning," the reporter murmurs.

There are tears in Janice's eyes. She sniffs and looks off into the distance. "I didn't want to fight with her. I want her to be happy. But I'm aware of the power of ideas, especially to a teenager. I knew I was losing her."

The scene cuts to a desolate shot of an empty playground. A swing blows. There's an abandoned Solo cup on the ground. In a voice-over, the reporter explains that a few days ago, Danny said she was going to a party. She never returned. That's when Janice knew something was wrong.

"I filed a police report," Janice says, the camera back on her. She looks wrecked now, her posture hunched, her eyes glassy. "I called all of her friends, everyone I knew. And then, a few days later, Danny left a voice message. I was thrilled . . . but then I listened to it. And because she's legally an adult, there's nothing I can do."

A grainy recording of a familiar voice begins to play. Tom's jaw drops. It's Danny. Definitely, *definitely* the young woman who was just in his house.

"*Hey, Mom. It's me.*" Danny sounds sober but controlled. Confident. And although there's static in the background, it doesn't sound like Danny's at a loud party. Tom can't hear any sounds in the background at all. "*I just want you to know that I'm okay. I'm safe. This is something I had to do. People . . . they were hurting me back there. I felt . . . stuck. Lost. I wasn't living up to the person I'm supposed to be. But here, it's better. I'm joyful. But I also think it's better if you don't contact me. You're going to have to be dead to me for a while. Maybe a long while. Have a good life.*"

When they return to the screen, Danny's mom's hands cover her face. The reporter waits a few moments while she silently sobs.

"Does this sound like the typical message your daughter would leave?" the reporter asks when Mrs. Martin has gotten over the worst of it.

Danny's mom shakes her head miserably. "This isn't the way Danny talks. Not her intonation, not choice of words—*joyful*? That's not a word she'd use."

"So you think she was reading off a script, maybe?"

"I do. It's like . . . well, I think someone coached her." Janice shrugs helplessly. "*Brainwashed* her."

"Who do you think might have done that?"

"This . . . man who led the group." Janice's voice lowers murderously. "This Ben person."

The clip ends. Tom chews on the inside of his cheek. The itch to use is really nagging at him today; it's making his skin crawl. So Danny got involved in this, what, new age youth group or something, and her mom didn't get it? Sure, that whole victimhood-isn't-real bullshit was kind of concerning, but maybe she said it to get a rise out of her mom—kids did that all the time. And then she went to Oregon? So what?

Below the news story are comments, though most are years old. *Praying for her*, one person wrote. But another commenter said, *Please. The girl is eighteen. She's allowed to explore. Mom sounds like she has a stick up her ass.* The original commenter fired back: *Actually, I know some people at her high school who joined up, too. After they were part of the group, they never seemed right in the head. Mom has a good reason to be worried. ISB, the place she went—it's a straight-up cult.*

Tom blinks. *Cult?* That seems a little extreme.

Still, now he has new keywords to try: An organization called *ISB*. And . . . *cult*. Also, Danny's mom referred someone named *Ben Rahm*.

Typing all of those into Google, he pulls up more hits. There aren't any more links to Danny's disappearance, but there does seem to be an ISB YouTube channel. When he clicks on it and looks through the thumbnails, he draws in a breath. There Danny is, sitting across from a guy with pasty skin and thinning hair. The caption says it's Ben Rahm.

Huh. The guy seems downright . . . *nerdy.*

He presses Play. They have wild, fake smiles, their lips stretched wide. Danny's voice seems higher pitched on camera than in real life, and she leans close to the guy, eager to please him. The words *Internal Spirit Map* and *victimhood* and *subservient* wash over him. And then the Ben guy mansplains how women shouldn't see their trauma as trauma but instead as a path to the divine, just like Danny's mother said to the news reporter. Tom scoffs and puts his hands behind his head. Guy has some nerve.

The thing is, Danny's smiling all the way through it, like it's all completely logical. For a moment, their bright voices and big smiles make Tom feel a little gaslighted, like maybe *he's* the one who has it wrong. But then he blinks. Nope. This is some weird, *weird* propaganda shit. He clicks it off.

He navigates to chat rooms and subreddits about ISB next. There are various posts lauding the group, the commenters celebrating how the program helped them get over fears and anxieties that had held them back. When he first sees *Ben* mentioned, it's positive. *Absolute genius*, someone writes. *Saved my life*, another poster says. *His story is so inspirational. How he came from nothing and grew up on the streets? Got tons of advanced degrees and almost made it to the Olympics? How he's the smartest man in the world?*

But then another poster chimes in: *He didn't grow up on the streets. That's a lie.*

And then another poster: *I heard he was home-schooled. Parents barely paid attention to him. They were more concerned with themselves. And he's not that smart. There are no degrees from those universities, and there's no evidence of some amazing IQ test.*

He's not a liar, someone tagged as the Moderator argues. *Spreading hateful speech on this sub will not be tolerated. This is your first warning.*

As for Ben, he was born a genius, with so much potential, but no one saw it, someone else wrote. *He learned to turn his pain and isolation into something transcendent—just like how he taught us. He refused to be a victim any longer. That's when he had this vision.*

Huh. There's that victim talk again. And it's a little creepy how the moderator chastised anyone commenting with opposing opinions. And people would probably be more likely to follow a leader if he came with all kinds of credentials and a superhero backstory and godlike qualities. Grew up poor, pulled himself up from nothing, genius IQ... hell, *Tom* would read that dude's book.

Tom clicks through the whole ISB subreddit. Some posts have since been deleted—did the moderator deem them too negative? Some of the posts talk of a place in Oregon where a lot of people involved with ISB live—a compound of sorts, like an intentional community. Rebecca said Danny disappeared to Oregon—it's got to be to this place. Someone else mentions a wonderful event called Celebration Weekend, a three-day festival of workshops and community. Another post writes, *I'm thinking of going to this but is it true we can't bring any medicine? I have epilepsy, and I take something for seizures.* Below that, a reply: *No medicine is allowed. You'll be taught how to control your seizures and overcome them.*

"Yeah fucking right," Tom mutters. He hopes the person with epilepsy came to their senses and didn't go.

There's also a topic titled "Dealing with Difficult Family Members." When Tom clicks on that, he reads a heartfelt account about how the particular poster wants to be more involved in ISB's programs, but her parents aren't supportive. Everyone who chimes in is supportive and sympathetic, saying that *their* families didn't get it at first, either. Someone writes, *Sometimes, you have to create distance between those who are trying to hold you back. Think of what Ben teaches. These people might be secretly toxic. They are standing in your way.*

He scrolls to the bottom of the comment box. A new comment has come in only a few days before that seems to have slipped in under the moderator's nose.

Please, OP, turn back now. What they have told you is all a lie. Do not join this group. It seems great on the surface, but it will SUCK YOU IN. The people involved are just as evil. The leader doesn't have your best interest at heart. He only wants to manipulate you. And that whole "transcendence from pain, no one is a victim" bullshit? That's just to get him off the hook when he's the one who inflicts the suffering.

This group will pressure you to do terrible things. They'll make you work only for the organization—you'll have to teach, recruit, slave, and undo all of the things that you've learned in a normal educational setting. They will make you give away all your money, sacrifice your body, sacrifice your soul. They will starve you. They will make you hurt yourself. They'll mark your thigh with a scar. They will convince you to stop taking medications and stop going to doctors. They will make you offer up terrible secrets about your life to prove that you're loyal. They will subject you to humiliation. You will be scarred for life. You may even be asked to have the leader's children, but when you do, the leader will take the child from you. You won't have normal maternal rights. Some of the mothers there aren't even able to see their babies without him around.

I hope this has scared you. Move away if you can. I beg of you. Those people are spiders. They will catch you. And they'll stop for nothing to keep you in their web.

Tom's heart is pounding now. Sweat prickles on his brow. A few things stick out: *They will starve you.* Danny is skin and bones. His gaze catches on the line *You may even be asked to have the leader's children, but when you do, the leader will take the child from you.* No wonder Rebecca is worried. Only . . . how does she actually *know* that? Does she look at these message boards, too?

Something else needles at him. *They'll mark your thigh with a scar.* Rebecca has a scar on her thigh. She always said it was a burn accident, something about a campfire, but . . .

"Daddy?" Roscoe has paused from his Lego. "You just made a weird noise. Like the sound the baby makes when he's gurgling his spit."

"Sorry, buddy," Tom says in a low voice. He had no idea he'd been making any sounds at all. "Just, um . . . reading something . . ."

The crawling feeling in his gut is getting to be too much. He can't handle this revelation sober. He needs something to take the edge off. Jittery, he turns back to his phone and dials Rebecca again.

He dials and waits. The phone rings and rings . . . and then goes to voicemail. Tom bites down hard on his lip. He sends a text next. *Can you call me?*

Then he stands. "Actually, your brother and I need to run upstairs for a sec. Be good, 'kay?" He scoops up Charlie, who isn't thrilled. He wants down so he can explore.

Charlie in his arms, Tom heads up to the bathroom and looks around. There, in a low cabinet, pushed far, far, *far* to the back, is a bottle. Inside is something he only wants to use in an emergency. He picks up the bottle and stares at the tiny pill inside. It's so tempting. All he needs to do is twist the cap, shake it into his hand, swallow it.

The baby reaches out and squeezes his nose. It brings him back to earth. Fuck. *No*. He can't go down this road again. He needs to call his sponsor. One rocky moment with Rebecca, and he's over the edge?

But this *isn't* a rocky moment. This feels bigger. Whatever Rebecca's friend was involved in, it's something that was dangerous and toxic. And is this why Rebecca never talks about her past? Was she involved in this thing, too? His head spins at the notion. He wants to trust his wife. He wants to believe her. The idea that she's kept . . . *this* . . . from him—well, it's staggering.

But still, he puts the pill bottle back. He has to keep a calm head. A *sober* head. He'll go down and call her again. Tell her to come back. He wants to talk. They can figure it out together, whatever this is.

But as he heads back downstairs, his gaze drifts toward the closet door, which is still ajar. Rebecca had been up here earlier. Doing . . . something. She definitely wasn't just looking for shoes.

He opens the closet and stares at Rebecca's organized racks of shirts, skirts, and dresses. Her shoes are mostly lined up on the floor in neat rows, though a few have been kicked over. She claimed she was rummaging around to find shoes to go out, but she'd chosen the Nike Pegasus that doesn't even have a mate. The whole thing is fishy.

Charlie's foot gets him in the chest. "Down we go, buddy." Tom drops to his knees and sits the baby on his butt. Charlie starts inspecting the dust bunnies while Tom peers at the closet again. Then, he spots it: a cardboard box shoved haphazardly into the corner. There's a high-heeled boot on top of it to weigh it down.

Frowning, he glances at her upper shelves. That's usually where Rebecca stores all of her boxes. And he thinks he saw her shoving something into this corner earlier, just as he'd walked into the room.

His fingers touch the edge of the box, but then he draws back. He trusts his wife. His wife trusts him. If there is something bigger going on, she'd tell him. Or would she?

He pulls the box toward him and removes the boot from the top. The flaps gape open. The box has a faintly musty smell. Tom's heart pounds as he peers inside. It's filled with rumpled T-shirts. There's also a ziplock bag containing a USB stick. He looks at the T-shirts, pulling them out one by one. The first bears a logo of the Davis High School Raptors. Rebecca's old school, probably. He drops it to the floor. The second T-shirt also seems to be from high school: a shirt from a drama club production of *Oklahoma!* Funny. Tom never knew Rebecca was in the drama club.

He digs down, finding a few more shirts. He's about to stop when his hand touches something hard and solid. He glances at the baby, now inspecting a shoelace. Holding his breath, Tom parts the T-shirts to expose a corner of what he fears the thick, solid item might be. He stares at the long, dark barrel. He pulls away more T-shirts until he unveils the handle, the chamber, the trigger.

Rebecca has a gun.

CHAPTER FOURTEEN

BEND, OREGON
EIGHT YEARS BEFORE

The grass is wet beneath Danny's butt, but she doesn't mind. She would sit in a puddle of water to get a front-row seat. She stares up at the makeshift stage, admiring the bursts of balloons and the banner that hangs overhead: *Celebration Weekend*, and then looks around at the crowds of people. How many people are here—a thousand? Two?

The stage is empty, but soon it will be filled. Danny feels exactly like she used to when she was waiting for her favorite band to start at the local amphitheater—the same buzz, that feeling she might faint the moment the lead singer breaks into song. What's even better is that in this case, she *knows* the lead singer.

Toby taps her shoulder; he's sitting behind her. "Wanna beer?" he asks, cracking one himself.

"I'm good," Danny says primly.

Toby sniffs. "More for me, then."

He recently dyed his hair blue. Before Toby met Ben—and he was one of the people who convinced Danny to talk to Ben, too—he wore tutus, but now he says that was just an "experimental phase of his masculinity." He's been working on those feelings in his latest sessions with Ben.

"Beer's allowed, you know," Toby adds after he takes a long sip. "Never knew *you* to turn one down."

That was the old *me*, Danny thinks. The version of herself who numbed her brain to avoid facing the truth. Sure, alcohol is allowed in ISB, but it isn't *encouraged*. Ben said he stopped drinking the moment he realized that booze was another trapping of victimhood, a way to dull him down and keep him quiet. People who have transcended beyond that way of thinking don't need alcohol anymore, he told her.

And so Danny doesn't need it either. She wants to be clear-headed for Ben's speech. It's the last item on the program at Celebration Weekend, the camping trip that's lasted several glorious days. It's been an awesome time so far: three days of nature, great food, introspection, workshops, trust exercises, therapy sessions . . . and of course, three days with Ben.

Danny wonders if everyone is as bummed about going home as she is.

Others settle down on blankets around her. There are people from Arizona, Colorado, and beyond, and some of them carry state flags or wear T-shirts proclaiming where they're from as a source of pride that ISB has such a far reach. It's thrilling to think the philosophy is gaining traction. Some people are brand new to the group, but some of them, like Danny, are Seeds, those who have committed to eventually teaching ISB's philosophies and practices—though, as Ben says, it will take some time to get there. Though many of the group are the same rank as Danny, she can't help but think she's a tiny bit special. ISB is headquartered in her hometown, and Ben has taken the time, over the last year, to counsel her *personally*. Not everyone gets that privilege. She wonders how many of the others got their first few sessions comped like she did. Anyone? Not that Ben can offer that to her anymore—which is fine. Danny is happy to pay for ISB with her savings.

Throughout the weekend, Danny has caught sight of quite a few women in Ben's presence. First there's Barb, Ben's partner and ISB cocreator—she's tall and gangly and wears oversized glasses and no makeup.

But there's something larger than life about her, a strong, steady, intimidating confidence. Maybe it's because she created so many of the ISB tenets. Maybe it's because, with the Inner Strength program she came up with, she was able to shrink her cancer tumors and go into remission without getting any treatment. Whatever it is, Danny has been a little afraid to speak to her, despite Ben saying they'd hit it off.

Then there are a group of women who have ascended to become Ben's Seedlings, the next level to which Danny aspires. These women teach the workshops with an air of confidence and calm. They're all so thin, and they seem to wear their thinness like a badge of pride. Most are beautiful, too. They flock around Ben, laughing, talking seriously and deeply, and Ben looks at them with special attention. They're spreading his word. Making tons of money, too. Danny knows she shouldn't have covetous feelings—it goes against the group's philosophy—but she's caught herself glancing enviously at their pretty jewelry and clothes, knowing that they probably afforded those things with the salaries they collected from running their own workshops.

Toby drains his beer. "Sure is beautiful today," he remarks, looking out at the giant trees that surround them. "So what're you thinking? You gonna do the compound?"

The reason this Celebration Weekend is being held in the Oregon woods near Bend is because Ben has been working to create an ISB community here. An intensive, immersive living experience for only the most faithful of ISB devotees—or, as Ben describes it privately, *the most highly evolved* of the people ascribing to his way of living. Seeds and Seedlings only, and from the way he describes it, it'll be a utopia. They'll grow their own food and live sustainably. They'll swim in the pond on the property, run through the meadows, or hike in the woods. They'll work on themselves every day. They'll be at their healthiest because of the site's location far from the pollutants of cities or highways. And they'll get to earn an income by teaching ISB ways to those who come for weekend retreats and workshops. Danny has only been a Seed for a little while, but she already feels like a hugely different person. Cleaner, stronger, more focused, all because of Ben's shifts in thinking—and because of the people and habits she's shed. The idea of making money off this—as Ben says, *lots* of money—well, she'd love for it to be her career. *Take that, Mom,* she thinks with a smirk. *There are other ways to succeed without going to college.*

Of course, moving there will come with a high price tag—at first. Rent plus meals plus round-the-clock ISB classes costs practically six figures. But it's a spend-money-to-make-money kind of thing—after a while, Danny wouldn't need quite as many classes and would be teaching them herself. And anyway, can you put a price on investing in yourself?

"I want to," Danny admits, trying not to sound as eager as she feels. High emotions aren't really applauded around here. "I mean, school's almost over. It seems like the right time."

"Yeah, same," Toby says. "We could go together." He smiles at her. Toby has been in this group longer than she has. Danny's pretty sure he got a little bonus for introducing her to Ben; she received a small payment for the acquaintance in her neighborhood who signed up for a weekend workshop. Danny wishes she knew more people to recruit; problem was, her friends were either already involved, or they weren't really the types who wanted to become better versions of themselves.

Toby sighs. "But the money's tricky, you know? But Barb's really trying to work it out for me."

Danny nods. "That's nice of her. And I heard Barb say that, too. We all can find it somewhere. There are ways."

Say you had an infected tooth, Barb had told all of them at the campfire last night. *You'd find the money to pay for that, wouldn't you? There's always ways to find money. What about family? Friends?*

Everyone had started murmuring.

"My grandma has a nest egg that she wants me to use for college," Toby goes on, probably thinking about that same conversation. "But . . . I only applied to one place, and I didn't get in."

"Yeah," Danny says, pulling her knees to her chest. She has done even less. She *told* her mom she applied to a few places—just to shut her up—and was rejected from all of them, but, in truth, she never even filled out the applications.

"It's my money," Toby goes on. "Seems like I'd get farther with ISB than I would in some sort of business associate's degree where you aren't even guaranteed a career at the end."

"Agreed," Danny murmurs. Ben has promised, over and over, that they will be teaching their own workshops within six months or so. She likes the way Toby has phrased that: *It's my money*.

Like Toby, she has a nest egg too. Her grandfather left her some cash when he passed away a few years ago, not that she has access to it. Her mom says it's better in the investment account; if she gave it to Danny, Danny would piss it away. She needs to use it for college.

But the money is in her name, not her mom's. Danny told Barb about this, and Barb let out a long breath. "To be honest, it's downright cruel that your mom is holding your future hostage. She isn't looking out for your interests. She doesn't care about your dreams."

"I know," Danny said softly.

The more sessions she took in ISB principles, the more she understood the patterns she and her mom had established when Danny was very young—and how dysfunctional they are now. They'd gotten into how Danny's dad had abandoned them when she was young, walking out the door one day for gas and never coming back. It was a shock, a wound, but Danny had found herself propping her mother up, not the other way around. She never had a chance to grieve her dad being gone because it was all about making sure her mom didn't have a nervous breakdown. Worse, instead of Danny's mother lauding Danny's inner fortitude to others, she instead said they *both* were barely keeping their heads above water. She turned her father's disappearance into a crutch, making them *both* into victims. It sapped their strength. A clean break from Mom is the only thing that would save Danny from being overrun by negative entities, Ben says. She will be able to undo those patterns, but it'll take work, and time, and patience.

Since Danny joined, she feels so much less . . . *terrified*. She rarely has that precarious feeling that she's going to forget who she is anymore, and the autoscopic feelings have dissipated almost entirely. She feels like she's in her body now instead of watching it, disgusted, from a distance.

And she certainly no longer sees her past pain as something she should dwell on. It happened, but she's rising above it.

And it feels incredible. So incredible, she wants to shout from the rooftops. So incredible that she wants to hand out flyers at school, begging other people to join ISB, too. She pictures herself teaching this to others, standing confidently at the front of a workshop room just like the glamorous Seedlings do now. And, yes, maybe wearing beautiful earrings and owning a nice car. Or putting all that cash in the bank. Or maybe money won't even *matter* . . . because she'll be with Ben. It's a secret thought, wanting to be with Ben. She's embarrassed to even think it. But she definitely feels it. It's kind of her ultimate goal, even beyond making an amazing salary.

But ugh, Danny's mom. Her choice of words when talking about Ben is infuriating. *I don't trust a man who wants to spend so much time with teenagers.* And, *There's something off about his eyes.* And, *Why does he insist you call him Scion? I don't like the sound of that, Danny.*

Last week was the worst. Just as Danny was off to another session, her mother intercepted her at the front door. "You've changed. You've lost weight. Is he making you do that? Is he telling you what to do?"

Danny shrugged. "Not at all. He's *inspiring*, Mom. A good person." *Better than you*, she'd wanted to add.

She moved to leave, but her mother grabbed her wrist. Danny didn't fight back. It was important, Ben had taught her, to stay calm and not let her emotions take over.

"You need to leave that group," her mother said. "You don't even have to go to college. There are so many other things you could do. It seems dangerous. I'm afraid you're going to get hurt."

Danny took a deep breath and said, calmly, "But, Mom, *you* were the one who said I needed therapy."

"That man is *not a therapist*. I've heard things about him, Danny. He isn't telling the truth—about anything. And that's just the tip of the iceberg."

"Could it be that you don't want me to feel better?" Danny looked at her innocently. "It's okay. You might not even know that's what you think. If I'm not happy, Mom, you can control me. You like it that way."

Her mother's hand had shot out then, a blur through the air. Danny heard the slap to her face before she felt the sting. She reared back, her eyes wide.

Her mother looked stricken. "I-I'm sorry. Honey, I didn't mean to do that. I'm just stressed, and I love you, and I'm afraid I'm losing you, and *of course* I don't want to control you! Why would you even *think* that!"

Danny's cheek throbbed. The more it hurt, the more her hate grew. But she wouldn't lash out. She wouldn't fight back. She was in charge of her feelings, not the other way around. And so, she whirled around and went through the door . . . *calmly*.

It's all normal behavior, Ben told her later. Danny shouldn't blame her mother—she should pity her. She doesn't know better. Her feelings are ruling her. She doesn't know how to change.

There's a hubbub on the stage. A cheer rises up, and Danny leaps to her feet, eager to see what's happening. The women step onto the stage first. There's Barb, of course, and then Amelia, who is twenty-five, her pale skin glowing, her flossy white-blond hair shining, her clothes hanging perfectly off her lithe body. Rue, just as thin, with her almond-colored skin and braids and beautiful singing voice. Sophia, possibly *thinner*, the actress, with her model-beautiful cheekbones and long dark hair and mysterious smile. Danny has heard that their lives were hard before they joined. Amelia was plagued with career pitfalls and toxic relationships. Rue had terrible paranoia, though it's miraculously vanished. Sophia was on the rise as an actress, though since she became part of ISB, her career has exploded both onstage and in the workshop sphere. She's killing it *everywhere*.

The women glance into the wings, beckoning the final individuals to proceed. As each person emerges, a new cheer breaks out. The cheers intensify as Ben finally emerges.

Ben faces the crowd and waves. "Are we ready to do hard things? Are we ready to be our best selves?"

Thousands in the crowd rise to their feet and put their hands together in prayer. "Strength be your guide!" Ben's catchphrase, from one of his most famous workshops. They scream it. Danny yells so loudly her throat feels raw.

Ben looks more handsome than ever. To be near him all weekend, to absorb his wisdom not daily but *hourly*—it's made Danny realize how brilliant he really is. People in the crowd are clasping their hands, falling to their knees, nearly exploding with gratitude. What must it be like to be Ben? To have helped so many people? To have turned so many moths into butterflies?

"Whoa, look who's with him," Toby says over the sounds of the cheers.

Danny's mouth drops. Trailing behind Ben, holding his hand, is Bex. Her *friend* Bex. She beams and waves to the crowd. And Ben is looking at her adoringly, like he thinks she's the best thing in the universe.

Toby stares at Danny, agog. "Did you know she was that high up in the program?"

Danny licks her lips. Bex was the one who really pushed Danny to join ISB, even more than Toby. She sang Ben's praises any chance she got. She said that it would help Danny so much and be an amazing thing they'd share. She was the one who'd said that the videos Ben took were helpful, not creepy, and that Danny should stick it out.

But Danny has barely seen Bex the whole weekend. She actually thought Bex was tiring of the group—it didn't occur to Danny that Bex was AWOL because she was in Ben's inner circle. It also makes her feel kind of betrayed; was Bex *hiding* this from her?

But above all this is another feeling roiling in her gut—desire. *Drive.* Danny wants to be on that stage. *She* wants to be the one holding Ben's hand. Basking in his light. She doesn't care what kind of sacrifice it requires. Spending the rest of her money on ISB sessions. Moving to the compound in Oregon. Breaking free of her mother entirely. Trusting Ben *completely.* Whittling herself down to the smallest girl she can be. She's heard whispers about other sacrifices, too—*major* sacrifices, ones that prove total loyalty and honor.

Danny will do all of that. She will do anything to continue to feel the way she feels. She will be the best student. She will score straight As. She'll blow everyone out of the water. Or she'll die trying.

CHAPTER FIFTEEN

CARSON CITY, NEVADA
PRESENT DAY

To Rebecca's relief, Dr. Salley's office does have cancelations this morning—the storm has caused a lot of damage, and quite a few roads are closed because of downed trees. It's a stroke of luck. When Rebecca was pregnant, she sometimes had to book weeks in advance for a scan or checkup. At least she can get Danny in quickly.

Dread washes through her. *Danny. Pregnant.*

When Danny steps out of the bathroom, Rebecca can't help it—she ambushes her right there in the middle of Maude's cute wood-paneled seating area. "We're going to an OB. I already called. It's in a half hour."

Danny's eyes widen. "I . . . I can't."

"You need to. It's the healthy thing to do."

"I *am* healthy."

"No, you aren't." Rebecca isn't an idiot. Then she thinks to ask something else. "Is he still allowing you to stay in the house?" she whispers, leaning close. "You're not . . . somewhere else on the property? Like, he isn't making you camp forever?"

Danny leans unsteadily against the battered leather couch. "Of course I'm in the house. I share a room with him."

That's something Rebeca doesn't want to visualize.

Then, Danny takes something out of her backpack. "Do you think I can get some water for this?" she asks, holding it up. It's a medicine bottle. Pills rattle inside.

Rebecca frowns. "What's that for?"

"Herbs." Danny smiles at her crookedly. "It's supposed to be good for pregnancy."

Panic shoots through her. "*He* gave it to you, didn't he?" Frantic, she grabs the entire bottle and tosses it in the nearby trash.

"Hey!" Danny cries. "What the hell?"

"Do you have more pills? You should throw them all away. I'm serious, Danny. They're not safe."

Danny scoffs, giving her a weird look. Rebecca can feel her heart beating in her chest. *Pump the brakes*, she tells herself. It's a reaction to Danny's news. So many memories and fears have flooded her all of a sudden. At the same time, Danny is skittish. She might flee if Rebecca comes on too strong.

"We should get going," she says in a softer voice, offering her hand to pull Danny up from her perch on the couch. "You'll like my doctor. He's just going to do a scan, maybe, or use this thing over your belly to hear a heartbeat."

"Of course there's a heartbeat," Danny insists. "I'm having a baby."

"Right. Yes. So this is just to see if everything looks okay for your peace of mind. *My* peace of mind. You want me to help you? This is how I'll help."

Amazingly, Danny stands. "Okay. But if at any point I feel uncomfortable, can I leave?"

"Yes. Of course." Rebecca is beyond grateful. And buoyed, too, that Danny has agreed to this fairly willingly. It feels like a good sign. Maybe Danny is telling the truth about sneaking away without telling anyone. Maybe she really is scared and desperate. She wants out. She's starting to wake up.

It's Rebecca's plan to make her wake up all the way.

As they leave, she peeks at Danny's midsection again. She would have had no idea had Danny not told her. She must not be that far along. But who, why, *how*? At the same time, does Rebecca really need most of those answers? She already knows them. Ben is the who, the why, and the how.

Ben, to whom Rebecca introduced Danny. Ben, whom Rebecca knew so well herself, once upon a time.

———

ISB had been so innocent at first. Rebecca's parents had joined the organization for professional growth when Rebecca was in grade school. Both worked at major corporations, her dad in finance, her mom in marketing, and they wanted to gain even more confidence, climb the ladder, all of that bullshit. Ben had all kinds of tools to reframe their thinking; he also had tons of testimonials from other professionals whose careers took off after his training programs. Her parents were very, *very* into their jobs. As an only child, you'd think they would dote on her, but it was the opposite; she was expected to take care of herself. She knew she should be grateful for what she had: There was always food on the table, she always had new clothes, and her house was big and nice and clean. She never *wanted* for anything . . . but her parents never helped her with her homework. They never knew her teachers' names. They barely knew her *friends'* names.

Still, she was okay with it for a while. She was independent and resourceful and had lots of friends and friends' parents around, so it didn't matter. For a while, ISB just lurked quietly in the background of her family's life, just some job seminars her parents went to a lot. Her parents were never interested in the mentorship program to become Seeds or Seedlings—they were too busy with their own careers. But in eighth grade, something happened. That summer, she went on a family trip to Mexico—which was laughable, as her parents were on conference calls nearly the whole time. Not once did they all go to the beach together; a lot of their dinners were with some colleagues who were also vacationing there. Bored, Rebecca snuck out every night that week for a walk alone on the beach. The last night, a cute stranger came up to her on the sand; he said he'd been watching her. At first, she enjoyed his flirtation, but then things turned pushy. She suddenly found herself shoved down against the pier pilings, his hands doing terrible things to her body. As much as she begged for it not to happen, it happened anyway.

She didn't dare tell her parents. What if they found it an annoyance, a distraction? Or maybe they'd blame her—Why had she thought it was safe to walk the beach alone at night? Why had she giggled at the guy's awful jokes? Why hadn't she just run?

When they returned home, Rebecca was much less sure of herself. She didn't want to go out. She didn't talk much. She developed a stutter—so bad she had a hard time speaking up in a class taught by a male teacher, or getting through a conversation with her grandfather on the phone, or even placing an order to a male Starbucks employee. It happened only around men—*All men are dangerous now*, she'd thought. Men had taken away her voice. Not that she understood this consciously.

Right around that time, Rebecca's mom and dad started encouraging her to talk to Ben. He had a large youth following, apparently. It was Ben who teased the traumatic event out of Rebecca. At first, she didn't want him to. She especially didn't want him to film the confession, terrified her parents would see—though, thinking on this later, maybe her parents were more perceptive than she gave them credit; perhaps they sensed something was wrong and, completely unequipped to, you know, *be parents*, they enlisted Ben instead.

But Ben said it would be important to capture the moment on video. He swore no one would see it. Rebecca could look back on it. Also, the videos were hers—after, she could do with them what she wished.

Famous last words.

They explored the triggers, the fear she felt, the helplessness she experienced. He helped unlock the notion that her stutter was directly related to what had happened. He also emphasized that she needed to stop thinking of herself as a victim, but in a way that Rebecca finally understood. Yes, what had happened wasn't good. Still, she had to stop living in the shadow of it. She had to stop letting it *define* her. A victim will continue being a victim indefinitely, Ben explained, but according to his teachings, we are all responsible for the things that happen to us. We chose whether we became victims, not the other way around.

At the time, it felt empowering. Rebecca liked the idea of rejecting the label of victim. She rewrote the narrative, imagining herself walking away from the man—*screaming* at him, actually, without stuttering, her voice loud and strong. *You need to be in control*, Ben explained. *You can't have other people speak for you.* Her stutter, he explained, was her relinquishing control. Saying, *I give up.*

On video, she worked through all of this. On video, she also told her attacker that he no longer was to blame—actions were actions, but she wouldn't be his victim anymore. At the time, she felt lighter. Better. *In control.* Ben was proud, and that felt good.

But here's the red flag Rebecca ignored: when she asked for her videos for her own safekeeping, Ben said that she couldn't have them. "I want to graduate you, actually," he said. "From a Seed to a Seedling."

Rebecca felt honored. Usually, Seedlings were older members, but Ben said he saw something special in her. Something inspiring. "But there's one thing," he said. "The group is founded on loyalty and trust. And one way to know that I trust you and you trust me is that I keep one of your secrets. In this case, it could be your videos. Think of it as a security deposit, sort of—and don't worry, *everyone* has given security deposits. Including me."

Rebecca wasn't sure. Was he *positive* no one else would watch the videos? Ben said yes—of course. "I made my own secret video, too," he said. "I'd be humiliated if someone watched it. But the only way someone would is if I betrayed the group. Left, maybe. Or did something really harmful like spoke badly about us or told lies. Broke your trust, in other words."

"But I'd never do anything bad," Rebecca protested. "I'd just rather keep the videos." She wanted to destroy them. She didn't want to think about that secret, ever.

Ben twisted his mouth. "You don't get it, then. Maybe you aren't right for the Seedlings after all."

"No, I am right! I want to do it!" Rebecca cried, her heart thumping. She felt tears fill her eyes, but she willed herself not to cry. "I'm loyal. I swear, I'm loyal."

"Then you have nothing to worry about with that video," Ben said, shrugging. "You need to trust us, and we'll trust you. Think about the bond you'll form with the other Seedlings just knowing you all have security deposits that make you feel extremely vulnerable—you've all entered this pact together. There's real power in that. Your actions are meaningful. It gives weight to your loyalty." Ben turned to look at her hard and then added, "I'm part of that bond, too."

That was what got her. The way Ben looked at her. The promise that seemed to dangle there for her to reach out and grab.

Soon enough, she was more involved in ISB than her parents. Ben's programs for younger people had a different structure than the career courses; they were more about shaping lives and trajectories. He took her under his wing as sort of a youth ambassador—she got several kids at school to join, including Toby Sherman, one of her friends. She remembers begging Danny to talk to Ben, too. *You seem so sad. He could help you. He's amazing. He helps with all kinds of things.*

She'd even told Danny her own story about the assault. Danny was the only person she told, actually, besides Ben. She didn't even know if she was supposed to tell Danny or if it was a breach of Ben's trust—he hadn't exactly said she *couldn't* share what had happened, but he'd made it out like it was an important secret between *them*, a key he held that unlocked her power.

But she thought it could help convince Danny. After she told, though, Danny looked at her strangely. "But, I mean, you *were* a victim, Bex," she said slowly. "You were raped. You should have pressed charges."

"What? No." Rebecca shook her head. "There's no point. I don't see myself as a victim anymore. Pressing charges—that would hold me back. *I* set the course of my life. I'm only a victim if I choose to be."

She remembers how Danny stared at her like she was nuts. But at the time, she thought she was doing such good. Rebecca thought she was *helping* her. Danny was so miserable. She needed guidance and light. *Rebecca* was happy, meanwhile—of course she wanted to share the joy.

And then Ben provided so much joy. It was like joy just flowed from his fingers. How could you not admire a man like that? How could you not see him as some sort of god? Of course Rebecca wanted to be more like Ben. And part of his inner circle. And *close* to him, closer than just student and teacher. For a while, that's what they were, and it was blissful. To be with a man who'd saved her? Ben felt so powerful; she felt safe under his wing. He never let her forget that he'd saved her—but that was okay! She appreciated him. She adored him. She *loved* him.

Until she didn't. Until she realized he wasn't who he said he was at all.

———

A red light takes her by surprise. She slams on the brakes, sending Danny jolting forward against her seat belt.

"Sorry, sorry," Rebecca says.

"It's okay," Danny says in a small voice.

Danny goes back to huddling against the window. She looks broken since she admitted why she's here. Because she told the truth about being scared? Maybe she's questioning the huge life change ahead of her? Rebecca certainly knows *that* feeling. Memories rush back. Unwelcome ones. She rubs her temples and shoves them away. She cannot think about this right now. She has to just push forward. Try and get this girl the care she needs.

She looks over at Danny, wondering if she should somehow lighten the mood. "Maybe we should pretend we're back in high school. You're the one driving. I'm texting the boys."

Danny gives her the thinnest smile. "I was a really bad driver back then."

"I know it."

"Remember that time I crashed into that boulder in Kayla's front yard? It was right in my rearview, and I backed into it anyway like it wasn't there?"

Rebecca laughs. "You had some problems with depth perception. To be honest, I used to pray whenever I got in the car with you."

"Oh yeah? To whom?"

"Buddha. Jesus. The universe." Rebecca feels her cheeks redden. She'd taken a lot of ISB courses by the time she and Danny became friends. She'd even expressed interest in starting the Seed program. It was possible, by then, Rebecca had prayed to *Ben*.

They pass a strip mall. There are few cars in the lot, probably because of the storm. The wind has let up, but the rain is still really coming down. Huge puddles have gathered on the road's shoulder.

"Remember how you used to let randos drive your car, even kids who didn't have licenses?" Danny breaks the silence.

Rebecca smiles. "Yeah. I was kind of a pushover."

"Like Justin McGinley—you were totally crushing on him. And he almost wrecked?"

Rebecca squeezes her eyes shut. "I can't believe I let him get behind the wheel."

She puts on her turn signal. "I can't remember. Did Justin work at Cinema Palace or 7-Eleven?"

"Neither!" Danny sounds outraged she doesn't remember. "Dylan Black was at Cinema Palace . . . I don't think we knew anyone at 7-Eleven."

"Oh, right, right," Rebecca says. "Dylan Black. Huh."

Danny clears her throat. "You talk to anyone from back then?"

Rebecca scoffs. "What do you think?"

Danny drops her chin. An awkward silence falls. Is she thinking about high school, too? Their friendship? How tight they felt, how close, how *bonded*?

Danny's phone buzzes softly, punctuating the silence. Her eyes dart to the screen. She licks her lips and turns the phone over on her lap without answering it.

The phone buzzes again. It seems more urgent. Rebecca checks her speed gauge. She's so keyed up; she's driving nearly fifteen miles over the limit.

"Is that . . . him?" she dares to ask.

Danny doesn't answer. Rebecca notices her tapping the wood paneling on the door. Once, twice, three times . . . after more than ten taps, she finally stops.

The phone doesn't make another sound for the rest of the drive to the doctor's office. Rebecca pulls into a space close to the door, and the two of them sprint through the rain to the lobby. They stand inside for a moment, wiping their wet faces, breathing hard. Rebecca presses the elevator button. Danny looks at the glowing light warily. When the doors open, she doesn't get in right away.

"Were you scared for your first doctor visit?" Danny whispers. "With, um, Roscoe?"

Rebecca nods. "Yeah. Really scared." Her mind was so twisted back then that she worried that simply walking into a doctor's office would bring on a spontaneous miscarriage. The gel Dr. Salley had dispensed on her belly so he could Doppler for a heartbeat was cold and slimy and had sent shivers down her legs and bad feelings—*familiar* feelings—coursing through her veins. But the nurse smiled kindly when the sound of the baby's heart resonated through the room. The baby was healthy, apparently. Rebecca was deemed healthy, too—albeit too thin. They'd prescribed her a high-calorie diet. Slowly but surely, Rebecca forced herself to eat more for the baby's sake. Things got so much better after that.

Now Rebecca steps into the elevator. After a beat, Danny blessedly follows. Rebecca hits the button for level three, and the car lifts. Danny jiggles on the balls of her feet, looking like she might be sick. Rebecca stares at her friend's sneakers. The tops have a few holes in them. The laces are gray. The bottoms look flattened, all the cushioning worn away. Rebecca wonders if she dressed especially shabbily to tug on her and Tom's heartstrings, or if conditions are that bad at the compound in Oregon.

Danny's phone buzzes again. Finally, she just shuts it off. Rebecca's heart jumps. *Good.*

The elevator dings, spitting them straight into a peach-toned waiting room. Only one other woman, cradling a pregnant belly, sits in a chair in a corner, scribbling something on a clipboard. Rebecca bustles over to the check-in desk and leans toward Samantha, the same friendly nurse who was there when she first came in with Roscoe. *It's okay you don't have insurance, honey*, she'd said in a soft voice. *We'll work it out.*

"Rebecca!" Samantha crows, her whole face lighting up. "Haven't seen you in a while! How are the boys?"

"They're great. Charlie's getting so big. And Roscoe is in first grade!" She fumbles for her phone to show some pictures.

"Adorable." Samantha sighs, then gives Rebecca her phone back. "You ever join that mom's group I was talking about? They go on walks through the trails, but they're stroller-friendly. You'd love it."

"Um, things got busy, but I'll definitely try and drop in."

Samantha has a daughter around Charlie's age, and Rebecca vaguely recalls a flyer being pushed into her hands, Samantha saying that moms need community and friendship. Rebecca doesn't doubt those things are true—there are so many times when she's home alone and just wants to have an adult conversation—but she's always so hesitant. No mom has a history like hers. She'd be mortified if anyone found out about her juicy past. *Could* they find something? She doesn't think so. Tom never has, but maybe he hasn't looked that hard. Other than Tom, she doesn't trust anyone. ISB did that. *Ben* did that.

"Anyway," Rebecca says quietly, glancing over her shoulder at Danny, praying the nurse offers her friend the same kindness. "This is the friend I was talking about, Danielle. I'll pay for her visit." Surreptitiously, she passes the nurse a credit card.

"Of course." Samantha grabs some papers. "She can come right through. What's her last name?"

"Danielle Martin," Rebecca says, figuring that's still the name Danny goes by. She leans closer. "I'm not sure she has ID, though."

Samantha waves her hand. "It's okay." She turns to Danny. "Hun? You can go back."

Danny's eyes widen as if to say, *already?* She hefts up her bag. Rebecca waves a hand. "I'll hold that for you."

Danny looks unsure. "I'll just grab my phone."

"Honey? Let's get your weight and height," the nurse calls.

"Go on," Rebecca says, shooing her toward the nurse. "I'll keep your stuff." She busies herself looking at her own phone. Tom has texted. *Where are you? What's going on?* She doesn't answer. She can't write to Tom yet. Every word out of her mouth just digs her deeper into a ditch of lies. She feels dizzy. It's like the seams of her life are coming apart.

Danny purses her lips and turns. The nurse gestures to a scale. Danny's eyes widen.

"I don't want to," she whispers.

"You don't have to look at the number, and I won't say it out loud," the nurse insists. "It's just to track your progress." But Rebecca can see the concern flicker across Samantha's face. For a millisecond, her gaze lifts, and their eyes lock. *I know*, Rebecca tries to telegraph. *I'm worried about her, too.*

"I'm gonna head to the bathroom quickly," Rebecca chirps. "But then I'll be right in there with you, Danny." She shoulders Danny's bag along with her own and walks toward the door down the hall. She hears the metal clicks of Danny stepping on the scale. There's another *clunk* as she steps off again, and the nurse gently murmurs for Danny to step into an exam room.

"My phone, though," she hears Danny saying. "I want to check something."

"I'll have your friend bring it in when she's done."

To Rebecca's surprise, Danny doesn't protest. There's talk about how to put on the cloth gown, and then the nurse shuts the door. Rebecca flushes the toilet even though she didn't have to pee. She just wanted an excuse not to give Danny's phone back right away. She turns on the faucet so the nurse—and Danny—thinks she's washing her hands. Then she turns Danny's phone back on. The moment she does, it starts to buzz again. If she's going to look, she needs to look fast—Danny wants her phone back. Withholding it from her, manipulating her—that's no better than what *he* does.

Five new texts have rolled in, all of them available to read even on the locked screen, all of them from a caller Danny has named Scion. Rebecca's blood curdles.

Scion: *Check in.*

Scion: *Check in.*

Scion: *Can I trust you?*

Scion: *ANSWER ME.*

Scion: *You'd better not be putting my son in danger!*

Rebecca groans under her breath. A knock sounds on the door, and she jumps. "Rebecca?" It's the nurse. "Your friend wants her bag."

"Oh! Yes! Coming!" Rebecca stands and turns off the taps. Her heart is pounding.

She exits into the hall. Danny's exam room door is ajar, but Rebecca doesn't trust her expression at the moment, so she hands the nurse the bag instead. "Here you go."

The nurse gives her a tight smile. "Thank you, dear. You can wait in the hall if you like."

And then she turns away. Slipping into Danny's room. Giving her phone back. And then Danny will see all that on the screen from Scion.

You'd better not be putting my son in danger!

Fuck. *Fuck.* She knew this, she did. But she was hoping she was wrong.

CHAPTER SIXTEEN

Bile rises in Tom's throat. He backs away from the closet, lurches toward the bathroom, and vomits into the toilet.

He breathes hard, ratcheting breaths, coughing out the remaining bile. But he doesn't feel better. All this time, there has been a gun in her closet. Not properly stored. Easily accessible to their children. And what if the thing's loaded? He knows how to check. He's never owned a gun himself, but some of the people he used to hang out with did—there were lots of times when they had the things out, practically waving them around, everyone so fucking foolish. Aiming the gun away, he pulls the chamber back. There are actual bullets inside. Actual goddamn bullets.

Why does she have a loaded gun? Where did she even get the thing? They'd never talked about their opinion on guns—suddenly, Rebecca seems like a total stranger. Is she secretly into them or something—is this part of her whole life? But Rebecca seems too cautious, especially involving their kids. She still hovers over Roscoe when he's on the playground and isn't like some of the other parents on their street who let their kids play outside without supervision. Would she really allow a deadly weapon within reach of them?

Tom wipes his mouth. What he really wants is to get rid of the thing entirely—throw it into a dumpster, *something*. Instead, he shakes the bullets into his palm and grabs his backpack from the closet. They rattle into the side pocket. Good for now. But then something occurs to him. When Rebecca was up here earlier, digging through this box—was this what she was looking for?

And now he's let her drive off with that girl alone.

He pauses before leaving the closet completely and looks into the box again. There's something about that ziplock bag, the one containing the USB stick. He pockets it and then tosses the empty gun back into the box and puts it back on the shelf.

"Dad?" Roscoe calls from downstairs.

"Coming!" Tom calls in the most cheerful voice he can find. He scoops up the baby once more and heads down the stairs. Halfway down, he grabs his phone and sends a text to Rebecca. *Can we talk?*

Roscoe is sitting where Tom left him, still slogging his way through the Lego set.

"Can you help?" Roscoe asks. "I can't find a Lego piece."

"Hang on, buddy."

He plops Charlie into his Pack 'n Play for a moment so he can think. His head feels detached. He needs to think this through. Rebecca had to be looking for that gun earlier. It completely explains why she was acting so jumpy. Meaning . . . what? She thinks Danny is going to hurt her? She needs to protect herself? But why would she leave without it, then? Why would she merely *look* for the thing, shove it back into the closet—in a precarious spot, no less—and then leave with this random, potentially dangerous person?

"Dad?" Roscoe whines. "You said you'd help."

"Just a *sec*, buddy," Tom says through gritted teeth.

He checks his phone. Rebecca hasn't written back yet. It makes him seethe—it feels deliberate, *all* of this is deliberate, everything she might be hiding. He grips the phone hard. *Why are you not writing me back*, he types. But then he erases it. *Why is there a fucking GUN in our house?* But he erases this too. Not over a text.

Part of him really, *really* wants to believe Rebecca has her reasons to own a weapon. Reasons for not telling him, too, and reasons for getting Danny out of the house, and reasons for keeping him out of the drama. Maybe he shouldn't text Rebecca about the gun because Danny can see her screen. Then Danny will *know* about the gun, know Rebecca's . . . *what*? It's not like she's taken the gun with her.

"Found it!" Roscoe cries gleefully, breaking Tom from his thoughts. "The piece was on the carpet! It blended in! Mommy's going to be so proud of me. She always says that I sometimes need to look harder for stuff."

"Good, good," Tom says, relieved at this small reprieve. "I'm sure Mommy will be proud." But just mentioning Rebecca fills him with uncertainty. He loves Rebecca. She's a wonderful mom. They're good parents *together*. And now he's opened a box—*literally*—that he can't close. Does he want to know these things about her? Clearly there's a reason she's hidden it from him all this time. He wants to be able to continue to trust her, to want to make a life with her. But suddenly, it feels like the gun and whatever is on this USB might throw all that into jeopardy.

He touches the USB drive in his pocket and reaches for his laptop on the counter. The USB drive is completely nondescript: black and silver, giving nothing away. Maybe it's nothing. Maybe he should trust Rebecca that whatever it is, it doesn't matter. Maybe they should move forward, not back.

But . . . but he just found a loaded gun in their closet. A friend belonging to what people are calling a cult has just shown up and Rebecca has *disappeared* with her. He feels like a jackass for not pushing her to tell him some of these things sooner. But it also feels irresponsible—for his children, for himself, and even for Rebecca—*not* to see what this is.

He glances at Roscoe in the other room. "I'll be right there, buddy," he murmurs.

Taking a deep breath, Tom slides it into the slot on the side of the laptop and waits. A file folder appears on the desktop. *D*, it's labeled. That's all.

D?

Tom clicks on it. Inside the folder are two video files. Videos? *That* he hadn't expected. He hovers the mouse over the first file, which has no title.

His finger double-clicks the mouse. The video slowly loads, a small square in the corner of the screen. Tom pulls at the edge of the square with the mouse to make it larger, and the video quality becomes grainier.

At first, he doesn't understand what he's seeing. The camera is shaky. The room is dark. A figure is curled up on the floor, the crown of her blond head visible. Her hands are wrapped around her knees, and she's breathing hard, maybe in the middle of a panic attack. It's only when Tom notices a particular large-stoned ring on the person's pointer finger does he realize who it might be. He's seen this ring before—in his own house. Danny wore it on her thumb. She shows her face for a moment, and Tom takes in her sharp chin, her big eyes. It *is* Danny. A younger Danny. Her cheeks are fuller. She looks healthier.

"Just lie there," a man says loudly from somewhere off-screen. *Too loudly.* Tom fumbles for the volume button. Then, on second thought, he grabs his wireless headphones from their charging case and pops them in his ears. He presses Play again.

A man comes into view—part of him, anyway. Tom spies the edge of a charcoal-gray T-shirt, a hairy forearm. It's definitely the same dude from the YouTube video. Ben.

"Lie there," Ben says again. "Don't move."

"Sorry," Danny whimpers.

Tom edges away from the screen. *Why does Rebecca have this?*

"Stop apologizing," Ben says, his voice sharp. But then he adds, more compassionately, "I needed to see one of your episodes to help you stop them. Just focus on your breathing, okay?"

Danny nods. She tries to breathe as she lies down on the floor, but she still seems agitated, her muscles tensing.

"Close your eyes now," Ben says. "Keep breathing."

"Okay, Ben," Danny whispers.

A chill shoots through Tom's bones. *Ben.* Danny says his name with such reverence.

"Nothing bad will happen to you. You understand that, right? *Nothing bad will happen.*"

Not so sure about that, Tom thinks. But Danny nods. She's calming down a little. Her breath comes out in short puffs.

"I'm going to start scanning you now," Ben goes on. "Let yourself go."

Danny's eyes open halfway. "Will it hurt?"

"It's okay. Everyone goes through this."

"Dad?"

Tom rips out the earbud, terrified that Roscoe might be standing behind, watching too. Luckily, he's still on the carpet, though he's looking at Tom with perplexed impatience. "Now I put a piece on the wrong way."

"Hang on, bud," Tom says as gently as he can. "I just need to finish watching this thing."

"Can I watch?"

"Nah. It's boring. For work."

Tom's tactic works; Roscoe turns away, disinterested. Tom looks at the screen again. He'd forgotten to pause it. Now, on the video, Ben is massaging Danny's feet. He has a pervy look on his face like he's getting off on it. Tom wants to throw something at the screen. Reach in and strangle this guy.

"I'm already getting a lot of feedback," Ben says, the soles of Danny's feet mashed between his palms. "Keep breathing. I'm going to have to move up now."

Ben's hands travel to Danny's bare leg. It's definitely not a massage. His fingers move closer and closer to the space between her legs until they're *there*, pushing inside. Tom closes his eyes; he feels like he's violating Danny by watching. Those posts on Reddit were right—whatever Danny is mixed up in is toxic. Damaging. *Illegal.* Is she still part of it? And Rebecca being in possession of this tape—what does *that* mean?

He glares at the man's face on the screen. Ben, the guru, has sandy hair. He's balding a little, and there's a little bit of a paunch at his waist. And yet, the video has paused at the very moment one of Danny's legs has flopped to the side, letting him in. Tom's heart breaks.

And then he sees something else on the paused screen.

It's a shadow. A third figure in the background, standing against the wall, watching this all unfold. It's a face so familiar, a face Tom loves, but it's so incongruous, so *impossible*, he thinks he's seeing things that aren't there. He leans in closer. Blinks hard. With a trembling finger, he presses Play again on the video. But this time, he doesn't focus on what Ben is doing to Danny in the foreground. He's looking at the figure in the background. The figure standing just behind Ben, seemingly holding something in her hand that Ben can't see. She's watching all of this placidly, as if she, too, buys into Ben's every word.

It's his wife. Rebecca.

CHAPTER SEVENTEEN

BEND, OREGON
PRESENT DAY

Danielle is not answering Ben's check-in requests. And though Ben tries to keep his emotions at a steady state at all times, he has to admit he's a little worried.

Here's why. Danielle is on a protocol. Like all of his other Seeds and Seedlings, Ben has set up their response schedule this way for a reason, one that fits her particular trajectory. It's important she holds herself accountable, and regularly checking in on the phone when she's not in the house does just that. It's also important she has discipline—she'll need it once she becomes a mother. Really, Ben is trying to help make Danielle her best. He cares about her so much—he cares about *all* of his group. He can picture Danielle's path so clearly. If only she'd see it, too. He wishes that Danielle—and everyone else—would stop being their own worst enemies.

He sits back at his desk, rubs his temples, and peers outside. His windows open to the front lawn, where he watches many of the women as they rake up fallen leaves. Jessica. Mirabelle. Raven. Amelia. Most of the Seeds and Seedlings are in their early twenties to midthirties, a decade to two younger than Ben's forty-five, but they move with wisdom and consciousness. They are absolutely in the moment. Perfectly Zen.

He smiles, comforted. It's his teaching philosophy that has allowed them to find their inner calm and dedicated commitment to daily tasks. They glow with health because they all complete their daily practice harnessing their inner strength, which cleanses their organs, blood, and mind. So many have benefited from this way of life. Around him, on the walls, is proof of that: plaques, awards, certificates of merit. There is the one from the Guinness Book of World Records proclaiming that he'd received the highest score of any US citizen on the national IQ test for problem-solving. There are photographs of him shaking hands with heads of state, great philosophers, Olympians, celebrities. There is the Oscar a famous actor gave him because he was so indebted and grateful for Ben's help.

He's helped tons of people because his teachings work. He's grown ISB into a multimillion-dollar giant. He has workshops all over the world, thousands of people reporting to him. As for the work they're doing in Oregon—running the weekends, creating this community, coming up with new workshops and modules and ways to reach out to the world to share their message—it's been thrilling to see his project and vision take shape. They've really built something here . . . and this is just the tip of the iceberg. Because he doesn't want to just build a movement. He wants to build a *people*. A next generation. He's already started that. He thinks of Quentin and Adam, safe in the other house, living this hallowed life from the very start. *His boys.* And there's Jax, too, and Mason, and Ford. Danny's son, too, when he comes.

There's a knock at his door, and Smyrna, a new Seed, pokes her head in. "You wanted to see me, Scion?"

"Yes." Ben straightens. "I've heard that there's going to be some sort of event tonight. And that I'm invited."

Smyrna lowers her eyes. "Oh. I've heard a little about that, but I didn't plan it, and—"

"I've also heard," Ben interrupts, "that you are a bit resistant to this event."

Smyrna looks stricken. Her fingers fidget at her sides. "I . . . I guess

I'm not sure I agree. Or feel comfortable." She glances at him nervously. "The way the women were saying it, it sounded like . . . *group sex*." She whispers this last part.

Ben doesn't flinch. "And is that such a problem?"

"I mean . . ." Smyrna draws her bottom lip into her mouth.

"You have blocks inside you, Smyrna. Blocks that hold you back. You know that, right?"

Smyrna nods, looking ashamed.

"To release those blocks, to *truly* be free, you have to be up for anything. *Willing* for anything. Including what the women are asking of you."

"But . . ." Smyrna's gaze falls to her thigh. "I thought what I did with . . . *this*"—she gestures to her pant leg; Ben knows what is beneath the layer of cloth—"I thought that was the ultimate sacrifice. I already proved I was bonded. That I was willing."

"Aren't we always trying to prove ourselves? Again and again?"

Smyrna's mouth wobbles, which gives Ben a little jolt of pleasure. She's undeniably beautiful, with wide eyes and a high forehead and plump, sumptuous lips he wants to touch. She seems eager to grow within ISB, but she pushes back about certain things. First, it was the buy-in fees. Long ago, that used to always be Barb's territory. Now that Barb is gone, a guy named Chuck smooths all that over now, but he doesn't have the same light, easy touch. Not that Ben misses Barb. Barb ended up being a traitorous bitch. May she rest in peace.

He steps toward Smyrna and touches her arm. "Don't you want to spend more time together? Don't you want to open up, as a person?"

"I want to spend time with you, yes," Smyrna murmurs, her gaze fluttering to him for a beat before she looks shyly away. Desire snaps beneath Ben's skin. He's always been a sucker for women who haven't yet found their confidence. There's something so beautiful and feminine about a soft voice, a downturned chin. He has the power to build them up, make them strong. They give themselves over to him once he's done this for them. They'll do anything.

"Then what's the problem?" he whispers, bringing his face closer to hers.

After a beat, Smyrna shakes her head. "There is no problem, Scion. No problem at all."

She scuttles out. Ben sits back. He wonders how uninhibited Smyrna will be for the ceremony, now that she knows he has his eye on her. How willing she'll feel to prove herself. He glances into the gardens. A few of the women are pulling weeds and preparing for the harvest, talking giddily amongst themselves. It was their idea, this ceremony tonight. He'd only given them the tiniest of suggestions. Better they think it was their plan—down to the date it's happening—versus a carefully planted seed in their minds.

He's excited for the ceremony. *Beyond* excited. But then he thinks of a tiny moment with Danielle before he sent her off. Danielle wanted to wait to go. Said she wasn't thrilled about the weather—there were a lot of storms rolling through.

"No, no," Ben insisted. "It must be tonight. It must be this weekend."

"Is there . . ." Danielle hesitated before speaking. "Is there a reason it *has* to be this weekend?"

But there's no way she could know about the ceremony that's been scheduled. There's no way she could know that he'd deliberately left her out because . . . well, a pregnant woman shouldn't be involved in such things. The women here don't talk about the secrets they hold but . . . what if someone *did* talk? Maybe Danielle found out some other way. Is *that* why she's not responding now?

Only, that's ridiculous. Danielle knows what's at stake here. She's smarter than that. Besides, it's not as if Ben has ever declared his exclusivity with any one woman. Even when he was young, he's preferred to be with, care for, and love more than one woman at a time. Before he started ISB, he was more secretive about it, afraid that his various lovers would become angry or jealous. Eventually, he cast all of that aside and just decided to be honest.

And it's been fine. *More* than fine. Women have always accepted it. And those who haven't, well . . .

Ben hopes that Danielle isn't being purposefully defiant. She's pregnant, though, and pregnancy . . . it does strange things to a woman's mind. Women become irrational, unsteady, *sick*. Not truly sick, of course—sickness does not exist, it's just a confine of the mind—but *victims*. But hopefully Danielle will be the outlier, the one who won't succumb, though now he isn't so sure.

Maybe Danielle is weaker than he expected. He hopes he can help her through it, but if he can't, he'll have to do what he has to do. For the good of his future child.

He is, above all other things, a caring father.

CHAPTER EIGHTEEN

BEND, OREGON
SEVEN YEARS BEFORE

Danny awakes to three pairs of arms yanking her out of bed. She kicks her legs, trying to fight them off. Someone pushes her down by her shoulders and ties a blindfold around her eyes. She tries to scream, but someone else presses a hand over her mouth. Quickly, the hand is replaced by some sort of cloth gag.

She's disoriented. Is she in her bed in California? But no, *no*—she's in Oregon, on the compound. She's been here for almost a year. It's been wonderful, but not without hardship, and she's been apprised something like this might happen. She needs to trust the process. Not be afraid. This is a rite. A step forward.

Her body goes limp and compliant as they shove her down a hall. The floor is freezing. A draft wafts up her bare legs—she's wearing only a nightshirt and socks—and sends a shiver down her spine. Their ice-cold fingers aren't helping, either. They grip her hard, some of them lightly giggling. Later, she will find bruises.

She thinks she can smell breakfast cooking, but as quickly as the scent comes it disappears again, so maybe not. Danny has enjoyed the compound, though she has to admit the food sucks. There isn't enough of it, and it's way too healthy. This is not virtuous thinking, though. Food is a vice. Food is for fueling only. To overindulge is to let your emotions be in charge, not your conscious mind. She needs to forget she's so fucking hungry. She needs to transcend her burning desire for french fries.

"Good girl," a voice murmurs in her ear, likely because Danny is being so pliable. She's a quick study, and she laps up the praise. If only her mother could see how she's excelling here, how *good* this place is for her—and how, once she completes a few more classes and levels, she'll be able to host some of the sessions for the people traveling to the compound on the weekends. Wouldn't it be amazing if she amassed a huge nest egg? What would her mom say *then*?

She regrets leaving her mother without saying a proper goodbye right after graduation, but she knows that if she'd tried that, she would have never gotten away. Sometimes, in moments when she's not fully in charge of her thoughts, images of her mother flash into her mind. Word got to her that her mom was on the news and even cursed Ben's name.

It worries Danny. Ben doesn't like slander. Not many people have left ISB, but he's taken it so personally when they do. Danny has even heard stories of Ben striking back and getting even. There was this one girl in Danny's grade, Susan, that Bex recruited; she tried Ben's teachings but decided it wasn't for her. A few days later, Danny overheard Susan badmouthing Ben at a lunch table. "I only talked to him because I was dared," she was telling a friend. "He was so creepy. The guy's like fifty but preys on girls; he's a total perv. And that group he leads, they're all robots. He's not helping them. He's making them worse."

Danny wasn't sure why she turned around and told Ben what Susan said. Maybe because she thought it would show her loyalty. She was surprised how dark his expression became, but it quickly shifted to sadness. "I just feel so bad for her," he'd said mournfully. "She's lying. She doesn't understand. And now she's spreading lies, too. It's just so wrong. So tragic."

The next day, Susan was called into the principal's office. Suspended for two weeks—no one knew why. Danny graduated without ever finding out, though it baffled her—Susan was a goody-goody, never touched drugs, never got in trouble.

She told herself Ben couldn't have had anything to do with it. But Ben had talked about everyone giving a "security deposit" to the group, a secret to prove their loyalty. Had Susan given her own deposit? And since she'd quit, had he told her secret?

It was kind of terrifying . . . but also kind of dazzling. Ben was a person who wouldn't back down. Ben had *power*. It was why she wants her mother to stop talking to the news. Back away from Ben. Mom badmouthing ISB—Danny doesn't want that to come back on *her*. She wants her trajectory with Ben to climb—not plummet.

Another door opens. Danny's handlers are behind her now, and with a jolt, she feels them shoving at her back, pushing her inside. She falls down hard on her knees with a grunt, her wrist twisting awkwardly. The door slams behind her, but Danny doesn't hear their footsteps. She blinks through the blindfold, seeing only darkness, and spits out the gag.

"Hello?" she calls out.

No answer.

"Hello?" she calls again.

Experimentally, she reaches for the blindfold. It isn't even tied that tightly. She pulls it down and blinks in the darkness. She can't see a thing. She has no idea if this room is big or small, or where the door is, or if her handlers are coming back. Surely they're coming back, right?

She waits.

And waits.

The darkness hurts, as do her knees where she fell. "Hello?" she calls again.

The darkness seems to have fingers, tendrils. They snake around her, squeezing her chest. Danny has never liked the dark. It's a dumb thing, something she doesn't like to admit, a scared kid trait she hasn't even mentioned to Ben. It has something to do with her mom working long hours when she was a kid and leaving her home alone at night. Without an adult there to care for her, every sound was a terror, especially if she turned the lights off. One time, when her mom was gone, her house lost power, and she was *forced* to be in the dark. That was when the first panic attack came.

Just like one is, now.

It feels like there's a rubber band around her chest. As hard as she tries to suck in air, there isn't enough.

"Please," she croaks, but it's weak and ineffective—no one is going to come. Maybe they'll *never* come.

Was it a mistake to come to Oregon? Leave everything behind? Of course, she hasn't left *everything*—she has Bex. Being on this journey with her best friend has been incredible. Besides, Bex has left her family, too—although it's a little different for her, because Bex's parents are part of ISB, not fighting against it. Mr. and Mrs. Reyes hadn't come to Oregon, though. In fact, Bex always complains they're too focused on their careers and self-perfection and don't really spend any time with her. Sometimes, Danny wonders if Bex joined ISB to get closer to them.

Instead, she got closer to Ben.

It's the only point of contention for Danny, really—how much higher up Bex is in this organization, how much access she has to the Scion. At the same time, it's pushed her to be better. So she feels frustrated when elements of the person she used to be appear from deep within. Like now. As much as she tries to tamp down her panic—*she* is in charge of her emotions, *she* can choose how to react to this—her body has other ideas. Her teeth chatter. Her muscles quiver. With shame, she feels her bladder emptying. Warmth spreads across the back of her nightshirt. The sharp scent of urine is suddenly present in the room.

The door bursts open. Danny is both grateful and horrified—she is literally lying in a puddle of pee. *Couldn't they have come earlier?* Three figures, backlit by the light in the hall, stand in the doorway. Danny turns away and moans. She's still a slave to the panic. She can't get a handle on her breathing. Her arms tremble, and her hand bangs against the floor, making the costume ring she wears on her pointer finger clank.

"Just lie there," comes a familiar voice. "Try to be still."

Ben leans down. Danny doesn't want him to. He'll smell what she's done, feel the wetness. It shows how weak she is. Through her haze, she can make out a blinking red light in the room. The camera. Someone is recording. That's not unusual, though—they record everything here. Toby, maybe? Ben has put him in charge of recording everything, mostly because he's the one who understands how to work the cameras best.

Danny wishes they wouldn't record. Sure, Ben will say that she can look back on this and learn something, but she doubts she'll ever want to see this again.

She shifts away so the camera can't capture her expression. Ben clamps down on her wrist. "Don't move."

"Sorry," Danny whimpers, going still.

"Stop apologizing. I needed to see one of your episodes to help you stop them. Just focus on your breathing, okay?"

Danny feels herself nodding and tries to take deep, calming breaths, but she can still feel her muscles tensing, the rubber band tightening.

"Close your eyes," Ben says. "Keep breathing."

"Okay, Ben."

"Nothing bad can happen to you. You understand that, right? *Nothing bad can happen.*"

Danny knows. And she's starting to feel just a little bit better. Ben is here. Ben will take care of her. Ben will make her strong.

"I'm going to start scanning you now. Let yourself go."

Danny opens her eyes and looks at him. "Will it hurt?"

Ben shakes his head. "No. But I need to figure out where you are blocked, okay? See, we have negative and positive entities covering us. Think of it like energy. Somewhere inside you is a dark nucleus of bad entities bundled up, blocking the flow of the positive."

Danny wants to recoil. She thinks of the bad entities inside her, curled up like maggots. Disgusting.

"It's your turn for this. You're one of the last. You trust me, right?" Ben is saying. "Danielle, you trust me?"

"Yeah," Danny says, weakly. "Of course I do, Ben."

She tries to relax as she feels his hands move over her socked feet. All she can think, though, is what her bad entities must feel like. Are they wrinkly? Oily? Can he really feel it on her skin? She tries to think of light entities instead. Goodness, pureness, lightness, things Ben would find valuable and admirable. Not parts of her he needs to extract, like a blackhead.

You're one of the last, he'd said. Why has he waited to do this exercise with her? Did he think she wasn't ready before? Is there some sort of ranking of the ISB Seeds—is she at the bottom? She considers, too, other people going through this . . . whatever it is. Danny isn't close with everyone in the compound, not even remotely. She and Bex are some of the youngest students—there are a lot of women in their twenties and thirties, and that doesn't count all of the weekend people coming in and out for workshops, some of whom Ben seems quite intimate with as well. Danny sees so many people heading out early in the morning to go on runs and work tirelessly in the garden. They mostly keep their distance, maybe because they think Danny is too young—or maybe undeserving?

Besides Bex, one of the women who live on the property who was nice to her is Sophia, a beautiful dark-haired Seedling who'd been with Ben onstage at the end of Celebration Week all those months before. Sophia was the prettiest of Ben's inner circle. Aside from Bex, she stood the closest to Ben, and he whispered in her ear. But Sophia went out of her way to say hi to Danny the first week at the compound. Went out of her way to learn Danny's name. Since then, she's included Danny in projects, partnered with Danny during workshops, tried to take her under her wing. She always kept herself at a bit of a distance, acting more like a coworker than a confidante, never telling Danny anything about her past life, never badmouthing anyone else in the group, and always, *always* having nothing but praise for Ben.

About a month ago, though, Danny had come out the door to the back garden and discovered Sophia speaking heatedly with Ben. Sophia's hands moved quickly, frantically. At one point, Ben held her shoulders and tried to look her in the eye, but Sophia kept turning away. Danny had ducked back inside the house, wondering if this was something she wasn't supposed to see. She'd never seen Sophia act with such emotion. How dare she speak that way to Ben! It unnerved her.

That night at dinner, Sophia wasn't at her usual place at the head table with Ben. Nor was she anywhere else. Maybe she was embarrassed, Danny figured. Maybe she was working off a sort of penance, the way the rest of them did when they had too many negative thoughts or gave into their victimhood. Danny lingered in the doorway where Sophia and another woman slept; when she got a peek into the room, she saw that Sophia's bed was stripped and bare.

The next day, when she didn't see Sophia at breakfast, she mustered up the courage to casually ask Ben where Sophia was.

Ben smiled wanly. "A goddess retreat. She's so lucky."

"What's a goddess retreat?"

"Something very special. You'll learn about it, eventually."

So, wait, yelling at Ben got *rewarded*?

Ben has taken off her socks. His fingers wrap around her feet. She bites down hard on her lip so she won't laugh. Her feet have always been ticklish, but she knows that's the wrong response. His fingers thankfully leave her feet and move on to her calves. This feels better, though it surprises her how sensual his touch is, how his hands linger. It's unlike any massage she's ever gotten. Does she like it? She's not sure. Maybe liking it or not isn't the point. Ben is the expert. She has to trust him.

Someone exhales. It isn't Ben. Danny remembers the others who came into the room. Someone must be holding the camera. What are *they* thinking, watching Ben touch her? She wishes they were alone. On the other hand, these rituals must be performed in front of people to strip her down.

Ben's hands travel up her leg until they're at her bare thigh. Danny tries to stay still, but she isn't sure a boy—or man—has ever touched her thigh before, not even a doctor. And she can only imagine how her leg must feel in his hands. Heavy and thick, probably, not sinewy and lithe like the women Ben surrounds himself with. And goosefleshy, and sticky with urine. Disgusting.

She wishes she could shrink her thigh just by willing it so. But when she opens her eyes a crack, Ben has his head tilted back. He looks peaceful. Certainly not disgusted that her leg is ungainly and fat. This calms her, too.

But his fingers don't stay there. They move up more, *definitely* into a realm no one has touched. Danny can't help it—she tenses. He's getting so close to her underwear.

Ben doesn't pull his hands away. "Don't run from it."

Danny feels her legs pressing together. "But it feels . . . bad." What if he touches something that's not supposed to be there? What if she makes a strange noise? Does she *want* him to touch there? Does *he* want to?

"Uncross your legs, please."

This must mean he likes her. Why else would he want to touch her there? She shuts her eyes and tries to go with it. Ben's fingers are deft. He moves with purpose. She feels him shift her underwear aside and touch her most delicate skin. She holds her breath. She shuts her eyes as he pushes his fingers inside her. It hurts, kind of. No one has done this to Danny before. Can Ben tell? Is she supposed to enjoy it? Should she be making some noises? She thought she'd feel differently about Ben touching her. She thought her whole body would ripple with some kind of . . . *release*. But this feels awkward and unwelcome. Ben is being so clinical. And people are *watching* . . .

She waits for it to be over. She waits for some sort of transcendence. Maybe she feels something. She wants to. She's never wanted anything more than she wants to be part of Ben's inner circle. Ben is the key to everything. Ben is the key to freedom.

"This is going to hurt," Ben says next. "Do you accept the pain?"

Hurt? Like *more*? But Ben's gaze is locked onto her. Danny nods. "Yes. Sure."

Then something happens that she doesn't expect—a searing, white-hot pain on the inside of her thigh so surprising that she cries out in terror. Irrationally, she wonders if this is Ben's penis—is this what they *feel* like? But when she opens her eyes, Ben still has his clothes on. But something is *biting* her, maybe, something huge. And then she sees Bex there, too. Bex is so close, maybe *doing* the biting, with something in her hand . . . and the *smell*. It's like meat left too long on the grill.

"What the hell?" she screams, trying to sit up. Why isn't anyone helping her, getting it off?

"It's okay, Danny," Bex says soothingly. "You're doing great."

And Ben pushes her down by her shoulders. "You look at me. You live through this pain. This will make you stronger."

The smell of charred flesh is overpowering now. *Meat.* The spot where she was bitten—or burned?—is so painful that Danny feels faint. "What did you do to me?" she asks, looking from Ben to Bex. "Why did you do that?"

"It's over. It's done. Just breathe. You're doing well, Danielle. Really well. You're doing it. You're growing as a human."

She tries to breathe, but she wants to puke. She wants to roll over and curl into a ball, not lie exposed like this, a video camera on her.

"Look at me," Ben orders. "Just look at me, no one else."

Danny looks at him. He doesn't blink. His attention is fully on her. She wants to do well, and doing well means fighting through this excruciating pain. She takes sips of air into her lungs. She ignores the throbbing on her thigh. She pushes out the images of blood, or skin melting away, or bones exposed, and just stares into the depths of Ben's eyes.

"Good," Ben says. "Really good."

Out of the corner of her eye, Danny can see the camera edging closer, but her gaze is locked with Ben's. His confidence gives her power. She feels her heartbeat slowing. She tries to smile, and then, she really *is* smiling. Later, she will peel back the gauze and look at what was done to her—how hideous it is, how *vicious*—but she won't feel sorry for herself. She'll feel proud. Like a badass. *I got through that. I fucking did it.*

Ben leaves quickly once the session is over, giving Danny's shoulder a squeeze and saying he'll see her later. She was hoping for more from him—like he'd invite her to a sunrise breakfast, maybe, or make another sort of declaration, something to pin them together—but she takes what she can get. Another woman, who she realizes is Amelia, another Seedling, meets Ben in the hall. Through the doorway, she sees Ben pulling her close and whispering something in her ear. Amelia brightens. A second woman named Chelsea pecks him on the cheek.

And then there's the other woman in the room—Bex. But she isn't looking at Ben. Her gaze is still on Danny. She looks kind of concerned. "Are you okay?"

Danny nods. "I think so. What was that?"

"I know it was a little shocking, but it's a way for us to connect. I have a scar, too. And now I feel so connected to you." Bex grabs Danny's hand. "I'm so glad you did this. And there's more where that came from. A group of us. A group of strong women. We're all in this together."

Danny lets Bex help her to her feet. Ben is in the hall, now, walking slowly and contemplatively with Amelia into the sanctuary. Danny can feel Bex's arm on her elbow, but suddenly, her friend slips back and crumples against the wall.

"Bex?" Danny turns back. Bex's skin is gray, suddenly. Her eyes are closed. "Are you all right?"

Bex grits her teeth and nods. But then she grabs her stomach and vomits on the floor. "Bex!" Danny whispers. A fine pair the two of them make. Urine and puke.

"Are you sick?" she whispers. "What's going on?"

"I'm fine," Bex says, swishing her away. "Just . . . equilibrium's off."

"You were sick like this yesterday, too," Danny whispers, remembering Bex in the same exact pose on the front lawn. "Maybe it's a bug."

"It's nothing. I'm fine."

"She's fine," says a voice behind them. Ben is at their side. And Toby is suddenly there, too, wearing a blue ISB T-shirt and carrying a mop and bucket. How Ben mobilized him so quickly, Danny isn't sure, but Ben doesn't look worried.

He helps Bex to stand. "You're fine," he tells her again. Emphatically. "Don't give in to it."

"I know," Bex says, a tiny waver in her voice.

And then, just like that, the two of them walk off, arms around each other's shoulders. Fresh envy blooms inside Danny. But for now, she is left in this dark hallway, still stinking of her own fear, standing in her best friend's vomit. Toby exchanges an empty glance with her before tracking Bex and Ben as they round the corner. And then he gets to work cleaning up the mess.

CHAPTER NINETEEN

CARSON CITY, NEVADA
PRESENT DAY

The hard plastic chair digs into Rebecca's spine. She listens for sounds coming from inside the exam room. It's still just the nurse in there, taking Danny's blood pressure and things like that. Is that a *ding* of another incoming text?

It still feels like Danny's phone is in her hands. She can feel its heat, and those words she read on the screen are burned into her brain. Ben hasn't changed. It sounds like Ben has gotten even worse. This *is Ben's baby.*

Danny is in great danger.

She shuts her eyes and thinks of the pull Ben used to have on her. At eighteen years old, she'd thought she was going to marry Ben. She really did. Asinine to think of that now. All the promises he made. All the promises he broke. She's sure they're the same promises he made to Danny, too. How devoted is Danny to him? It *seems* she's on the fence . . . or is that an act? Ben seems angry that she's not checking in, but is it just average Ben wrath, or something worse?

The door to the exam room opens, startling her. The nurse pokes her head out. "Want to come in for the doctor's scan? Your friend says it's okay."

Rebecca practically runs inside. "Yeah. Of course."

In the room, Danny is sitting on the table, her socked feet resting near the stirrups but not in them. A blanket covers her body, but the bottoms of her painfully thin legs are exposed. Rebecca meets Danny's gaze, and Danny frowns.

"How's it going?" Rebecca asks.

"I don't like this."

"I know. But it'll be over soon. And I promise: Dr. Salley is really nice."

"But this really isn't necessary."

"I know you *think* that, but it actually is."

The sheet covering Danny shifts, and before Danny can yank it back up, Rebecca catches a glimpse of her bare torso and thigh where the gown is too loose. It's like her gaze is magnetized instantly to the tattoo on the inside of her leg, the circular scar with two lines through the center. She looks away quickly. At the same time, Danny pulls the blanket back over and sets her mouth in a line, knowing exactly what Rebecca saw. For as angry as Rebecca is about Danny showing up and bombing her life, Danny's tattoo is a wake-up call. *Rebecca* did that. *Rebecca* allowed that to happen to her.

The door creaks open again, and here is Dr. Salley in his white coat and loafers, pulling on a pair of exam gloves. "Rebecca," he says, smiling at her warmly. "Good to see you. How's the family?"

"We're great." She gestures to the table. "This is my friend Danny. Thanks for getting her in so quickly."

"Some storm, huh?" Dr. Salley gestures to the window, though by now the storm has died down to a drizzle. He strides over to Danny to shake her hand. When Rebecca turns back, she notices that Danny's expression is guarded. It looks like she's ready to jump off the table. Rebecca meets her gaze. "It's okay," she mouths.

"Vitals look good, though your weight is low," Dr. Salley says as he looks at the notations the nurse has put in Danny's chart. "You taking prenatals?"

"I eat really well," Danny says in a pious tone. "I don't believe in vitamins."

"Yes, but you've been taking herbs," Rebecca butts in.

They turn and look at her. Dr. Salley glances at Danny questioningly. Danny shrugs. "They're supposed to be good for pregnancy."

Rebecca breathes in, wanting to say that they probably *aren't*, but maybe now isn't the time to get into this. So she waves her hand. "Okay. Whatever."

"Well." Dr. Salley clears his throat. "I can't speak to herbal teas, though most aren't encouraged during pregnancy. But we do recommend prenatals, especially for the folic acid. I'd also like to see your weight up by at least fifteen pounds. You need enough energy stores to support the baby."

Danny blinks innocently. "I think I'm fine at the weight I'm at."

Rebecca presses her fingernails into her palm. A flash comes to her: the compound in Oregon, dinnertime. A line of pin-thin women at the tables, waiting to be served. Funny: Ben always said it was up to the individual to take charge of their choices, but no one seemed to protest when Ben served minuscule portions and didn't let any of them ask for seconds. It was a virtuous thing, eating less. It was what Ben wanted, and he made them think that they wanted it, too.

Rebecca can tell there are questions swirling in Dr. Salley's mind. "Don't worry," she blurts loudly, the sound of her voice startling everyone. "I'm going to make sure Danny cleans her plate and goes back for seconds."

Dr. Salley nods, though his gaze remains on Rebecca for an extra beat. Does he share her concerns? Does he remember when *Rebecca* first came to him, how similar she looked and acted?

He gets to work feeling Danny's belly. As he places his hands on her skin, Danny's ankles flex and tense. "It's okay. Just feeling on the outside. Just measuring how far along you are. I'd say nineteen weeks, thereabouts?"

Nineteen weeks! Rebecca is horrified. Danny barely looks pregnant. How can she be halfway through?

"We have an ultrasound," Dr. Salley says. Though the question is meant for Danny, he's looking at Rebecca. "How about a quick peek, while you're here?"

"No, thank you," Danny says.

"*Yes*," Rebecca says at the same time.

Danny frowns. "I don't need it. The baby is healthy."

"So you *have* had an exam?" Dr. Salley sounds confused.

Rebecca's heart is banging. She isn't going to touch that one. "Danny, it's right in the room next door. *I* had one, for Roscoe and Charlie—it doesn't hurt. It's peace of mind, really. And it's fun—don't you want to see what your baby looks like?"

"We could confirm the gender," Dr. Salley says.

Danny looks between the two of them. In her purse, her phone buzzes. Again. It's like Ben *knows*. Then Rebecca feels a frisson. *Could* he?

"I already know the gender," Danny is saying, "but fine."

Danny slides off the table. The paper covering the exam table crinkles as she sits up, pulls the gown around her, and starts for the other room. Though her leg isn't exposed again, Rebecca can't help but think of the tattoo that's there. She wonders if Danny and the other women still take naked pictures daily, showing off their tattoos to the camera. She wonders, too, if Danny's tattoo hurts sometimes.

The way hers does.

Danny is compliant enough as she lies down on the ultrasound table and the doctor dims the lights. She flinches when the doctor squirts the ultrasound gel on her belly, though when the baby appears on the monitor, she gazes at it with wonder. Rebecca breathes out. As far as she can tell, the baby looks fine. Dr. Salley turns on the Doppler, and a strong heartbeat booms through the room.

"Heartbeat is one hundred fifty-four beats per minute," he reports. "Very good."

"Look at the profile!" Rebecca coos. "See?"

Danny blinks, flabbergasted. "Does he really look like that?"

"He?" Rebecca sniffs. She remembers Ben's text: *You'd better not be putting my son in danger!*

"I know it's a boy," Danny echoes. She sounds like a robot. "It has to be a boy."

The doctor's brow furrows, the wand stills. "Miss . . . Martin. I'm obligated to ask. Things are . . . *safe*, at home?"

Danny looks apprehensive. "What do you mean?"

Dr. Salley shares a secret look with Rebecca. She so, *so* badly wants to shake her head, or scream that no, things are *not* safe for Danny. Dr. Salley is a mandatory reporter—he could actually get Danny some real help.

But if she speaks up, Danny will bolt. "She's fine," she says reluctantly, even though her tone of voice implies anything but. "Aren't you, Danny?"

Quietly, Dr. Salley continues the scan, taking pictures and measurements every so often. Rebecca distracts herself by staring at the ultrasound screen as the doctor takes images of different angles. Finally, she can tell the doctor is determining the sex. She isn't that skilled in ultrasound technology, but she has had two boys. The image is blurry and vague. She clocks the doctor's expression. His mouth is a straight line. His eyes cast downward. He glances warily in Danny's direction.

Danny looks around at both of them. "Why is no one saying anything? Why do you look like that? What's wrong with my baby?"

"Don't worry, your baby is healthy." Dr. Salley's voice cracks. "But, my dear, you're having a healthy baby girl."

Danny's expression turns to stone.

———

Dr. Salley rushes through the exam from then on, practically sprinting from the room once he's checked out all he needs to check. Rebecca has no idea how she'll explain this at her next visit. Part of her hopes he's reporting Danny's psychological state regardless of her reassurance that everything was fine. But then she hears his voice in another exam room, speaking to another patient, so maybe not.

Danny's legs dangle over the side of the ultrasound table. Her head is in her hands. She looks like she might faint.

"What am I going to do?" she moans.

"Danny." Rebecca strokes her shoulder. "Hey. This is all good news."

Danny looks up at her, wild-eyed. "*Good news?* What the fuck, Bex? What did you just subject me to? And, worst of all, that guy got the gender all wrong. I'm not having a girl. I'm *not*."

Rebecca stares at her. "Danny, yes you are. Ultrasounds . . . they're literally pictures of the inside of your body. There's no way Ben knew the gender without that."

Danny's eyes flash. "He did."

"How? He isn't a doctor."

"Doctors don't know anything." She grits her teeth. "Now he's going to know I had an ultrasound. If the baby comes out a girl, it'll be my fault because the scan . . . *messed things up*, or something."

Rebecca's heart feels cracked in two. "Danny. Come on. You're not even making any sense. Think of seventh-grade health class. You know that's not how it works." She also can't help but think, *Wait, after coming all this way, you're still thinking about going back to him?*

Danny leaps from the table and grabs her clothes, pulling them on quickly. Rebecca walks toward her, but Danny holds out an arm. "*Don't.*" She stuffs her feet into her wrecked shoes and barrels out of the room and into the hall.

"Danny!" Rebecca clambers after her, nearly knocking over a nurse. "Wait!"

Danny storms through the waiting room and out the front door. Rebecca follows, though she realizes something and turns back. She can feel the receptionists staring.

She clears her throat and tries to smile. "Uh, sorry. Thanks for everything."

Then she bursts out the door, thunders down the stairs, and looks around the lobby. It's quiet and empty. Rebecca listens for footsteps in the stairwell, but she hears nothing.

"Danny!" she screams. "Danny, come on! I'm your ride!"

Still no answer. Rebecca presses her fingers against her temples and tries to focus, but her thoughts are scattered. Scenes from the ultrasound room keep flashing in her mind. And then they merge with scenes from a long time ago—another dark room, once again Danny lying flat on her back, but this time, in Oregon.

The day Ben first touched Danny—and then ordered them to give her the tattoo—isn't something she likes thinking about. She was part of the ceremony . . . but then, she was part of a lot of ceremonies. Ben told her that because she was so high-ranking, her energy was vital to the ceremonies working. Rebecca wanted to be tough and unflinching around Ben, and when she had a hard time watching him do certain things to certain people, she just sort of . . . disassociated. Even her own brand: she barely remembers the experience of having it done. It's like she was out of her body, watching the painful process but not really living it. Ben praised her for that, of course, but only now does she realize how fucked up that is.

It never occurred to her to tell him to stop, either. You didn't really tell Ben that. If she had, he would have taken great offense. He would have cut her out of his life.

With Danny, though, she almost put her foot down. Ben gave her a heads-up that they would be performing the ritual, but he hadn't prepped her that it would be Danny who was next. For all the other ceremonies, the women had some sort of inkling that they would be going through a rite of passage that would strengthen them within the ISB community. Rebecca had never seen someone be taken completely by surprise, like Danny. In fact, before they entered Danny's bedroom, Rebecca had grabbed Ben's arm.

"Shouldn't we wait until she wakes up?" she'd whispered. "She's dreaming."

Ben had squared his shoulders. "Danielle's too much of an overthinker. I don't want her to resist."

"If it's such a positive thing, why *should* she resist?"

The words had flown out of her mouth. But this was Danny, her oldest friend. It hadn't seemed fair that they were ambushing her. What if Danny was scared?

Ben had waved his hand cavalierly. "If you don't want to be part of it, if you want to show your disloyalty to your friend and me and what we're doing here, fine. Is that what you're saying?"

Rebecca had swallowed hard. Ben knew best, she'd reminded herself. He did. She had to trust that.

But it was hard to see Danny in such a panic. Danny had told her that anxiety attacks were a thing of her past—why was she having one here, in their sacred space? But she was proud of Ben for pulling her out of it. And when he climbed on top of her and started to scan her body, just like he'd scanned Rebecca's body, and Amelia's, and Sophia's, and the other women whose ceremony she'd felt lucky enough to witness, she was rooting for Danny, praying for her not to reject the process, believing that this process, if you could even call it that, was going to be *healing*. Danny's nakedness, her vulnerability, she was so *open* to it, so accepting. Rebecca saw the fear in her eyes—but she saw the trust, too.

That trust for Ben was still there. And it was blinding her. This, too, is Rebecca's fault. She'd stood there. Idly. She'd stood there and let it all happen, thinking it was all *okay*.

Drizzle falls on her face. The parking lot is strangely empty of cars. "Danny!" she screams into the void. "Danny!" Could Danny have just *run off*? Is that *it*?

But then, she spies a hunched, wretched figure near the trees at the back of the parking lot. Just standing there, her face in her hands. Rebecca lets out a breath. "*Danny*," she whispers. And then she starts to run toward her.

CHAPTER TWENTY

DAVIS, CALIFORNIA
PRESENT DAY

It takes a whole cup of mint tea for Janice's heartbeat to return to normal levels. Even then, she's agitated. It's even more frustrating to have a hunch about something but not know what to do about it.

Bex. Could that be where her daughter went? To *her* . . . instead of to her mother?

Ironically, when Danny first met Bex, Janice had liked the girl. She'd thought Bex was a good influence on Danny, all bubbly and ambitious, optimistic and determined. The girl radiated good health and a good attitude; Janice figured she wasn't the type to do drugs or get in trouble. She was right about that, she supposed, in the general sense. But it all depends on how one defines *trouble.*

One day after school, maybe when the girls were in tenth grade, Bex was over at their apartment; she and Danny were listening to music in Danny's room. Janice tried not to interfere, though she was curious about what they were talking about. Danny had made so much sense as her little girl, but as a teenager? Not so much. Every move Janice made, every decision, it all felt like a misstep. She wondered endlessly if the lingering pain of Dave's absence might have made a difference. She thinks of the night he left. Said he was going to get gas. The first few hours, she paced, worried he'd been in a car accident. She called every emergency room around. Then, she found the note in his study, right there on his desk. *I can't do this anymore.* What the hell was she supposed to tell Danny? How do you spare a child the truth that their own parent, who's supposed to love and protect them, has essentially thrown them away? She avoided Danny's questions for a few days. She made excuses. But then she just broke down and told Danny the truth because she didn't know what else to do. Of course it broke Danny. She'd always connected more with her father than Janice. It wasn't like the note gave any reasons, either, that she could point to. They swam in confusion. Danny, unfortunately, clung to hope that he'd come back. Ironic, Janice thinks—it's the same hope *she* clings to now, for Danny.

Eventually, Janice pulled herself together and tried to get Danny to do so as well. Her grades had plummeted after Dave vanished. But the problem was, Danny didn't want to listen to her. Danny's hurt had turned to defiant anger. Janice pushed Danny to do well in school and get involved and volunteer and do all the right things that would look good on a college application, but it went in one ear and out the other. There was a part of Janice that wondered if Danny was fucking up deliberately because she thought it would get Dave's attention, wherever the hell he was. There was also a part of her that missed her little girl desperately and kind of hated this new, sullen, grumbling, defiant young woman who'd come along. What could Janice even say to a person like teenage Danny? She'd been afraid of girls like Danny in high school, moody and sharp, their eyes always narrowed, always slouching around like they just didn't care.

At five that evening, the apartment buzzer sounded. When Janice answered the door, a smiling woman in a red pantsuit stood in the pitifully dingy hallway.

"Hi!" she said brightly. "I'm Rebecca's mother! Candace."

She stuck out her hand. Janice stared at her manicured red nails.

They matched her outfit perfectly. Did she paint them every night, Janice wondered, to coordinate with everything she wore?

Bex appeared from the back room and cheerfully greeted her mother. When Candace asked if Bex had homework that night, Bex dutifully replied that she'd finished it in study hall, but that maybe she'd get a jump on an essay due for English later in the week. Janice tried not to gawk. As Rebecca left, she'd said goodbye to Danny *and* to Janice, which officially meant she'd said more words to Janice that day than her own daughter had.

Janice couldn't help herself. She grabbed Candace in the hallway. "I have to know. What's your secret?"

"Secret?" Candace's brow furrowed.

"With her." She tried to laugh. Tried to make this less of a deal than it was. "I mean, teenagers, you know? Bex seems so . . . well-adjusted. I can't even get Danny to talk to me."

Candace relaxed. "Well, Rebecca has really had some breakthroughs lately. She went through some struggles, but she has a wonderful teacher."

"You mean . . . a tutor?"

"No, more like a guide. We all work with him, actually—my husband and I, too. The organization is called ISB. For my husband and me, it's more like career training—a sort of reprogramming of doubts, high-achieving corporate track. But it's also a way of thinking, a way of life, and it can be helpful for younger people, too." She looked beyond Janice, back through the open door to the apartment, a glimmer of pity in her eyes. "Danny can always come to an intensive, if she's interested. There's a fee, but there are also scholarships."

Janice's heart sank. Intensive? *Guide?* It sounded like a multi-level marketing scheme selling happiness. Danny would never agree to that sort of thing. She'd already tried a therapist, a psychiatrist, a guidance counselor, tutors, and even a Unitarian minister, though she had been the most disastrous of all.

So she didn't even bother asking Danny if she'd want to do it. It didn't seem legit, anyway. But Bex's family was a big influence on Danny. Her daughter spent more time at Bex's house than Bex did at their apartment, and sometimes Danny would drop little hints about how much she admired Bex's parents, how *clean* their house was, how they had a television in every room, how Mrs. Reyes made delicious salmon for dinner. Salmon! Danny wouldn't touch fish at home. She knew she should be happy—it could be so much worse, Danny could be running wild, at least she was safe—but she also felt so resentful.

And curious. What was so great about Bex's family anyway? She scoured for information about them online. Candace and Michael Reyes were all over LinkedIn; they both also had their own websites where they did "corporate counseling" and talked about "human potential." They had Facebook accounts, too, though they weren't personal in the slightest. There were no pictures of them on hikes or visiting family for the holidays or hanging out with Rebecca—their posts were all links to corporatebabble blogs about productivity and ambition, or else brags about their latest promotions or other work wins. Everyone who commented on their posts were either people within their workplace—Janice googled them, too—or tied, it seemed, to this ISB group. And, interestingly, when Janice clicked on *their* profiles, the ISB members had little personal information on their pages, too—just motivational memes and bulletins about upcoming workshops and retreats. If you didn't know them, you'd think they had no personal lives at all. No families. No children.

Which was weird, Janice thought. *Her* Facebook was filled with nothing but Danny. She loved taking family portraits and preserving memories. So who did Candace think she was, peering into Janice's life with such judgment? And what, did she expect Janice to believe this group they were part of was some sort of miracle robotic machine? Life didn't work like that.

So when Danny suddenly said, at the end of junior year, she was doing "a few sessions" with Ben Rahm, the man who'd founded ISB, Janice already had her hackles up. Oh, of *course* she'd take Rebecca's parents' advice. Meanwhile, the man wasn't even a real therapist. But she'd cooled her jets, especially because Danny came home from the sessions calmer, more cheerful, not quite so dark. Maybe this *would* change her. Maybe this Ben guy would convince her to buckle down in school, apply for college. If only she just *applied*, Janice thought. She'd get in somewhere. And that would give her confidence. And Janice's worries would be over.

The morning before one of her sessions, she'd tried to talk to Danny about what she and Ben talked about. "Stuff," Danny said, shrugging. "Life."

"Like . . . where you're going with your life?" Janice asked, hopefully.

Danny's mouth twisted into a smirk. "It's a little deeper than what sort of job I'm going to have, Mom."

But wasn't ISB corporate training? Wasn't it about careers? She watched as Danny leaned forward to swipe mascara on her eyelashes. "Don't see you putting on makeup that often," she said, pointedly. As in *never*. She had wished Danny took more stock in her appearance.

"Yeah, well, my sessions are recorded. I don't want to look like a total slob on camera."

Janice straightened. "Why are your sessions recorded? Who's watching them?"

Danny rolled her newly made-up eyes. "Only me, Mom. It's for me to look at in the future. To see how far I've come."

Alarms blared in Janice's mind. Could that actually be true? Maybe that was how certain therapies worked? It wasn't like she knew.

She tried to play it cool. "So do you talk about . . . me? Our family?"

Danny looked away, which told Janice that they did. A lump formed in her throat. "What do you say?" she pressed.

"It's private," Danny had muttered.

"Yes, but maybe it would help if I knew."

"It wouldn't." Danny's eyes flashed. "You wouldn't understand. You *don't* understand."

And then she threw down her mascara wand and stormed out of the room.

Janice felt breathless. *Help* me understand, she wanted to yell after Danny. Who was this man who had cracked the locked box that was her daughter within a few hour-long sessions? Maybe he was charismatic and handsome. Hollywood gorgeous, probably—did she have a little crush?

What she did next is something she isn't proud of, but she wouldn't take it back. Janice took the afternoon off from work and drove to the high school. Danny hadn't said where the sessions took place, but Janice knew it was right after school ended. She waited in the parking lot when the bell rang and Danny emerged from the front double doors. Then, stealthily, she followed her daughter on foot as Danny walked from the high school to the public library. She'd wondered if it was a scheduling mistake—maybe Danny was just going to study! But then Danny walked with purpose to a study room at the back. She knocked on one of the doors, and the door opened to let her in. There was a man there. A short, burly guy with outdated glasses and downturned eyes who wore ugly desert boots. Danny's whole body went electric when she saw him. They moved to each other, and he kissed her. *On the lips.* It was a peck, but still.

But it didn't make sense. None of it made sense. And Janice couldn't help herself—she gasped from her spot behind the stacks.

Danny froze. Then she whirled around, pinpointing exactly where Janice was hiding. Her expression morphed into something ugly. "*Mom?*"

Janice revealed herself. Her arms hung at her sides. "I . . . I just . . ."

Her gaze bounced between Danny and the man she was with. *Ben.* He stepped forward gruffly. "Mrs. Martin. Ben Rahm." But he didn't shake her hand. He pressed his palms together and sort of bowed at her in a permissive way, as if to say, *I respect you, but move aside.*

"What are you doing here?" Danny snapped. "Did you follow me?"

"I just . . ." Janice looked at Ben. "I'm sorry, I need to take my daughter now. What I just saw—you're totally out of line."

"Mom!" Danny looked mortified. "What are you *talking* about?"

"The man *kissed* you." Janice's heart was beating wildly. Rage coursed through her veins. "I saw. He is an adult, Danny, and you're a child." She pointed at Ben. "I could have you arrested, sir."

"*Arrested?*" Danny shrieked. "Are you *mental?*"

"It's okay, Danielle," Ben told her. (*Danielle?* Janice thought. *Who's that?*) "Your mother just doesn't understand that this is normal."

What's normal? Janice wanted to scream. Who was this man? Who was this adult, kissing her daughter on the lips? How on earth was that *okay?*

But then a librarian came around the corner, giving Janice a strange look. Other patrons were staring, too. It all felt like too much. Janice looked at Danny. "You're coming with me."

"Hell no, I'm not," Danny growled.

"Danielle, it's fine," Ben said in a tempered voice. "You should go."

Only then did Danny relent. Janice hated that he was the one who gave her permission. Danny walked hunched to the car and didn't speak to Janice all the way home. Janice's mind hummed. "You can't talk to him anymore," she said. "That's wrong, you realize. Very, very wrong. That man should not be kissing you."

"He didn't kiss me, Mom. Your eyes were playing tricks on you."

Janice gawked at her. "No, they weren't!"

Danny crossed her arms and looked pointedly out the window. There was no getting through to her. By the time they were back at the apartment complex, Janice was second-guessing herself. Was Danny right? *Had* she hallucinated that kiss?

Their relationship deteriorated after that. If they did talk, it was only to fight. Her critiques of Ben only riled Danny up more. It went on the whole fall of senior year, and then winter. Janice forbade Danny to see Ben, but she had no control over her—she knew Danny was going to the appointments anyway. There was no point in encouraging her to fill out college applications or even study anymore—Janice's opinions no longer mattered. At one point, Janice had even thought about threatening to kick Danny out, but the idea terrified her. Because what if she went and lived with Ben?

Janice had no one to turn to—the only other people she knew who had knowledge of Ben were Bex and her parents. She had called Candace, delicately asking if Ben had ever seemed . . . *touchy-feely* with Bex. Candace had shut her down immediately. "You definitely have some bad data," she'd said. (*Bad data*. Like this was some kind of computer program.) "Ben wouldn't do that. He's all about human potential. There is nothing untoward about his methods."

"But I saw him kiss Danny on the lips. And that was just the one time—who knows what else is going on? She's saying it's not a big deal, but I swear—I saw it."

Then Candace laughed lightly. "Oh! Kissing on the lips! Ben kisses everyone in the group on the lips. We all do."

"*What?*"

"It's not a big deal. Seriously. Even men. I promise, it's nothing more than that."

Janice felt breathless. "Okay, well, Danny won't tell me what they talk about in their sessions."

"How is that any different than a girl speaking with her therapist?" Candace had asked.

But he's *not* a therapist, Janice wanted to argue, but it was like yelling at a brick wall.

After graduation, Danny disappeared to Oregon. Bex did, too. From what Janice understood, Bex's parents did not—but when she'd tried to contact them to ask if they were worried about this strange *community* their daughter had joined, her calls went unreturned. She tried sending them messages on Facebook—nothing. She even went to Candace's office, figuring she'd just ambush her face-to-face, but when the receptionist called up, Candace said she was busy. Janice considered waiting but then decided against it. Even if she did accost Candace in the parking lot, Candace clearly wasn't going to tell her anything. She wasn't on her side.

And forget about her pleas on the news having any impact. She'd felt so energized that the reporter was doing a piece about Danny, but the day after the clip aired, she came home to a message on her machine. Not from Danny. Not even from Ben. It was another woman's voice—though not Bex's either—and she'd said, robotically, "Please leave your daughter be. We will take action if you try and spread lies about her again. We're not afraid. We feel sorry for you, but we also won't back down."

And, well, that had kind of stopped her in her tracks. *Action?* What did that mean? What kind of messed-up group *was* this? She considered calling the police—she'd already filed a missing persons report before she got Danny's message. She'd considered calling a lawyer, too, because there had to be some kind of action she could take. But now she worried.

If she tried to get Danny back . . . what if something bad happened?

Now, she finishes the last of her tea. She still has that message. Her answering machine isn't in use anymore, but she'd recorded it onto her phone; she makes sure, whenever transferring devices, not to lose it. She thinks it might be useful in the future. Like one day she'll wake up and realize who the voice is . . . and that will solve everything. She's even shared it with a few trusted members of the group, and they don't recognize the voice, either. That's one bright spot, anyway—over the years, thanks to obsessive searching, Janice has connected with people who either have loved ones trapped by ISB or who were part of the group but left. It's been hit or miss, getting them to talk to her—quite a few are worried that she's some sort of ISB mole trying to find out where they've fled to or looking to see how much they'll say. But at least she knows she's not crazy anymore. The group sucked lots of people in with their promises of unlocking potential and happiness, alleviating fear, and making tons of money. But once you were theirs, you had to promise a lot. You were coerced. Manipulated. Worked to death. *Starved.* There are rumors, too, that certain women are getting tattoos on their bodies in some sort of commitment ceremony. *To him*, the whispers say. *To Ben.*

It's heartbreaking. *Sickening.* Eight long years, a prisoner of that place. And the most infuriating of it all? She'd found out, through her grapevine, that about a year after they left for Oregon, Bex defected. Bex, who'd dragged Danny in. She left . . . though Janice doesn't know where Bex went, or why, or how, or why she didn't take Danny with her. Sometimes, she thinks she hates Bex more than she hates Ben. Why did she abandon Danny? And where the hell did she go? Not home to her parents. They're still in Davis, too—Janice would have seen Bex around, surely. Only once did she have a sighting of Candace Reyes, at the grocery store. She'd come around the corner with her cart and there she was, staring blankly at shelves of crackers. Janice backed away before she could be seen, peering at Candace from behind a display. Candace's hair was shorter and had more gray. She looked like she'd put on a little weight, and there was sadness and wariness in her eyes. Janice didn't know if Candace and her husband were still part of ISB, but if they were—and if Bex defected—she was sure Bex wasn't in touch with them. So Candace, too, was a mother who lost her daughter. It was Janice's turn to feel smug. *Doesn't feel so good, does it*, she thought at Candace's straight back. Her eyes burned into her blazer. Or maybe it was Candace she hated the most, for her self-righteousness, for how she'd insisted that Ben was well-intentioned, that she'd had *bad data*.

But now, an opening. She wants to believe the intel she's received is correct and that Danny is no longer on the compound. She wants to trust her gut that Danny somehow knows where Bex is and has gone to find her. *Why* she'd do that, Janice isn't sure—her daughter should be furious at her for leaving, shouldn't she? But maybe their bonds of friendship are still strong. At least Janice has a mission, now. A purpose, something to work for.

Shakily, she sits down at her computer and starts to type. She has a few active, trusted contacts—Shay, a mother whose daughter also went to Oregon, and Vanessa, who extricated herself from ISB about a year ago but still knows people on the inside and sometimes hears gossip. Vanessa was tight-lipped about why she left and what she saw there, only that it wasn't good and that she was concerned for those who'd stayed. Now she was working three different jobs just to make ends meet; Janice got the sense that Vanessa had sunk a lot of money into joining the compound and came out with absolutely nothing. This was a common thread Janice heard—ISB members made lots of money at first, and supposedly earned tons of money while teaching and mentoring in Oregon. But once they left the group, once they *betrayed Ben*, they no longer had access to that bank account. How this was legal, Janice had no idea. But she had a pretty good idea of where it went: right into Ben's ever-growing portfolio.

It had been a while since Janice reached out to Vanessa, though—three, four months. It's possible Vanessa wouldn't even want to talk. But she had to try. Heart pounding, Janice picked up her phone and made the call. The phone rang several times before Vanessa picked up. Some loud TV program blared in the background. When Janice explained who she was, Vanessa's bright tone vanished, but she stayed on the phone, telling Janice to hold on until she moved into another room.

"I'm sorry," Janice blurts when Vanessa comes back on the line. "I just . . . I think Danny has left. I think she's gone to see Rebecca Reyes. They were friends. You might not even know her, but . . ."

"I've heard of her," Vanessa interrupts. Her tone is flat, wary.

"Y-You have?"

"Sure. Everyone has heard of Rebecca. She was one of his chosen, long ago."

Janice holds a breath. In the mirror across the room, she sees her wide-eyed reflection. This isn't such a surprise, really. "Why do *you* think Rebecca left?" This isn't the first time she's asked one of the contacts. One of these days, they're going to give Janice the answer she knows in her heart is true.

"I didn't know her. Our paths never crossed. I want to think she left because she was starting to see how dysfunctional and dangerous the community is, but I really don't know."

"Yes, but she was so devoted," Janice argues. "So *committed*. I think she started her own group somewhere else. Got greedy. Wanted to make more money." There was no way Rebecca left with nothing. She was as rigid and ambitious and bloodless as her parents and left, Janice knows, on *her* terms. Not the fleeing-in-the-night situation the others had to endure.

Vanessa clears her throat. "Funny you bring her up, though. Her name's come up lately anyway."

"Rebecca's name? Why?"

"I think for a long time, people had no idea what happened to her. She just . . . vanished." Vanessa falls silent a moment. Maybe she's thinking, like Janice is, about how messed up that is—to have to *disappear* after leaving the group, for fear they'll come after you. "But I think someone figured out where she is. Someone within the group, I mean."

"You do? *How?*"

"I don't know. Again, this is just a rumor. But I heard that violence was involved. Like, they had to force it out of someone."

"Oh dear," Janice murmurs. "Why were they looking for her?" And then she realizes. Was *Danny* looking for the address? But the idea of

Danny hurting someone to get it . . . there's no way. Not her Danny. At least she doesn't want to think so.

"Do you think you could find out the address yourself?" Janice whispers. "Or a phone number for Rebecca? Something?"

There's a crying sound on the other end. "I have to go," Vanessa says.

Janice stands straighter. "Is that a baby I hear?" she blurts.

Vanessa is hesitant. "Yes," she says, in a caught sort of tone.

"When did you have a baby?" Janice asks, dropping her inhibitions.

"I have to go," Vanessa says. "I'll see what I can do."

The call cuts off. Janice sets down her phone, rubbing her temples. Why would Danny go to Bex? Janice can't trust that she's making a clean break. She can't trust anything.

The phone rings again, startling her. She fumbles for it, her heart jumping when she sees the familiar area code on the screen. "Vanessa?" she says when she answers. She hadn't expected Vanessa to call her back so quickly—if at all.

"I need to be fast," Vanessa says. There's an edge to her tone. In the background, that baby is screaming loudly. "But I have something for you."

CHAPTER TWENTY-ONE

CARSON CITY, NEVADA
PRESENT DAY

Tom has broken into a cold sweat. It's not unlike how he used to feel when he was coming down off a high and didn't have access to more pills. It didn't seem right that the pills could be prescribed to other people, that they could just be sitting in medicine cabinets, that certain people could take them and not be affected the way he was, not *need* them like he did. He hadn't even realized how hooked he was until he tried not to take them and all of the symptoms came. The shaking. The sweating. The *pain*. The delirium. He hadn't realized how dangerous the withdrawal was—that he *needed* to go to the ER so he could be safely medicated—until it was nearly too late. He could have died.

After he was in recovery, he heard all kinds of stories of pillheads like him, or alcoholics, all of them trying to ride it out at home, their friends finding them near dead. It terrifies him, how close he came to that same state. *Poof,* he might have vanished. And he wouldn't have these kids. He wouldn't have his wife.

His wife who, maybe, he doesn't know at all.

It has to be a dream. Some sort of sick joke. But at the same time, hasn't this been lingering in the background their whole relationship? Tom *knew* she had darkness. Problem was, he thought he knew what the darkness was. An abusive boyfriend, maybe. That she was running from some guy, not wanting him to find her, and that was why she was so covert about her life and her past and her parents and all of it. Which was all beyond awful, but it was something he could at least picture in his mind and try and . . . help her with.

And it was that, kind of. But it was much *more* than that.

He stares at the frozen image of his wife on the screen. Just standing there while this Ben dude feels up a barely legal Danny. Rebecca looks barely legal herself, actually. What the *actual* fuck? Rebecca doesn't even look disturbed by what's happening. She has this weird robotic *smile* on her face, like it's all copacetic. It sickens him. Which saddens him, because if his wife disgusts him . . . what then? How could she have done this? How could *this* be her past? And now, this woman has washed up on their doorstep, skinny and dirty and afraid . . . and the *gun* in Rebecca's shoebox . . .

"Roscoe?" He slams the computer shut and stands. "Pack up some toys, buddy."

Footsteps. Roscoe pokes his head, his sweet, innocent head, into the room. "Where are we going?"

"To Grandma's. For a sleepover."

"Really? We're going to drive in the storm, too?"

Outside, it's just a garden-variety rainstorm now, not the weird tornado conditions it had been earlier. But the roads could be flooded. He'd have to be careful. Still, he needs to keep his children safe. They can't stay here, not with what he now knows. He'll tell his mom Rebecca has the flu and doesn't want the kids around her. He'll come up with something, some stopgap until he thinks of something better.

But . . . where *is* Rebecca? Actually at the doctor's? He reaches for his phone and dials her number. It rings . . . and rings . . . and rings.

"*Fuck*," he whispers.

He thinks of how open he's been with her. More open than with his friends, his parents, his brother—anyone in his life. How, when they met, he was still so tempted to use. He was only weeks into recovery; everything felt so muddled. Rebecca waltzed in like a ray of sunshine, and with her, a whole new life. But he'd bared his soul. He'd explained the shaky ground he was on. He'd given her background, too—the shoulder injury he'd had out of high school, how it had jeopardized his baseball career, but how he'd pushed through the pain, playing ball as much as he could, maintaining his status on the team, working his shoulder to shreds. After a certain point, surgery was the only answer—but after that, there would be no baseball. There would be no baseball career.

He'd been in such a slump after he woke up in the hospital. The only thing that had made him feel happy were the pain pills. They'd fed them to him like they were candy during his hospital stay, but the moment he was discharged, they didn't want to refill his prescription. It had pissed him off. Why hook him on that shit when they were just going to yank it away from him? Didn't they realize it was the only thing that helped?

His doctor had given him a thirty-day supply after enough begging. Tom had blown through it in days. It was astonishing how quickly his tolerance ballooned. But then his doctor had put his foot down. So Tom had tried another doctor, who gave him another thirty days—but then that guy put his foot down, too. Then came buying the shit off the street. Raiding his parents' medicine cabinet for old Vicodins Dad had gotten after a root canal. It had made him manic, desperate; he was fucking up at work, but he didn't care. He had tried to hide his habit. He had tried to go off it, too, but the withdrawal would be so terrible that he'd wind up in the ER, where the doctors understood the only thing they could do to keep him alive would be to pump him full of the poison all over again. It was a vicious cycle; so many ER visits, so many people let down—he stole pills from his *grandmother*, at a certain point.

He'd told Rebecca all of this. He laid himself bare. And though it was true that one of the first things she said was that she didn't want to talk about her past, he wishes she would have given him *some* kind of indication of what she'd been through.

He rubs his temples. He's being too hard on her. Isn't devotion to a cult just like addiction to pills? Can he really judge her for being so deep into something she couldn't see the forest for the trees? She got out, that's the point—just like he did. She stood by while some monster assaulted her friend, but what terrible things did Tom do when he was high? Certainly nothing like that, but there are things he isn't proud of. Things he doesn't like thinking about.

He tries Rebecca again. "*Pick up, pick up,*" he murmurs. But still nothing.

Roscoe thunders back into the room with a stuffed canvas bag. A remote control car peeks out the top. "Ready!" he bellows.

Tom smiles weakly. Kid loves Grandma and Grandpa's house. Thank God his parents even welcomed him back into the family after he made their lives such hell. It will be okay. He and Rebecca can talk through this. She was a kid back then. Probably couldn't stand up to the guy. She was just a pawn. A victim.

"Let's go," he says, grabbing his keys. Then he strides over to the baby to get him ready. A mental checklist forms in his mind: diapers, a few changes of clothes. The visit can't be for *that* long—just until he and Rebecca can talk things out and he makes sure things are safe. Bottles, formula. God, a baby needs so much. He searches the hooks for the diaper bags. He'll call his parents on the way over, but even if they aren't home, it's fine. There's a key under the mat.

The phone rings, and he looks up. But it's not his cell—it's the phone attached to the wall, the landline they barely use anymore. Tom eyes it warily. Weird that it's ringing. They have no ID for this line; the phone is old, from when his parents owned the house. Is it Rebecca? Is it that guy, *Ben*? If Rebecca ran from him—and she must have—is he pissed? *Is he looking for her?*

The ringing continues. Swallowing hard, puffing out his chest, Tom yanks it from the wall. "Hello," he says gruffly.

There's scratching on the other end. Breathing. "Hello?" Tom demands. "Who is this?"

"Is this where Rebecca Reyes lives?"

It's a woman's voice. Shaky. Thin. Still, Tom's hackles are up. *Reyes?* No one had used Rebecca's maiden name in a long time.

"Who is this?" he demands.

In his mind's eye, he sees that dingy room from the video. That dirty floor where Danny lay. That terrible lighting. Where even *was* that? Is this person calling from there?

The person on the other end hasn't responded. "I said, who is this?" Tom repeats. "What do you want? How did you get this number?"

"I'm sorry, I'm sorry, just—please." The woman lets out a small moan. "My name is Janice Martin. I'm looking for my daughter. Danielle—Danny. Is she there? Is she with Bex? Rebecca?"

The phone feels strange against Tom's ear. Too heavy, too plastic. "You're her mother. Danny's mother."

"So you've seen her? You've seen my Danny?" The woman makes a little whimpering sound on the other end. "Why would she go to *her*, of all people? She's the reason for all of Danny's problems. A terrible person, probably still doing terrible things, and this is who my daughter runs to?"

"*Excuse* me?" Tom grips the phone. "Watch how you talk about my wife!" Then he freezes. What if this is a con? What if this woman isn't Danny's mom at all, but some sort of . . . *spy* . . . within the organization, trying to get information out of him? And he just said Rebecca is his wife. And that she lives here.

"I need to go," he says, ready to slam the phone back down. "Don't call here again."

"Wait!" the woman cries. "I'm sorry. I shouldn't have said those things. I'm . . . it's been so terrible, waiting all these years for any kind of answer. Waiting for Danny to come to her senses. Is she with you? Has she finally left the group? Has she left *him*?"

Tom knows the *him* she means. He also is almost certain that this is the same voice from the news report he watched only a half hour before. The desperate, sobbing mother who didn't understand.

"She visited my wife this morning, yes," he admits in a softer voice. "But I don't know why. And I don't know if she's left the group for good. I didn't even know the group existed, to be honest with you. I only found out just now." He clears his throat. "So Danny's been there the whole time? With these ISB people?"

"She has," Janice says. "Not that I've talked to her in eight years. I tried to get Danny to tell me something, *anything* before she left, but I never got anywhere. But it's dangerous. I've heard he breaks the women down. Makes them comply. Makes them answer to him. If they don't text back, they're punished. If they overeat, they're punished. And they're all . . . head over heels for him. Not that I understand why." Then she seems to catch herself. "Wait, did you say you were Rebecca's husband?"

"Yes. I'm Tom."

A strange laugh sounds from the other end. "Rebecca got *married*? To someone other than that guru? *That's* interesting."

"She was young when she was part of all that," Tom says. "And . . . you're making it sound like they were in a relationship or something."

There's an uncomfortable silence. Tom's stomach twists. "*Was* she?"

Danny's mother sighs. "From what I've heard, he was in a relationship with all of them. They were all having sex with him. Every last woman he invited to that place in Bend."

Tom rises to his feet, turning his back to Roscoe so the boy can't see his expression. "That can't be true. It *can't*." But he thinks of Danny in that video. Ben's fingers snaking up her leg. How naive is he if he thinks the guy didn't do the same thing to Rebecca?

"Thinks he's a polygamist or something, I don't know. He's trying to build some sort of master species. But if he gets a woman pregnant? It's the goal, but forget about her ever seeing that baby. That's what I've heard, anyway."

"What do you mean?" Tom whispers. "What does he do to the babies?"

"Oh, nothing terrible—well, besides raising them on his own. Thinks he's totally capable."

"But what about the mothers? What happens to them?"

Danny's mother doesn't answer.

"*What happens?*" Tom repeats. "If you know, you need to tell me!"

"I-I don't know," she finally answers. "Not for sure."

He feels dizzy. *Ben was getting them all pregnant?* And then what would he do after they had the babies? Rebecca, earlier, frantically rushing Danny off to the OB. Is *that* why she's here?

And Rebecca, for that matter, all those years ago, looking so lost in the frozen section at the Price Chopper. Maybe it all makes horrible sense.

"I . . . I think your daughter's pregnant," Tom whispers. He doesn't mean to say it. The words just pop out of his mouth.

"Oh, God," Danny's mother whispers. "Oh, sweet Jesus. You have to help her. *Please.*"

"Rebecca . . . she's trying. They're at the doctor. I think they're making sure everything is safe."

"Everything is *not* safe," Danny's mother screeches. "Not if Danny's with *her*. You need to find them. You need to get her away from your wife."

"But . . . why? Why would you say that? Rebecca isn't going to hurt her. She was looking out for her."

"You poor, *poor* man." Mrs. Martin sounds defeated. "Your wife? She was complicit in all of it. Everyone has told me that. There's even a rumor she was the one who came up with the baby-making idea in the first place."

CHAPTER TWENTY-TWO

Danny slumps as Rebecca strides across the parking lot toward her. She looks so small inside her sweatshirt. It's hard to imagine there's a baby inside her; the width of her body is practically the same as the width of the No Parking sign. An exaggeration, fine, but not much of one.

Rebecca approaches Danny but doesn't say anything for a beat. The two of them stand side by side, staring at a nondescript block of senior living apartments. Birds chirp guilelessly. There's a layer of mist around the mountains. Traffic swishes past, ordinary people doing ordinary Saturday-morning things. It's barely raining anymore. And maybe it's good to be outside, in the fresh air, instead of confined by walls. Back in Oregon, whenever someone had something important to discuss, they always did it outside. In the garden. In the woods. Walking one of the dogs. Movement helped brain flow, at least that's what Ben said. Maybe there was some truth to that.

"I told Tom I'd pick up food," she says, finally. "What should we get for dinner? Your choice. Anything you want."

"I don't want anything," Danny answers.

"You have to eat, Danny."

Danny sets her jaw. "You said you had things to do this afternoon. I should get going anyway. It's a long way back."

Frustration explodes inside Rebecca. "You can't go back there. And you're definitely not caring for yourself. It's not just for you anymore. You know that, right?"

One of Danny's shoulders lifts. Slightly.

"As that child's auntie, I demand you feed her and treat her better."

Rebecca tries to make her voice sound light, but it cracks all the same. Danny winces at how Rebecca has used *her*. It breaks Rebecca's heart.

"It's all good news, Danny," she says softly. "You saying there's something you could have done—*what*? You're having a girl. A beautiful, healthy girl." Danny's scowl deepens. "Why is that such a terrible thing? And, what, you're going to starve her to death? Because she's a girl?"

Danny covers her face in her hands.

"I think this is why you're here. Because you know it's a good thing, but you're scared. You're so scared, Danny. I can see it. You told me yourself."

Danny removes her hands. The tip of her nose is red, and her eyes water. "This was a bad idea."

"It wasn't," Rebecca begs. "Listen. You and I both know whose baby this is. But how can it be good for you that he's making you check in? Not letting you breathe, go to a *doctor*? And let's not mention eating, sleeping . . . and he thinks you're *camping*? What pregnant woman should be doing *that*?"

"You act like you didn't do these things, too, back in the day." Danny's eyes flash. "Like you didn't totally buy into this—create it, even, and force it on others?"

"I didn't—"

"Cut the bullshit, Bex. You've made Ben into a monster only because it suits you now. Only because you love someone else. You adored him for *years*. And then you just . . . *left*. Without saying goodbye."

Rebecca's mouth drops. She takes a big step away, feeling defensive. "You think I didn't regret leaving you there? I had to run, Danny. I was in danger. It'll be dangerous for you, too."

Danny turns away. "Why didn't you tell me you were pregnant?" she asks in a small, defeated voice.

"I . . ." Rebecca feels disarmed. It's not like they'd ever had a chance to discuss it—she just didn't think Danny would come straight out and ask. "I mean, I wanted to. I really did. But Ben told me I couldn't tell anyone yet. Not even you. And also . . ." She pauses uncomfortably. "I thought it would be another thing that came between us. Everyone was competitive for Ben's attention . . ." She sighs. "Including both of us. There was friction between you and me once we got to Oregon. You can't deny that."

Danny shrugs. "You still should have said something."

"I'm sorry. I really am." But then something needles at Rebecca. "When did you find that out? About Roscoe, I mean?"

"I don't know," Danny keeps her gaze on the ground. "Not so long ago."

Rebecca mulls this over, then says, "Is that why you felt like you could come see me? Because of what we . . . share?"

Danny hugs her chest and shrugs. "I just . . . I can't think straight. I feel lost."

"It's because you've relied on Ben to tell you what to do for the past eight years. Of course you're lost. But you don't have to be, Danny. Don't go back. It's really dangerous there."

Danny scoffs. "That's a little dramatic."

"Is it? Or do you know, deep down, that I'm telling the truth?" Rebecca crosses her arms. "Why else did you come? Why else did you cry on my shoulder and let me take you to Dr. Salley? Why are you talking to me *right now*? I'm thankful I got out. I have no idea what my life would be like if I was still there, but I know one thing: my relationship with Roscoe *would not exist*."

Danny's chin trembles. Rebecca thinks that maybe she's gotten through, but then Danny rolls her eyes. "It's not like that. It really isn't."

"Jesus, Danny." Rebecca slaps her sides. "Fine. Do you remember Sophia?"

Danny frowns. "She went on a goddess retreat? About the time you left?"

Rebecca flinches. *Goddess retreat my ass.* "Not much later, did a baby—Ben's son—arrive at the compound? Alone?"

Danny's eyes shift back and forth. "How did you know that? You were gone by then."

"Because that was Sophia's baby." She puts her hands on her hips. "And I'm guessing the baby was raised in the same part of the house as Quentin and Adam, Ben's other kids? All by a bunch of women who *aren't* their moms? Why did we never question that? And I'm also guessing Sophia *didn't* return to be with him?"

"Sophia couldn't handle being a mother," Danny answers immediately. "Ben said she was weak. She gave up her rights."

Unbelievable. Danny just *buys* it. "Danny! How many more times has this happened? How many more babies just showed up randomly—without their mothers?"

"What are you saying?" Danny looks angry. "What are you implying?"

Rebecca's head is pounding. "You've got to know what's happening. You've got to at least *suspect*. How many children are on the compound now?"

Danny licks her lips. "Some."

"And how many of their birth mothers are actually taking care of them?"

Danny looks away. "They couldn't handle it. Pregnancy, motherhood—it's not for everyone. Ben always says so. It makes a lot of people weak. They lose themselves."

"Danny, that's ridiculous. Every single mother who was part of the ISB Oregon community, *really*? What about all the mothers all over the world who *can* handle it? What are they, superheroes? I thought ISB women were the strong ones and everyone else was weak." Rebecca crosses her arms. "You're smarter than this. They're all Ben's kids. Ben pushed them out. And now he's gotten around to you, and the same thing is going to happen."

Danny's mouth drops open. "He loves me."

Rebecca quickly realizes she's gone too far. "I'm sorry. I didn't mean for it to come out like that. It's just . . ." Everyone wanted to be with Ben. It was a badge of pride and attention, it meant *everything*. But after Ben got what he needed from someone, after Ben tired of a woman and her complaints and *emotions*—or, God forbid, she got pregnant—he moved on to the next waiting devotee down the line. Danny has always had low self-esteem. Maybe Ben knew she would stick around for the long haul, so he wasn't in any hurry with her. And love? Absolutely not. Ben wasn't capable.

Danny's lips part like Rebecca has said all of this out loud. But then her phone rings. Her gaze drops to her pocket. "I need to go."

Rebecca touches her arm, desperate. "He took everything from me," she whispers. "He made me think I was sick—for *years*. He tried to make me believe that the assault that happened to me was *my fault*—for years! That I wasn't a victim of it—I was making myself *think* I was a victim, and how wrong that was." She shakes her head. "It nearly ruined me, Danny."

"Don't be dramatic," Danny spits.

"*Dramatic*? You think *I'm* the one being dramatic?" Images of Ben standing on the stage at Celebration Weekend, riling up the crowd, basking in everyone's admiration flare in her mind. She lets the picture fade. She doesn't want to waste mental energy thinking about Ben like that. She peers at Danny again. She looks so tiny, slumped against the parking sign. There's a tennis match in Rebecca's brain. On one hand, there's the broken, scared, vulnerable Danny who maybe has doubts. On the other, there's the sneaky, whispering, conniving Danny who showed up on her doorstep, waltzed her way into Rebecca's house, and sweet-talked her husband and son. She can't figure out Danny's agenda, and what Ben thinks Danny's agenda is, and what Danny really *wants* her agenda to be. Maybe Danny doesn't even know.

The phone rings again. Danny's fingers touch it through her pocket.

"Please don't answer it," Rebecca begs. "Ignore him. You want my side of the story? You want me to finally explain why I had to leave that night? I'll explain. I *will*. As a friend. I should have tried harder before I left. Even if it would have meant his wrath." She glances at the ringing phone. "Just turn that off, okay? Just for a little while? I won't take it from you. I won't judge you anymore. But I want some time with just you and me. To tell you my story."

Fear flashes across Danny's face. She's worrying about the

repercussions. What Ben will do because she hasn't obeyed. But in Rebecca's mind, it doesn't matter. It's her job, she knows, to make sure Ben doesn't see Danny ever again.

Danny's mouth wobbles. Then her shoulders lower. "Okay. Let's hear it."

Yes, Rebecca thinks. It feels like the biggest victory in the world.

CHAPTER TWENTY-THREE

For a few minutes, the only sound in the car is the *swish, swish, swish* of the windshield wipers. Danny is curled up against the window, trying to make herself small. But Rebecca grips the steering wheel with purpose. At least Danny has agreed to get into the car with her. At least she's agreed to listen.

Rebecca takes a deep breath, keeping her eyes on the road ahead. She's navigated onto an empty highway so that she doesn't have to concentrate too hard on driving. She's never told anyone the logistics of this story. She always thought the less she talked about ISB, the less reason they'd want to come after her. But now here she is, telling this to someone who's still technically part of the group. She has a lot to lose here.

At the same time, maybe just telling her story will be the thing that truly pushes Danny over the edge.

"It's not like I woke up one day and realized it was all bad," Rebecca starts. "It was little by little, bit by bit. Ben was so nice when we all first started, as I'm sure you know."

"Of course."

"It's like . . . he really wanted to *build* something with us, you know? And we were all together, and happy, and he valued our opinions and ideas . . . and I mean, we were all earning money. Remember all those bookings? How expensive the workshops were—people who wanted to see *us*?"

Danny sniffs. "You had rich parents. You were set regardless."

Rebecca gives her an even stare. "Do you not remember that my parents essentially threw me into the deep end to just . . . figure it out? Sure, I had money, but they didn't give a shit. I never felt loved, Danny. Not one single day."

Danny lifts her head from her arm and looks at Rebecca. It's clear she didn't know this. Rebecca gets a pang—why hadn't she shared this with Danny? But she'd felt ashamed, kind of. It became yet another chasm between them, another thing they didn't discuss.

"Anyway, it was exciting for a little while," Rebecca went on. "But the more I was involved, the more I realized that Ben never let me forget that he'd helped me through my dark times and that I owed him. You remember me talking about that. The assault?"

Danny shrugs one shoulder.

"And do you remember you asking me why I hadn't pressed charges?"

Danny frowns. "I never asked you that."

"Sure you did. But it was before ISB. Before you talked to . . . *him*. Before he *got* to you and made you think that something that happened to you wasn't anyone's fault other than your own. He already had me so confused. He had me thinking that I had somehow *caused* that assault on my own. Maybe by talking to the guy, or going on the walk by myself—I'd made it happen. There were no repercussions for the guy who did it to me, but I didn't question Ben's thinking. But I started to see how he got away with certain things. Certain *actions*, people just let him do, even though he was preying on them—they just let him because they didn't want to think of themselves as victims."

"Like what?"

"Like . . . he would pick on some of the guys, for example. Like really needle them, be a total asshole. But the guys just sort of took it. Whenever any of them pushed back, Ben was always like 'I never said that to you' or 'I think you misunderstood.' And even if there were other people in the room who'd clearly heard what Ben had said, no one spoke up. They were all afraid."

"Or they all respected Ben. I mean, look, he can come on strong sometimes," Danny says. "Some people can't handle that."

"Sure. People couldn't imagine Ben being a predator because he's the smartest and most moral person they'd ever met. He was the Scion. But that's just one example."

Road signs swish past. One exit, then the next.

Danny shuts her eyes. "What else, exactly, does he do that you think is so predatory?"

Rebecca considers her words. *Everything*, she wants to say. *The way he talks to you now. The way he texts you. The control he has over you. You don't even have access to your own money!* Danny thinks it's a choice, a privilege, but that's what he's enchanted her into believing.

"I didn't feel safe anymore. I didn't even feel *me* anymore. And then I started to realize, I'd been part of ISB since I was sixteen years old. I didn't even have time to figure myself out. Was this even my path? Who even *was* I? My parents just threw me in—*they* didn't give a shit. But I didn't have anyone within the organization to ask. They'd just say I needed to take more classes, or that I was weak, or that I was getting sick again." She glances at Danny. "That was one of his favorite go-tos. Saying that I was sick when I came to him. He threw all these psychology terms at me—I was *depersonalizing*, I was *black-and-white thinking*, I was *autoscopic*."

Suddenly, Danny sits up. Her eyes widen. "What?" Rebecca asks. "Did he say that to you, too?"

Danny looks away.

"It's Greek, he said," Rebecca goes on. "*Self-watcher*. We made a whole module out of it, but then Ben wasn't satisfied, so we threw it out. Anyway, he said that he'd cured me, but that if I left, I'd be sick again for sure."

They pass a long stretch of strip malls on the highway. For a while, there are no cars at all. Suddenly, Danny sits up and looks around. "Where are we? This isn't the same way back to your house."

"Um, I . . . We'll take the long way," Rebecca says.

Danny sets her mouth in a line. "Can we just get back? I need the bathroom again."

"We can stop somewhere. A McDonald's or whatever."

Danny wrinkles her nose. "Public bathrooms are gross. Please?"

Rebecca clenches her molars. She was hoping to drive around for a while so they could talk this out without involving Tom again. She almost considers taking them to a hotel, but then the exit for their house appears on the highway.

Danny points at it. "There. Let's get off."

Rebecca glances at her, alarms going off in her head. "How do you know your way around Carson City?"

Danny shrugs. "This was the way my cab came. I remember the name of the street."

If Rebecca doesn't take the exit, it might spook Danny, make her think she has other plans. She might even jump out of the car. Reluctantly, she puts on her blinker and moves into the right lane. She wonders what Tom is doing. Her house feels so distant right now. Like another world. He's called a few times, she's seen, but she hasn't answered.

"You certainly didn't act like any of this was bothering you," Danny finally mutters. "I mean, you were always up there with him, part of the ceremonies, teaching, guiding, even doing . . . you know."

She meets Rebecca's gaze. Rebecca shivers. She thinks she knows what Danny means. That hot branding iron. That sizzle on flesh. The screams.

Everything inside her clenches.

"You certainly didn't show if you were uncomfortable," Danny continues.

"How could I have shown it? He would have punished me!"

Danny makes a face. "I wouldn't call it punishment."

"Oh, right, so making you go on all-night marches isn't punishment? Or turning to someone *else* for affection to make you jealous? Or—oh yeah, this is a good one—one time, he threatened to *resign from the community* because of something I did. I can't even remember what it was, but he acted so upset and betrayed, he was like, 'Clearly I'm not getting through to anyone here. I might as well walk.' It's class A manipulating, Danny. And it's one hundred percent punishment."

"So you left because he rejected you," Danny says, her voice rising in an *aha* kind of way. "Because you weren't his one and only anymore."

"*That's* the only thing you heard?" Rebecca wants to bang her head against the steering wheel, though she supposes she could see why Danny latched on to that example. At first, Ben treated Rebecca like a queen, and she knew Danny was jealous. And, okay, it made her feel special. Deep down, Rebecca was always comparing herself to Danny. She was so much prettier than Rebecca. And Danny, once you brushed the cobwebs and darkness from her, was so . . . *captivating*. She was pretty and bubbly and had this starry-eyed optimism that Rebecca sometimes couldn't muster. She sang the group songs loudly, in a beautiful voice, and she was artistic, and she always said she had big plans for the world, even if she didn't know what they were. Danny also had a mom that adored and celebrated her, versus Rebecca's mother who didn't even notice when she got an A on a test. Yeah, some crappy things had happened to Danny—like the stuff about her dad leaving—and, fine, Danny lived in an apartment instead of Rebecca's enormous house, but who cared about that?

She was thrilled when Danny joined ISB so they could be together all the time and share everything at a much deeper level . . . but at the same time, did she want Danny to be *as* happy as she was, *as* fulfilled? It was a dark part of her that she didn't like looking at, but she had to wonder if she felt better about herself when she was on top and Danny was slightly rushing to catch up. But Rebecca had always seen the potential in Danny, and she'd always known that someday soon, everyone else would, too. That time began once Danny got to Oregon. The community wasn't as close-knit before they all moved there; not everyone knew Danny the way they knew Rebecca. But Danny really blossomed there. People wanted to be around her—and that included Ben.

Had Rebecca been jealous? Had she felt Ben slipping away from her? Had it scared her, especially because of the condition she was newly in? Of course she'd thought about it. But she'd also suppressed it. The feelings were so tangled in guilt and envy and confusion and fear, she really didn't know what to make of her decisions and actions surrounding Danny. She remembered, though, how tenderly Ben had touched Danny after she worked through her panic attack. Rebecca had seen it then—that look he was giving Danny was the same look he used to give to her. But when she'd had her dizzy spell—for reasons Ben understood, but for reasons he also thought were troubling, like she wasn't *strong* enough to handle it—he'd looked at her with a completely different expression. Doubt. Disgust, even. Like maybe he'd made the wrong choice.

She clears her throat. "I knew I was pregnant before I left. I was afraid of what it would be like if I stayed."

"You should have told me, Bex."

"What would have happened if I did? What would it have changed? Anything? Would you have stayed away from him? I doubt it."

Danny smirks. "So you *were* jealous, then."

"Danny, *no*. I don't mean it like that, not really. Look, I saw something that made me leave. Something Ben was doing. Something I was afraid he'd do to me next."

Danny turns to her. Rebecca doesn't know what it is she's said, exactly, but suddenly Danny looks like she's actually paying attention. "What did you see?" she asks in a quiet voice.

Before she can explain this, her driveway comes into view. Rebecca wants to pull the car over to the curb just a few houses away—it feels like she *has Danny*, and she doesn't want to lose her—but then Roscoe spots their car. "Mommy!" he cries, and starts running toward her. Rebecca groans and eases the car forward.

"I'll tell you in a minute," she mutters to Danny.

She notices Tom is in the driveway too, loading the baby's rear-facing car seat into his car. A duffel is slung over his shoulder, and there's a shell-shocked expression on his face. Her stomach swoops. This feels wrong.

"Where's *he* going?" Danny sounds just as surprised.

Rebecca pulls up next to him and hops out the moment she shuts off the engine. Roscoe reaches her and hugs her waist. "Mommy! We're going to Grandma's!"

"Oh?" Rebecca's heart is pounding. She looks at Tom, who has now straightened and is looking at her . . . *strangely*. No, accusingly. Like he doesn't know her anymore.

She dares to walk over to him. "What's going on? Roscoe says you're going to your mom's?"

Tom's lip quivers. There's something pent up about him, like he might explode. "I can't believe this. Lying is one thing. But exposing us to danger? Letting her in, fully *knowing*?"

Rebecca's heart starts to bang. No. *No.* "Wait. Whatever you think you know, it isn't true."

"Whatever I think I know? *Bex*?" Tom steps closer and says, in a hissed whisper, "I found the gun. In the shoebox you were looking through, actually, *on the floor, loaded*, where our children could get it. And I found some fucked up videos, too. Of *her*." His eyes flick to indicate Danny, somewhere behind them. "Some kind of . . . ritual, or something. Some asshole guy feeling her up. She looks barely legal. And you're just . . . standing there, right behind him. Danny's having his kid, I take it? Guru guy? And you were part of this group? This *cult*?"

Rebecca can feel the tears blurring her vision. *This can't be happening. Tom saw Danny's video. Did he see everything? The worst part?*

"I didn't know how to tell you," she blurts. "I knew you wouldn't understand. It doesn't make any sense, and I hate myself for it, and I wanted to escape all of that—I *did* escape all of that. To come to you. I had to save myself."

"And your baby." Tom puts his hands on his hips and stares at her, but Rebecca can't meet his gaze. "It's why you fled, right? Is Roscoe . . ."

Rebecca holds up her hand. "Don't say it. I don't want you to. I don't think of Roscoe that way. I think of Roscoe as yours, and us as a family."

Tom looks shattered. Maybe he didn't actually think it was true. It's finally sinking in. "Jesus," he says. "I might be sick. Why didn't you tell me?"

"Would you have understood? Or would you have looked at me exactly how you're looking at me now?" Rebecca wipes away a tear. "I wasn't in my right mind, Tom. I was brainwashed. But I still think of them every single day. They haunt me."

"I read stuff online." Tom leans against the car, his arms crossed tightly over his chest. "And I read what they do if you leave. How they find you and want to hurt you. You knew all of this, too. And yet you let Danny in anyway?"

"She's my friend," Rebecca whispers. "I left her behind when I escaped. I always felt bad about that. And I think I can help her now, so she doesn't have to go through what I did. I'm sorry. I know we need to talk more. A *lot* more. But I need to make sure she never goes back there. I need to get *through* to her. I need to—"

There's a *slam*.

Tom whirls around and screams. Rebecca turns, too. At first, she doesn't understand what she's seeing. She swore she'd turned the car off, but the headlights are blazing, and the engine has growled to life. Then she realizes Danny is sitting in the driver's seat. Even more disconcerting, there's someone in the back. A figure staring out the window, a confused look on his little face. *Roscoe.*

Rebecca doesn't get this, either, but in a sickening instant, as the tires squeal and Danny pulls away, she does.

"Danny!" she screams, running after her. The taillights vanish into the gloomy day. Then she wheels around to Tom. "Give me the keys!"

"What are you going to do?" Tom screams.

"What do you *think*? Give me your keys. Get the baby out of the back. I have to go after them!"

Of course this is what's happening. Of course this is why Danny has come. The pregnancy was only a decoy. *This* was what she wanted.

Roscoe. Because he's Rebecca's . . . but he's also Ben's.

And Ben wants his child back.

"Wait," Tom says, grabbing her arm before she swings into the driver's seat. "You're not going after her."

"Are you insane?" Rebecca screeches. "She's stealing Roscoe! I should have fucking seen this coming! I should have *known*!"

Tom lowers his head, his jaw clenched. "What I meant was, you're not driving." He yanks open the driver's door and throws himself inside. "I am."

CHAPTER TWENTY-FOUR

BEND, OREGON
SEVEN YEARS BEFORE

"Hey, Bex. Up for a walk?"

Rebecca is face down in bed, trying to stop the constant spinning in her head, wishing there wasn't such a terrible taste of rotting fruit in her mouth. She has to twist around to see her friend in the doorway. Toby's cheerful expression startles her. He's been so withdrawn lately. Also, it's Ben who initiates walks, not anyone else. She isn't even sure they're *allowed* without him.

Maybe Toby senses Rebecca's confusion, because he gestures outside as if to explain. "It's so nice out. The sunset is gonna be really pretty, I bet."

"Um, okay." Something tells Rebecca it's important. Only, can she manage standing? She isn't certain.

The world wobbles but then rights itself. Ben told her that the first trimester, for most women, is the hardest. And according to him, she's about eleven weeks along—which means only a few more weeks of this disabling queasiness she's having a hard time hiding from the group. It's complicated because the ISB community is all about self-healing.

Everyone has the power within to overcome illness, and Rebecca is supposed to be a role model for the others—what will they think of her if she's sweaty and pale and puking all the time? Ben seems baffled that she can't use his teachings to make her nausea go away. He has also given her some herbal pills that are supposed to help, along with daily inner-strength meditation sessions. But she's felt queasier and dizzier as the days go on.

And surely, at some point, she'll be allowed to tell people—she's just waiting for Ben to give the go-ahead. Rebecca wonders if there were restrictions with the mothers of Ben's other children back in the day. There are two little boys here, four- and five-year-old Quentin and Adam, who are also Ben's. That was a shock. The first few years of Rebecca being part of the group and developing a relationship with Ben, she had no idea he even *had* kids. But then, about a year ago, when the ISB community moved here, a few children appeared, too—*surprise!*

She'd tried to hide her reaction when it happened, but in the last twelve months, she and Ben have grown much closer. Now, they tell each other everything. It's only a formality now that he asks her to join him in his bed; she's there almost every night. And so, not long ago, Rebecca broached the subject about the boys' mother being part of the community, too. She said it in an objective, nonjealous tone, because jealousy is victimization. "Perhaps I know her?" she said lightly. "Perhaps we garden together!"

"Oh no, the mothers aren't here," Ben answered coolly. "They chose to give up their rights because they each thought the children would be better suited here, in this wonderful community, with me."

The mothers, he'd said. So . . . different mothers, then. She wanted to ask about that, but Ben's expression was so closed off, she decided against it.

Quentin and Adam are clearly Ben's, there's no doubt about that; they look just like him with their sandy hair and solid, strong, sturdy bodies. They're the only kids here—the compound is full of single people, otherwise—and they're housed separately from the rest of the group and cared for full-time by two Seedlings who were dismissed from workshop duties. At first, Rebecca wondered if maybe these women *were* the kids' mothers and Ben just wasn't saying so—though *why*, she had no idea—but she'd seen them interact from afar, and something about their body language told her that they weren't. They were just caretakers. Doing the work Scion asked.

Rebecca is happy that Quentin and Adam have someone else to play with, anyway—it isn't exactly that it's lonely here in the wilds, because it isn't, but a single kid might get bored all by himself. And she's happy they get to be with their father—Ben spends a lot of time with them, and he's very attentive. But Rebecca's shocked their mothers aren't here. What kind of mother gives up her children? Were these mothers ISB members and then left? *Why?*

But she tries to let it go. Asking questions and digging into the past isn't really the ISB way.

Anyway. Now she is pregnant with Ben's child, but no one else knows yet. It's tough. Rebecca would love to tell Danny, at least, despite the fact that she and Danny have grown apart since they've come here. They've both been really busy . . . and Rebecca senses that Danny resents her. Maybe for her closeness with Ben, her position within the community, like it's all a competition. Maybe it is.

And forget about telling her parents. Rebecca has chosen to put more distance between herself and her parents since coming to Oregon. She's offended they didn't choose to come to Oregon with her to be part of ISB's next chapter. But they chose their careers, *just like always*. They could have made more money teaching here, but when Rebecca told her mother this, she shrugged and said Oregon was more suited for Rebecca's lifestyle, not hers. And then she patted Rebecca on the shoulder and said good luck.

It was *icy*, the whole thing. In the dark moments when Ben isn't around to monitor her feelings, she seethes with resentment. Rebecca sensed her mother was relieved, like she continued to be happy that Ben had taken over caring for her and she was out of their hair. She hasn't reached out to them since she's come—nearly a year. She saw it as a game of chicken: if she didn't reach out, how long would it take them to call her? Except . . . months went by, and they just *didn't* call her. Which told her everything she needed to know. So why would she tell them they're going to be grandparents? Why would she let them share in the joy of this baby at all?

But these thoughts aren't within the ISB philosophy. She's victimizing herself. She should go to Barb, maybe, who is an expert at unpacking the negativity and transforming it into something powerful she can use to better herself . . . but Rebecca feels so embarrassed. She's so high up within this group—a role model. She shouldn't even be *having* these feelings.

It is beautiful outside, the humidity chased away after the rain, the trees making a dark, ethereal green curtain across the sky. The air smells clean. They head toward the woods, off the trail. Ben typically likes the trail, says the woods are hard on his knees. Well. He doesn't *say* it's hard on his knees, exactly, but Rebecca sometimes sees how he struggles over roots and rocks, winces when he steps wrong. An old injury from when he was a diver, maybe.

Birds flap skyward. Their feet crunch on the path. For a little while, Toby simply walks at her pace with his hands in his pockets. She's going slow, she knows, way slower than she used to walk back in high school. Toby doesn't seem to mind.

This is nice, Rebecca thinks. When did she last have a normal, quiet walk? Everything has felt so heightened lately, every uttered word so important and weighty.

"I feel like I've hardly seen you around," she says after a while.

"I've been here. Probably more than you think. Always behind the camera or cleaning up a mess."

"True. So are you . . . ?"

Rebecca isn't sure how to phrase her question. *Happy*, she wants to say, but that feels . . . obvious. It's unspoken that they're all happy. That's the point of ISB. And Toby is the community's official videographer, documenting everything about how they live and Ben's teachings. Ben encouraged him to do it, and it's a natural role for him since he's always wanted to make movies. He's even getting paid to do it as his formal responsibility in the community.

Yet Toby seems less boisterous than he used to be. Back in the day, he was always making videos of pranks he pulled or stunts he tried to reenact. He had dreams of playing bass in a rock band; he even had a name for it picked out: Black Animals, because he was always drawn to black cats and dogs. He kept trying to recruit Rebecca and Danny to sing lead as a duet, and Rebecca and Danny went along with it for a while—with Danny at the mike, they were even kind of good. They practiced in Toby's grandma's dinky, cluttered garage—there was barely any room for the equipment. They covered Nirvana songs and other grunge. Sometimes, Toby's grandma came out of her living room to listen. She was cool for an older lady, way more open-minded than Danny's mom or Rebecca's parents. Grandma always said Toby played bass beautifully even though he was terrible. She bopped her head at every awful cover and cheered loudly when they shuddered to a finish.

"How is your grandma?" she asks suddenly, her thoughts flowing over.

Toby gives her a strange look. "Huh?"

"I was just thinking of her. Have you spoken to her lately?"

Branches crack underfoot. "I mean, *no*, obviously."

Rebecca skirts around a tree stump. She hadn't realized that Toby was encouraged to cut off his grandma. It's one thing for Danny to cut off her mom—Janice Martin was so adamantly against ISB, so that made sense. But Toby's grandma always seemed encouraging about anything Toby threw himself into. Maybe Rebecca doesn't know the whole story.

And anyway, letting go of certain relationships is for the good of growth. Ben always says that people have to do hard things to become better humans. A lot of things around here are hard. Like all the chores they do daily to keep the place looking beautiful and running smoothly—the washing, the food-growing, the weeding, the tilling, the housecleaning, the building, the caring for of the chickens and goats, the security duty, the food prep, and so on. And then there are the morning long-distance runs they're required to take to purify their mind—even Toby, which is funny, because he always hated running in gym class. And don't forget the quota of workshop ideas they need to come up with every week. The number of classes they need to teach to the disciples who visit the compound on the weekends. The counseling sessions they must undergo themselves *and* take part in to counsel others. The recruitment requirements to inspire the philosophy in others and build their own teams—including getting more people to come to Oregon. The administrative work they're forced to do at all hours of the night, whenever Ben needs it, all on what seems like not quite enough food...

But it's exhilarating. Really. It gives Rebecca a high to inspire so many people, to push her body to its limits, to realize what she has the capacity for. She reminds herself of this all the time.

"Remember our band?" she says now. "Remember how she always brought us snacks on a cute little tray?"

"Yeah, they were crap, though."

"Generic cookies, tasted like dust." Rebecca giggles but then gets a twinge of sadness. How free she used to be to just *eat a cookie* without thinking of the repercussions. "And those weird cheese crackers from the dollar bin."

"Those were totally expired." Toby twitches. "Are we supposed to be talking about the past?"

"It's positive stuff. We were a good group, in high school. Still are."

Toby looks down. When Rebecca looks over, she's stunned to see there's a tear rolling down his cheek. She stops. "What is it?"

Toby stops, too, and suddenly faces her. He's chewing on his lip, and the color has drained from his face. Rebecca feels frightened, suddenly. "I need to tell you something, and I need to tell you fast," he says. "I'm leaving tomorrow. I'm getting out. I don't know where the hell I'm going, because nowhere is safe, but I have to leave."

Rebecca blinks hard. It feels like she's been punched. "W-Why would you leave?"

"You can't tell anyone I'm going. I'm begging you. But . . . you should come, too."

Rebecca laughs. "I can't. Neither should you. You need to stay, Toby! We'll take care of you! We're your people!"

"You're pregnant, aren't you?" Toby blurts.

A jolt goes through her. They are, she realizes, quite deep in the woods. The trees form a dark canopy around them. The thing is, Ben told her not to tell anyone yet. That it was never good to reveal a pregnancy before a certain gestational date.

"You are," Toby insists when she doesn't answer. "I saw you after we were filming Danny the other day—when you were throwing up. At first I thought it was because of what happened to Danny, and I totally wouldn't blame you. But then I realized maybe it was something else, too. I have a cousin who was pregnant last year, she acted exactly the same. Dizzy. Nauseous. Breathing heavy. We've known each other a long time, Bex. Don't try and deny it."

"It's none of your business," Rebecca says tightly. Then she turns to go. She shouldn't be here.

Toby touches her arm. "Wait. Look, I'm not . . . I saw something, okay? Something I can't wrap my head around. That's why I'm getting out of this place."

"What are you talking about?"

He moves closer. "I was filming B-roll stuff around the community for some of our promotional materials," he whispers. "I sort of got lost in the woods, got off track. I didn't mean to be by that cabin, but I was turned around. Alone. Anyway, I turned to leave, but then I saw Ben burst down the path with this weird look on his face. He was being . . . *sketchy*. Like he didn't want anyone to know what he was doing. Something told me to hide. He walked right by me to that old cabin. And . . . I don't know why, but I followed him."

Anxiousness fills Rebecca. "You should have trusted him, Toby!"

Toby holds up his hand, *hold on*. "Well, yeah, but something felt off. Ben was carrying a picnic basket. He went right up to the cabin and went inside. I heard him talking to someone in there. With the door open, I could hear that someone was crying. And I peeked through the window, and . . ." He winces. "It was Sophia."

Rebecca blinked at him. "Sophia's at a goddess retreat. She left a while ago. I *saw* her get into a car." Ben had told the whole group about the goddess retreat in Arizona Sophia had been chosen to attend. "It's for self-betterment; she's working closely with a guru I'm very connected with," he'd boasted to them. "She'll have all kinds of wisdom for us when she returns. Maybe, if you prove yourself, you'll get to go someday, too."

The way he said it brought up more shameful, envious feelings in Rebecca—Sophia was so beautiful and effortless, and she saw the way Ben looked at her. She'd been part of the group longer than Rebecca had and seemed so mature and put-together, but she'd always kind of held herself at arm's length from Rebecca. Not like she was better, exactly, just like she was on a different plane.

"I don't think so," Toby says, breaking Rebecca from her thoughts. "Because she's in a *room*, Bex. Here. In the cabin up the hill. Ben's keeping her there *all alone*."

Rebecca bleats out a laugh. "What are you talking about?"

"I'm telling you. Things here aren't what they seem."

Rebecca stiffens. "Toby. You've misunderstood. It isn't what you think. It can't be."

"Do you want to bet? She's there. Right now."

There's conviction in Toby's eyes. Rebecca glances through the woods in the direction he's pointing. There is a cabin up there, though she's only seen it from far away. Ben says it's unusable and structurally unsound. It was part of the land when he bought it; he intends to restore it at some point, but not now.

"There's more," Toby said. "Sophia looked different. Her body was really thin, but her belly . . . she's pregnant, too, Bex."

Rebecca stares at him. "She's what?"

"Pregnant. Farther along than you."

Rebecca shakes her head. "Sophia isn't . . ." She trails off, unable to say the last part.

"Why?" Toby puts his hands on his hips. "Because you're Ben's one and only? Even you know that's not true."

Rebecca lowers her eyes. She's seen Ben flirt with other women . . . even kiss them. Amelia. Chelsea. Sex isn't about ownership, he often said. Coupledom was imprisonment. Jealousy was victimization. To set oneself free, to be enlightened, you had to let go of all of that.

But she thought . . . well, she thought it was just flirtation. She thought she kind of *was* his one and only. Sure, he had kids with other women before they came here; sure, he'd been in other relationships . . . but not *now*. Not with her in the picture. Not with her having his next baby. And Sophia? She didn't pick up that their relationship was that intimate. But then again, her and Sophia's paths barely crossed. They were both always teaching different workshops. They were usually on different chore rotations. Ben even assigned them to separate morning running groups. Was this deliberate?

Her body feels hot, then cold. She starts to tremble. "Maybe there's a reason her belly is . . . like that." She swallows hard. Toby puts his hands on his hips and gives her a level stare. She shuts her eyes. "Okay, if what you're saying is true—if she's *pregnant*"—she whispers this last part, ashamed that she's ashamed—"maybe there's a reason he's keeping her in that cabin. Like, maybe it's better for the baby?"

"A cabin with no heat or running water?" Toby's throat bobs as he swallows. "Would *you* like to be in there?"

"I . . ." Rebecca looks away. *No*, her mind screams. The conditions in Oregon are challenging enough. Her twin bed is too firm, nothing like her comfy bed at home. The house as a whole is too cold. The water is often not hot; it's difficult to bathe. It isn't a matter of money, either. According to Ben, ISB has tons of money. They could have all of it repaired, they could swap out better mattresses. It's the principle. *We can do hard things.*

Is it possible Sophia is even *more* principled? Like, she's chosen this cabin for herself as a test? She asks Toby this, but he shrugs. "I wanted to think that. But it almost seemed like she couldn't get out of the bed. Like she was . . . tied there. And, Bex, she looked miserable. Her skin was gray. There was nothing in that room. Just the bed. Certainly not any food. I don't think she chose it for herself. It's been a *month*."

"So what are you saying?"

"I've videoed Sophia enough. She can be outspoken. I think he's keeping her there because she challenged him, and he wants to control her," Toby whispers. "I think this is punishment, not reward."

Rebecca's heart twists. This doesn't make sense. She saw, from the window, Sophia getting into a car to go to the retreat—she looked fine, happy. Had she gone and come back? Or had she not gone at *all*? But why would Ben send her away? A horrible thought strikes her. She thinks of those little boys, Quentin and Adam, here without mothers. How their mothers aren't even *spoken* of.

Is Sophia hidden there because she's *pregnant*? It's certainly not like Ben announced *that* to the community yet, and if she's farther along than Rebecca is . . .

She pushes the thought to the side. That's ridiculous.

"If it's so bad, she could leave," she says to Toby, squaring her shoulders. "Walk out of there, go somewhere else. I mean, c'mon. Has Ben actually locked the doors? Is he actually holding her hostage?"

"Metaphorically, he is! Why don't any of us just leave? Why don't you? How easy do you think that could be? And I heard him talking to her, through the window. Telling her this was the right thing for her character and growth and all of that. That she needed to expunge her negativity, that it wasn't good for the group. It didn't feel right, Bex. None of it did. And . . . what if it happens to you, too?"

Rebecca's mouth feels dry, suddenly. So Toby came to the same conclusion she did: that this was some kind of hidden-away pregnancy thing. She shakes her head. "You must have this all wrong." She feels trapped in a dream, maybe, encased in a tomb. "Did you . . . did you *talk* to her?"

Toby shakes his head. "I wanted to. But then Ben shot out of there and saw me. He came out of the cabin before I could get away, and he saw the look on my face. He was *furious*, Bex. Said that I was too unevolved to understand what I was seeing, and if I told anyone, he'd release my secret."

She blinks at him. "Your . . . secret?"

Toby looks away and shrugs.

"What are you talking about?" Rebecca presses. "What secret does he know about you?"

Toby twists his mouth. "Come on. We all had to give one. Mine just isn't a permanent mark on my skin."

Rebecca swallows hard. She thinks of the first video she made, the one about her assault. She'd thought it was enough, actually, but shortly after they came here, Ben had asked for more.

"I need to know you on a deeper layer," he had demanded. "I need to know that I'm the one you trust the most. You need to go through something truly transforming, and I want it recorded for my posterity. Something painful, something that rocks the depths of your soul, to prove that you're my one and only."

"But I've already told you everything," Rebecca had protested. "There's nothing about me you don't know. I swear."

"Then make something up," Ben had said, shrugging. "Something that could really hurt someone were it to be released. About your parents, maybe. Your family. Someone you really, really love."

Rebecca had shivered, then. They were on Ben's bed, naked; she didn't have any covers over her because Ben liked to admire her body at all times. She didn't mind, and she loved Ben's attention, but sometimes she got cold. "But that would just be hurtful," she said, confused.

"It's not like I'm going to release it, my darling. That's not what this is about. It would only be between you and me. To show your devotion." He'd taken her hands and looked deeply into her eyes. "It's part of ascending to the next level of consciousness. The only way to get there is to chip away at yourself. To lay yourself bare. I want to go there with you."

But Rebecca couldn't think of any lies to tell that would ruin her or her family. So that's when Ben came up with the idea of putting a mark on her skin. Pushing a hot iron into her flesh with a design of his choosing—that would be her secret. It would prove she was his forever.

They came up with the brand's design together: an abstract zigzag that, if looked at a certain way, looked like the initials *ISB*. The day Rebecca was marked, Ben set up the camera in the corner of the room and hung a bright bulb from the ceiling that gave her a headache. Then he made Rebecca strip off her clothes and lie down on her back on a massage table. She remembers the goose bumps rising on her skin. The hot sizzle of the iron as it got warm under a flame. She also remembers the casual tune Ben hummed as he twirled the brand. He was enjoying this.

When it happened, she'd wanted to cry out in pain, but she was afraid it would make her look weak. The sensation seemed to stretch on forever—it felt like her whole *body* was burning. She bit down on her lip so hard she nearly chomped through it, and the next day, her calves ached from being tensed for so long. The smell of it made her want to puke.

"Say you're mine forever," Ben chanted above her as he pushed the iron into her skin.

"I'm yours forever," she said back, teeth clenched, tears in her eyes.

The site of the burn throbbed and oozed and sent spasms through her for minutes, hours after it was over. And yet, once she stepped off the table, she'd felt strangely exhilarated. It felt like the hardest thing she'd ever done, harder than death, and she'd gotten through it. Ben was keyed up, too. "I think this could be good," he said. "I think we should share this experience with the others. Slowly. One by one."

Rebecca blinked at him. She felt a little disappointed. She'd thought this was *their* thing, not something for the whole community.

But Ben kept going. "We'll all be linked. There are others who would benefit by going on this kind of journey. You can help them through." He held up the iron poker. "You will be their shepherd, guiding them into the light."

And Rebecca did it. For the first few women, her hand shook as she lowered the iron to their bodies. She felt like she was going to vomit. She wasn't sure she could actually go through with it. But there was Ben, always watching, and so she had to. Again and again.

Afterward, some of the women came to her with gratitude and appreciation, thanking her for being the one to give them the experience. Of course, there were also the women who looked at her, forever after, with resentment and betrayal. Even if they felt some catharsis or epiphany, even if they were all in on ISB and Ben, in the animal parts of their brains, they would always link Rebecca to that distinct, gasp-inducing pain. They hated her on a primal level, she could tell.

She looks up at Toby, wondering how long she was in her own head. Toby keeps talking. "My secret is about my grandma. I felt pushed in a corner, should have said *anything* other than what I said—because it's true. She could get in a lot of trouble, if she hasn't already."

"W-What is it?"

He shakes his head and looks away. "I don't want to get into it. Just some illegal stuff she was mixed up in . . . insurance fraud. She doesn't even know I know. I hate that I even told Ben, but he was pressuring me, and I couldn't think of anything else. If he finds out I told you, he'll release what happened for sure."

"So you're just going to leave instead?"

"Why would I hang around here? And you should leave, too. There's this contact on the outside. This woman named Kristen. She can hide people."

"What, in her house?"

"No, it's almost like witness protection. She finds places for people to live far away, where they can't be found. The trade-off is you can't talk to family . . . but, I mean, it's not like we're doing that anyway. And obviously you'd have no access to any of the money you made here. Although . . ." He looks away. "How do we even know we've *made* any money?"

"Of course we've made money!" Rebecca cries. "You know as well as I do how much the workshop packages we teach cost people! And the counseling, and the new classes we come up with . . . Ben set up accounts for all of us!"

"Have you actually *checked* your account lately? Or ever? How do you actually know there is an account at all?"

Rebecca crosses her arms. "You're saying he's scamming us? Ben takes care of our money, so what? He says it's compounding more and more by the day. He handles it because . . . Well, I sure as heck don't know anything about investing—do you?"

"Do you know your account number? The bank it's at? Anything?"

Rebecca blinks. She doesn't. But so what? Why does she need money right now anyway?

She trusts Ben. She *does*.

"Toby, this makes no sense," she says. "You're telling me you're going to leave . . . and go where? Also, if you go, Ben will still release the secret about your grandma anyway. Why not stay and try and work this out? Understand what's happening."

"It's hard to understand you're being brainwashed when you're right in the thick of it," Toby says, dejectedly. "It's hard to break through Ben's barrier. I don't *want* to stay, Bex. I don't give a shit about the money I made—because let's face it, the money isn't there. We're penniless *here*. My eyes are open, and I can't shut them again. If he releases that information about Gram—well, he's probably going to do it anyway. Even if I stay, even if I go. My only hope is that I get out and warn her before that happens. If she's still alive, that is. It's not like I've talked to her for months." They're quiet a moment, but then he adds, "So you won't even think about it? Coming with me, I mean?"

Just considering leaving fills Rebecca with trepidation. She doesn't know who she is without ISB and Ben. Her whole life is here. Where would she even go? Certainly not to her parents. They'd made it clear they don't care.

And her baby. The baby she's having *with Ben*. Pregnancy has been awful, but she sees the end result as so hopeful, a beautiful start for them. There's no way she could raise a child on her own. Who will she rely on? Ben's the one who knows everything.

But what if everything Toby told her is true? What if that cabin, just up that path—what if Ben plans to hide *her* there, next? A sick little incubator. Shut away, forced to gestate their child, and then . . . what? Also, Sophia is pregnant, too—and that stings. She can't be that much farther along than Bex is. So Ben is going to have *two* babies, then? Will hers even be that special?

Her head is spinning. She realizes Toby is staring at her, waiting for her to answer. She thinks of his grandma. He must have felt pushed to the brink to tell Ben that secret. His grandmother doesn't deserve to be exposed for whatever she's done.

"You go," she says quietly. "Get away if you need to. I won't tell anyone."

"But what about you?" He sounds heartbroken.

"I think it's easier this way." She places a hand on his arm. "But thank you for telling me."

"Wait," Toby says, before she can turn. He gestures to the house. "One-six-five-seven."

Rebecca blinks. "W-What's that?"

"The code to the video room. Your secret is on a USB. Find it. Don't leave it here."

Then he turns around and heads into the woods, leaving Rebecca stunned. It's the last time she'll see Toby, she's sure of it.

―

She's antsy the rest of the day, but she tries to hide it, especially around Ben. She has to do a few recruiting calls, following up with people who are interested but haven't yet joined ISB, and she puts on her best, most inspirational voice when she tells the well-worn stories of transformation, success, and enlightenment the group can bring. "We have so many people who were lost in their careers before following Ben's teachings," she says in a video call to a woman in her early twenties. "But now they've become so successful, either in their chosen career path or working with us and ISB. This way of life isn't about the money, but if you graduate to the Seedling level in the group, you're paid handsomely to share the wisdom with others."

But her words catch on that last bit: *paid handsomely*. She thinks of how Toby doubts the money is even in any of their accounts. *Is* it strange that Ben controls all of that and hasn't even shared account information with them? But Rebecca is barely out of high school. She never even had a bank account before this; her parents handled all of the finances. Letting Ben take over . . . well, it felt the same. The only difference was that she likes Ben. *Loves* him.

"Hello?" the woman on the other end of the video call says.

Rebecca jumps, realizing she'd trailed off midspeech. And then another wave of queasiness hits her, the baby reminding her that he's still alive and kicking. "Let's pick this up another time," she says hurriedly, and clicks off the call with just enough time to run to the hallway bathroom and slam the door before puking.

When it feels like everything is out of her, she looks at her cell phone. Ben has texted.

Check in.

She sits up and wipes her mouth. It's important that she respond within a certain amount of time, otherwise she's punished. Sometimes it's an early wake-up call. Sometimes it's a long run. Others, including Danny, must adhere to this regimen as well. It's good for their mental training.

She types a text back: *Here.* Then she sends another text full of lies about her amazing recruitment call that just happened. She expects Ben to praise her, but instead, he responds with a single sentence.

Have you seen Toby?

The phone trembles in her fingers. *No*, she types.

But then she regrets sending it. Can Ben tell she's lying? Rebecca isn't positive, but she suspects this place has hidden security cameras. What if one picked up her and Toby talking in the woods? What if someone saw them?

Ben doesn't respond. It makes her jittery and paranoid, but when she sees him an hour later at dinner, he's affectionate enough, though distant. But the news is circulating. Toby is gone. He left his cell phone at the door, walked through the gate, and hasn't returned.

At first, everyone else thinks this is an accident. They wonder if Toby is hurt. Except for Ben. Ben rampages around the compound, screaming at people, talking on his cell phone, demanding answers. He rounds up a few guys, younger people Toby hung around with, accusing them of knowing what really happened, calling them terrible names, names Rebecca has never heard come out of his mouth before—gross profanities about women's and men's bodies she doesn't even want to repeat in her mind. When they shake their heads and swear they have no idea what happened to him or why, Ben takes one of them by the shoulders and shakes him hard, screaming, "What did he say to you? What kind of lies came out of his mouth? And you better not have believed them!"

It's a side of Ben she's never seen. If Ben were truly blameless, would he be so up in arms and asking these questions? It might not mean Toby was right about what he saw with Ben and Sophia, but Toby must have seen *something* Ben feels guilty about. Afraid, even. Or maybe not afraid—fear is victimization—maybe just frustrated because it'll be misinterpreted?

She shivers and ducks around a corner before he can see her. Across the room, Danny stands at a sink, washing vegetables. She looks up and meets Rebecca's gaze for a split second, her eyes widening briefly with confusion. Rebecca looks away. Should she tell Danny she knows more than she's letting on? But what will Danny do with that information? Will she keep the secret . . . or will she turn Rebecca in to Ben?

She thinks of Danny's fervent, subservient expression as Ben went through his ritual with her the other day. Since coming here, she's become so devoted to ISB and Ben. Especially the Ben part. In Ben's presence, she showers him with praise, boasts about her progress, doesn't stray even a millimeter from his prescribed actions and behaviors. It's like what Rebecca suggested for her worked *too* well. She might choose Ben over Rebecca in this situation. Rebecca hasn't told her she's pregnant yet—Danny might seethe at that, might do something to spite her. At the very least, she'd tell Rebecca that Toby was wrong, that he misunderstood, that what he was saying was ridiculous—all the things Rebecca wanted to believe, too.

The thing is, she doesn't know why Toby would lie. He's not that kind of person, especially because of what's at stake—having the secret about his grandma come out *and* potentially losing all the money he earned here. Why would he make that up and make his life worse? So does that mean . . . *it's true*? She squeezes her eyes shut, wishing this were a dream. Ben is her everything. She doesn't want to doubt him. The thing she wants to check on—if he caught her, he would feel so betrayed. He might even cut her off. He might even . . . She hesitates before continuing the thought. Ben would never hurt her. Ben *loves* her . . . and their baby.

Does he love Sophia, too?

Her heart pounds as she slips out one of the compound's side doors. It seems like everyone else is caught up with Toby going missing—or else completely oblivious to it and working on their chores, or in ISB sessions—that not a single person notices. She darts to the wooded path where she and Toby had walked. She thinks she knows the path to the cabin, but she keeps on her hands and knees, in between the trees, on the off chance she catches someone on the trail. Twice, she hits the dirt when she hears a twig *snap*, terrified it's Ben—or anyone else, really, because they're all accountable to one another, and everyone is supposed to tell if someone is doing something out of line. Technically, she should have told on Toby—*immediately*.

But she didn't.

Finally, the brown structure rises into view. It's more dilapidated than Rebecca realized—the windows are cracked and look burned, the roof is caving in, and weeds have grown so high they block half the door. Surely no one is living here. It feels like such a mistake to have come that she spins on her heel and turns back for the compound. She can still salvage this. If Ben catches her now, she can claim she wanted a walk for the fresh air. She'll even tell him about Toby, maybe. What he told her, and his plans—as much as she doesn't want anything to happen to his poor grandma, her devotion lies with Ben, and she has to honor that.

Behind her, someone lets out a tiny cry.

She whirls around, her ears pricked. It's coming from inside the shed. She moves a little closer, edging through the grass. There it is again. It's a cross between a moan and a sigh. Rebecca scuttles to the half-broken window. It's covered in soot and dirt and spiderwebs, and the glass is so dirty it's almost impossible to see through. She cups her hands against it anyway and peeks inside. And she draws in a breath.

There's a dark shape of what looks like a bed in the middle of the room. Someone is lying in the bed, barely moving. She sees a tendril of dark hair falling toward the floor. *Sophia's* dark hair. As Sophia writhes, Rebecca sees her swollen stomach. A slightly louder moan sounds. Weakly, Sophia brings her hands to her face and tears them down the length of her cheeks. Her fingers are bone thin. She looks skeletal. The woman, Rebecca realizes, is barely clinging to life.

She presses her hands against the window. She needs to call out Sophia's name. She has to save her from this. Is she chained? Is she drugged? Her gaze darts to an overturned milk crate next to the bed. Is that . . .

a bottle on top? It has a cheerful red lid—the very same lid on the pills Ben now has *her* taking. Not vitamins, he told her. Not that bullshit doctors force on their patients to get kickbacks from big pharma. This stuff he made himself. All-natural, totally holistic. Actual healing chemicals to support mother and baby the *right* way.

Are they vitamins? Because she has felt so sick. And scattered. And *tired*. So much more tired than she even imagined. It could just be pregnancy symptoms. It *could*.

But what if it isn't?

But just as she's about to open her mouth, she hears footsteps on the path for real this time. Terror darts through her veins. She shoots from the window and ducks around the other side of the cabin, her heart in her throat. Voices carry from the trees—it's Ben and Vincent, who is Ben's go-to guy for everything. They're grumbling about something, and they bang noisily into the shed, sending the door flying against the outside wall loudly enough that Rebecca jumps. And though she can't see them inside, she certainly can hear what they're doing. The shouting. The banging. Sophia's crying. And then, the telltale sound of someone's hand hitting a cheek—or worse.

"*This is all your fault, you bitch!*" Ben screams. "*You are worthless! Beyond worthless! You have betrayed me, and you have betrayed everyone here, and you don't deserve this child! Never!* Ever!"

Sophia wails weakly from inside the tiny, terrible room. A rattling cough follows—it sounds like she doesn't even have enough energy to expel air from her lungs. Rebecca feels her knees buckle, and while she wants to help Sophia, she knows she needs to get out of there—*now*. Ben cannot know that she knows this. Ben cannot see her. *Otherwise, she might really end up in this shack, too.*

She tears down the trail like a wild animal. Mercifully, no one comes up the path and sees her, and she is able to return to her room unnoticed. But something makes her pause before going inside. Next to her room is Danny's. The door is open. Rebecca peeks in. Danny's bed is made, but she isn't there. Rebecca wishes she were. She needs to talk to her about this. Even if it gets her in trouble. That shack. Ben yelling those things. The sound of that *slap*, Sophia's death rattle cough. But maybe Danny wouldn't believe her. It hurts, realizing she can't trust Danny anymore. It's nothing Danny's done, is the worst part—it's Rebecca's fault she's even in ISB.

She sits down on her bed, hugs her torso, and starts to rock. What is she going to do? Should she help Sophia? *How?* Maybe Toby is going to get help? And can she really believe that if she stays, she'll be treated differently than Sophia? Sophia used to be *beautiful*. Way more beautiful than Rebecca. If Sophia didn't stand a chance, does she?

She doesn't know if she should sob or scream. Maybe she should escape, then. But the idea exhausts her; she has no idea how she might do it. The name Toby told her, Kristen, pops in her mind. *Like witness protection*, he'd said. The only Kristen she knows is an ISB member, a charismatic actress who started a chapter of the movement up in Seattle. She hasn't heard a thing about her since moving here . . . which is unusual, maybe, because Ben has started to involve Rebecca more in the ISB operations, including the branches. So . . . does that mean Kristen *isn't* part of the organization anymore? What happened? And was Ben angered that she left? Did he release *her* secrets?

Text Kristen, Toby had said. *She'll know what to do.*

Rebecca pulls out the cell phone she uses to answer Ben's orders. He hasn't made any requests of her at the moment—probably, she thinks with a wince, because he's still busy punishing Sophia. Does she dare use this phone to contact someone else on the outside? What if Ben is tracing it, somehow? What if Kristen is a setup? A mole on the inside, snuffing out the defectors? But then, Toby left. So maybe not.

Maybe she has to try.

With shaking hands, she scrolls through her phone and finds Kristen's number. Everyone in the ISB community has everyone else's numbers for easy access; they're all one big family. Her heart thuds fast as she sends the text.

Toby told me to contact you. I need help. Can you help?

It's like throwing a bomb. She expects alarms to go off, for the door to fly open and Ben or one of his devotees to tackle her. She imagines her body pushed to the ground, her baby squashed, her bones breaking. *Her baby.* She has to think of her baby.

But eerily, none of that happens. The compound is as still as ever. And then, a tiny *bloop* sounds from her phone.

You must follow my instructions to the letter. Delete this message after reading.

CHAPTER TWENTY-FIVE

For the next few days after Rebecca makes the decision to blow up her and her child's life at ISB, she waits.

And waits.

And waits.

Kristen says she'll text instructions, but they don't come. Every minute that passes, Rebecca fears she's made a terrible mistake.

Or that someone is going to find out.

She lies in her bed much of the time she isn't doing chores, barely able to contain her anxiety. It claws at her. It snaps beneath her skin. She can't tell if the nausea she feels is from morning sickness or panic—and that's without the pills Ben has been giving her. For the past two days, she's been only pretending to take them, slipping them under her tongue and feigning swallowing but then spitting them out when his back is turned and crushing them into her palm. She's examined their powdered contents, trying to figure out what they might be. Have they been making her sicker? She thinks of her baby swimming inside her and gets a twinge of grief. A pill that hurts her would hurt him, too, wouldn't it? *Why would Ben do that?*

She's also ambivalent and guilty. What if this is all a misunderstanding?

Is that possible? Maybe Sophia is doing this to herself on purpose? Maybe it isn't Sophia at all but some sort of . . . *animatronic*? Maybe this is a test, somehow—for *her*? And maybe, doing what she's about to do, she's about to fail. Is she making herself into a victim? Is she descending into weakness? In doing this, will Ben release her secrets? Will she be broke? Is it right to leave a child's father? Quentin and Adam seem okay . . .

But then her mind returns to their mothers. Was it simply a decision they made not to come, or did something more . . . *sinister* happen? Rebecca wishes she could get close to the boys and ask them, but what would she say? *So do you ever talk to your mommy? Do you remember your mommy at all? Was Daddy* . . . torturing *Mommy? Do you remember that, too?*

If she stays, what will happen to her and her baby? She can't feel the baby moving yet, but she pictures him growing bigger every day. Sprouting arms. Legs. Opening his eyes. Breathing in and out. He depends on her. She can't let him down.

As for Ben, Rebecca is astounded he can't sense her doubt and impending betrayal. Ben always claimed to be so in tune with people, so good at reading what people are feeling. Then again, he's distracted by the Toby situation. Since they've come to Oregon, no one has left the compound unannounced before. Sure, there were a few weekend visitors who didn't fit the vibe, and it was Ben who kicked them out. But Toby was an integral part of the group. Everyone is shocked that he deserted ISB. Now, the wagons have circled. Everyone is whispering. Some people are even crying—people who didn't even seem to know Toby. And Ben is taking Toby's leaving especially personally. It's been Rebecca's role to comfort him, among others. She's tried her best.

"He always seemed a little less than devoted, like he never completely believed in the cause," she told him last night in his room, while she lay naked on his bed. She felt a mix of guilt and confusion about Ben looking at her, touching her. She's supposed to hate this man, isn't she? Why is she still leaning in for his kisses?

"It's just such a bad PR issue," Ben grumbled. "I don't want him to give anyone the wrong idea about ISB's mission. Recruitment is up. We can't mess with that."

Rebecca nodded evenly, squashing down her reaction. Naturally, Ben wouldn't admit to her that the thing he feared most was what Toby would tell people about Sophia. In his mind, Rebecca had no idea about Sophia. Which swung the pendulum in her mind back to revulsion again. *You're holding a woman you got pregnant hostage in a cold cabin at the top of the hill,* she wanted to scream. Guru or not, that was just . . . fucked up.

Now, her phone chimes. She tries to lift her head from the pillow. The room spins. "Ugh," she moans. She looks at the screen. It's Kristen. Her stomach drops.

It's time. You have twenty minutes.

Rebecca's heart jumps into her throat. *Now?* She thought she'd have a little more warning. She thinks about the schedule. Where is Ben? Where are the others? Is it a weekend or a weekday? For a moment nothing is straight in her mind. *She can't do this.*

She forces herself to sit up. The room lurches but then steadies. She sucks in breath after breath. She imagines the blood rushing through her body, nourishing her baby. She's all he has. If Kristen says now, then it's now.

She dresses and steps into the hall. But then her gaze moves guiltily to Danny's open door. As usual, Danny's bed is empty; Rebecca guesses she slipped out of bed at four a.m. to start her run. It's when she used to get up, too, before she was pregnant. Now Ben lets her sleep a little later.

She feels a twist of dread. Is she really leaving Danny here? She's tried to talk to her friend several times over the past few days, hoping to give her some inkling of what was going on, but every time she worked up the courage to bring it up, she chickened out. She has only been able to ask tangential questions, things like, "Do you know what bank our funds are being held at?" (Danny had no idea, though she said she was sure Ben would tell her—he always said that they had access to all information whenever they wanted.) Or, "Where was that goddess retreat Sophia's at, again?" (Danny didn't know this either, but she stressed how amazing it probably was, and how Ben knew such incredible spiritual leaders.)

That's the problem. Danny's eyes light up whenever she sees Ben.

Even worse, last night, when Ben broke up their talk prematurely, Rebecca must have made some sort of disgusted face, because after he walked off, Danny looked at her sharply. "I don't like the way you're treating him," she said.

"Huh?" Rebecca blurted.

"It's like you don't appreciate what you have—and all the light he's brought to you."

Danny was right. Or was she wrong? *So* wrong? Rebecca felt muddled. She mumbled some excuse about her expression not being directed at Ben at all but something that was on her mind. Danny clucked her tongue. "Your mind doesn't seem particularly clear lately. Maybe you need to do a session with Barb—or better yet, Ben."

And have them pick open her brain until she spilled the truth? *No thank you.* The sessions are designed to wear a person down to their most vulnerable state only to build them back up again. Rebecca knows—she's been a session leader herself.

She shrugged. "You're right—I need to get my head clearer. I'll probably go on an extra-long run." Not that she would. Even before Toby told her about Sophia, she's been peeling off a few miles in, telling her running group she needs to make a bathroom stop and that they can go on without her. They trust her enough not to wait—she's Ben's chosen! Instead of continuing on her own, Rebecca would sit in the woods until the group circled back around, then fall back in with them, pretending she'd been running the whole time. Whenever she'd return, she'd clutch her lower belly, profusely apologizing to her baby for putting him through so much pounding.

Should she write Danny a letter? Warn her, somehow? But she looks at her watch. Kristen said *twenty minutes*. If she's really going to do this, if she's really going to save her baby and herself, she needs to go now. Besides, she doesn't even know where Danny is on the compound. There's no way she's going to just leave a letter in her room. Anyone could find it.

A sob rises in her throat. She hates leaving her friend here, but she has to think of her baby. *I'll come back for her*, she swears silently. *Once I'm safe, I'll make sure she's safe.*

And with that, she slips out into the hall. Though not before grabbing one thing first.

Kristen told her to bring nothing except the clothes on her back. *We can provide you some things*, read the text, before Rebecca deleted it and deleted *that* from her Deleted folder. It's not like she's brought much to this place anyway, but she still feels a sense of longing when she looks at the old, soft sweatshirt from high school, and the stuffed rhinoceros her mom gave her when she was a kid that she still likes to sleep with. There are items that remind her that not everything here has been bad, too: the trail running shoes tossed in a corner, which logged hundreds of miles on them, most of them over beautiful terrain. Running has been a salve here. There's her gardening hat, too, and she thinks of all the days she spent on her hands and knees in the soil, laughing and singing with the other women—including Danny. The community here is good. It isn't all terrible. Could she just stay? Is there some sort of workaround?

Then she thinks of something else Toby said. She steps into the hall, walks to the end, makes a left. The door to the video room is shut, and the lights are off. Ben uses the room to make videos for the workshops, but from what Toby indicated, it's also where their secrets are stored.

There is a keypad next to the knob. Rebecca looks right and left; the hallway is empty. She sucks in a breath, and then taps the digits Toby told her. *One. Six. Five. Seven.* A green light glows, and she hears the lock release.

The inside of the room is dark and humming. There are a few security screens overhead, views of places Rebecca didn't even know Ben was watching, like the library just down the hall from this room. The library is empty now. There's a fire burning in the fireplace, the sun slanting gently across the floor. It looks oddly peaceful, so incongruous to Rebecca's racing heart and churning thoughts.

She eyes a laptop on the desk, some organized files, and then a small cabinet with tiny drawers to the right. The drawers look USB sized, and when Rebecca slides one open, that's exactly what's inside. Her guts twist. Could all their secrets really be *here*? It's terrifying, the idea that they're loaded and ready. One false move, and they'll be released to the world.

She touches the drive on top. It's labeled with initials, *PM*, but doesn't know what it means. She riffles through more; there are others with initials as well, but she doesn't see on labeled *RR*, her own. She keeps digging.

Then, a flash on the security camera catches her eye. She stands up, squinting. One of the men, Bailey, has just walked into the library. It's so *close*. What if he hears her?

Rebecca tears open another drawer of USBs, scanning the initials on each. *SF. JO. BGB.* Not hers, not hers, not hers. *GG. MQR. FV.* Some of these initials are those of women who are on the compound—are they their secrets? Their *brands*? She thinks of Toby behind the camera, filming their branding sessions, and a terrifying thought strikes her heart. If the branding ceremonies are on these thumb drives, then *she* is also on these thumb drives. As the one doing the branding. Again. And again. And again.

Her hand flies to her mouth. She's implicated in so many of these. If she leaves, Ben might release one in retaliation. Maybe he'll twist things to make it look like it was all her idea. Her heart sinks. She's doomed. Can she steal *all* of them?

She eyes the library cam. To her horror, Bailey is now frowning at something just outside the library. Does he hear *her*? She watches as he walks toward the arched door. She has to get out of here. Bailey cannot see her. She has no idea if he has access to this room, but if he thinks something weird is going on, he'll alert the others—he's loyal like that. *Everyone* here is.

She looks at the USBs again. She doesn't have time to gather them all up. Then, her gaze lands on a thumb drive marked *DM*. She swallows hard. *Danny Martin.* Her hand flies out; she grabs it, stuffs it into her pocket, and then closes the drawer before she can talk herself out of this. She twists the doorknob and slides out of the media room mere seconds before Bailey steps around the corner from the library. It takes every ounce of control to walk calmly and casually past him.

"Hello," she says. Bailey smiles back. Rebecca lets out a breath.

Next, she walks with purpose into the kitchen, where she finds

Freddy, the community's dog. He's a spry, fit Labrador retriever, healthy from swims in the nearby lake and walks and runs with all of the residents. He looks up hopefully when he sees Rebecca walk in.

"Hey, buddy," she murmurs. "Want some exercise?"

The dog rises, tail wagging. But first, Rebecca must ask permission. She pulls out her phone and writes to Ben: *Okay to walk Freddy?*

Even though Ben is teaching right now, dots appear right away. *Yes. But only for twenty minutes. Check in when you are back.*

Rebecca breathes out. Hurdle number one, done. Twenty minutes is plenty of time. Though instead of slipping her phone into her jacket pocket, she places it in a kitchen drawer, all the way to the back. It takes her a moment to actually close the drawer. It's been so long since she's been separated from her phone.

But she won't need it where she's going.

Her hands shake as she reaches for the dog's leash on a hook by the door. Perhaps to anyone else passing by, she seems upbeat as she coos to the dog and maneuvers him outside. She gulps in fresh air and tries to fight back tears. It's like her body is moving without her, on autopilot. She finds herself walking toward the woods, as Kristen instructed in her first series of messages the other day. *When I tell you to go, there will be a phone planted in a knot of a tree with a branch that curls around like the letter J.*

Rebecca knows this tree. She's spent so much time outside that she knows all the trees. She gets to it and looks around, terrified that someone is watching. The woods are eerily silent; the only sounds are birdcalls and the wind. Taking a deep breath, she plunges her hand into the knot. When she touches hard, cold plastic, her heart races. The phone is actually here. She pulls her fingers away. What if it's a setup? How could Kristen have gotten back on the property? Is this a test?

The woods are still so quiet. After another minute of breathing, she reaches into the knot again and pulls out the phone. It's an ordinary flip phone. Probably a burner.

The dog pants patiently as Rebecca, hands shaking, turns the phone on. It's slow to boot up. Every snap of a twig, every gust of wind, she looks up in terror, certain she's been found out. Finally, a list of contacts appears. There are only two numbers: Kristen's and a cab company's.

A bead of sweat rolls down Rebecca's forehead. This is next on the list of instructions. Her hands are so sweaty she can barely hit the button to call. The phone rings once, twice, and then a voice blares so loud through the receiver that Rebecca startles.

"JoJo at JoJo's Cab Company. Can I help you?"

Rebecca just stares at the phone. JoJo's voice seems to echo through the woods, a beacon.

"Hello? Someone there?"

"Uh, yes," Rebecca says, her voice sounding croaky. "C-Can you send a cab to pick me up at highway marker seventeen in Freeborn?"

"Mile marker?" JoJo sounds skeptical. "You mean, like, on the side of the road? You break down or something? Need a tow?"

Of course this seems bizarre to a cabbie. "Um, no. Or, well, I've got it covered. But right now, I just need a ride. Mile marker seventeen. Can you do it?"

"Sure, we can do it. On our way."

Rebecca claps the phone shut and stares crazily into the middle distance. There's no turning back now. But she knows there are another few steps she needs to accomplish.

She steels herself, grips the dog's leash hard, and marches toward the front gate, which is the only way out with the dog. There's a huge chain link fence around the rest of the property, and it's regularly monitored for gaps or holes for Freddy's safety as well as Ben's two boys. The adults are allowed to request permission to leave through the front gate to walk the dog or go on their regular runs on pavement. And so Rebecca strides there, acting like this is all no big deal. But then she sees who's on guard today. *Barb.*

Don't be afraid, don't be afraid. They all have to take guard duty every once in a while, even Barb—but she has such a tight bond with Ben as one of the earliest adopters of ISB and a creator of many of its philosophies. Barb, who never married, with her marathon-runner body, short haircut, and keen, narrowed eyes, lives and breathes ISB and its tenets. She was the one who found this compound, and she acts kind of as a den mother to everyone here, though half the members are afraid of her because of all the power she holds. Rebecca has witnessed plenty of Barb's counseling sessions; she's scarily good at eking out negative feelings and vulnerabilities in people. It's pretty obvious most of the members figure Barb reports what they say straight to Ben. Surely, Rebecca thinks, *her* finances aren't in some nameless account only Ben knows about.

Today, Barb sits in the gate house, a little shack at the front of the fence that contains a phone, a radio, a portable heater, and a motorized button to open and close the gate at will. There's also a gun in there. Ben prepped all of them it was there and showed them how to use it; he said that it was primarily for wild animals, as the woods were full of bears.

Rebecca can't stop thinking of the gun now.

Her feet crunch on the crushed gravel. Barb looks up, and Rebecca tries to smile. "Keeping us safe, Barb?" she says in a cheerful voice.

Barb smiles back. "No safer place, babe."

"Enjoying gate duty?" *Make chitchat*, the text had said.

"Just trying to relax," Barb says.

"You feeling okay?" Rebecca asks.

"Sure."

But when Barb meets her gaze, there's a flicker of pain in her eyes. Everyone has heard about how valiantly Barb cured herself of cancer using ISB's techniques. But now that everything else about ISB has been thrown into doubt, Rebecca can't help but notice that Barb's skin seems awfully pale, and her sweatshirt hangs on her.

Barb's gaze darts to the dog. "Ben not taking this big lug himself?"

"He's tied up. Requesting permission to take him over to the meadow."

"He didn't alert me of that . . ."

A tense moment passes. Will Barb call him to check? Rebecca didn't ask Ben to leave the property; they have to do so explicitly, and she feared that saying she was leaving the area would tip him off. Barb will catch her in a lie.

But then, mercifully, Barb shrugs. "Sure he forgot. This Toby thing's thrown us all for a loop."

Rebecca nods. "I know it."

"You were close to him, huh?"

Barb doesn't seem to be looking at her suspiciously, but Rebecca feels a chill go through her all the same. "We went to high school together," she says carefully. "But I have no idea what he was thinking." Then she puts her hands in prayer pose, a gesture she adopted from Ben. "Strength be your guide." Their catchphrase.

"And yours," Barb says, copying the gesture.

And with that, to Rebecca's astonishment, Barb pops her head back into the little booth, turns to the button, and the motorized gate groans open.

"Enjoy, bud," Barb says to Freddy. She sends Rebecca a wink, too. A wink that almost seems . . . *conspiratorial.* Rebecca is puzzled for a moment—and then backs away without telling Barb goodbye. She regrets not doing that, when she looks back on this later. In a week's time, Barb will be dead.

Rebecca walks quickly away—though not *too* quickly. Down the dirt road, past the rows of trees—she can see the meadow in the distance. She glances over her shoulder and is astounded to see that Barb's head is bent down—she's reading her book, not even *watching.*

Walk 200 paces. Look for the stone in the ground marked 009.

After walking about two hundred steps, her feet land on something harder, with less give. She glances over her shoulder again to make sure Barb isn't watching, then crouches down and plunges her hand into the nearest bush. Her fingers close around something cloth. She pulls it out, and she lets out a sigh of relief. It's the go bag Kristen described. She dares to peek inside and sees bottled water, a change of clothes and shoes, toiletries . . . and *money.* Rolled-up bills at the very bottom.

Dust rises from the road ahead. Rebecca's eyes boggle. *The cab.*

She presses her hand over her mouth to contain both her joy and her deep, extreme sadness. She doesn't want to do this. She's abandoning the only family she's really felt close to. She's never going to be able to see them again. She knows it.

But then she thinks about the baby rolling around inside her. Despite her nausea, she feels clearer today. A burst of optimism shoots through her—she can *do* this. She has to.

She checks over her shoulder one more time. She can't see the guardhouse from here, which means the cab is out of Barb's view, too. She crouches down to the dog and pats his big head. "Okay, Freddy," she whispers. "Good boy." She wishes she could take him along, but she rolls up the note she wrote before she left and wedges it between the ring in his collar. "Go back," she says, swishing her hand toward the compound. "Go on. Find Ben."

The dog gives her an uncertain look, but when she tells him to go back again, he seems to understand and slowly trots back toward the compound. "Go!" Rebecca whispers to herself, sad she won't see Freddy ever again . . . but also anxious, terrified, and a tiny bit empowered about what she's written on the note for Ben. She pats the flash drive in her jacket pocket. She hopes it's enough.

Don't look for me. And don't release any videos. If you release anything of me, I have enough to ruin you, too.

CHAPTER TWENTY-SIX

Danny is on a break from her duties when she overhears the news.

She is in the potting shed, where she likes to go to think and get away from the others. Not that she doesn't like the others. They're fine. They're her family—and sometimes, she even feels that. But it seems like there are always people everywhere, and sometimes she just wants to be alone. She also likes the earthy, funky way the shed smells, and the way the light slants in through the breaks in the wood slats, and how quiet it is in here, quiet enough for her to gather her thoughts.

It's been a weird few days with Toby taking off. Came out of nowhere, that, and now everyone is touchy, especially Ben. Some of the workshops have even been canceled. They've had extra counseling sessions and emergency meetings to talk through feelings about why Toby did this . . . as well as reminders about the rules of the community. When they came to Oregon, Ben and a few of his male seconds-in-command like Carson and Vincent explained, they signed on to stay. There were certain conditions that would allow a person to leave and fulfill their ISB duties elsewhere, but those must be discussed with Ben beforehand—which Toby had not. Abandoning the compound in Oregon meant a breach of trust. By leaving, Toby's secret, whatever it might be, was now vulnerable.

It had sent an uncomfortable ripple through the crowd.

But Danny isn't rattled. They signed on for this. All of them. Yes, they'd given up secrets, but so had Ben—they are all in this together. She can't wrap her mind around what Toby was thinking. Then again, she's drifted from Toby since they came to Bend. She hasn't meant to; it's more like she went one way, and Toby went another. For Danny, it's been diving wholeheartedly into ISB and her Seedling duties. For Toby . . . well, clearly he became less invested.

Part of her wonders why he even came. Because he had nothing better to do? Clearly he took advantage of Ben's genius and goodwill. It pains her to think that Ben might be taking his leaving personally. She hates the idea of *anyone* hating Ben—deep down, he's quite sensitive. During a meeting last night, when he looked particularly forlorn, she wanted to rush over, wrap her arms around him, and tell him that this was the most amazing community ever. That they were building something new all because of *him*, and they were helping so many people all over the world, and that they felt so happy and fulfilled and powerful and strong. Who cared about one dumb kid who decided to leave? What did it matter? Ben, the Scion, was amazing. He shouldn't forget that.

Of course, Danny didn't get the chance to even talk to Ben last night. There were a lot of other women around him instead. And the woman closest to him was Bex.

Danny's feelings about Bex make her uncomfortable. Jealousy isn't a quality Ben encourages; it's just another way to make oneself a victim. And yet, seeing Bex in Ben's golden light feels like same-old same-old, same shit different day, not that different from seeing Rebecca as she'd been in high school, stepping out of the new car her parents bought for her or easily acing a math test or effortlessly attracting a group of friends. It all comes so naturally to Bex . . . but at the same time, does Bex even *believe* in ISB? Does she even like this kind of modest living, coming from her huge house and all her possessions? Does she like teaching and learning as much as Danny? Has this place transformed her into someone better, cleaner?

It has for Danny. Even that branding ceremony, though extremely strange, was transcendent in hindsight. She is part of something. She has confidence overflowing. She can do hard things, just like Ben says. It makes her feel like a badass. If only that were more acknowledged. Just a little. Like, if they were to be graded on who changed the most and worked the hardest, Danny has to be up there at the top of the leaderboard for sure.

Footsteps sound on the other side of the wall. Danny freezes. "Ben?" someone calls.

It's Vincent's voice. He's one of the older members of the community, often leading the group runs. It's also rumored that he pumped a lot of cash into ISB at its beginnings because he comes from a wealthy mining family. Not that ISB needs any financial support these days.

"What is it?" Ben asks.

Danny sits up straighter. Ben is right outside this little building. She shifts to the wall and looks through a tiny crack, and there Ben is, handsome in his plaid coat and hat, staring hard at Vincent. Should she show herself? Go outside? She doesn't want to seem like she's spying . . .

"I've been trying to find you." Vincent looks frazzled. "Something's happened."

The two men start to whisper. Danny still wonders if she should go out. She swears she hears *security system* . . . and then *Freddy*. As in . . . the dog?

"There's no way she'd do this," Ben says through his teeth. "Have you tried calling?"

"Yeah, and there was no answer."

Ben groans and squeezes his eyes shut. "This is exactly how it happened with Toby."

Toby? Danny grapples with what could be going on. Is someone else gone? That seems impossible.

"Try again," Ben says. "Put it on speaker."

Vincent dials. After three rings, a connection is made. "Hello?" a voice calls out, with uncertainty. It sounds like Rue.

"Who is this?" Ben demands.

"I-It's Rue. Is this . . . Scion?" She sounds afraid.

"Why are you answering Rebecca's phone?"

Rebecca? Danny gasps. No. No *way*.

There's a confused pause. "I'm so sorry, Scion. It was just in a drawer . . . in the kitchen? I was wondering where the ringing was coming from—I'm sorry, Scion. Was I not supposed to answer it?"

There's a *beep* as Vincent hangs up. Then silence. The men stare at each other. Then Ben says, "Don't just *stand* there. We need to talk to whoever's on gate duty. Who is it today?"

"Barb, I think."

Ben groans.

"As far as the note goes," Vincent says, and then clears his throat awkwardly. "Tech came to me earlier. Apparently, the door was breached. And there is a missing . . ." His voice drops to a whisper again. Through her crack in the wall, Danny sees Ben turn very, very pale.

What is missing?

"And you just thought to tell me about this now?" Ben roars.

"I'm sorry, Scion. I thought it was just misplaced."

"What about her parents?" Ben asks. "Maybe they know something."

"I have Carson trying to reach them now." There's a pause, and then a digital *bloop*. "Speak of the devil. Okay . . . Carson says that they haven't spoken to her in months."

"*Months?*" Ben sounds puzzled. (Danny is, too. Why wouldn't Bex talk to her parents? They're *part* of ISB.) "Call them back. Keep calling them. Tell them that this could be very, *very* bad for them if there's something they're not telling us."

Danny's mind swirls. It makes no sense. Bex would never betray the group, and on the heels of Toby leaving . . . it takes her breath away. And Bex just heard Ben's speech about the ramifications of abandoning ISB. If she leaves, Ben releases her secrets.

And also . . . Bex is leaving *her*. Danny's her best friend. But maybe Bex doesn't care about that anymore.

Maybe Danny doesn't know her at all.

She doesn't know what to do but go back to her bunk, sit there, and wait. Part of her thinks Bex will be in the room next door, safe and sound, but her side of the room is empty. If she's gone, she's taken nothing with her, at least not from what Danny can tell. She just doesn't understand why this is happening. Why wouldn't Bex have said something? Aren't they friends?

A knock comes. The door opens before she can speak; Ben pokes his head in. She rises to her feet, startled and a little nervous. Ben makes a leveling motion with his hands. "It's okay, Danielle. Sit," he says, and then comes to the bed and sits down next to her. *Sits down right next to her, on her bed.* Danny doesn't dare move. Ben has never been in her room before. Her heart pounds in her ears.

For a moment, he just stares at his lap. His shoulders heave.

"I . . . heard something," she dares to whisper. "About . . . Bex."

Ben nods, ever so slightly.

"I swear I didn't know," Danny pleads. "I've been sitting here, wondering why myself. Wondering why she'd leave this . . . paradise."

Ben turns to her, his expression turning even more serious. "I need to know I can believe you when you say that to me. But look at it logically. She was your best friend. I have to assume you know something. You knew Toby, too."

"I don't." Tears fill Danny's eyes. "I swear. Bex . . . I mean, we talked, but I'd been doing my thing, and she'd been doing hers . . . I thought she was *fine*." Is this true? She isn't sure. She looks down, feeling like she needs to be honest. "Looking back, it didn't seem like she was as committed. Just little things, here and there. But she never said anything to me, I swear. This is totally out of nowhere."

The reading lamp throws hard shadows across their faces. Ben looks angular in this light, dark circles under his eyes. "I found out some information about things she took when she left. It looks like she snapped."

"What did she take?" Danny thinks about what she'd overheard. Something about a note. Something about tech.

Ben waves his hand. "Nothing important. To be honest, she was sick. Very sick. And Toby leaving—maybe it's not a coincidence. We think maybe he got to her, somehow."

"Sick . . . how?" Danny gasps.

"In the way most people are. In the way you often can't see. I was helping her fight against it, harness that inner strength. Those who are truly focused can battle any illness inside them, even something mental. But I don't think Bex was particularly strong, in the end."

Danny nods. In their early sessions, beyond Ben talking about her autoscopy, they drilled into Danny's own sickness, which manifested itself as self-doubt, laziness, resentment. It's so easy for her to slide back into those patterns of thinking, so it's a choice to be well. Part of the ISB philosophy is that everyone is overcoming their own sicknesses; she just didn't realize Bex was really struggling with anything.

"She's self-sabotaging," Ben says sadly. "And leaving . . . it's the ultimate sabotage to the self. Basically, it's suicide."

A tear falls down Danny's cheek. "I'm so scared for her."

He pats her hand. "It's okay. We'll find her. But for the moment, things are gonna change around here—for you, Danielle. Looks like there's an opening with your name on it."

"An . . . opening? What do you mean?"

He smiles sadly. "As a matter of fact, I've had big plans for you for a while. They've just gotten fast-tracked."

Danny blinks. Does Ben mean what she thinks he means? Is this an invitation to . . . *the inner circle*? A mix of emotions overtakes her. Guilt . . . but also elation . . . *validation*, but also apprehension. It's uncomfortable to think she might benefit from Bex disappearing. And yet . . .

She sucks in a breath. "I'm not sure if I'm ready."

"Of course you are." He stares into her eyes. "Don't limit yourself." Then his phone beeps. He stands without checking it, though he's now holding the hand he'd previously patted. "Tomorrow, your life is going to change."

CHAPTER TWENTY-SEVEN

BEND, OREGON
PRESENT DAY

It's been hours. Danielle is officially off the grid. Out of contact. Out of touch. Not checking in like she said she would. Providing absolutely no updates. Maybe Ben should have never trusted her. His suspicions were correct. She's weak. She's sick. She'll never be able to take care of a child of her own, that's for sure.

But fine. It's fine. He can resort to other methods to find her.

Swiveling to his computer, he pulls up the tracking screen and refreshes the feed. Ah. There she is. Her phone blinks red on the map, a stable dot. Carson City, Nevada. Same place she was the last time he checked. Right where he needs her to be.

Well. Not exactly. She's not at the house anymore. About two hours ago, the dot traveled to a coffee place. Then, the dot moved to some kind of corporate building. It contains offices for an osteopath, an MRI scanning facility, and an ob-gyn, among other things. But Ben can't believe it. Is Danielle at a *doctor*? Did Rebecca convince her to do this? Her care is *here*, with them. Not from some quack. Some charlatan filling her head with terrible ideas.

His blood boils. He texts her again. *Check in, please. Now.*

Still no answer. To temper his annoyance, Ben drops to the floor and does a few push-ups. *Eight. Nine. Ten.* Anything to refocus. Anything to get the control back.

He thinks of the original plan. Danny would travel to Carson City, where they'd tracked Rebecca down. There, she'd disarm Rebecca enough with cheerful kindness and get into her house. Ben's hope was that Danielle could get in and out with what she needed, but if she had to stay longer, that was okay, too. As long as she got out of there with the child.

But already, things feel shaky. Why isn't she answering? She'd insisted she could get the job done. Swore Rebecca meant nothing to her anymore and that she could lie to her easily. But there has always been something about Rebecca that breaks Danny down. Eight years ago, when Rebecca was a dependable member of his community, Danny listened to her extra closely, always wanting to do whatever Rebecca did. It was probably why Danny met with Ben in the first place—because Rebecca was already part of ISB. At the time, Ben thought it was a *good* thing because Rebecca was such a positive influence.

That last day Ben saw Rebecca, he would have never guessed what she was planning to do. He thought Toby had no influence over her. It had stunned him. She was one of his best, a real beacon, a *model student.* He never thought she would have it in her, not considering all she had to lose.

He looked for her for a long time after she abandoned the group—both because of the threat she'd made and also because of what she'd stolen. Months passed. *Years.* He'd seethed. He'd threatened all those who'd left who could still be swayed. Said he'd release their security deposits to the world, said he'd cast them out, promised to harm their families, their loved ones, but they all swore they didn't have any information. Not Danny, not the other women Rebecca had bonded with, not even Rebecca's parents, who seemed more blindsided than even he was.

But Toby—Ben always suspected that kid was the key. Even before he absconded, the guy had always flown under the radar, lurking in the background, barely speaking, not really providing much benefit to the group. Ben didn't even know why he'd allowed him to join the community here, really—sure, he was a Seed technically, but he wasn't taking the proper courses and workshops to grow into a Seedling. Ben wasn't even that sad when he took off, not really. It was only once he realized the guy had taken something valuable of his—*and* that he'd spread misinformation—that he'd grown much angrier. He should have never allowed that kid to be around any of the videos or equipment. Especially now that he knows who he gave that footage to. *Rebecca.*

Only after he found out about Danielle having his child did his mind start working about Toby and Rebecca again. Suddenly, it was absolutely unconscionable that they were both out there. It lit a new flame under him, and he went on an all-out search—not for her, though, but for Toby. Toby would be easier to find. Toby had less to lose.

As it turned out, it was easier than he ever expected—a tech guy had been searching for him far and wide and finally found the kid posting gaming videos on YouTube. He probably thought he was in disguise with that different hairdo and glasses and posting under a fake name, but it all made Ben snicker. He had a few IT experts in his back pocket, and they traced the computer Toby was posting from in half an hour. And then, Ben had started to prepare.

He knew Toby would lead to Rebecca. He knew he could shake him down. But someone must have tipped the guy off about what Ben had in mind, because two weeks ago, he released the video talking about the community. It was absolutely a kamikaze effort—the guy would have never made himself such a target if he hadn't known they were already coming. Ben had gotten the alert about the live stream as he was in the car with the others on the way to Toby's house. IT guys were able to take it down about an hour after it posted—just about the time they got to Toby's front door—but Ben seethed at the damage it might still do. If he were to believe YouTube, which he wasn't sure if he did, twenty thousand people had viewed it. He had his guys monitoring all the social media channels to make sure no one had recorded snippets and reposted them or leaked anything to reporters. There were Discord groups and Reddit threads to troll. The fucking work and money he had to shell out, all because of this stupid kid. He was fired up by the time he got there. Now he had even more reasons to punish the little fucker. He'd stolen one more thing: Ben's reputation.

Ben didn't go inside Toby's house when it all went down. He remained in the car, listening. When it was all over, the world wouldn't be hearing from Toby again. As for the Toby part of it, that was easy enough to clean up—his guys were pros. Nobody even missed him, probably. His grandmother had died a few years back. Dude had online followers, but no family, no friends. No one to file a police report.

As for the video . . . well, no one had yet heard from reporters. Maybe they'd dodged a bullet. And they were able to get Rebecca's address, too— exactly what they'd come for. The plan was back on track, for the most part.

But the plan will only work, Ben thinks, if she *follows through*.

Ben finishes his push-ups and sits back on his knees. He hates mistrusting his own people. It's why they are all here, together—they're stronger as a group, without the influences and lies the outside world can force upon them. More than that, they're more *joyful* as a group. Ask any of the women out the window in the fields. Look how happy they seem, pulling the weeds! Look at their lithe, light bodies, their broad smiles! Look at how they smile upon one another, bonded for life, *sisters*! Danielle has been so faithful, too . . .

The phone rings, and he jumps. It's her. Finally.

"Where have you *been*?" he shrieks.

"I have him," Danny shouts into the speaker. The sound on her end is grainy. "I have him, and we're driving. I did it."

Ben drops to his knees, he feels so grateful. He looks at the computer again. The dot is moving quickly. Right toward the target, in fact.

"I did it, Scion," Danielle repeats. "It wasn't easy, but I did it."

"She made you go to a doctor, though, didn't she?"

"Yeah. I had to. I needed to earn her trust. It's not like I listened to his advice. I hardly let him do anything."

Ben grits his teeth. He's not thrilled that Danielle saw a doctor, but he'll have to let it go. "I was worried you were getting lost again. Getting foggy."

"No. It's good. I'm clear. Very clear, Scion."

Then, a thin, high-pitched voice sounds from Danny's end. "Where are we going?"

Ben's hand flutters to his mouth. It's *him*.

"Don't worry, honey," Danielle says to the boy. "We're fine."

"Why are you driving so fast?" The boy sounds worried.

"Be careful," Ben tells her. "Don't do anything rash." The last thing he wants is for her to crash the car with his son in the back.

"I won't," Danielle says. "I'm not far from the meeting point anyway. Is everything in place?"

Ben hurriedly clicks the mouse on another window on his computer, a chat with Kris, who's been waiting for his signal. All he needs to do is send one text. "Yes. You have the directions?"

"I do."

Out the window, some women pass by. Smyrna turns toward the glass and sees him. Her expression first grows nervous, like that of a slacking-off pupil in school. She straightens her posture. Sucks in her abdomen as best she can. Then she smiles at him. It's a dutiful smile. She's probably thinking of the ritual set for tonight. Ben hopes he can still make it. The world seems right again.

"Good," he says to Danielle. "I'm proud of you. This is for the best, you know?"

"I know," Danielle answers. "I'll see you soon."

CHAPTER TWENTY-EIGHT

CARSON CITY, NEVADA
PRESENT DAY

Tom swings into the driver's seat. Helplessly, Rebecca climbs into the passenger's side and slams the door shut. She glances at her baby son in the back in his rear-facing baby seat. Only by the little mirror propped up can she see his drowsy expression. The storm happening in their lives doesn't affect him at all.

Tom guns the engine, his jaw clenched. "You don't have to do this," she cries. "She's so far ahead already."

Tom's eyes flash. "What am I going to do, just sit here? I have to try. He's my son, too."

Rebecca can feel his disdain in her bones. She hates that he's learned about her past this way. She hates the way he's looking at her now like he doesn't know her. And most of all, she hates the mistake she's made.

"I should have known this was going to happen," she moans. "She set me up. She lied to me. I thought she was here because . . . because she was scared, and I felt for that. I just . . . I heard she was pregnant, and I just snapped. I wanted to help her."

A muscle twitches in Tom's jaw. "I wish we would have talked about this before you did anything. I mean, I thought your past was . . . I don't know." At the stop sign at the end of their road, he looks right, then left. "Do you have any idea where they might have gone?"

Rebecca shakes her head.

"Great." Tom slaps his thighs. "Maybe we should call the cops?"

Rebecca chews on her lip. "Maybe." But that would mean exposing her past to everyone, not just Tom. His parents. Their neighbors. Kids at Roscoe's school. Though why does it matter anymore? If it could get Roscoe back. Only, *would* the cops be able to find him?

Then an idea cuts through the noise. "Wait. My car keys. They're still in the car."

"Obviously. That's how she's driving."

"They have a tracker tile on them. Remember?"

Tom's eyes widen. "Oh."

Rebecca pulls out her phone and taps the screen for the tracker app. She bought a tracker for both their car keys when Roscoe was going through a race car driver phase; he loved stealing their keys and pretending he was a driver himself. Soon enough, a map appears on the screen.

"There she is!" Rebecca cries, pointing at the moving dot. "She's heading up Baker!"

"Got it," Tom says, gripping the wheel.

They follow the dot as it moves. Danny is still at least a mile ahead of them, though. Once they're on Baker, which Danny still hasn't turned off of—where is she *going*?—Tom clears his throat. "So. It really is a cult?"

She takes a deep breath and nods through the tears. "Yeah."

Tom goes hard over a pothole. Rebecca's gaze darts to the back seat again, but Charlie seems fine with all the jostling. "And that Ben guy . . . how in the world did you get mixed up with him?" Tom asks next.

"It's a long story. My parents . . . they were part of it first."

"Is that why you don't talk to them?"

"I don't talk to them because they only care about themselves and they always have. But I also *can't*. They might still be involved, and I don't want anyone from there to know where I am. I *fled*, Tom. I found out Ben was sleeping with everyone and poisoning the pregnant women and . . . and I don't know what else. I didn't know what he had in store for me and Roscoe. There was this woman there, hidden in a shed, a few months farther along than I was—I had no idea she was even pregnant. As soon as I saw that, I was gone."

"Jesus," Tom whispers.

There's traffic at a light. They can still track the dot on the app, but Rebecca doesn't like that Danny is getting farther away. *Please, please keep my baby safe*, she prays to the universe, thinking of Roscoe as Danny's prisoner in the back seat. What must he be thinking?

She looks at Tom. "I literally left with the clothes on my back and a go bag and had to break out of the compound. It was awful. This ex-member sent me a bus ticket to Carson City and a little bit of cash and a list of apartment rentals with management companies that asked no questions and didn't care about background checks. Today, I thought maybe that's what was happening with Danny. Like, maybe he'd hurt other pregnant women, too, and she figured that out and got scared for her and her baby. But I was wrong."

"You sure as shit were." Tom glares at the stopped traffic ahead. "So how *did* they find you now? If you were doing such a good job staying hidden."

Rebecca sighs. "Toby. He was part of the group, too, but he was the one who warned me that terrible stuff was going down. After I settled here, but before I met you, I was lonely. The ex-member set me up on this messaging app—you could chat securely, and your messages would vanish after they were read. It was less likely to be traceable that way. I messaged her for a bit, and then I went into this group chat . . . and Toby was there. I talked with him a little. He was so happy that I was out. I kept in touch with him from time to time. Like, I told him I had Charlie. But after that, conversation stopped."

"So he's known our address all along?"

Rebecca stares at her lap sheepishly. "No. But he knew when Charlie was born, and which hospital—there were details he could have put together to find me, if he was pushed."

"And you think he was pushed."

"He put out this weird video a couple of weeks back. It was *all* about ISB. It felt like . . . a suicide letter. Like he knew people had found him and were coming—and why. So he wanted to warn the world."

A garbage truck has stopped at the curb to pick up a few cans. All the other cars, including theirs, have to slow. Tom hits the brakes. "And that's when you think he told them?"

"It's certainly a coincidence that Danny showed up now, so . . ."

"But why didn't you say anything to me two fucking weeks ago, Rebecca? If you were so worried—this affects our family."

"I know. I just . . ." She stretches her neck and stares at the ceiling. "I guess I was in denial. It had been so many years. I was hoping it would just . . . go away." Then she looks at Tom. "What did you do with that USB drive? You didn't throw it away, did you?"

"That's what you're worried about? The USB drive?" He laughs mirthlessly. "How about the gun? How about the fact that a brainwashed psychopath has kidnapped our child?"

"Those videos are what's keeping our children out of danger. It's collateral, Tom. I took it with me when I left—I know how much power it has, and I think it's why they haven't come for me."

"Until now," Tom interrupts, just as the garbage truck finally pulls off the curb and traffic moves again. A light up ahead turns yellow. Gritting his teeth, he goes through the light, too, despite the fact that it's solidly red.

"Tom, be *careful*," Rebecca screeches, glancing at Charlie's reflection in the back seat mirror again.

"We're losing her!" he screams back.

Rebecca wishes she had Danny's number, though maybe she wouldn't answer anyway. "I can't believe she's doing this," she moans. "She should be afraid of Ben. And now she's going right back there? What is she thinking?" But then, as she's saying it, Rebecca thinks she might understand why Danny feels she has to kidnap Roscoe and bring him back to Ben. Maybe Danny *does* know what Ben does to most mothers. Adam and Quentin, those little boys who lived in Oregon when Rebecca was there—they must be twelve, thirteen by now—what really happened to their mothers? It's something Rebecca has thought about tons, especially after giving birth to Roscoe, not that she ever had any answers. The more she thought about it, the more she knew there was no way they walked away from their rights and let those kids live in Oregon with Ben. Nope, Ben did something to those mothers to change their minds. Maybe he had tortured them just like Sophia. Maybe he has done it to mothers after Rebecca, too.

Maybe Danny knew, in the back of her mind, what was happening. But maybe this was Danny's get out of jail free card. Maybe Ben promised that she would get to see her baby . . . but only if she brought Roscoe back, too.

"Oh, shit," Tom says.

Rebecca looks up. They're coming up to yet another red light. There are cars stopped ahead, but Tom is looking at something on the shoulder. It looks like *their* car. When she looks at the tracker app, the dot has stopped in this exact spot.

"There!" Rebecca screams.

Tom pulls off and parks behind their car. Rebecca jumps out her side, but that's when Rebecca realizes that Danny's driver door and Roscoe's back passenger door are flung open. She runs there anyway, praying Roscoe is still inside.

He isn't. The car is empty.

She steps back and looks around. "Roscoe?" she calls. No answer.

There's nothing on the side of the road. No businesses. Just a drainage ditch and a drainage tunnel. She glances at it uneasily. Could they have gone *there*?

Tom runs up to her and stares up and down the shoulder. "I sure as shit hope someone didn't pick the two of them up already."

Rebecca's chin wobbles. What if they did? The tracker on her car keys was her only lead on Danny and Roscoe. But the keys are still in the car. And Danny and her baby? Where are *they*?

But suddenly, cutting through the traffic sound, a little shriek. She perks up. It sounds like . . . *Roscoe.*

"He's here!" she cries. "I think he's through that tunnel!"

"Let's go," Tom says, pivoting to get the baby.

"Wait." Rebecca touches his arm. "No, Tom. We can't drag Charlie into this. Let me go."

"Alone?"

"Yes." Rebecca points back to their car a few paces away. "You stay here. Wait for me. It isn't safe for either of you."

Tom nods, but then he looks at her worriedly. "But what if you get hurt? What if Danny's with someone?"

It's what Rebecca suspects. Most likely, someone has been tailing Danny as backup all along. She shrugs. "I have my phone if I need you," she says quietly.

Tom looks at her helplessly. "I don't like this at all."

"I risked one kid's life, I can't risk another," Rebecca pleads. "And the longer we argue, the more time Danny has to get away. Look, this is what I was running from, but it's been a long time coming. Talking to Danny, really *explaining* to her—it feels like something I need to do. For all the mothers. Maybe I can save Roscoe *and* her."

Tom pushes the heels of his hands into his eye sockets and sighs. But then the baby starts crying. He turns back to the car. "Fine. If you're going to go alone, you'd better do it before I change my mind."

Rebecca nods and steps away from the car. When she looks into the ditch, there's no sign of Danny. She doesn't hear Roscoe again, either. Maybe she never did. Maybe it was just the wind.

Still, she turns and gives Tom an encouraging wave. He gives her a blank look back. He's still so dazed. In shock, probably. Will he even still be her husband when this is all over? She fights back tears as she turns around and braces herself for the steep decline into the drainage tunnel. She prays she sees her son on the other side.

But really, she has no idea.

CHAPTER TWENTY-NINE

"Come on, Roscoe," Danny says through clenched teeth, dragging the little boy through murky, foul-smelling water and into the drainage tunnel. "That's it. One foot in front of the other."

"Why are we going through the mud?" Roscoe's voice is high-pitched and scared. "Where's my mom?" He glances behind him again. To keep him calm, Danny had said his parents were coming on their little journey, just in a different car.

But now she doesn't know how to explain. "Um, your mom is waiting for us on the other side," she lies. "We're meeting someone else, too."

"Who?"

"A friend. Someone close to your real dad."

Roscoe's brow furrows. *Oops.* Danny hadn't meant to say that. The plan was for Ben to be the one to explain; Danny doesn't want to steal his thunder. But didn't Ben realize how hard this was going to be? Why had he given her a nearly impossible task? Roscoe is a thinking, perceptive, scared little kid who has tons of questions. If he starts screaming, what then?

Of course, what was Danny's other option? That's the problem. It's why she has to push forward. It's why she needs to get this done.

Ben was thrilled when he discovered Danny was pregnant. Danny had no illusions that she was the only woman in Ben's life—quite a few others on the property had been with him romantically, too, but they all sort of felt like sisters. But as far as Danny knew, no one else still living in Oregon had had Ben's child. Actually, the other women who'd been pregnant with his children ended up with health issues—like Sophia, who Bex had mentioned. Not that Danny believed what Bex said about Sophia. Pregnancy was hard on people. It did strange things to women's bodies, things that their strength and healing exercises couldn't touch. And, well, it made some people mentally ill. For people like Sophia—and then Rue after her, and then Jasmine after *her*—the pregnancies wreaked havoc on their minds, and they weren't strong enough, mentally, to climb out. That was the thing with self-healing, after all. You had to be strong in the first place. You had to put in the work. And if you didn't . . . well, that's why you got sick.

And so, the babies—Jax, Mason, and Ford—came to Oregon, but the mothers did not. It was their choice, though. Ben always said that. He didn't push them out—they decided that staying away would be the best thing for their children. Ben's children. The *community's* children, really. Because that's the thing: Ben has this grand, amazing idea that he wants Danny to be a part of now: they're building the next generation of ISB. A generation of children all sharing Ben's DNA . . . and now at least one of them will have Danny's DNA, too. It feels so important. Like she's really contributing to something.

Still, the fact that every mother suddenly lacked the mental fortitude in pregnancy worried Danny just a little bit. But when she told Ben, he wrapped his arms around her—she was sitting on his lap, in his office. "Don't think that way. *You're* going to be my healthy girl. My miracle mother." But, he added, she must keep herself in tip-top shape. He wasn't taking any chances. "Eating clean. Exercising. Purifying and strengthening your body with the right herbs."

"Prenatals?" she asked.

"Sort of, but better." He shifted a little to pull an unmarked bottle from his desk drawer. "These are special herbs to optimize the pregnant body. We grow them on this very land. You'll have to take at least four a day, all right? And get good sleep, and watch your stress."

Danny cupped her hands around the bottle. It was stuffed with little capsules. "Although—the exercise. I've been so tired lately. I don't know if I can do the runs like usual."

Ben frowned. "Pregnancy is when you need exercise the most. You have to transcend the pain and exhaustion. You're better than that."

"I know, but—"

"Now is not the time to doubt yourself," Ben said sharply. "Remember how you were before we were together? Remember how scattered, how foggy?"

Danny looked away. "I do."

"I don't want that happening to you again. Especially not now. Pregnancy is a delicate time, Danielle. The chance of sliding back into sickness is much, much greater. You have to be vigilant. And so do I. It's important for the community."

"But you're happy, right? About the baby? About . . . us?" She looks up at him hopefully.

"Of *course* I am," Ben stressed, and Danny's heart blossomed. But then Ben looked pensive again. "I want to tell you something. Something I've never told you before. It's about Rebecca."

"Bex?" Danny blinked. No one had talked about Bex in years. Danny still thought of her, occasionally, and she certainly wondered what happened to her after she left, and there were rumors that she started up a rival organization, but Danny doubted that was true. But then, ISB and this community had a way of filtering out the negativity and noise. After Toby and Bex left in rapid succession, Ben talked to the whole community about how it was a good thing, really, and how weak they both were, and how they didn't hold themselves accountable or to the ISB standards. He reiterated that their security deposits, the secrets they'd given, were at risk, and so it would be for anyone else if they chose to desert the group in such a dramatic way.

And then he told everyone not to think of them ever again. Danny tried her hardest not to. Things felt so strong for a while. Their community of women was growing. She participated in so many ceremonies now and got to witness women transforming before her eyes. Danny never got used to watching the ceremonies where Ben gave the women the scars, though she did like seeing the relief and disbelief in their faces once it was over.

"You did it," she said to each and every one of them, clutching their hands. "You did something really fucking hard. You're a total badass. Strength be your guide."

So it was strange, Ben bringing Bex up now. "What do you mean?" Danny pressed. "What about her?"

Ben fiddled with an imaginary piece of lint on his shirt, heaving a sigh. "Rebecca was supposed to have the community's baby, too."

Danny stared at him. "*What*?" Meaning . . . Bex and Ben? Danny always suspected, actually. Bex was one of his favorites. Holding his hand on the stage during Celebration. His chosen girl.

"But then she left. I think she was scared. Unable to continue the tasks of ISB. Ashamed that she was slipping, mentally. Once again, pregnancy was too much for her."

"She just left while pregnant?" Danny was flabbergasted. "Why didn't she let you—and all of us—take care of her? Or at least the baby?"

Ben shook his head. "I don't know. I've thought about it long and hard, on so many walks. I was so hopeful for her, for the baby. I knew it was going to be a boy—just like I know our baby is, too."

Danny blinked. Maybe it made sense that Ben could know that. After all, all his other children were boys. Maybe he only had boy sperm. Instead, she asked, "Do you think Bex had the baby on her own?"

Ben nodded thoughtfully. "I believe the child is out there, yes. Somewhere. I can sense it. With Rebecca, though, that worries me. It hurts my heart to think how she must be caring for him. My child, *our* child, a child of the community, out there somewhere, unfulfilled. I wish I could just . . . talk to her."

"Couldn't you try and find where she went? You deserve to see your child. You're his father."

"I could, probably. I have my sources." He turned over his palms. "But . . . it's a delicate thing, me talking to her. I'd rather someone else go in first. Someone she's always trusted. Never had a reason to doubt."

"I wish *I* could talk to her," Danny said after a moment.

Ben's eyes lit up. "Would you consider it?"

Danny pressed her lips together. "Oh. Wait. I mean . . ." She'd just sort of been saying words, actually. Did she want to talk to Bex? This new knowledge about her pregnancy—it was just another wound, another thing Bex kept from her. They were supposed to be best friends. But she did miss Bex, sometimes. Just a little . . .

"How would it work?" she asked. "How would I even do it? It's not like we even know where she lives."

"We have ways of finding out those things. But it may take you going to her, to get her coming to us."

"*Leave* here?" Danny's heart banged. She hadn't gone anywhere for eight years.

Ben took her hands. "If you could do that, if you'd go on this mission for me . . . Danielle, it would prove how steady you are. How *well*. As I've said, pregnancy can have a profound effect on the mind and body. I have hopes that you'll be my outlier, but this has happened so many times before . . . it's going to take a lot of effort."

"I'm ready to put in the effort," Danny said weakly. "I'll do anything."

"I know." His eyes shone. "And you know, you going out on a limb, talking to Rebecca—it would prove to me that you have the strength. And that you'll never falter."

Danny had stared down at their entwined hands. At that very moment, her belly lurched in much the same way it had been doing all week, protesting against hunger and smells and even movement, sometimes. But she bore down and rode it out. From now on, she told herself, she would bend over backward to show that she was strong and resilient. She could do whatever Ben asked.

She had to. She wasn't being sent away and separated from her child. She would be the healthy mother. The one who remained with her baby. She would be the winner.

The drainage tunnel is dark and damp. The ground is slippery, and there are constant *thumps* from the cars on the road above. Roscoe whimpers. "I don't want to walk anymore," he says. "I don't like the dark."

"It's okay. It's a really quick tunnel." Ben's instructions mandated that they meet on the other side, away from traffic. "See? There's light ahead again."

"I want my mom."

"Don't worry. She'll be here soon." Danny felt crappy lying. Almost as bad as she'd felt lying to Bex. She was astonished that Bex believed her so quickly. It was like as soon as Danny admitted she was pregnant, Bex's guard dropped. All she wanted was to help. It was nice, but it also kind of reminded Danny of how pitying Bex was in high school, always so worried about Danny's well-being, like Danny was some sort of delicate glass figurine.

Well, it isn't Danny who needs help now. It's Danny who has the power.

She drags the little boy by his wrist. He whimpers, but he walks along. When they emerge through the drainage tunnel and into daylight again, Danny has to squint to handle the brightness. They're standing in an ugly field full of puddles and litter. When she looks around, there isn't a soul here. Her heart jumps. This is wrong. Kris said he'd be waiting. He was supposedly watching her this whole time.

So where the heck is he now?

Roscoe kicks at a clump of dried grass. "I'm hungry," he whines.

"We'll get you food soon. All the food you want."

"What kind of food?"

"Real yummy stuff, okay? You like pizza?"

"Yeah." But Roscoe doesn't look comforted. "Where are we going?"

Danny crouches next to him. "Listen. What if I told you we're going to this amazing house in the woods, filled with people who teach amazing things? And that there are a few other little boys who live there, too—and they're your brothers?"

Roscoe looks confused. "Charlie's my brother."

"Well, these are your *real* brothers. They're named Quentin and

Adam and Jax and Mason. And they're super nice and love to play with toys, just like you."

Roscoe thinks a moment. "Do they like Lego?"

"I'm sure they do," Danny answers. "Best of all, they're your family. You'll get to be with your family again."

"I already live with my family," Roscoe says.

Danny bites her lip. "Yes, but this is *also* your family. This is where you're supposed to be. Somewhere truly amazing, where you can be your best self."

But something about that makes Roscoe's little brow furrow again. He glances toward the tunnel, and then at Danny, and then down at his feet. "I want to go home," he says.

Danny's head hurts. Before coming, she'd had this dumb notion that Roscoe would be so overjoyed after hearing he had brothers and would live in the woods. Ben made it sound like the kid was probably dying to get out of his family situation, Bex was probably still so sick. But it isn't that way at all.

"I want my mommy," Roscoe says, as if reading her mind. He looks at Danny sharply. "I don't want you. You're mean."

Danny's mouth wobbles. She can't help but take this personally. *You're a bad mother. You'll be a bad mother.* She gets the urge to tap something, somewhere, but there's nothing solid anywhere. She looks at her phone again. Where the hell *is* he? She just wants to get this over with.

Finally, footsteps sound through the tunnel. Danny swivels around, relieved. But then a figure emerges from the shadows, and Danny's stomach drops to her knees.

Bex.

"Come on, Roscoe," Danny says, taking his hand and starting to run. But it's too late. Bex has seen them. "Danny!" she screams. "Roscoe!"

"Mommy!" Roscoe drops Danny's hand. "Mommy!"

He runs for Bex and dive-bombs into her. Bex grabs him tight and hugs him hard. But Bex's eyes aren't on her little boy. They're on Danny, and they're full of hate.

All at once, Danny feels about an inch tall. Something strange happens, too: she puts herself in Bex's position. Tries to imagine her child on the outside and another woman taking the baby away. It makes her clench with terror. It makes her stare down at her boots—muddy from slogging through this tunnel, trying to escape—and feel a wash of shame.

"What the hell are you thinking?" Bex screams, marching over to her. "Where do you think you're going with him?"

Danny's eyes water. This isn't how this was supposed to go. "You need to leave, Bex. It's better this way."

"*Better this way?*" Bex's eyes are wild. "You really think I'm going to let you just take my son?"

"I don't want to go with her!" Roscoe cries into Bex's waist.

"It's okay," Bex says, stroking his hair. "You're not going anywhere with her." She stares murderously at Danny again and then gestures around the shabby, ugly field. "What are you doing here? Waiting for a spaceship? Someone's meeting you, isn't he?" Bex glances around nervously. "Who? Is it *Ben*?"

Danny shakes her head. The fight seeps out of her. This is a part of the day she hasn't rehearsed. "No," she says in a small voice. "Not Ben."

"Then *who*?"

She sighs. "Kris."

"Who's that?"

"This guy who's with us. He came after you left. Started a men's movement."

"And this Kris guy, he's been keeping tabs on you the whole time you've been here, hasn't he? And let me guess, he was your ride? Not some . . . *bus*?"

Danny bites her lip and looks away. "He dropped me at the bus station. And then I took a taxi to your house."

"So you lied to me. About everything. And I'm the sucker who believed you. So good job, Danny. Good powers of persuasion." Bex is crying now. "Tom's calling the police. You're not getting out of this. And by the way? I bet you a million dollars Ben won't bail you out—and this Kris guy won't rescue you either. They'll leave you high and dry, Danny, because they'd rather die than have bad press related to ISB. You're on your own."

Danny sucks in a gasp. She wants to refute Bex's prediction, but it's actually something Ben said before she left on the mission. *You will be a representative for ISB out in the world. If something happens, if you get in trouble and make a bad name for us, I have to consider it a breach of trust. I don't want to be cleaning up some PR nightmare on the news.*

"Tell Tom not to call the police," she whispers. "Bex, you don't understand. I can't fail. You don't know what it means for me to go back with nothing."

Bex puts her hands on her hips. "Sure I do. And I tried to warn you. So do you really expect me to feel bad for you right now? Oh, and by the way, it won't matter if you manage to get Roscoe away from me. Ben will take your baby away from you regardless. That's the endgame, Danny. It's always the endgame."

Danny shakes her head. "Not with me."

Bex's laugh is ugly. "I know you think you're special to him, but you're not."

Through the drainage tunnel, Danny can hear cars roaring on the highway. The wind blows the dead grass and kicks up dust.

"I want to be the healthy mother," Danny whispers. "The one who stays. Who makes it."

"Healthy?" Bex laughs. "You think you're healthy? Look at you! And, oh, those herbs you're taking? Guess what they really are. Sedatives."

Danny's eyes widen. "That's not possible."

"Have them tested. He gave me pills, too. Said they were grown right on the property. Nope, they were one hundred percent diazepam—Valium. You, me, Sophia, all those other women who never got to see their kids, the ones Ben said couldn't handle the mental rigors of being pregnant? *He* makes us like that. And here's the other thing." She looks at Roscoe and then claps her hands over his ears. "I only saw Sophia, Danny, but if she's any indication, I'm not sure she even made it off the property. I think Ben kept her alive only long enough so she could have his baby . . . and then he killed her."

"Stop it!" Danny screams, covering her ears. She doesn't want to believe her.

But Bex is looking at her with such conviction. And Danny can't stop thinking about all those kids at the compound without their moms, all the tiny pinpricks of questions like stabbing knives in her skin. Where *did* those mothers go? Why did she never think about that? They'd been so devoted before they left, integral members of the group, and suddenly . . . *gone*. Because they were pregnant? Because Ben didn't want them to get in the way of raising *his* children?

Did he actually kill them?

Bex has backed up all the way to the drainage tunnel now. She looks ready to dart through with Roscoe in tow. "Listen, I'm going to give you two choices," she says. "One, you continue to vow your allegiance to Ben, and tell the police exactly what went down."

Danny swallows hard. "And two?"

But then her phone rings. Ben's name flashes on the screen. Danny pales.

"Don't answer that," Bex warns.

"I can't just ignore him!"

"Sure you can. You've been doing it all day."

"Yeah, but now . . ." Danny winces at the next thing she has to tell her friend. "He's going to know something's really wrong if I don't respond to him now, Bex. And he'll come for me. For *us*. He knows where I am. Where *you* are."

Bex just stares. "You think I haven't figured it out already?"

The phone rings again. Danny's gaze darts to the screen, though she already knows who it'll be. *Ben. Ben. Ben. Ben. Ben.*

Danny looks at her. "What's option two?"

"Option two is you come with me, and we end this."

Danny doesn't move. She still imagines Kris somewhere, watching. Bex has to realize that, right? Has she lost her mind?

The phone rings again. Danny's heart pounds as she imagines Ben on the other end growing more and more impatient and furious and vengeful. And she swears, suddenly, she can feel a flip in her stomach that maybe isn't *her* body. Her skin prickles. Is that her baby? Has she felt her *move*?

She cannot lose her baby. There is no possible way.

She steps toward Bex. She feels weak and limp. "Okay," she says in a small voice. "I'll go with you."

"And I can trust you?"

Danny shrugs. She has no idea. Her phone rings again. "I can't have him calling like this. It'll drive me insane."

Bex raises her head. "Actually, I want you to answer it soon enough."

Danny's mouth drops open. "You *do*?"

"Yes. As long as you've chosen option two."

Danny stares at her blinking phone. She nods, ever so slightly. "I have."

"Okay, then," Bex says quietly. Her eyes are suddenly full of light. "I'm going to tell you exactly what to say."

CHAPTER THIRTY

BEND, OREGON
PRESENT DAY

Ben presses his palms together and tries to breathe. In, out. In, out. Years ago, before they moved to Oregon, a friend had invited him to a sensory deprivation chamber; he spent ninety minutes in a dark, soundless, windowless room, alone with his thoughts and feelings and being. He'd never felt so calm and composed as he had in that chamber. *In control.* He'd heard his blood swishing in his veins. He'd actually heard his *thoughts* electrically crackling and snapping. It had made him feel superhuman, having that sort of awareness. He tries to harness that presence of mind now, but it's proving to be difficult.

He tries Danny. The call goes to voicemail.

He swivels around to his computer screens. On one of them is a GPS tracker showing the blue dot. It's on the side of the road. This should be going well. He'd called Kris ten minutes ago and told him to mobilize. "She'll be there soon. She knows where to go." The ditch at mile marker 104. Through the tunnel. Get there at all costs.

So why hasn't someone called to confirm? Minutes tick by. Ben zooms in on Danny's tracker dot. Then he realizes something. *Fuck.*

He tries calling her again. No answer. So he calls Kris instead. "There's more than one drainage tunnel," he screams. "She's gone through the wrong one. She's waiting at the wrong place."

"But we told her the mile marker." There are footsteps on Kris's end. "How far is she?"

Danielle is only about a quarter of a mile away. Kris could run ten miles in a little over an hour; he'd get there easily. Ben says to call back when he gets there; he'd made the foolish mistake of not putting a tracking dot on Kris as well. When he hangs up, he sends Danielle a text that she's at the wrong tunnel, but Kris is on his way. *Stay put.*

Ninety seconds later, the phone rings again. Kris. "Shit," he says when Ben answers. "I'm here, but there's someone with her. Another woman."

"What?" Ben shoots to his feet. It's got to be Rebecca. "How?"

"Looks like she followed them."

"Damn it," Ben shrieks again. "Danielle was supposed to make a clean break."

"There's no way I'm approaching, Scion. It's not safe." There's a pause. "I gotta get out of here."

Ben lets out another groan. All Danielle had to do was get Ben's son to this drop-off point with enough of a head start. What, had Rebecca been in the fucking *car* with her? What is Danielle thinking?

He looks at the monitor again. Danielle's dot hasn't moved. He pictures Rebecca with her. Saying . . . *what*? Is she breaking? Is she *defecting*?

There is absolutely no way Ben is losing another son.

He zooms out and looks at the road she's on and then the highways that link to it. He needs a route from Bend. On another monitor is a map of Rebecca's neighborhood. With a click of a button, he can see either a map drawing of roads and turnpikes or a detailed, Google Earth–style photo of Rebecca's house. There's a windsock on the front porch. An oak tree in the front yard. And a tire swing, likely for *his son* to play on.

He can feel his blood starting to boil. He forces his thoughts back into that dark, blank chamber. There's no use getting angry about this.

Anger implies victimization. Anger implies *fear*. He is way beyond fear. He is *action*.

He rises from his desk and walks into the great room. A few of his Seedlings are doing "workups" on some of the younger, less experienced members of the group, sitting nose to nose with them, whispering softly straight into their psyches, as Ben has taught them. In another room, Seeds and Seedlings are working on their inner-strength exercises, the rhythmic breathing he'd come up with to rid the body of poison and inflammation, all without medication. In yet another room, Seedlings sit at a bank of computer terminals having video chats with some of their protégés outside the compound. Not everyone involved in ISB lives in Oregon, only the most devout. Ben has people running whole branches of the organization on the ground in those cities, making sure things run smoothly. Montreal. Miami. St. Louis. Austin. They are recruiting more people by the day, and best of all, a portion of all of the branches flows straight back here, to him.

It took him a while to figure out the proper terminology for the people in his hierarchy of teachers. It was Barb's idea to call him Scion—Barb had always had a knack with words, coming from a marketing background. She was also useful because she seemed so oblivious to certain things, only saw the method and the progress, which were as much her creation as they were Ben's. Scion, Barb said, can mean *heir*, but it can also denote *representative*. Ben likes to think that he has been chosen, because of his superior intelligence, to inherit the wisdom of understanding the principles of ISB and pass them on to others in an effective way. He considers himself the father plant and those who learn from him and teach the others his Seedlings. The lower rung, Seeds, are starting out on the ISB rungs—they do "practice sessions" where fictionalized scenarios are acted out and they teach and counsel accordingly.

When she came here, Danielle had been on the path to becoming a Seedling. Ben wasn't sure how she'd do. He liked her, but he always felt she seemed a little shaky, like her foundation hadn't firmly set. Rebecca had been a Seedling, the youngest Seedling ever. God, he'd been proud of her. Such tenacity. Such dedication. Perfect, too, that her family was already invested in the group—less chance of hysterical parents trying to pull her out of things—but also not that invested in *Rebecca*, so they wouldn't be watching too closely. They seemed happy to let her get more and more involved in ISB. It's why it hurt so badly when she vanished. Anyone else could have gone, but Rebecca—he had such hopes for her, and especially for their child. He aches for that boy. It hurts, not having him here. He wants all of his boys around him; it doesn't feel right that one is out there, fending for himself.

And though he tries very, very hard to clear his mind of the rage, whenever he thinks of Rebecca escaping . . . and getting away . . . and then having the baby . . . and *marrying someone else* . . . he wants to scream.

Carson, a Seedling, looks up as Ben passes. "Everything all right, Scion?"

Ben gestures to speak with him privately. Carson says something to the student he was working with and meets Ben in the corner. "What's going on?"

"We might be losing Danielle. I believe she's sick again."

Carson's lips part. "Jesus. At the goddess retreat?"

Ben nods. "Uh, yes." The goddess retreat has been a longtime placeholder for where certain worthy women have gone. He respects that they still trust him so implicitly, that no one questions its validity. "I feared this. She did, too. So I need to go in and get her and make her well. She needs to be here, back in the community—it's her only hope. So I need access to the car."

Carson looks worried. "But you said—"

"I know what I said. But it'll be all right. This is a special case. Can you handle things here while I'm gone?"

Carson nods, puffing up his chest. Guy lifts weights morning and night. He's a protector to these women and children. Ben trusts that.

He grabs car keys off the ring. They're in the kitchen, where a few people are preparing the afternoon meal; they all look up and greet him warmly, but he doesn't reply. If anyone is surprised that he's heading for the garage, they don't let on, though Ben thinks they must be. Their strict policies about leaving have become even stricter in the years since

Rebecca and Toby left. These days, they barely even host workshops at the compound anymore; most everything they do is virtual and they still charge the same fees. The only people who *do* leave, actually, are those who go on goddess retreats.

And even they don't *actually* leave.

Still, staying close is better. The world beyond their compound is tarnished and toxic, they all believe that. He knows Carson will think up something to tell the others that won't worry them, though. A speaking engagement. A TV appearance via satellite feed from Portland. He's left for such things before. No one is aware yet that Danielle is even pregnant, and for those who have asked, he's said that she, like some of the other women, has gone on the goddess retreat.

He yanks open the garage door. His cars gleam in their parking spots: the Lambo, the Benz, the Rolls, the Rover, and the 911. Cars have always been his vice—cars and connecting with people, he always joked to the group. And yes, antimaterialism is a big part of the ISB way, but they've flourished in the past ten years. Why not treat himself now and then? Besides, no group member has ever groused about going for a ride in one of these babies. The cars are for them all to enjoy.

Today, he needs four-wheel drive and a back seat, so the Rover will do. From the back of the garage, he pulls a child's car seat from the jumble of kid things—not that the other children on the property ever leave the compound, but they have this stuff here just in case there are serious medical needs that for some reason can't be treated on-property. He throws it into the back—he'll secure it later. Then he pulls open the driver's door, sits down, and takes a deep breath. Only thing is, when he goes on speaking engagements and TV appearances, he has a driver. It's been ages since he's driven himself. But it's fine. *Fine.*

He starts the engine and pulls out of the property. Fred's at the gate now, and Fred waves him through without question. He thinks of the day Rebecca vanished. *Barb* had been working the gate that day. He can't believe she'd let something like that happen . . . but then, Barb had really changed after they moved to Bend. She still loved the community and took care of everyone, but there were moments, here and there, where he saw slips in loyalty, even questioning of their principles. Certain times, she seemed downright meek in his presence, cowering back like he was going to hit her—and then resentful. Everyone needs stern words sometimes, though. Barb had always been able to take it before.

Most disturbing of all, just a month before Rebecca left, Barb's cancer came back. But instead of treating herself with the patented breathing program like she had before, she wanted chemo. She requested special permission to leave the grounds to go to the doctor in Bend. To anyone else, Ben would have said absolutely not . . . but Barb was a unique case. There were special provisions for her anyway, including granting her access to her finances. Ben rationalized that he did this because Barb had been with him so long . . . but it was also because she owned half of the ISB workshop copyrights; there wasn't much he could do, legally or business-wise, without her. And there was this, too: Barb announced to him that she'd recorded new security deposit secrets recently, overriding the old stuff she'd submitted years before. "They're about how I faked my healing." She'd looked Ben dead in the eye. "I never had cancer before. I just pretended I did. But this time, I actually do, and I'm scared shitless."

Touché, Ben had wanted to say to her, not that he'd ever give her the satisfaction. It was brilliant, though, a secret that was still shameful but would also delegitimize the group were he to release it. He was stuck. He had no power over her. So he let her go to her stupid appointments. He did *not*, however, let her take any of his cars.

But Barb letting Rebecca leave . . . that was a whole other ballpark of betrayal.

He'd grilled Barb hard about it, questioning her over and over about whether Rebecca had seemed nervous, and why Barb hadn't double-checked that Rebecca was able to leave the property—which she wasn't—and why Barb had missed the moment Rebecca ducked around that turn, dropped the dog's leash, and slipped into that taxi. Barb swore up and down that it was a lapse in judgment was all—Ben and Rebecca were so close, she just thought Rebecca was following orders, and as for not seeing Rebecca vanish . . . well, everyone made mistakes, didn't they?

Admittedly, Ben had gotten angry. *Really* angry. It wasn't his finest hour, but he felt like his community was crumbling at the edges. He lashed out at Barb, and though he didn't strike her, she'd cried out in terror and then said, defeated, that she hated this place, hated *him*.

The next day, he found her in her room. Cold. Still. Unmoving. Ben leaned down; she was breathing, but only faintly, like maybe she'd taken something to knock her out. They grew all kinds of herbs in the garden.

He stood back, thinking. Barb was a liability now. A ticking time bomb. The fact that she co-owned so much of ISB pissed him off. The fact that there was so much money in her bank account, money that technically didn't deserve to be hers—what had she *done* for it, exactly?—made him antsy. He turned back to Barb, and, well, that extra pillow was just *there*, and suddenly he was pushing it over Barb's face. She didn't resist. She wanted to go anyway. She'd said so herself the night before, in so many words.

After, Ben let everyone think that Barb's cancer had returned, that he himself had diagnosed it. She'd done her best to self-heal, but she'd decided to endure medical treatments against Ben's advisement. It was the chemo that killed her. They had a massive funeral; thousands of ISB devotees came to pay homage. Barb got a proper send-off. And Ben got his just desserts in the end. Barb had no one in her life except ISB. Even if she'd come to hate the group, she hadn't thought to update her will. Upon her death, Ben took ownership of her half of the copyright for all the workshops. The money she'd earned and that her estate would earn into the future—it all went to his organization. To *him*.

That's what you get for being a lying, deceiving bitch.

God, he's agitated today. He needs to settle his nerves, otherwise he's going to swerve off the road. He reaches into the center console and rummages for cassette tapes. Finally, he finds the one he wants and pops it into the player. Tony Robbins's voice blares through the cabin, talking about the invisible forces of internal drives and emotion being the force of life. The man is talking to a crowd of hundreds of thousands of people, far more than Ben has even spoken to, and sometimes it makes him seethe to think about it. *Most of us are great minds, right?* Tony says, but Ben grits his teeth because he knows, technically, *his* mind is greater than Tony's—and anyone else's.

But still, it calms him for the moment. He turns off the dirt road onto the highway. The route is etched into his mind because he has that sort of photographic memory. Strip malls pass, then big box stores, and then he gets on another highway, heading west to Nevada. Tony's voice drones on, but after a few minutes, it isn't enough. Ben glances at the center console, recalling what else he noticed there when he was rummaging—gummy candies. A driver must have left them behind, certainly not anyone affiliated with ISB, as candy is forbidden. All sugar, in fact—it's a poison. A vice. A crutch. So many people have trouble breaking from it, but then they talk about how *clean* they feel, how reborn.

But all of a sudden, he can't stop thinking about the candies. His mouth starts to water for them. A minute later, the urge is too great. He plunges his hand back into the center console, rips open the package with his teeth, and pours them all into his mouth at once. The rush of sugar almost *hurts*. His teeth zing in protest. But he chews and chews, working the gummies into gelatin pulp, and then swallows it all down. His stomach aches, and he thinks he might puke, but at the same time he wants to buy four more packs and eat them one after another.

He's so distracted that he swerves into the neighboring lane where another car is fast approaching. The other driver lays on his horn, gesturing rudely. "Learn to drive, fucker!"

Ben rolls down his window, too. "Don't you know who I *am*?" he roars.

The guy looks at him like he's nuts. Then he laughs and drives away.

Ben balls his fists. He flexes his calf muscles and does a few fire breaths. *Anger is fear. Anger is fear.* He cranks up Tony Robbins again, and when he sees a rest stop in the distance, he thinks *Fuck it*—he's going in for more sweets.

And then his phone rings. *Danny.* Well, well, well.

Ben eyes it. He shouldn't answer, it would serve her right. But then his gaze flicks to the car seat in the back. He hits the green button. "I already know, Danielle."

"Scion, I'm so sorry," she whispers. "But she—"

"Are we on a safe line?" he interrupts. "I know she was with you. Kris saw you both. Did she call the police?"

"No. I talked her out of it. And, yes, I'm on a safe line. She's close, but she can't hear me. I'm telling her that I'm calling you to say that I'm not going through with it. I'm making her think that I'm defecting."

"*Are* you?"

"Of course not. But I have to say that so she trusts me. I'm still trying to make this happen. It was a mistake trying to drive their car, but don't worry. I didn't bring any negative attention to the group. We're fine."

Ben shuts his eyes. "We're moving on to plan B."

"I know." Danny clears her throat. "But I think that's okay."

Ben raises his chin. "Where is the boy?"

"We're going back to the house now. Bex thinks I'm broken. She's taking me in. That's where we'll be. I'm sorry I screwed up."

He groans. "Stop apologizing. It's exhausting." Then he sighs. "I'm in Bend, but I could be there in about seven hours."

Danielle is silent. All Ben hears is static. Finally, she says, "Her neighborhood is really quiet. I don't think you'll have any trouble."

"That's good," Ben asks. "Got any nosy neighbors?"

"Not that I noticed."

"The kind of place where they leave the doors unlocked?" Ben prompts.

"I'll make sure of it," Danielle says, her voice full of eagerness—almost mirth.

Ben smiles to himself, despite all the snafus. "I'll update Kris with his instructions. Because of how things are changing, I'll likely have him lie low."

He hangs up and checks his map. And then, after a moment's thought, he dials another number. Kris answers on the first ring.

"I need you to stay in town and track them," he says. "But lie low, too. Monitor the 911 calls. I can't fully trust she's on our side. She says this'll be an ambush . . . but I just need to make sure she's telling the truth."

"Got it," Kris says. "No problem, Scion."

He cranks Tony back up and passes the rest stop. Funny, his need for sugar is suddenly gone.

CHAPTER THIRTY-ONE

CARSON CITY, NEVADA
PRESENT DAY

Danny is hyperventilating. She keeps checking her phone, certain Ben is going to call back and *know*. She can't believe the lie she just told. She can't believe he *bought* it.

Bex stands next to her and pats her arm. "You did well."

But Danny's hands are shaking. She needs to punish herself for lying to Ben. Run for two hours. Inhale poison. Walk into traffic. Should she walk into traffic? The highway is right there. She needs to pay what she did. She wishes she had something to tap against, but they're in the grass with not even a tree trunk near them. She slaps the side of her face.

"What the hell?" Bex grabs her arm. "What are you doing?"

"I'm a bad person," Danny whispers shakily. "Lying is weak."

"Danny. *Stop.* You're not weak. You're saving yourself. This man is coming to steal my kid and yours. I know that's hard to believe, but it's true. Think about what you almost just did for him, with Roscoe. He's going to do exactly the same thing. We've been over this."

"I know," Danny whispers, but somehow she can't quite get it through her head.

They walk back through the tunnel. When they get to the other side, Danny sees Bex's other car waiting behind the one she stole. Tom leaps out and grabs Roscoe quickly, as if he's afraid Danny's going to snatch him again. He doesn't even look at her. It fills Danny with humiliation. Did she seriously think these people were just going to give up their kid without a fight?

Bex steps over to Tom, and they exchange a few quiet words. Tom doesn't look happy, but Bex seems to be convincing him that she has this covered. Danny waits a polite distance away, trying to silence the screaming in her brain. *Are you actually doing this? Are you actually leaving? What if this is a mistake?* If she'd met Kris at the right drop point, where would she be right now? It's so destabilizing, having Ben upset with her. On the other hand, there are all the warnings Bex gave her about Ben purposefully making her sick. Could they be true? She *does* feel sleepy after taking those herbs. Unsteady on her feet, her thinking slow, all of it. She'd blamed herself, the pregnancy hormones. So had Ben, in fact . . .

If she went back, would he take her child from her? Would she become like all the other women who'd had his children? Cut off? *Gone?*

A door slams, and she looks up. Tom is back in the car and peeling down the road with both kids in the back seat.

She turns to her old friend. "What is your plan, Bex? What are we going to do?"

Bex walks to her car and opens the driver's door. "We're going home. I have something important there. And then we'll wait for Ben to get close. And then we'll call the police."

"You make it sound like it's easy."

Bex swings into the driver's seat. "You just have to trust me. I want the best for you and your baby, Danny. And I want you to be free."

The car roars to life, and Bex pulls onto the highway toward her home. Danny gazes at the ditch and the drainage tunnel, feeling a strange mix of feelings. Regret. Trepidation. But maybe also like she dodged a bullet.

They're silent as Bex navigates the few miles home. Seeing how little distance she'd traveled, Danny is once again plunged into despair. She can't do anything right. She can't even steal a kid. She's *weak*.

Back at the house, the yard is strewn with branches from the storm. A particularly large one lies across the driveway; Bex has to get out and manually push it out of the way so they can pull into the garage. Tom's car is there, too. He sits in the driver's seat, staring straight ahead. In the back seat, the baby is crying.

Wordlessly, Rebecca closes the garage door, filling the garage with darkness. Then she gets out, opens the door, and speaks to Roscoe. After a moment, he ducks down so he can't be seen through the back windows. Rebecca throws a blanket over him and pulls down a baby sunshade to block the back window. She slams the car door again and presses the button to open the garage door, pulling Danny into the house.

"What are you doing?" Danny asks.

"Tom is taking the kids to his mom's, but don't you dare tell anyone that. I'm having Roscoe hide in case your guy is tailing him. Then I'm going to go upstairs to Roscoe's room and turn on a bedroom light to make it look like Roscoe is staying here. It might not fool him completely, but at least your guy won't have proof that Roscoe left."

Danny shakes her head. "O-Okay."

Bex steps through the door but pauses a moment, her shoulders tensing, her ear cocked. "What is it?" Danny whispers.

"I still don't fully trust you," Bex says. "Not after the shit you pulled. You're one hundred percent telling me the truth that Ben isn't already inside the house?"

"I swear. He's in Bend." Danny shifts her weight. "I mean, I guess he could have lied to *me* and started for here earlier. But he doesn't like to leave the house. These days, he barely leaves at all."

Bex crosses her arms. "That's interesting. He used to go off the property all the time. But let me guess: he doesn't like putting other people in charge?"

Danny shrugs. "Maybe."

"Well, I'm not taking any chances."

Bex grabs Roscoe's baseball bat, which is tilted against the wall in the foyer. Danny watches as she marches though each room, bat raised. After opening every closet door and thoroughly checking the basement and even the attic, Bex seems satisfied. She sweeps back through the living room toward the stairs, but then her gaze travels to a laptop sitting on the couch. Her expression shifts.

"What?" Danny asks.

"Tom's laptop." She rushes over and pales at the sight of something sticking out of the side. Wordlessly, Bex walks to the laptop and pulls out a thumb drive and hands it to Danny.

"What's this?" Danny asks.

"It's *yours*, Danny. Your video. From ISB. Your . . . you know . . . branding."

Danny stares at the little device in Bex's hand. Her mouth falls open. "Wait . . . *how*?"

"Toby told me where to find the videos. I was looking for mine, but I found yours," Bex explains. "I just . . . grabbed it."

Danny blinks. She can't muster a single word, she's so startled. She thinks about what's on that video: The ritual shortly after she arrived. The one where she's naked and they—*Rebecca*—burned her. Then she looks at the laptop on the counter. "Tom watched this, too? The whole *thing*?"

Bex's eyes lower. "He obviously didn't know what it was. And . . . I kind of get the sense he didn't see *me*, at the end . . ."

Danny crosses her arms. "Oh, and I bet you just won't tell him, right?"

Bex swallows hard. "I think I have to. Everything's changed, now."

Danny can't wrap her mind around this. The idea of Bex's husband seeing her naked . . . on that floor . . . Ben *touching* her. Ben said those videos would be safe, always, and that no one else would ever see them. "You just *took* it?" Danny's voice cracks. "Without asking me first?"

Bex sinks into a chair. "I'm sorry. I just . . . I was desperate and running out of time. I needed something that would ruin him. I said I'd release it if he ever came after me."

"You were going to release *my video*? That's my choice! Not yours!"

Bex looks caught and sheepish. "I never *did*. I mean, I *wanted* to—I wanted to expose ISB—but I didn't want to do that to you."

"Wow, thanks." Danny scowls, feeling numb. "That makes me feel a lot better."

"Danny, I'm sorry. I wanted to find mine. I thought I was doing you a favor. It seemed safer with me than with him. And it's good we have it now. You can give to the cops. They'll put Ben away."

Danny can feel her heart pounding. "What? *No!*"

"But it proves you were a victim. We can blur out your face. We don't have to release your name. And as for my role on the video . . . well, maybe I should just face what I did."

"Bex . . ." Danny paces around the living room, passing those same cheerful family photos. The idea of the whole world seeing her getting marked makes her stomach churn. Then she realizes something else. She remembers Ben talking about some files that went missing after Toby vanished. Ben was so type A, surely he'd gone through all the videos to see *which* file was gone. Did Ben *know* that *it was Danny's*? But why hadn't he gone after Rebecca to get it back? He always talked about how sacred those videos were, how they were only for them.

But maybe he hadn't gone after Rebecca because he feared she'd release it. What about that scared him, though? That it would humiliate Danny, or that it would humiliate *him*?

She collapses to the couch and pulls a cushion to her chest.

Danny stares at the drive in her palm. It's so light. She thinks back on that day for a moment. How honored she'd felt, but also how disoriented and scared. What had even *happened*? She hadn't wanted Ben touching her where he'd touched her. At the same time, she'd been so thrilled to be initiated, she didn't care. And the Bex of it all, the fact that Bex branded her? That part was weird, sort of, and confusing, but Danny was just so happy to be part of things, she'd kind of compartmentalized it.

A tear falls down her cheek. It doesn't make sense how that was the best day of her life and also one of the worst. But maybe that's been every day since. Could it be that she's just pushing the pain down, telling herself it'll make her stronger, convincing herself it isn't all that bad?

"I'm so sorry, Danny," Bex says softly. "About all of it. I'm sorry I roped you into ISB in the first place. I should have never told you to talk to Ben. I wish I'd known."

"You were just trying to help me," Danny says miserably.

"But I knew what Ben was like—a little, anyway. I knew he could have power over people. I knew he could be . . . well, the way he is. Yeah, I thought he could help you on some level. But maybe, also, I wanted us to be in it together, to not have to go through it alone."

Bex's voice cracks, and she covers her face with her hands. It's a different sort of anguish than when Danny showed up, or when Bex found out Danny was pregnant, or when Danny stole the car with Roscoe inside. This anguish turns inward. Danny swallows hard. She is angry with Bex, yes . . . but not that angry. Not really.

Then Danny realizes something else about what's on the video. It doesn't just make Ben look like a criminal.

She lets out a breath. Her fingers release the drive. It clangs to the wood floor. Then Danny stands and stomps down on it with the heel of her sneaker. She puts all her weight into the movement, and the drive makes a satisfying *crunch* under her shoe.

"Danny!" Bex leaps to her feet. "What are you doing?"

"You're in that video, too."

Bex stares at her. "So?"

"*So?* You'll get in trouble, too! Child protective services could get involved. I might be sheltered, but I at least know that. You could even lose your kids." Danny feels a pull in her chest. "I can't let that happen."

Bex's eyes boggle. Her mouth makes an O. But then she stares down at the mangled plastic and metal on the ground. "But this was how we were going to get him. I was going to make sure he was close and then call the police, saying I had this video *and* Ben was close by." She looks at Danny. "You didn't do this to *save* Ben, did you? You don't want him to come here so he can kill me?"

Danny shakes her head. "I didn't. I swear. I just . . . I didn't want you to get in trouble . . ." She takes a deep breath, wondering if she just screwed up something else. She thinks of Ben on the road now. Coming for them. Getting closer.

"Should we run?" Bex whispers. "He knows where this house is. Where we are. Probably where Tom is, too."

"You should," Danny says, and then looks away. "But me . . . he'll always know where I am."

Bex stares at her. "Why?"

Danny lets out a breath. She was hoping she wouldn't have to do this. Ashamed, she raises her wrist and touches something just below the skin. "It's a tracker. He installed them a while back. So he can't lose us."

Bex's jaw drops. "Jesus," she whispers.

"Unless I cut it out, he'll be able to follow me. And he will, I think. I'm carrying his child. He won't let another one of us go." Danny swallows hard. "But you should run. It's okay."

Bex blinks. Then she shakes her head. "No. No way. I . . . I think I have a plan B."

"What?"

"Pretty sure this is a stand your ground state," Bex murmurs.

"What?"

But Bex shakes her head, snapping out of her reverie. "It's probably better you don't know. All I need you to do is hide. I'll handle the rest."

CHAPTER THIRTY-TWO

Tom walks into the little bedroom in his parents' condo and inhales in a deep, overexaggerated way. "Even though I never lived here, this still smells like home," he says to Roscoe.

"What does home smell like?" Roscoe sounds amused.

"Hard to explain, buddy. Maybe it's the detergent my folks use . . . whatever it is, it takes me right back."

Experimentally, Roscoe inhales, too. "I think it smells like dust."

"Are you saying Grandma and Gramps are *dusty*?"

"Maybe." Roscoe giggles.

"Too bad this is your new bed, then."

Roscoe's eyes widen. "It is?"

Tom looks away. *Maybe*, he thinks. *For a little while.*

He can't fathom the idea of things returning to normal back at home. Then again, maybe he's got that all backward. He has never technically adopted Roscoe—mostly because he never thought he had to. In that case, this wouldn't be Roscoe's new bed . . . because Roscoe would no longer be his.

It makes his heart twist. He curses his wife and all her secrets. Why hadn't she said something? Why hadn't she warned him this day might come? What, did she think it would push him over the edge as far as his addiction went, like maybe he was too *delicate* to handle it? That was such bullshit. She's put their whole family at risk. Children he loves. Even Tom *himself.*

He realizes Roscoe is still looking at him, waiting for an answer about the bed. "No, no, buddy," he says. "I was just kidding."

He pulls the covers back. This is always the bed Roscoe sleeps in when he comes for a visit, and his mother has bought special baseball-themed sheets. Tom's grateful for her. Grateful that there's room here for Roscoe and Charlie and himself. In the living room, down a small hallway, his mom coos to Charlie, hopefully getting him settled down for bed. She says something to Tom's father, and then they hear the remote switch off.

"In you go," Tom urges Roscoe. Finally, the boy eases under the covers and adjusts his head on the pillow. Just looking at his young features gives Tom a pang of hurt deep in his chest. Some serious shit went down today. He could have lost Roscoe forever. He hates even thinking about it.

"You want a story before sleep?" he asks Roscoe gently.

Roscoe shrugs and then shakes his head.

"Not even *Where the Wild Things Are?*"

Roscoe makes a face. "That's not my favorite anymore."

Tom crosses his arms. "It was your favorite two days ago. What, you too big for it now? Too much of a man?"

Roscoe shrugs again and looks away. Maybe he's more troubled than he lets on.

Tom clears his throat. "Wanna talk about what happened today? With Mommy's . . . friend?"

The boy's gaze darts to Tom, then finds his lap again. "Are they really friends?"

They shouldn't be. "Well, I think they were a long time ago. Mommy definitely didn't expect she was coming . . . but maybe she should have."

"What do you mean?"

"Never mind. Anyway, I think her friend might be troubled. She didn't quite know what she was doing when she drove off with you like that. Were you scared?"

"Sort of," Roscoe says in a small voice. "She didn't drive very good. And I kept asking her where we were going, but she didn't answer. And I didn't like walking through that dark tunnel at all."

"I hear you, buddy. And I'm so sorry that happened to you and we weren't there." Tom fights back tears. "But we were right behind you. Me and Mommy. You know that, right? We were making sure nothing bad happened to you."

"That woman made it sound like I was going somewhere else. To some other family."

"We'd never let that happen. She's sick, buddy."

"Sick? Like dying?"

"No . . . a different kind of sick. But don't worry. She's getting help."

Such flimsy lies. Tom has no control of that woman. He hates Danny, hates her for coming this morning and disrupting their lives, hates for what she did to Roscoe, and maybe even hates her because she cracked open the truth about who his wife used to be. He doesn't feel relief knowing that Rebecca was part of some . . . *cult*, or that she'd had the cult leader's baby. Of all the things he'd imagined about her past and pregnancy—shitty boyfriends, abusive situations, the result of a one-night stand—cult hadn't been on his bingo card. And while he doesn't wish one of the other scenarios to be true instead . . . well, it's just so . . . *strange*. He wonders if he'll ever get used to it.

Of course she kept it a secret, though. It's bizarre. And of course Tom feels for Rebecca. Did she have anyone to talk to about any of this in the aftermath? Probably not. She just had to . . . *swallow* it. But meanwhile, all this time, she's been living in low-grade fear that this Ben guy was going to find her.

Tom rubs Roscoe's head in gentle circles. He thinks Roscoe is falling asleep, but then he suddenly says, "Do I have to tell the police?"

"About what happened today?" Tom asks.

"Uh-huh."

"I'm not sure yet, buddy. Maybe."

"Do you think they'll arrest that lady? Mommy's friend?"

I wish they would, Tom thinks bitterly. But then he says, "I'm leaving that for your mom to decide. Miss Danny is an old friend of your mom's. And I think your mom wants to help get her better. That's why she's with her now."

"Do you think Mom will be safe?"

"I think they're just talking." *And luring Ben here*, he thinks. Rebecca had explained to him that they'd wait until Ben broke in, call the cops, and then hand over the damning video evidence on that thumb drive. If they just gave the cops the video without Ben, it would allow him ample time to flee the country, especially since he knows Rebecca has evidence on him. They need him here. They need to catch him red-handed.

Tom has no idea if it's a good plan or not, but it feels like his hands are tied. He feels trapped in this house. He can't do anything to give away Roscoe's location. He has no idea how many more guys this Ben dude has in Carson City, potentially watching, waiting, hoping to snatch Roscoe away.

He can't let that happen.

Finally, Roscoe falls asleep. Tom creeps out of the room and closes the door softly. He's so lost in his thoughts that he almost collides with his mother, who is just finishing putting the baby to bed.

"Oops," Tom says. He points to the guest room door. "All good in there?"

"He went down fast," his mom says, smiling. "He's a champion sleeper, that one."

"Thanks, Mom," Tom says sadly, patting her arm.

He tries to move on, but his mom doesn't let him pass right away. She looks at him carefully, then clears her throat.

"What's going on?" she blurts. "With you and Rebecca, I mean."

"I told you. She has a friend over. I was just giving them some space."

His mom puts her hands on her hips. She seems shorter than she was when Tom was a teenager—maybe there really is something to people shrinking as they age—but she's no less intimidating when she wants to be. "Bullshit."

"Mom, I—"

"You can tell me, Tommy. She's a good woman. Whatever this is, you can get through it. Don't ruin it."

"*Me*, ruin it?" That did it. He turns to his mother and splutters, "Rebecca kept something really . . . *important* from me. I feel totally betrayed. This isn't me messing up the marriage. It's absolutely her."

"Is this about her past?"

Tom wilts to the couch and puts his head in his hands. "Maybe."

"Does it really matter?"

"*Sort* of. I just don't know how to forgive her."

He feels his mom sitting next to him and letting out a sigh. "If you love someone, you find ways to forgive them for almost anything."

"It's not as easy as that, Mom."

"It isn't? What did you think I had to do for all the years you were in the thick of all your stuff? You probably don't even remember the ways you lied to us and broke our hearts. And sure, you can say that it's different because you were our *child*, but believe me, Thomas, there were definitely times when I wished you weren't."

"Thanks a lot!"

"I'm not saying this to make you feel bad. I'm saying it because we battled through it. All of us. Together. Whatever this is with Rebecca, you can't just run away. I know it's tempting. But think of all you'll lose if you do that."

Miserably, Tom's gaze drifts toward the closed bedroom door where Roscoe sleeps.

"It's not going to be easy. It's going to be terrible. I know from experience. But I also know you love her. You do, right?"

Tom closes his eyes. Despite everything, despite how angry he is, he nods.

"You have to hold that close. You have to *remember*. People are broken in all sorts of ways. You have to try and find your way through."

"And if I can't?"

"Don't decide that after just one night of being away. Go to her, Tommy. She needs you."

His mother says this with such conviction—and worry—that it makes the hairs on Tom's arms rise. Does she *know* something? He thinks again of Danny and all those things they said about the cult and its dangers. His mom can't possibly know any of that, but still, her words . . . they strike a nerve.

"Anyway." She pats his knee. "I got those corn chips you like, if you're hungry." And then she pads down the hall to the back room. Before she shuts the door, Tom mouths *thank you* to her back. He should say it out loud, but he's afraid his voice will break.

Tom sits for a while feeling dazed and lost. The house is still. He can hear his father's light snores. Outside the window, the neighborhood is dead and peaceful. It became nighttime so quickly. Twenty-four hours ago, he was living in a blissful existence—a dad with a wife and two sons. And now?

Fight through it. God, he so wants to run away. But maybe his mom has a point.

There are no new messages on his phone, but suddenly he wants to reach out to Rebecca—it's his mother's strange, emphatic command that she needs his help that's done it.

Everything okay there?

She doesn't reply.

He jiggles his foot nervously. He needs to be doing something, but he doesn't know what. He picks up his phone and starts googling. The very first thing he looks for? *Ben Rahm.* He wants another look at that guy's face.

Images pop up. Tom stares at the guy's thinning hair, his muscular shoulders. Sure, he's smiling, but there's no light or kindness in his eyes. He seethes with hatred. Rebecca slept with this guy and had to flee from him. And now he's slept with her friend. And clearly he's deranged and maniacal because he planned some sort of kidnapping plot for Rebecca's son. He is a monster. Not worthy of living, in Tom's opinion.

After staring at various pictures of Ben—teaching, midspeech, headshots, posing with what looks like the Dalai Lama, which immediately makes Tom lose respect for the guy—he navigates back to the ISB YouTube page. There are a lot of video uploads, and some parts of the channel are behind a paywall. ISB touts itself as a "personal growth and development program" with shiny videos of smiling people looking totally enlightened and like they're living their best lives. And, same as his search from before, it seems like if anyone posted something negative about ISB in the video comments, an army of people attack. It's like someone in ISB is constantly moderating the group's online presence, making sure it remains squeaky clean.

Then he notices a video on YouTube that he didn't see earlier. *Is ISB a Cult?* The video had only been posted a few hours ago. Tom clicks on it; after a few ads, a chubby millennial-age guy with a beard sitting in a computer chair appears. He turns the sound down low enough for him to hear but not to alert his parents.

"Thanks for joining us on *Conspiracy Today*," the guy says, gesturing to the banner behind him, which reads the same thing. "Today, we're looking at another group that just might be a cult. I bet you've heard of ISB—which stands for *Infinite Spiritual Being*. It's the personal growth program run by Ben Rahm. Anyway, it's garnered quite a lot of attention over the past few years, both for starting a community in Oregon and for whispers that some of the teachings and rituals are sexual in nature and extremely coercive. But never before has someone actually come out and blown the whistle—until we uncovered this."

In the corner of the screen is a still video of a floppy-haired guy in a dark room. "This is Toby Sherman," the millennial guy explains. (*The* Toby? Tom wonders.) "This was only posted a couple weeks ago. Toby is normally a gaming YouTuber. Never talked about anything else on the record. But in this video, he makes some serious allegations. The video was almost immediately taken down, but lucky for us, someone had been watching and screen recorded—and sent it along. Let's see what this dude has to say."

The video shifts to a clip of the guy in the dark room. Behind him are gaming posters and consoles. His gaze darts back and forth nervously. And then he starts talking about how he was secretly in a cult called ISB.

Tom stares, agape. This must be the video Rebecca was talking about.

After a minute of Toby talking about how terrifying ISB was, the millennial conspiracy theorist returns to the screen. "Interesting that Toby seems to know, instinctively, that ISB is going to give him shit for what he's saying. He's almost on what's like a kamikaze mission. But here's the thing—my sources now tell me that maybe ISB didn't just punish him by taking that video down. No one has *seen* Toby since it uploaded. We tracked down the convenience store where he works—guy has missed all of his shifts since this post. Could he have left town? Or did something *else* happen?" He crosses his arms. "This Ben Rahm, he means business. I've talked before about how he can be litigious, but I also think he takes matters into his own hands—and they get violent."

Tom leaps to his feet. Does Rebecca know what Ben is capable of? She must. She's seen Toby's video. Why hadn't Tom asked her what Ben might have *done* to Toby after he shook their address out of him? He isn't using his head.

He tries Rebecca again. Still no answer. Should he just drive over there? Only, what if Ben is tracking *him*, too, and knows he's brought the kids to his parents'—there's no way his mom and dad can defend themselves against that guy alone. He needs to be here. The first line of defense.

He stares maddeningly at his phone. Then, the call from California pops into his mind. Danny's mom. He'd made a note on his phone of the woman's number even though she'd called on the landline, thinking he might need it. He can only imagine the terror she must be feeling about her daughter. He has to talk to *someone.*

He types the phone number into his parents' landline—thank God they're old-fashioned and still have one.

The phone rings once, twice. Danny's mother picks up, her voice sounding groggy. "It's Tom again," he says, trying to keep the tremble out of his own voice. "We spoke earlier today."

"Where's my daughter?" Mrs. Martin demands. "Have you found her?"

"She's . . . she's with my wife," Tom explains. "At our house."

"Your wife is part of the problem!"

"No. She's not. I swear she's not and hasn't been for some time. She's trying to help Danny. But listen—I have this horrible feeling that Ben is coming for them. Danny, probably . . . but also my son. Rebecca's baby, when she came here. Ben . . . wants him, for himself. And he's coming. He's on his way."

Mrs. Martin inhales sharply. "Why aren't you calling the police?"

"I'm not sure I can myself. I have our son. And I'm calling from a landline, and as far as I know, they're not tracking it. But they seem savvy. They could be tracing 911 calls, who knows what kind of shit. I can't have them knowing where my kids are."

"So you're just going to *not report this*?"

"I'm hoping maybe . . . *you* could," Tom says.

There's a pause. "So his people would trace the call to me instead."

"Well, possibly . . ."

Mrs. Martin doesn't speak for a few beats. Finally, she sighs. "All right. I'll do it."

Tom quickly gives her his home address and the local police station's number. "But listen, I don't want you calling right yet," he goes on. "We have video surveillance on our doors. Rebecca insisted we get it—I never really understood why, as our neighborhood is really safe, but maybe now I do. We only want to call the police once we see Ben on the property. Sneaking in somehow. Or trying to force his way in. My wife said she'd call the police, too—but I'm not sure she knows how dangerous he can be. We need the cops to actually have a reason to arrest him for something."

"I hate the idea of them being there alone." Mrs. Martin sounds near tears.

Tom swallows hard. "I do too. I'm going to monitor the situation, and I'll call you when it's time. Okay?"

Mrs. Martin agrees, and Tom hangs up. Then, on his phone, he opens the app for the video doorbell at his house. There is a camera at both doors, the front and the back. He prays Ben won't see them. They're fairly hidden. And maybe, living in Oregon for so long without neighbors, Ben isn't aware of the technology.

Both of the live video images are blurry, and there's no movement. The front yard still has tree branches strewn everywhere from the storm this morning—it's not like Tom has had time to clear them. In the backyard, Roscoe has left behind a few of his trucks and a kid-sized baseball glove. Tom's throat tightens. But Roscoe is safe here. With him. What about Rebecca, though? Where is *she*?

He stares at the two feeds without blinking for fear he'll miss something. *Come on, buddy*, he wills, though it feels wrong to hope for a madman to try and break into your house with your wife inside. But Rebecca will be able to hold her own, at least until the cops come. It's got to be why she has that gun. He wants to end this. He wants this guy to fry.

He's so keyed up that he needs something to do with his mouth—gum or something. Usually he keeps some in the backpack he's brought, so he reaches for it and starts to rummage around. But then, something strange and rattling bumps against his fingers, stuffed deep into one of the bag's pockets. He frowns. What is *that*? When his hands close around the pieces of hard metal, his heart sinks. *No.* It can't be. But when he pulls it out . . . it *is*.

The bullets from Rebecca's gun.

CHAPTER THIRTY-THREE

Ben is close. He knows this not just from what his GPS tells him, but also a sense deep in his bones. He's always known he's perceptive and excellent at sensing energy. It's like he can *feel* Rebecca and Danielle . . . and his children. He is coming for them. He will have them. No matter what.

Slowly, he drives the car down the dark street of identical houses. It makes him sad, how generic they all look. Rebecca left their beautiful world for . . . *this*? She's fooled herself into thinking she's happy here. She's probably a terrible mother, too, sick and vulnerable and emotional and certainly, *certainly* not giving his son what he needs. And that man who's raising him alongside her? Well, just thinking about that guy makes Ben sick. It's unconscionable, really. The wrong needs to be righted. Roscoe will be so happy to be with his real father. He will *thrive*. And he'll grow up *properly*, with good values, back in Bend. Not the way he's growing up here.

GPS says the house is at the end of the block. Danielle's GPS tracker says she's there as well. He reaches for his phone and texts Danielle. *Here*, he writes.

To his relief, she responds immediately. *Back door.*

He smiles to himself as he pulls up to the curb. Not quite at the house, of course—he doesn't want to alert them, and surely Rebecca is on high alert—but a few doors down. He wonders how it went down with Danielle today—and where Danielle actually is. Surely not in the house anymore. Rebecca is probably furious with her and turned her away. Hiding in the woods, maybe? Ben is eager to reunite with her. There is a lot of work she needs done, a lot of healing for her mind. Still, he's proud of Danielle for being brave and following through. He knows it had to be difficult. He'll go easy on her, he figures. She's stronger than he thought. And Rebecca—it's a wonder she didn't call the police. But at the same time, Ben knows why she didn't. Rebecca isn't innocent in all this. Rebecca is guilty of lots of things, too, allegations Danielle could turn on her. Scared little mouse. Of course she kept quiet.

He steps out of the car and pulls on a pair of gloves. Then he starts down the dark street, his footsteps echoing softly on the sidewalk. It's the kind of neighborhood without streetlights, which suits him just fine. When he reaches Rebecca's house, he stares at it a moment, relishing the fact that he's so *close*. The windows are dark. There's no movement inside. They're sleeping blissfully in there. Just like babies.

But not for long.

CHAPTER THIRTY-FOUR

Shit. Tom stares at the bullets in his palm. He'd completely, *completely* forgotten he'd taken them out of the gun . . . but of course he did. He didn't want the kids getting hold of a loaded weapon. And after Danny drove off with Roscoe, things happened so quickly—he wasn't thinking to give the bullets back to Rebecca. All he wanted was to get Roscoe away from her friend.

He checks the video doorbell again. Still nothing. No movement. Then he reaches for the phone on the wall once more and dials his wife's number. She still doesn't answer. Does he leave her a voicemail, warning her the gun isn't loaded? How will she be able to defend herself?

Suddenly, a flicker on the screen. Tom slams the phone down and turns to it, his mouth agape. It's the back door. There's something . . . some*one* . . . at the edge of the yard. His heart starts to pound. Even though he's been anticipating this, it's terrifying to see that Ben has *actually shown up.* He doesn't seem to notice the camera, either, because he walks right up to the porch.

Tom lurches backward as though Ben can actually see him. *Mrs. Martin.* He needs to call her. *Now.*

"Dad?"

Tom whips around, heart in his throat. Roscoe stands in the hallway, blanket dragging behind him. He looks upset. "Yeah, buddy?" Tom asks, turning over his phone so Roscoe can't see what he's looking at.

"I can't sleep. Can you snuggle with me?"

"Uh . . ." Tom glances at his phone. "Just a sec, okay? I just need to do something out here, and then I'll come in."

"What are you doing?" Roscoe frowns at the face-down phone on the table.

"Nothing!" Tom's voice jumps an octave. "Just, um, adult stuff—seriously, go back to bed, and I'll come in before you know it. Okay?"

"Okay . . ." Roscoe hangs his head and trudges back into the little bedroom. The moment he disappears through the door, Tom turns the phone back over and stares in horror at the screen. Ben . . . is *gone*.

But the back door hangs open. *Wide*.

"Shit, shit, *shit*," Tom moans, reaching for the phone to call Mrs. Martin . . . and reaching for his car keys.

He prays he isn't too late.

CHAPTER THIRTY-FIVE

There it is. The back door Danielle was talking about. Ben creeps closer, one ear cocked for sounds. A dog barking. A gasp from a neighbor. A window opening and someone calling out. This isn't the type of neighborhood that gets crime, he can tell. Not that this is a crime he's committing. He's righting a wrong, and that's very different. Same as it was with Toby, if you want to get right down to it. Toby had stolen something from him. Something precious. He also blasphemed the whole community on the internet, attempting to spread horrible lies and ruin their characters. And he told his guys not to hurt Toby upon entering. To *reason* with him. Was it really Ben's fault that the kid lashed out, almost like he *wanted* something bad to happen? Really, his guys acted in self-defense.

His fingers grasp the knob. It turns. His heart lifts. The bolt releases, and the door swings open. He's *in*. For a moment, he can't believe it. In Rebecca's house, after all this time. *He's so close.* This is the way this is supposed to be, obviously—it's why this is so easy. The universe is intervening, paving him an easy path.

The room he enters—a kitchen, it looks like—is dark, but he doesn't dare turn on any lights. Instead, he moves slowly, feeling his way around the counters and table. As his eyes adjust, he takes in a plastic cereal bowl drying next to the sink. His son's, probably. His heart lurches. There are signs of the boy everywhere—trucks and Lego bricks on the floor, little shoes on a mat, drawings on the refrigerator with his signature scrawled messily at the bottom. *Roscoe.* Ben doesn't really care for that name. With all of his children, he only names them after they are born, when he can sense their beings. He doubts, though, that Roscoe was a name he would have picked—perhaps he'll change it, when this is all said and done.

The first floor is eerily quiet. Ben is aware of every footstep. He spots a staircase through the kitchen and knows he needs to climb it. Danielle didn't tell him specifically, but this looks like the kind of house where all the bedrooms are upstairs. He tiptoes on the risers, avoiding the piles of laundry and other detritus sitting on the steps, waiting to be carried up. Clearly Rebecca isn't as tidy as he mandated everyone be at the big house in Bend. A pity. What must her husband think?

At the top of the stairs, he pauses and looks at the series of doors. Really, she has made it so easy. The bathroom door is ajar, a nightlight illuminating aged blue tile and a small bathtub. The door right next to it has a big truck sticker on the outside along with Roscoe's name spelled out in bubble letters. Ben can't help but grin. Rolling back his shoulders, he edges into the room as quietly as he can. He can just make out a shape under the covers. Ben tries to control his excitement and sense of redemption, because this is going to be the hardest part.

He approaches his son and sits at the edge of the bed, gently enough so that the kid doesn't stir. "There you are," he whispers. "Rest easy. Everything is okay. It must have been hard without me, huh? But it's all right. I'm here now."

He waits. Assesses. The boy still sleeps.

"Feeling the call, I know you felt it," he whispers. "It's promised to people like us, you and me. So listen, we'll only need to pack a few things. When you're home, everything will be new. New clothes, toys . . ."

A crackle of static. He looks up. What was *that*? He scans the room. Nothing. Probably just his mind playing tricks. An engine cough outside. The wind.

He leans a little closer to the mountain of blankets, wanting to touch his boy's shoulder but suddenly a little afraid. "You'll be the prince of our new world. Anything you want. Whenever you want it. It's your birthright. A man must be around his father. His father is the most important thing. You'll understand someday."

The boy starts to move, first his shoulder, then his hip. The excitement in Ben's stomach grows. Here is the moment. Here is his chance. "Come on," he whispers, moving his hand up the shoulder and toward his chin. "Let me see that face."

He pulls the blankets back a little just as the child turns. Only, it's not a boy in the bed—but a woman. Ben is completely disoriented by Rebecca's dark eyebrows and hair, and she springs up so vigorously that he jumps back in fright. Somehow, she suddenly has him flat on his back on the ground before he can even make a sound. And something is pressed to his chest. He angles his chin and stares at it in horror.

It's a *gun*.

"Surprise," Rebecca hisses, her breath smelling like rot and evil. And just like the degenerate Ben always knew she was, she has no trouble pulling the trigger.

Click.

Pain shoots through Ben's jaw. Only, it's not from the gun—it's from how badly he's clenching his teeth. He opens his eyes again. Rebecca is staring at the gun in confusion. Her gaze trains on him again, and her eyes narrow. Once again, she pulls the trigger.

Click.

No shot again.

Rebecca groans. And then, five more *clicks*, five more shots to the chest, five empty chambers. By the third or fourth shot, Ben is laughing. After the fifth, he smacks the useless weapon out of Rebecca's hands, tightens his core, and leaps to his feet. Now it's his turn to shove her to the ground. He outweighs her by quite a bit. And he definitely, definitely isn't letting her go.

"You made a big, big mistake," he whispers.

CHAPTER THIRTY-SIX

Ben's knee is directly on Rebecca's sternum, making it hard to breathe. She's so stunned by what has happened that she can't quite figure out what to do next—but she *must*. She was sure the gun had bullets in it when she checked on it after Danny arrived. But Tom—*Tom*. He said he'd found the gun, too. He must have taken the bullets out. Why, *why* hadn't she checked? She'd seen Tom's number flash on her phone—maybe that's why he was calling. To warn her. But Ben was already in the house by then, or at least very close. She was afraid to answer and give herself away. Her plan to surprise him had worked . . . until it absolutely hadn't.

Ben leers over her. It is a reunion Rebecca has never wished for. His hair is longer and a little more gray and much thinner. He has a beard, and his glasses have changed, and he might be a little bit softer in the midsection, but she can tell he is still as obsessive about his health as ever, and just as strong. He is like a rock pressing on her torso. Her lungs feel flattened. It's inconceivable to think that this is a man she worshipped, undressed for, laid herself bare. Just thinking about it makes bile rise in her throat.

"Where is he, Rebecca?" he growls.

"Fuck you," Rebecca says through gritted teeth.

"Just tell me where he is, and I won't hurt you."

Yeah, right. She thinks of the things Ben said at the bedside when he thought she was Roscoe. Rage courses through her veins and makes her brave. She manages to roll out from his grip, destabilizing him. Then she pivots and punches him, hard. It's enough to move him off her, and she scrambles for the gun he has thrown aside. When she turns, Ben is coming for her again, hands headed toward her throat. She cracks him hard in the temple with the gun's handle, and he goes flying against the wall.

"What the *fuck?*" Ben screams, clutching his head.

"Get out of here. I'm calling the police." Still holding the gun, Rebecca scurries to her son's bed, fumbling to open the bedside drawer where she's stashed her phone. She's already cued up 911—all she has to do is hit the green Call button. Her fingers shake as she unlocks the device.

"No, you won't," Ben hisses. His hand shoots out, knocking the phone from her grasp. Rebecca screams and lurches for it, but it skids under the bed. Ben grabs her at the knees, and she falls forward, cracking her head on the bedpost. Then he slams her hard on her back, her spine digging into the wood floor. She feels his fist on her jaw, then her temple, then her cheek. Her mouth tastes like blood.

"You. Are. Not. Better. Than. Me," Ben groans, timing his words with his blows. Rebecca tries to fight back, but he has her pinned. With every punch, she grows weaker and weaker. Her vision starts to blur at the corners. She can feel blood trickling from her ear. The noises Ben makes above her are feral and senseless and terrifying. It's all too much, suddenly. She feels herself slipping away. *Danny*, she thinks. But there's no way she can call for her. Who knows where Danny even is. Maybe Rebecca was wrong—maybe she really isn't strong enough to leave. Maybe Danny was part of this as a setup, still . . . and maybe Rebecca has made a huge mistake.

"I'm sorry," Rebecca croaks. She doesn't say this to Ben—absolutely not. But to Roscoe. To Tom. To herself. She hasn't tried hard enough. Maybe she trusted her friend too implicitly. And now the wrong side is going to win.

CHAPTER THIRTY-SEVEN

Danny crouches in Bex's basement, staring at the little black-and-white monitor in her hands. On the screen are blurry shapes of a dark little boy's bedroom. Before Bex sent her down here, Danny grabbed Roscoe's video monitor so she could keep track of what was happening up there. Both the kids have a monitor, it seems, and Danny remembers using monitors when she used to babysit in high school. She turned on the camera in Roscoe's room and then carried the monitor to the basement. She hopes this doesn't mess up Bex's plans . . . but Bex has got to be crazy if she thinks Danny is just going to hide down here knowing absolutely nothing. She needs to see this for herself. Whatever Ben plans to do. Whatever Bex plans to do to him.

The image on the screen wobbles and then rights itself. It's dead quiet. Moments before, Danny saw Bex hide herself under the little boy's covers to wait. Danny waits, too. It's driving her mind mad. She taps against a box of Christmas ornaments, but it gives her no sense of control or calm. She closes her eyes and tries to do her strength exercise, the one that's supposed to harness and purify every organ and give someone ultimate control of their body, but suddenly, she feels some doubt about the ritual. It certainly isn't working right now.

Bex said it was for her own good that she hide; she'd rather Danny not get her hands dirty—and it wasn't good for Danny's baby. But Danny feels so helpless. She also doesn't know exactly what Bex intends to do. The plan is for Ben to come into the house and then head to Roscoe's bedroom; he'll think he's stealing the kid away. Instead, he'll find Bex? Danny isn't sure. She wishes she could reach out to Bex to tell her she doesn't think this plan is a good one. Problem is, she doesn't dare call her in case Ben is already here.

Is she really doing this? Is she really setting Ben up? The man she thought she loved. The man she's spent eight years with. It makes her want to throw up. It makes her want to break free from this hiding spot and throw herself at his feet, begging for his forgiveness. Intellectually, Danny understands that what Bex told her is probably true, to some extent: there's no way Ben is blameless. But her heart doesn't know that yet. Her heart still longs for him, misses him, wants to be near him. It's taking every ounce of her resolve to stay put and not move. To just . . . *let this happen*.

A *crack* makes her turn. She peers at the baby monitor again, but it's the same image—a still life of Roscoe's room, Bex huddling under the covers of Roscoe's little bed. But then a noise sounds from directly above her. Danny stares at the ceiling. Is that . . . ? *Yes*. Someone has just opened the back door. She waits. If it's Tom, he'd call out . . . but there are no voices.

A shiver goes through her. *Ben, then?* She'd told him the door was unlocked. He won't come down to the basement, will he? He can't possibly know she's here . . .

Ben's footsteps sound on the ceiling. The floorboards creak as he walks toward what Danny figures are the stairs. She hears his first footfalls on the risers, but then can't hear anything else. He's on the second floor, then. *So close to Bex*. What is he going to do when he realizes it isn't Roscoe in the bed? *Is this a terrible idea?*

She looks at her phone. Should she turn it on and call the police? What if something pings on Ben's end, alerting her that she's here? She doesn't know what to do. She feels stuck. She listens for sounds, but there are none. Not that she can hear with her own ears, anyway.

But then a shape appears on the monitor screen.

Danny's jaw drops as a fuzzy image of Ben creeps into Roscoe's little room. It's dark, and it's hard to make out his expression completely, but it looks like one of . . . *rapture*. Slowly, Ben walks over to the little bed. Danny's heart pounds. Bex has a plan, but Danny has only halfway acknowledged the terrible suspicion of what the plan *is*. She heard Tom mention a gun. This is what she's letting happen, sitting here silently. She's letting her true love, her beacon, her Scion . . . *die*.

Turn on your phone, she wills her fingers. But they're like blocks of lead. She can't get them to move.

"There you are," Ben coos through the speaker.

Danny rears back. At first, she thinks he's talking to *her*.

He's still talking. He must think it's Roscoe in the bed, judging by his soft voice. He says something about how everything is okay now. How it must have been hard without him. Danny bites her bottom lip. She isn't so sure about that. Roscoe seems happy here. This is his family.

"We'll only need to pack a few things," Ben murmurs. "When you're home, everything will be new. You'll be the prince of our new world."

Danny watches as he leans down and touches Bex's shoulder, giving the figure in the bed a loving, knowing look. The image on the monitor is almost crisp now, eerily precise. "A man must be around his father," he whispers. "His father is the most important thing."

Danny's mouth drops open. He didn't just say that. He *couldn't* have. All this time, even though she's listened to Bex, even though she's nodded her head and tried to let it sink in, maybe she didn't believe her—not completely. Ben loved the women in ISB. Ben loved *her*. He wouldn't take away Danny's baby. He didn't have a deranged opinion of women as mothers. It just wasn't possible.

A man must be around his father. His father is the most important thing.

It's what he must think about Danny's baby, too.

When Bex shoots up in bed, Danny calls out and almost drops the monitor. Things happen so fast, then—she pushes Ben backward. There's a loud *thump*, and then a groan, and then something clicking. *The gun*, Danny realizes, her stomach dropping to her knees. Except . . . something is wrong. The gun doesn't make a *bang* . . . just an impotent little clicking sound. Then there's another click, and another. Danny stares at the screen, but Bex and Ben are off camera—she can't tell what's happening.

But then Ben chuckles. "You made a big, big mistake."

Bex screams. Danny's hand flutters to her mouth. "Fuck you!" she hears Bex yell, and then a loud blow and a crash, and then Ben reappears for a moment as he careers across the carpet.

When he rounds on Bex again, he lets out a furious, animalistic grunt Danny has never heard from him before. Ben's anger is potent. Overflowing. It has, Danny realizes, lurked inside him always, festering, *building*.

He's going to kill her.

Danny drops the monitor and clambers up the stairs. Fuck hiding. Fuck keeping her hands clean. She can't stand by and let this guy murder her best friend. No community is worth that. As she climbs the stairs, she dials 911. Her heart is pounding so hard she can barely hear the dispatcher, and she has no idea what she even says because for the life of her she can't remember Bex's address. When she hangs up, she hears screaming coming from above—and something far worse, a banging sound against the floor. Bex's body? Bex's *head*? Danny's body goes hot, then cold. She looks around for a weapon. A kitchen knife? But it's all the way around the island. She needs to get upstairs *now*. Then, she spots a wooden baseball bat hanging on the living room wall. She yanks it from its hooks, possibly tearing out some plaster, but no matter. She takes the stairs two at a time, feeling tears streaming down her cheeks. She's almost too afraid to approach Roscoe's bedroom, because the sounds coming from the inside are terrible, and she isn't sure she can handle this. But then she hears Ben grunting, "You are not better than me," and something turns over inside her. Who *is* this man? They can't let him win.

When she steps into the room, Ben's back is to her, and Bex is on the ground. Danny tells herself not to look directly at her friend for fear she might scream, so instead she advances toward the man she thought she loved. The baseball bat quivers in her hands, but she manages to swing it hard and make contact with his head. *Thwack.*

Ben's hands release from Bex's body and fly to his ears. He spins around, and his eyes widen when he sees her. "Danielle!" he screams. "What are you doing?"

She can't speak. She can't think. She swings again, this time missing his head by an inch. "Danielle, stop!" he screams. "This isn't what it looks like!"

"Did you kill her?" Danny screams back. "You killed your son's mother?"

"She came after me, she—"

But Danny doesn't care. She swings again, this time clocking Ben across the forehead. He howls and staggers backward. "Danielle, *stop!*"

Out of the corner of her eye, Danny notices Bex coming to. There's blood all over her face, and her eyes aren't quite focusing. Danny feels a rush of gratitude—at least he hasn't killed her yet—but turns to Ben to whack at him some more. Ben ducks her swing. Then he starts to laugh.

"You picked the wrong side, Danielle," he teases. "Bad, bad choice."

"No, I didn't," Danny sneers, raising the bat once more like she's swinging in the World Series . . . and hitting him square in the chest. Ben's eyes widen. He wheels backward, trying to grab onto something, but the force of the blow is too great. His body crashes into—and then through—Roscoe's bedroom window. Before Danny even knows what's happening, glass shatters and Ben's body disappears out and then down, down, down.

"Oh my God," Danny whispers.

"*Danny?*" Bex sits up groggily. "How did you . . . What's happening?"

Danny's heart is pounding. "He . . . I . . ."

She hurries to the window and looks out. There, on the dark lawn, Ben lies on his back, groaning.

Bex gasps. "Did *you* do that?"

"I had to," Danny says in a small voice. "He was going to kill you."

Bex stares at her, amazed. "I thought . . . you were . . . I thought he and you . . ." But then she trails off. "Danny. *Thank* you."

Danny waves her hand. There's no time for that now. She looks out the window again. Ben is alive . . . and now he's slowly trying to get up. *No*, Danny thinks. She grabs Bex's hand. "C'mon."

They hurry down the stairs, Bex trailing blood, and out the front door. Broken glass sparkles on the lawn. Ben twists and moans in the side yard, and he's slowly making his way to his feet. He's covered in blood and grass. When he sees Danny and Bex, he starts to crawl on all fours toward the street. He's surprisingly fast, and Danny thinks he's going to get away, when suddenly Bex breaks into a sprint and tackles him from behind. Danny follows behind as Ben groans and collapses on his belly. The sharp smells of blood and piss fill the air. Bex looks around and grabs the metal nozzle of a garden hose and starts to bash his head with it. Ben's eyes close. Blood pours from his mouth. He's barely conscious, his head lolling to one side. Blood oozes from his mouth and wounds on his head.

But then a pompous smirk settles over his face. "You're both worthless," he slurs. "You're both *weak*."

"No, we're not," Bex says, her eyes streaming with tears.

"All I want is my boy."

"You can't have him," Bex moans. "You can *never* have him!"

To Danny's horror, Ben staggers to his feet, lunges for Danny, yanking the bat from her hands. Danny wheels back, but it's too late—he whacks her with it on her shoulder and then again at her hip, dangerously close to her baby bump. Danny screams and falls to the ground. She shields her bump and shuts her eyes, sure he's going to hit her again and again.

"Ben!" Bex then screams from somewhere to the left. "Come on, you pussy. You want me instead. You know you do. So come get me."

Danny opens one eye. Murderously, Ben turns in Bex's direction. He's gripping the bat so hard his knuckles are white. And Bex is just staring at him, weaponless, vulnerable, but seemingly unafraid. Time seems to slow down—Danny can see him advancing for Bex, and then raising the bat over his head, and Bex's stalwart features blurring before her.

"Bex!" Danny cries out, but it's like her voice doesn't work. And the whole *world* is blurry, actually—not just Bex's face. She can feel herself falling, both from fear and the pain from where Ben hit her. She wants to move, wants to defend her friend, but it's like her body doesn't work anymore.

"Bex!" she says weakly, mostly just inside her brain. But the world is clouding around her. And then, to her dismay, it all goes terrifyingly dark.

CHAPTER THIRTY-EIGHT

Tom has never driven so fast in his life. Unbuckled, his phone pressed to his ear, screaming first to Danny's mother and then to 911 himself—who the fuck cares if Ben's minions know where he is now, as his wife's life is on the line—he speeds through stop signs and red lights, praying he doesn't get stopped. As he approaches his neighborhood, he hears sirens wailing, and his heart leaps to his throat. He steps on the gas on the final turn and almost pukes when he sees several ambulances and police cars at his curb.

He parks on the grass and leaps out. Cops are standing around the yard, looking at . . . *something*. A body on the grass. Oh God, is it *Rebecca*? He can't see. He can't tell. He walks like a zombie, his brain not quite connecting with his legs. He might faint. It doesn't matter what Rebecca withheld from him. They can get past this. But please, *please*, he needs his wife alive. He doesn't know what he'll do without her. If that asshole did something to her, if he *killed* her . . .

He goes to push through the throng of officers when an arm shoots out, stopping him. "Whoa, buddy."

"I need to see my wife!" Tom screams. His gaze focuses on the guy's badge. *Detective Yates.* Shit, there's a *detective* involved? "This is my house! Where's my wife? Where's Rebecca?" *Is she that body under the sheet?*

Yates puts his hands on Tom's shoulders. "Calm down, sir. Your wife is over there. Giving her statement."

He points to the left. And there, sitting on the back of an ambulance with a blanket around her shoulders, is Rebecca. There's blood on her face, and her eye is bruised, and she looks dazed, but she's *here*. Alive.

So then . . . who's that body on the grass?

No matter. Tom runs to her. When Rebecca sees him, her mouth contorts into an ugly cry. She launches off the back of the ambulance to fall into his arms. Immediately, she's sobbing.

"I'm okay," she says into his ear. "I'm okay."

"Thank God," Tom whispers, caressing her hair. "Thank fucking God."

"She's a tough girl," says a voice behind him. Tom pulls away from his wife just a little to see another officer, a woman, with a notepad in her hand. "Defended her home," the woman goes on. "And her friend."

Tom glances again at the body on the grass. It's *him*. Eerie that he's actually right next to this Ben guy after obsessing over him for the past day. The only feature sticking out from under the sheet is a few tufts of his thinning hair. Blood has soaked through the thin cotton. And the shape of his skull under the sheet doesn't look quite right, like some of his jaw has caved in. *Holy fuck*, he thinks.

Then he looks back at Rebecca, who is crying so hard she can barely breathe.

"He . . . he came for Danny and me," she chokes out.

"I know," Tom says. "I took the bullets from the gun. I'm so sorry, baby. I thought I was doing the right thing. I was trying to protect the kids."

Rebecca nods. "I know. And you were. But . . . oh God, Tom, I was so scared."

"She did what she had to do," the cop breaks in. "She fought back. Her friend came after him with a bat. He fell out the window."

"I-I didn't mean for that to happen." Rebecca looks apologetic.

Tom scoffs. "Are you kidding? You were just doing what you had to do."

But Rebecca seems so afraid for some reason, like she did something wrong. The officer with her, whose badge reads *Smith*, shakes her head.

"We have quite a file on this guy, it seems. Complaints from family members, allegations of abuse—the FBI was watching him carefully. They'll be along shortly, as this is a matter that spans several states. We're just sorry you ladies had to take matters into your own hands."

The detective moves on to talk to Danny. Rebecca leans her head on Tom's shoulder. Her body is still trembling. Tom's is, too.

But then Rebecca backs up, seems to check to make sure the cop has really moved on, and then looks at him. "Tom, I want to start over. I want us to tell each other everything."

"I know," Tom assures her. "But we can talk about all of that later. You need to get checked out. You're kind of banged up."

"Tom, no." She clutches his hands. "There's something I need to tell you. *Now.*"

"Rebecca, really. Right now, I'm just glad you're okay. Safe. I'm glad that madman—" He glances toward the flares and the officers on the lawn and *the body*. It's hard to believe it's the same yard where Tom and his family picnicked, and he and his brothers played hide and seek, and he built tiny snowmen the few times it snowed a few inches—all of it was marred now by this terrible man and his terrible death. Sadness floods over him. The sadness of what he did to his wife for so many years. "I'm so glad he fell."

"That's the thing, Tom." Rebecca's voice quivers. "He . . . he didn't fall out the window. I mean, he did, but that's not what killed him. He got back up when he was outside. He had your bat. He . . . he hit Danny with it. The woman carrying his child. Danny was knocked out. Then he came for me, and . . ." She shuts her eyes. "I don't know what came over me. I just . . . *snapped*. I don't know how I got that bat. I know I should have just knocked him out—I heard the sirens. But that's not what I did."

"It's okay," Tom insists. "You were scared. For yourself. For your friend. And you were *angry*. Listen, I want you to tell me about what you went through—as much as you feel you can and want to, anyway. But you don't have to now. And please, there is nothing wrong with what you did."

"But what if the police see the bruises, his head bashed in? They're going to question what happened. It's one thing to defend yourself. But to do what I did? I went overboard, Tom."

Tom crosses his arms. "I'll help protect you if you're questioned. We'll get through this together."

Rebecca blinks. "But it might not be as easy as that."

"I'll make sure you're safe. This guy ruined your life. You aren't going down for this. There's no way."

Rebecca seems shocked. She shifts her weight, then takes a breath in. "After the way I've lied to you? After everything I've kept from you—and the *gun* . . . ?"

Tom pulls her to him again. "I'm here for you. I promise."

She shudders as he holds her. Maybe she doesn't think she deserves him. He's sensed this, he realizes, from her, not that he ever knew what she was feeling. Her whole life with Ben she probably walked on eggshells, never sure if she was doing the right thing, never sure if he truly loved her. She carried that baggage into this relationship, maybe figuring everyone was like Ben and would only love conditionally. Tom would spend the rest of his life proving to her that she was worth so much more.

He slings his arm around her as they turn and watch the EMTs load the body into the ambulance on its way to the morgue. He wants to ask his wife what she's thinking, knowing it's her old abuser's body under that sheet, but he lets her disappear into her thoughts. It's hard to know what the road ahead will be for her—and them. But in some ways, now knowing her past, at least he knows what he's working with.

The ambulance doors slam, sealing Ben inside. Rebecca grimaces, but as soon as the ambulance pulls away, something inside her seems to release. "There he goes," he says gently. "It's over."

Tears stream down Rebecca's face, but then she nods. "It's over," she says. "It's really over."

CHAPTER THIRTY-NINE

Beep. Beep. Beep.

Rebecca opens her eyes to a stark white room and a marker board bearing her name. *Welcome to Room 304*, it reads, as well as displaying the emblem for the local hospital. And then it rushes back to her. *Ben. The attack.*

"Oh my God," she says, sitting up.

"Mommy!" a voice cries. Rebecca looks over: Roscoe. He's *here*.

She gestures him over, and he runs to her, carefully wrapping his arms around her shoulders. Nothing has ever smelled so amazing in her life as the scent of the top of his head. Tears fill her eyes.

"Mommy, are you okay?" Roscoe asks.

"Mommy's okay," Rebecca says weakly, kissing his cheek. "I was just sleeping." She looks down at the IV line in the crook of her elbow. "This is just fluid, that's all. And I just have a little bump on my head, but it's going to be fine."

Roscoe presses his little mouth together with a look of concern. "You have bruises, though. On your face."

"I know. I fell. But it's no big deal."

But Ben. He *isn't* fine. The realization hits her hard again. *Dead. The fall out the window.* That's their story, and they're sticking to it.

She looks over. Tom is sitting on a hard plastic chair in the corner, the baby on his lap. She's never seen anything lovelier than her whole family together. When he sees her, he gives her an encouraging smile. "Morning," he says, bringing Charlie over. "Thought you might like some visitors."

Rebecca shifts up—painfully, as her whole body feels bruised—to kiss the baby. "What time is it?" she murmurs.

Tom swivels around to check the clock. "Nine a.m. I think they're bringing breakfast around soon. Maybe pancakes!"

Rebecca smiles, but she can't fathom eating. She's still so keyed up. Everything still feels so raw.

Last night, there was talk of Rebecca and Danny going to the police station so they could give more official statements and receive more official questioning. But after a few minutes, word started to leak throughout the entire force what sort of man Ben was. Soon enough, they were all looking at his profile on Instagram and YouTube as well as the terrified parents' comments about the rumored abuse, torture, and control. Briefly, Rebecca shared her story about seeing Sophia in that wrecked cabin, and how Ben gave the pregnant women things he called vitamins but were probably far from it, and how she feared for her life after she escaped. And then Danny jumped in, telling them to investigate a person named Toby Sherman, who also left the group but was shaken down for some information and might have been killed.

It seemed to sway them away from charging Rebecca or Danny with anything. And, as Rebecca notices, there is no officer posted outside her door, waiting to arrest her.

Still, the secret pulsates inside her now. She kind of can't *believe* she did what she did. Talking Danny into luring Ben there. Springing out of that bed to shoot him. Danny hitting Ben and him falling out the window—well, yes, that was sort of an accident, and it truly was self-defense.

But on the lawn? After she heard the sirens? All she had to do was stave Ben off. Hold out for a few more seconds. But something had snapped in her mind that made her do what she did, especially when she saw him standing over Danny, ready to hurt her and her baby. She thought not only of the things Ben did to her but to all the women, and Toby, and all the *families*, the poor families missing their loved ones because Ben deemed them too *toxic* to keep in touch with. The man was truly, *truly* psychotic, and she had this terrible fear that if she didn't end his life, he would wriggle his way out of an arrest. She thought of the people still on the compound in Oregon, slowly wasting away. She thought of the women whose babies had been taken from them—and, yes, they would be without a father, but that term was too good for someone like Ben. She thought about Roscoe, too, and how if Ben lived, there was a chance that he might someday lay *eyes* on Roscoe, and suddenly she just couldn't bear it.

She didn't want Ben to live.

He was so shocked when she grabbed the bat from his hands and started pummeling him. He begged for her to stop. He clutched his head and dropped to the ground, and she didn't even stop when he went still. She only dropped the bat after the sirens were close. The evidence of what she'd done was obvious—his whole face was a bloody pulp. It was the first thing the cops looked at when they came on the scene. They saw the bat, too, and the blood, and Rebecca stammered something about how she'd hit him inside the house, when he was an intruder, before he fell. And Danny had no idea because she'd passed out and hadn't seen any of it.

Did the cops buy it, *really*? What about that Kris guy, the one who'd brought Danny here and was waiting to steal Roscoe? Rebecca figured that any minute now, the guy would come forward, saying he'd witnessed Rebecca's brutal beating. But there seems to be no word from him. The police would have told her by now.

And, oh God, everything else floods her mind, too. She lets out a sob. Tom rushes to her side with Roscoe. "What is it?" Tom asks.

Rebecca looks at Roscoe. "You must have been scared, with Miss Danny."

Roscoe stares at his shoes. "She made me walk through the mud. My shoes got all messed up."

"We'll get you new shoes, buddy, I promise," Rebecca says through tears. "You were so brave. But you knew Mommy and Daddy were coming for you, right?"

"Yeah, I knew," Roscoe says, smiling sadly.

"He's a tough one," Tom says, clapping Roscoe on his little shoulder. "Just like his mom."

Rebecca feels a lump in her throat. *And just like his dad?* It's a thought she can't turn away from anymore. Roscoe's heritage is something she's pushed away for the past seven years, but now it's the only thing she sees. Yet, just because he's the child of a monster doesn't mean he'll grow up to be that way, too. She'll go to the ends of the earth to make sure of it.

But then something terrible occurs to her. She touches Roscoe's hand. "Can I talk to Daddy alone for a minute, baby?"

Obediently, Roscoe returns to the little plastic chair, entertaining himself with a Lego figurine. Rebecca looks at Tom as he shifts the baby onto the other hip. "This is going to come out," she says in a low voice. "About me. Everyone's going to know who I used to be."

Tom is quiet for a moment. He looks uncomfortable. "There was a reporter who called already. I do think people are getting wind of the story, considering who Ben was."

"Meaning they'll know who I am and what I did. Parents at Roscoe's school. Our neighbors. Your parents!" She winces. It's almost painful. If this goes public, Roscoe will find out once he gets older. This is exactly what she didn't want to happen.

Tom sits down on the edge of the bed and strokes her hand. "It's your story to tell," he says. "Not Ben's. You can tell it however you want."

"But it'll come out that I was there for those awful rituals . . . that I was *complicit*."

"Were you? Or were you under his spell? I've read some of his philosophies, baby. His whole 'no one is a victim' thing. But guess what? You *were* a victim. You were his victim. He victimized all of you. And it's okay to tell that story."

Rebecca pulls her bottom lip into her mouth and squirms.

"Is that the reason you don't want it to come out?" Tom presses. "Because you're still conditioned that being a victim of something is bad? It's something that happened. It's fact. He abused you. He mind-controlled you." Tom pauses a moment, thoughtfully. "I'll stand by you whether you want to talk about what happened or not. If you want to go on the record, that's great, but you also don't have to. You already took control by leaving and defending yourself against the guy. No one can take that away from you. Though, I have to say, maybe it would be poetic justice if you truly painted how much of a victim all of you were in a big way. It would turn all of his teachings on their head."

"I know. And it's tempting. I just . . ." Rebecca breathes out. "All these years, I've felt so guilty about what I was part of. And I've tried to tell myself that I didn't *know* what I was part of, that I was really young, but I just look back on it, and I don't know what I was thinking. I worry about other people wondering that about me, too. Wondering what sort of idiot would get wrapped up in a cult." She glances at him. "You certainly did."

"At first," Tom says. "But the more you talk about it, the more I understand." He turns his wrists and stares at his palms. "People probably will judge you. But everyone judges. People judge me, especially people I used to know when I was using. They still think I'm that person, even though I'm not anymore. Some people don't believe that we can change. But obviously, we can."

"We've been through a lot," Rebecca says softly. "Both of us."

"We have." Tom pushes her hair off her forehead. "I think it's why we work together. We make each other stronger."

"So, you're staying with me, then?" Rebecca's voice cracks on the last word.

Tom chuckles lightly. "I'm willing to give it a try if you are."

She squeezes his hand. There will be hard days, she knows. Tom will feel the sting of her betrayal over and over, and they'll both have to face people's judgment and scorn. But maybe they can be strong together. Maybe they can weather this.

She can only hope.

"Bex?"

She opens her eyes again. Still in the same hospital room. Still hooked up to machines. But now Tom isn't in his chair. There's someone new in the doorway. Unlike Rebecca, Danny isn't wearing a hospital gown but a T-shirt and leggings. They can't be her own clothes, Rebecca realizes—they're way too oversized, even for modest Danny.

Danny notices her looking. "Hospital gave me some stuff. My other clothes were sort of . . ." She makes a face. "Bloody, I guess."

Danny tries to laugh, but then her expression contorts into something almost grief-stricken. Rebecca swallows hard and tries to push herself higher up the bed. "They didn't admit you?"

"Nah, amazingly, I had no broken bones. They checked the baby out, even. I did get a stern talking-to; apparently I'm way too underweight." She bites her lip. "My knee-jerk reaction is to say that isn't true, but when a lot of doctors say the same thing . . ."

". . . maybe you should listen," Rebecca finishes for her. "But I'm glad you made it through okay."

"You did, too." Danny smiles at her sadly. "They say your concussion isn't that bad. You just need to rest." There's another awkward pause, and then she adds, "I'm sorry, Bex. About all this. Has this ruined things with Tom?"

Rebecca sighs. "I don't know, honestly. He doesn't seem mad now. But I know that's going to change. His whole version of me is different now."

"You could always go to a therapist. Like, a *real* one."

Rebecca raises her eyebrows. "Is that a dig on Ben? So soon?"

Danny looks away. "Yes. No. Maybe."

"Do you . . . miss him?"

Danny shakes her head. But then a tear rolls down her cheek.

Rebecca stares at the marker board with her name on it until her vision blurs. Danny has got to know, deep down, what Rebecca did to Ben. She wonders if she's a tiny bit resentful that she didn't let the man live. What Danny did, coming to Rebecca's rescue at the end, even participating in the trap at *all*—it astounds Rebecca. She never thought Danny's eyes would open so quickly. She's so proud of her; maybe she's underestimated her friend all this time. Then again, she knows how the process was for her when she realized Ben wasn't who he said he was. It wasn't linear. It wasn't binary—one day Ben was good, the next he was bad. Even after she saw Sophia in that shed, even after she escaped, there were many days where she feared she'd made the wrong choice. Living in the shitty apartment here in Carson City, trying to subsist off the tiny stipend Kristen loaded into her account, terrified at the thought of raising a baby alone—there were days she almost called Ben up and told him she was coming back if he'd take her. Of course Danny probably felt that way, too. It was only normal.

"I'm sorry, too, Danny," she whispers.

Danny glances over at her. "It's okay."

They stare at each other for a moment, and Rebecca feels like Danny actually understands what she was apologizing for. She killed Ben because it was necessary. But she knows Danny saw his bloody face. Danny must have put two and two together. Yesterday she was still devoted to him. You can't let go of those feelings so fast.

She reaches out and squeezes Danny's hand. Then she looks down at Danny's backpack on her lap. "You're leaving?"

Danny breaks her gaze. "I got a call from my mom. I guess she was tipped off, somehow, and then she got in touch with Tom?"

"Tom? *My* Tom?" This is news to Rebecca.

"Yeah. Yesterday. I don't know how it went down."

"And you *talked* to her?"

Danny lets out a shaky breath. "It was okay, actually. Nice to hear her voice. And unlike what I thought she was going to do, she didn't lecture me about the dumb mistake I'd made or tell me that she'd been right all along."

"Did you tell her what happened with Ben? Like, why you'd come here?"

"Why did I come here?" Danny shrugs. "I mean, yes, Ben sent me. I was supposed to steal Roscoe. But it's not what happened, is it? I told her some of it, I guess. And I also told her I was pregnant. And she . . ." Danny smiles a little. "She's excited for me."

"Of course she is." Tears blur Rebecca's vision, suddenly. She could contact her parents, too, she supposes. But she doesn't want to. Their relationship maybe isn't one that can be salvaged. It leaves her feeling hollow inside. *Danny's luckier than she realizes*, she thinks. But maybe Danny will realize that now. And anyway, she has a good family, here. Tom. Her children. Tom's parents, too. It's enough.

She looks at Danny again. "So, wait, are you going to stay with your mom?"

"God, I don't know. That still seems like a step backward. I mean, she really *did* drive me crazy." Danny bites her lip. "I said I'd visit her, though. After, um, I clear up a few things elsewhere."

"So you're leaving Carson City? Are you *sure*?"

Danny laughs sadly. "This isn't the place for me. Besides, you don't want me around."

Rebecca opens her mouth, then shuts it again. Though it's certainly how she felt yesterday, it isn't quite as true anymore. She isn't sure who Danny can be to her now, though. She'll never fully forgive Danny for trying to steal her child. But she also owes Danny her life.

"I want to make sure you're safe," Rebecca says. "Are you sure you feel strong enough to leave?"

"I'm fine, Bex. Really. I came all the way here, didn't I?"

"I know, but . . . I just remember how hard it was. When I left. I was in exactly your position. You could stay with us. Really. We have a spare room." She has no idea if Tom will go for this, but she feels protective of Danny—and Danny's baby.

"I think I need to do this on my own," Danny says quietly. "But I'll stay in touch."

"You *promise*?" This still feels so soon. And Danny's still so *delicate*.

But then a nurse appears behind Danny, telling her that her cab to the bus station is here. Danny turns and gives Rebecca one last look. Regret rises in Rebecca's chest. "Are you sure I can't convince you to stay? At least until you have your baby?"

"Bex. No. I can't interfere with your family any more than I already have."

"But you'll definitely go to your mom's? For a little while? She'll make sure you go to appointments, things like that."

"I'll go to my appointments."

"But who will be with you for the birth?" Rebecca cries out.

"Bex." Danny puts her hands on her hips. "I'll figure it out. And we'll talk. Okay?"

"Okay." Rebecca doesn't like letting her go, but it seems she has no choice. There's a lump in her throat. "Danny, I'm sorry."

"You have nothing to be sorry for."

"But I do. For all of this. And—I never said this—but for what I did to you." Her gaze darts to the spot on Danny's thigh where the hot poker hit her skin. "I hate myself for that."

Danny's gaze falls there, too. Her shoulders rise and fall. "It's not like you had a choice."

"Sure I did."

"No, you didn't." She gives Rebecca a knowing look. "You know you didn't." Then she clears her throat. "You're going to talk to Tom about that?"

Rebecca shuts her eyes. "I'm going to try," she whispers. She wonders how Tom is going to understand all this. How *anyone* could, who hasn't gone through it.

They sit for a while in silence. Then, she realizes she wants to ask one more thing: "What do you think will happen to the videos?"

Danny has already turned halfway, but now she stops.

"There are so many," Rebecca says. "Of all of us." Someone could release them. Someone who still felt Ben's pull and was deeply angry that he was gone.

But Danny seems to have an answer for this, too. "My mom knows people," Danny says. "There's a whole group, I guess, who have been wanting to get us all out for a while. She says that they have lawyers. They'll fight anything that comes out—any videos, whatever. They know how to take them down, I guess, and sue those who post anything. We're the innocent ones here."

"We're the victims," Rebecca agrees, trying out the word.

Danny's lips pucker in distaste. Then she brightens. "No," she says. "We're *free*."

Her voice lifts as she says this like she's suddenly ecstatic. Like she *believes* it. And then, just like that, she waves goodbye as though this is an ordinary day and they're ordinary friends, and then she's gone.

CHAPTER FORTY

CARSON CITY, NEVADA, AND BEND, OREGON
PRESENT DAY

By the time Danny is ready to leave, she and Tom feel like friends. Well, maybe that's pushing it, but at least he doesn't hate her anymore. And the guy has a lot of kindness inside him. Case in point: he gave her five hundred bucks to head back to California. Enough for a plane ticket. That's tricky, of course, because Danny's ID expired years ago, and she doubts she'd be able to get past airport security. It's one thing on a long list of tasks she needs to accomplish in her so-called brand-new life, she supposes. It all feels so overwhelming.

A bus makes more sense. She stands at the bus station for real this time, looking at the schedules, trying to understand them. Danny has never actually been on a bus alone before.

After some puzzlement, she figures out that there's a bus leaving for Sacramento in three hours; then she'll connect to a local bus that will take her to Davis. Danny wonders if they'll be pulling up to the same bus station she remembers from when she went to high school; sometimes Toby and some other boys used to skateboard around the parking lot because they had good obstacles and curbs and Danny and Bex went to watch. Once she returns to her hometown, she'll be confronted with all sorts of ghosts like that, she supposes. Is she even *ready* for that? Is she ready to see her mom again?

Her mom was nice. So grateful. So *relieved*. She said nothing on the phone about how pissed she was that Danny had wasted her life or that she'd *told* Danny that ISB was a disaster—all she cared about was if Danny and her baby were safe. And she seemed absolutely thrilled when Danny said she'd come back and visit her. Maybe she'd changed. But how long would that last? How long would it take her mom to start nagging her about going back to school or getting a job, or maybe that she wasn't a perfect mother? And would she love Danny's daughter completely, or would there always be a little bit of resentment there—and even disgust—because she's Ben's?

It terrifies her. *I'm not ready*, her mind screams. *I can't do this alone.* Maybe Bex was right. Maybe she should have taken her up on her offer to stay in their guest room until the baby is born. But then what? She can't live with them forever. *You got yourself into this mess, you gotta get yourself out.*

But did she get herself into this mess? She doesn't even know anymore. She doesn't know *anything*.

"Next!" the clerk at the bus station ticket window calls.

It's Danny's turn, and there are people behind her waiting. She almost considers stepping out of line to collect her thoughts, but now the ticket agent is waving her up. "Um, hi," Danny says. "Can I get a ticket to Bend, please?"

She can't believe she's going back. And yet, the station doesn't collapse. Lightning doesn't strike. The agent doesn't even look at her strangely; Bend isn't setting off red flags, nor is Danny. It seems no one knows yet that she is the member of the ISB cult who took down its leader, or that it's completely bizarre that she is heading right back to the ISB compound. Calmly, the agent takes her cash and prints a paper ticket.

"Stairwell four," she says. "Leaving in thirty minutes."

Danny is a robot as she heads down the stairs to wait for the bus. It's like her thoughts have flatlined and she is just moving by muscle memory. At the end of the platform is a small snack bar with candy, chips, and soda. She drifts toward it, touching some of the remaining bills in her pocket. It's weird to think she can buy something to eat, anything she *craves*, without repercussion. She doesn't have to ask Ben's permission. She can eat ten bags of chips if she wants. Not that she wants to. Chips are bad. Candy is bad. When will she stop feeling that way? *Ever?*

"You buying something?" the clerk manning the snack shop asks. His voice makes Danny jump.

All the food options blur before Danny's eyes. There are too many choices. She can't make a decision, even though her stomach is growling and she knows her baby needs it. Hurriedly, she grabs an orange soda and hands over some bills. But as soon as she twists off the top and takes a drink of the fizzy liquid, her stomach revolts. She isn't allowed to have this. It just feels wrong. It wasn't the correct decision to choose this drink. She should have chosen something else. She should have had someone else choose for her. She tosses the soda away after only a sip.

It astonishes her when she gets on the bus. She keeps looking at her hand, figuring Ben is tracking her by the little device under her skin, knowing she's returning. It takes a moment each time to re-remember that while her tracker is still active, Ben isn't looking at it at all. Ben is dead. A death *she* played a part in.

Experimentally, she tries to feel emotions about this, but nothing comes. Not yet, anyway. But she knows it will. She knows the grief will be endless. Not that Ben is dead, exactly, but that he duped her so badly. Duped *all* of them. She loved her little community in Oregon. They aren't bad people. They were all trying to make themselves better. But then her mind shifts to the rituals she forced women to perform. The mark on her thigh . . . and the marks she made on others' thighs after her. It hadn't seemed like a bad thing at the time. It was a secret they all shared in, something strong they'd gone through together. But maybe it wasn't at all.

Flat landscape passes. Once they get into Oregon, trees begin to rise up and swallow the road. She's getting closer, she can feel it. The air *smells* like ISB. Ben started his practice right in Danny's hometown, but he told the group that he always felt like an Oregonian at heart. The woods were so tranquil, best for deep, contemplative thought and change. In nature, he always said, one became their best self. Only, maybe they weren't becoming their best selves—they were becoming identical copies of Ben, thinking his same thoughts, following his rules. That's what Bex wants her to believe, anyway. That's what makes sense, *logically*. But it's so hard to feel it in her heart. Weren't they happy there? What about all the laughter, the fun? What about the videos she made with Ben talking about empowerment and strength? What about the promises he made to her and her baby?

But then she thinks of his words crackling over the baby monitor: *A man must be around his father. His father is the most important thing.* And she shudders.

He wasn't who he said he was. He *wasn't*. Who knows who he was, really, except someone who liked to control others. Now she'll never know his true, deep-down self. Probably Barb didn't even know, before she died. She wonders what Barb knew about Ben, in the end. Maybe someone will come out of the woodwork verifying his great accomplishments as a child—scoring genius level on tests, qualifying for the Olympic team in diving. Or maybe someone will refute them. It's not like anyone went back and checked Ben's facts—Danny certainly didn't. People got up in arms if you said anything bad about Ben, let alone challenge who he said he was. Did he even love her? Did he love any of them? Or did he just want a lineage?

At the bus station, she finds a cab parked at the curb. When she gives him the address of the compound, he gives her a strange look. "You sure you want to go out there?" ISB has a reputation in these parts. People know what it is.

"Yes," Danny answers.

The cabdriver doesn't speak to her the whole ride, but that's fine with her. On the drive, she gets the urge to pull up the directions so she can follow them turn by turn, just like she did when she went to

Bex's house. A left here, a right there, follow the winding road past all the mile markers. Even though she follows the turns exactly, it doesn't comfort her like it used to. Perhaps because she has no one to check in with—well, except for herself. But what does it matter if *she* condones her actions? She doesn't trust her judgment. Not after Ben making all the decisions for her for so many years.

It's dark when the cab pulls up to the compound. Genevieve, a Seed she doesn't know well, is in the little gate booth. Danny freezes, unsure how she's going to explain herself, but to her surprise, Genevieve gives her a benign smile.

"Welcome."

Just like that, Genevieve unlocks the gate for her. Danny's heart hammers. What does this *mean*? Do they really not know Ben's gone?

She shoulders her backpack and starts up the path to the main house. There are no lights on. No sounds from inside. It unnerves her, and she fears something is going to jump out from behind a tree and grab her like in a horror movie. People must know what she's done. What if some of them are furious? Ben's true disciples, like Vincent. Or maybe Kris has come back? Or there are others . . .

Her heart bangs. She looks around. Listens. This might not be entirely safe. Maybe this was a terrible idea.

"*Psst!*"

Danny freezes. She hadn't expected anyone to be awake. A figure steps out from the shadows, and she raises her weak, skinny arms in defense. But then a woman steps forward.

"It's Smyrna," she whispers. "Danielle, yes?"

Danny blinks. She doesn't know Smyrna well. The woman is fairly new, though Ben has taken a shine to her lately. Danny has to assume she wouldn't be here if she weren't devoted.

"I knew you weren't at a goddess retreat," Smyrna whispers. "I just knew it."

Danny runs her tongue over her teeth, feeling a chill.

"I was afraid something terrible happened to you. I've . . . I've *heard* things, and seen things, and . . ." Smyrna suddenly throws herself at Danny, hugging her tightly, shaking with sobs. "I'm glad you're okay."

Slowly, suspiciously, Danny wraps her arms around the woman, too. She's so afraid, Danny realizes. The woman is literally shaking. And... goddess retreat? *That's* where Ben told everyone she was? But women who go to goddess retreats never come back to Oregon. Maybe that was Ben's plan, too. *All along.*

"I'm fine," she tells Smyrna. She looks around. "Is anyone else here?"

Smyrna blinks. "Many of us are. Though..." She leans forward, her voice lower. "*A few have left.* And there have been... rumors."

Danny runs her tongue over her teeth. "Rumors?" she says in the calmest voice she can muster. *The police told her that because of the volatile nature of ISB—and because of Danny and Rebecca's involvement with the group—they're taking their time before releasing the news to the media. But things have a way of getting around. There's no way Danny can stay here for more than one night. Soon enough, they might know she was involved. She'll have to prepare for that.*

Smyrna is nodding. "Yes, Scion isn't here right now. He had to go somewhere important, but people are concerned because he hasn't checked in. He missed this... ceremony we were supposed to have." She looks relieved.

Ceremony? Danny wonders what that means. But it doesn't matter.

"Anyway, a few people have just... *left*." Smyrna's eyes are wide. "I didn't know we could do that!"

Danny takes her hands. "We can do that, now," she says gently. "We can do whatever we want."

When she pulls back, saying she has chores to do, Smyrna still has that fragile, skittish expression like she's going to get in trouble at any moment. *Tomorrow, I will take her with me,* Danny decides. *Tomorrow, we'll leave together.*

With Smyrna gone, the front room is dark and still. There are hints of life—music at the piano, books strewn around, a broom leaning against the wall. All the bedroom doors are closed, but Danny can hear some fans whirring. She wonders who has left. Kris? Did he bolt at the first sign of trouble? Seems that way. And as far as Danny knows, Kris was the only one clued in to the operation. Ben wanted it that way; he liked secrets. Liked there only being a select few who knew the whole story.

She pushes past and turns down another hallway. It leads to her own bedroom . . . but she's not going there yet. The first thing she does is walk to the video room with a keypad on the doorknob. She's never been in here before, but she types in the code Bex gave her, and the door opens.

She slips inside, eyeing the computer terminals and the little drawers Bex described. There are so many of them, though. She picks up one of the drives and looks at the laptop sitting open. It gives her an idea. Quickly, she slides it into the port at the back of the monitor. When the drive loads, she copies the entire contents of the desktop and dumps it onto the drive. *Processing time: 20 minutes*, it reads. Danny sits back, chewing on her lip. You'd think that this laptop would contain the same data as on the USBs, but what if she's wrong? What if this is an idiotic thing to do?

But there's got to be something. Even something minor. Evidence that he tattooed all of them. A hint linking him to Toby's death. Proof that Toby *is* dead. The made-up logo for the goddess retreat. *Something.*

Blessedly, it takes only ten minutes to copy all the files, not twenty. When the transfer is complete, Danny removes the drive and drops it into her pocket. Insurance, she thinks. Just in case she needs it against anyone.

Creak. She freezes and looks up at the surveillance monitors overhead. Someone is walking the floor. Someone is always guarding this place. She ducks under the desk and watches as a figure walks right past, down the hall. It's a guy—Victor, maybe, she isn't sure. He doesn't even pause by this room.

Fatigue is weighing on her, but she still isn't ready for bed. She walks to a large room with several child-sized beds. It's where the children sleep. Three-year-old Ford. Twelve-year-old Adam. Seven-year-old Jax. And others. But not her daughter. Never her daughter.

Danny walks over and peers at their sleeping forms. Before, she never really thought hard about the kids—just that they were special because they were Ben's, and because their mothers had gotten sick. It's what he told her, and she used to believe everything he said.

She pauses at Jax's bed. Looking at the boy now, it's so obvious he has Sophia's eyebrows and coloring. *Sophia*. It was like one day she was here, arguing with Ben, and the next she was at the goddess retreat . . . and she never returned. Bex said she was in the cabin up the hill—*could* she have been? A while later, Jax arrived, and all that was said was that Sophia wanted Jax to be at the compound, with Ben. It enrages her, now. A baby separated from his mother. A baby and mother possibly tormented—and for what? Because she didn't comply? Because Ben deemed her weak? Because Ben was *afraid* of her? Afraid of mothers, maybe. Afraid of them making better decisions. Afraid of them realizing what ISB was and leaving with his children. Maybe it was that.

Danny will find Sophia if she's still alive. And she will reunite the child with her if she can. She will find all these kids' mothers. Maybe she'll enlist Bex to help her. But these kids need to be back where they belong. They need to be free.

But for now, she has to trust the kids are cared for. She'll think about the details tomorrow. She's exhausted, suddenly—she's been up for far too many hours, first traveling to see Bex, hashing it all out, then the long bus ride back here. All she wants to do is sleep. And so, she goes to the place she knows best: her tiny room at the end of the hall. She opens the door and breathes in. It smells like lavender in here from the gardens. The bed is spare and hard—Ben insists they sleep in uncomfortable circumstances because it "builds character." She sits on the mattress and stares at the room, marveling over the fact that she barely has anything on the walls. Here for eight years, and not much to show for it. She reaches for the blanket to pull it up, but a voice inside her says she should go without blankets tonight because she needs to be punished. She winces, stops the thought. *You need the blanket*, she screams to her addled mind. *Your baby needs it, too*. Every thought, every action—it'll all need to be retrained. But she'll try.

And so she pulls up the covers. They're soft and warm. Welcoming. *I deserve this*, she tells herself. *Or I want to think I do, anyway*.

Her breathing slows. And to her astonishment, she falls safely and deeply into sleep.